P9-CEJ-594

A Knight in
Shining Armor

Books by Jude Deveraux

The Velvet Promise
Highland Velvet
Velvet Song
Velvet Angel
Sweetbriar
Counterfeit Lady
Lost Lady
Twin of Ice
Twin of Fire
River Lady
The Temptress
The Raider
The Princess
The Awakening
The Maiden
The Taming
A Knight in Shining Armor
Wishes
Mountain Laurel
The Conquest
The Duchess
Eternity
Sweet Liar
The Invitation
Remembrance
The Heiress
Legend
An Angel for Emily
The Blessing
High Tide
Temptation
The Summerhouse
Forever . . . A Novel of Good and Evil, Love and Hope

Published by POCKET BOOKS

JUDE DEVERAUX

A Knight in Shining Armor

POCKET BOOKS

New York London Toronto Sydney Singapore

This book is a work of fiction. Names, characters, places and
incidents are products of the author's imagination or are used
fictitiously. Any resemblance to actual events or locales or persons,
living or dead, is entirely coincidental.

POCKET BOOKS, a division of Simon & Schuster, Inc.
1230 Avenue of the Americas, New York, NY 10020

Copyright © 1989, 2002 by Deveraux, Inc.

All rights reserved, including the right to reproduce
this book or portions thereof in any form whatsoever.
For information address Pocket Books, 1230 Avenue
of the Americas, New York, NY 10020

ISBN: 0-7434-3972-4

POCKET and colophon are registered trademarks of
Simon & Schuster, Inc.

Designed by Jaime Putorti

Printed in the U.S.A.

*I dedicate this book with love
to my editor and, more importantly,
to my friend,
Linda Marrow.*

A Knight in Shining Armor

PROLOGUE

ENGLAND
1564

*N*icholas *was trying to concentrate* on the letter to his mother, a letter that was probably the most important document he would ever write. Everything depended upon this letter: his honor, his estates, his family's future—and his life.

But as he wrote, he began to hear a woman weeping. Annoyed, he got up from the crude little table and looked out the tiny open window to the courtyard below. There were four men walking about, but there was no woman. Besides, Nicholas was three stories up, so he could not have heard her. The room he was in had walls so thick he could hear nothing from outside, and the oak door was heavy and bound with iron.

"She is not of this world," he told himself, then gave a shiver as he crossed himself. He sat back down at the table and again began to write.

But the moment he sat down, he heard her again. Her weeping had been soft at first, but it was growing louder.

For a moment, Nicholas cocked his head to one side and listened.

Yes, she was weeping, but her tears were not from fear, or even from grief. No, he could feel that the source of her pain came from something deeper.

"No!" he said aloud. He did not have the time to try to understand this woman, whether she was of flesh or spirit. Right now, his need was as great as hers. He gave his attention back to the letter, but he could not concentrate. The woman's tears were pulling him to her. She needed something, but he could not tell what. Did she need comfort? Soothing? What did she want of him?

Putting down his quill, he ran his hand over his eyes. The woman's tears were filling his head. No, he thought, what she needed was hope. The weeping was from a person who no longer had hope.

Determined to turn his mind back to his own problems, Nicholas looked back at the letter. The woman's problems were not his. If he did not finish this letter and give it to the waiting messenger soon, his own life would be without hope.

Nicholas wrote two more lines, but then he had to stop. The crying was increasing, growing louder. As it increased in volume, it seemed to grow inside until it filled every corner of the room—and every nook inside his brain.

"Lady," he whispered, his voice filled with desperation, "give me peace. I would give my life to help you, but I cannot. My life is pledged elsewhere."

Again, he picked up the pen and tried to write, this time with his other hand over his ear, doing his best to block out the sounds from the woman.

But Nicholas couldn't stop hearing her. He dropped the quill, ink running across the document as he put both hands over his ears and closed his eyes tight. "What would you have of me?" he cried. "I would give you all that I can, but I have nothing left to give."

But his pleas meant nothing, for the woman's weeping grew and grew until the inside of Nicholas's head began to go round and round. Slowly, he opened his eyes, but he saw nothing. Before him was only darkness. He could not see the walls of the room or the door. He could feel the chair beneath him, but he could no longer see the table or the letter that was so important to him.

But as he sat there, a small, bright light appeared in the far distance, and Nicholas felt himself drawn to the light. As he looked at that tiny speck so far away, it was as though nothing in his life had ever mattered but that light.

"Yes," he whispered. Then he closed his eyes and gave himself over to the sound of the woman's tears. Slowly, his body relaxed and he put his head down beside the letter he had been writing. "Yes," he whispered again as he surrendered himself.

ONE

ENGLAND
1988

Dougless Montgomery sat in the backseat of the rental car, Robert and his pudgy thirteen-year-old daughter, Gloria, in the front. As usual, Gloria was eating. Dougless shifted her slim legs to try to make herself more comfortable around Gloria's luggage. There were six large pieces of matched leather luggage to hold Gloria's belongings, and since they wouldn't fit in the trunk of the little car, they were piled in the back with Dougless. There was a makeup case under her feet and a big wardrobe on the seat beside her. Every time she moved, she scraped against a buckle, a welt, or a handle. Right now, she had an itch under her left knee, but she couldn't reach it.

"Daddy," Gloria whined, sounding like an invalid four-year-old, "she's scratching the pretty suitcases you bought me."

Dougless clenched her fists, closed her eyes, and counted to ten. *She.* Gloria never said Dougless's name, but just called her *She.*

Robert glanced over his shoulder at Dougless. "Dougless, could you please be a bit more careful? That luggage is quite expensive."

"I am aware of that," Dougless said, trying to keep the anger out of her voice. "It's just that I'm having a difficult time sitting back here. There isn't much room."

Robert gave a great sigh of weariness. "Dougless, do you have to complain about everything? Can't you even allow a vacation to be pleasant? All I asked was that you make an effort."

Dougless opened her mouth to reply but closed it. She didn't want to start another argument. Besides, she knew that it would do no good. So, instead of replying, she swallowed her anger—then rubbed her stomach. It was hurting again. She wanted to ask Robert to stop to get something to drink so she could take one of the tranquilizers the doctor had prescribed for her nervous stomach. "Keep this up and you'll give yourself an ulcer," the doctor had warned her. But Dougless wouldn't give Gloria the satisfaction of knowing that she'd yet again managed to upset Dougless and to, yet again, drive a wedge between Dougless and Robert.

But when Dougless glanced up, she saw Gloria smirking at her in the makeup mirror on the sun visor. With determination, Dougless looked away and tried to concentrate on the beauty of the English countryside.

Outside the car window she saw green fields, old stone fences, cows and more cows, picturesque little houses, magnificent mansions, and . . . and Gloria, she thought. Dougless seemed to see Gloria everywhere. Robert kept saying, "She's just a child and her daddy has left her. It's only natural that she's going to have some hostility toward you. But please try to show some sympathy for her, will you? She's really a sweet kid when you get to know her."

A sweet kid, Dougless thought as she looked out the window. At thirteen, Gloria wore more makeup than Dougless did at twenty-six—and Gloria spent hours in the hotel bathroom applying it. Gloria sat in the front of the car. "She's just a kid and it's her first trip to England," Robert said. "And you've been to England before, so why not be generous?" That Dougless was supposed to read the road map when she could hardly see around Gloria's head didn't seem to count for much.

Dougless tried to concentrate on the scenery. Robert said Dougless was jealous of his daughter. He said that she didn't want to share him with anyone else, but that if she'd just relax, they'd be a very happy threesome. "We could be a second family for a little girl who has lost so much," he said.

Dougless had tried to like Gloria. She'd tried hard to be an adult and ignore, and even understand, Gloria's hostility, but it was more than Dougless could do. In the year she and Robert had been living together, Dougless had made every possible effort to find that "sweet kid" that Robert had told her of. Several times, she'd taken Gloria shopping and spent more money on Gloria than Dougless's small elementary school teacher's salary allowed her to spend on herself. Several Saturday nights Dougless had stayed at the house she shared with Robert, babysitting Gloria while he went to professional functions, usually cocktail parties or dinners. When Dougless had said she'd like to attend with him, Robert had said, "But time alone is what you two need. You need to get to know each other. And, remember, babe, I'm a package deal. Love me, love my kid."

Sometimes Dougless had started to believe that it was beginning to work because she and Gloria were cordial, even friendly, to each other when they were alone. But the minute Robert appeared, Gloria changed into a whining, lying brat. She sat on Robert's lap, all five foot two inches, one hundred and forty pounds of her, and wailed that *She* had been "awfully mean" to her.

At first Dougless had laughed at what Gloria was saying. How absurd to think she would ever harm a child! Anyone could see that the girl was just trying to get her father's attention.

But to Dougless's utter disbelief, Robert believed every word his daughter said. He didn't accuse Dougless. No, instead, he just asked her to be a "little kinder" to "the poor kid." Immediately, Dougless's defenses had gone up. "Is that supposed to mean you don't think I'm a kind person? You *do* think I would mistreat a child?"

"I'm just asking you to be the adult and have a little patience and understanding, that's all."

When Dougless asked what he meant by that, Robert had thrown up his hands and said that he couldn't talk to her; then he'd walked out of the room. Dougless had taken two of her stomach tranquilizers.

After the arguments, Dougless had wavered between guilt and

rage. She had a classroom of children who adored her, yet Gloria seemed to hate her. *Was* Dougless jealous? Was she somehow unconsciously letting this child know she didn't want to share Robert with his own daughter? Every time Dougless thought of her possible jealousy she vowed to try harder to make Gloria like her, which usually meant she bought Gloria another expensive gift. And she'd again agree to babysit on the weekends when Gloria stayed with them. While Gloria's mother had a *life,* Dougless thought with bitterness.

At other times, all Dougless felt was rage. Couldn't Robert just once—*one* time—take Dougless's side? Couldn't he tell Gloria that Dougless's comfort was more important than the blasted suitcases? Or maybe he could tell Gloria that Dougless had a name and wasn't always to be referred to as *she* or *her?* But every time Dougless said something like that to Robert, she ended up apologizing. Robert said, "My God, Dougless, you're the adult. And I only see her on alternate weekends, so of course I'm going to favor her over you. You and I are together every day, so why can't you stand to play second fiddle now and then?"

His words sounded right, but at the same time, Dougless fantasized about Robert telling his daughter to "be more respectful" toward the "woman I love."

But that didn't happen, so Dougless kept her mouth shut and enjoyed the time she and Robert had when Gloria wasn't around. When Gloria wasn't with them, she and Robert were perfectly suited, and she knew, through age old intuition, that very soon she was going to receive what she wanted so much: a marriage proposal.

Truthfully, marriage was what Dougless wanted most in life. She'd never been burning with ambition the way her older sisters were. Dougless just wanted a nice home and a husband, and a few children. Maybe someday, after the kids were in school, she'd write children's books, something about talking animals, but she had no desire to fight her way up a corporate ladder.

Already, she'd invested eighteen months of her life in Robert, and he was perfect husband material. He was tall, handsome, well-dressed, and an excellent orthopedic surgeon. He always hung up his clothes, and he helped with the housework; he didn't chase after women, and he always came home when he said he would. He was reliable, dependable, faithful—but, most important, he needed her so very much.

Not long after they met, Robert had told Dougless his life story. As a child, he hadn't been loved very much, and he told Dougless that her sweet, generous heart was what he'd been looking for all his life. His first wife, whom he'd divorced over four years ago, was a cold fish, a woman who Robert said was incapable of love. Just three months after he met Dougless, he told her he wanted a "permanent relationship" with her—which she took to mean marriage—but first he wanted to know how they "related" to each other. After all, he'd been hurt so badly the first time. In other words, he wanted them to live together.

What he said made sense to her, and since Dougless had had a number of "unfortunate" previous relationships with men, she happily moved into Robert's big, beautiful, expensive house, then set about doing everything she could to prove to Robert that she was as warm and generous and loving as his mother and wife had been cold.

With the exception of dealing with Gloria, living with Robert had been great. He was an energetic man and they often went dancing, hiking, bicycle riding. They entertained a great deal and often went to parties. She'd never lived with a man before, but she had easily settled into a domestic routine, feeling as though it was what she was made for.

They had problems other than Gloria, of course, but Robert was so much better than any of the other men Dougless had dated that she forgave him his little quirks—most of which revolved around money. True, it was annoying that when they went to the grocery together he nearly always "forgot" his checkbook. And at the ticket window of theaters and when the check was presented in restaurants, half the time Robert found he'd left his wallet at home. If Dougless complained, he'd talk to her about the new age of liberated women and how most women were fighting to pay half the expenses. Then he'd kiss her sweetly and take her somewhere expensive for dinner—and he'd pay. And Dougless forgave him.

Dougless knew she could stand the small problems—everyone had idiosyncracies—but it was Gloria that sent her screaming. When Gloria was with them, their life turned into a battleground. According to Robert, his daughter was perfection on earth, and because Dougless didn't see her that way, Robert began to see Dougless as the enemy. When the three of them were together, it was Robert and Gloria on one team and Dougless on the other.

Now, on this holiday in England, in the front seat Gloria offered her father a piece of candy from the box on her lap. Neither of them seemed to think of offering any to Dougless.

Still looking out the window, Dougless gritted her teeth. Perhaps it was the combination of Gloria and money that was making her so angry, because, with this trip, Robert's little "money quirk" as Dougless had always thought of it, had turned into something more.

When Dougless had first met Robert, they had talked for hours about their dreams and they'd talked many times of taking a trip to England. As a child, she had often traveled to England with her family, but she hadn't been back in years. When she and Robert had moved in together, in September of last year, Robert had said, "Let's go to England one year from today. By then we'll know." He hadn't elaborated on what they would "know," but Dougless was sure that he meant that, in a year, they'd know whether or not they were compatible for marriage.

For a whole year, Dougless had worked on planning the trip, which she'd come to think of as their honeymoon. A "pre-honeymoon," she called it in her mind. "The decision maker," she said to herself, then smiled. She made reservations at the most romantic, most exclusive country house hotels England had to offer. When she had asked Robert's opinion of a hotel, he'd winked at her and said, "Spare no expense for *this* trip." She had ordered brochures, bought travel books, read and researched until she knew the names of half the villages in England. Robert's only stipulation had been that he wanted an educational trip as well as fun, so she'd compiled a list of many things to do that were close to their lovely hotels—which was easy to do, since Great Britain is like a Disneyland for history lovers.

Then, three months before they were to leave, Robert said that he had a surprise for her on this trip, a very, very special surprise that was going to fill her with joy. His words had made Dougless work even harder on the plans, and she found their little game of secrecy exciting. As Dougless planned, she thought, Will he propose here? Or maybe here. This place would be nice.

Three weeks before they left, she was balancing Robert's household-accounts checkbook when she saw a canceled check for five thousand dollars made out to a jewelry store.

As she held the check, tears of happiness came to her eyes. "An engagement ring," she'd whispered. That Robert had spent so much was proof that even though he was a tad stingy on small things, when something really counted, he was generous.

For the next few weeks Dougless had walked on clouds. She cooked wonderful meals for Robert and had been especially energetic in the bedroom, doing everything she could think of to please him.

Two days before they were to leave, Robert punctured her bubble a bit—not enough to burst it, but it had certainly been deflated. He had asked to see the bills for the trip, plane tickets, advance reservations, whatever she had. He had then added the amounts and handed her the calculator tape.

"This is your half of the cost," he'd said.

"Mine?" she'd asked stupidly, not understanding what he was saying.

"I know how important it is to you women today to pay your own way, so I don't want to be accused of being a male chauvinist pig," he'd said with a smile. "You don't want to be a burden to a man, do you? You don't want to add to all my responsibilities at the hospital and to my ex-wife, do you?"

"No, no, of course not," Dougless had mumbled, feeling confused, as she often did when confronted with Robert's reasoning. "It's just that I don't have any money."

"Dougless, baby, please tell me that you don't spend everything you make. Maybe you should take a course in accounting." He lowered his voice. "But then your family has money, doesn't it?"

That was one of the times Dougless's stomach had begun to hurt, and she remembered the doctor's warning about giving herself an ulcer. She had explained to Robert about her family a hundred times. Yes, her family had money—lots of it—but her father believed his daughters should know how to support themselves, so Dougless was on her own until she was thirty-five; then she'd inherit. She knew that if there was an emergency, her father would help her, but a pleasure trip to England hardly counted as an emergency.

"Come on, Dougless," Robert had said with a smile when Dougless didn't reply to his question. "I keep hearing what a paragon of love and support that family of yours is, so why can't they help you now?" Before she could speak, Robert raised her hand to his lips and kissed it. "Ah, baby, please try to get the money. I so much want us to go on this trip because I have such a very, very special surprise for you."

Part of Dougless had wanted to shout that he wasn't being fair. He should have made it clear that she was going to be required to pay for half of the trip before she'd made reservations at such expensive hotels. But another part of her asked why she'd expected him to pay for her share. They weren't married. They were, as Robert often called them, "partners." "Sounds like John Wayne and a sidekick," Dougless had muttered the first time he'd said that, but Robert had just laughed.

In the end Dougless couldn't bear to ask her father for money. It would be like admitting defeat to him. Instead, she'd called a cousin in Colorado and asked him for a loan. The money had been given to her freely, no interest, but she'd had to endure her cousin's lecture. "He's a surgeon, you're an underpaid teacher, you've been living together for a year, but he expects you to pay for *half* of an expensive trip?" her cousin had said. Dougless had wanted to explain about Robert's mother, who had used money to punish her son, and about his cold ex-wife, who had spent everything Robert earned. Dougless had wanted to explain that money was just a small part of their lives and that she was pretty sure that Robert was going to propose marriage on this trip.

But Dougless said none of that. "Just send the money, will you?" she'd snapped.

But her cousin's words had upset her, so, during the few days remaining before they left, Dougless gave herself several little lectures. It was only fair that she pay her own way, wasn't it? And Robert was right: it *was* the day of the liberated woman. Her father, by not dropping millions in her lap before she could handle them, was teaching her to take care of herself and, now, so was Robert. And, most of all, she told herself that she had been an idiot for not realizing beforehand that she was supposed to pay her own way.

After Dougless had contributed her half to the bills, for the most part, she recovered her good humor, and by the time she'd packed their suitcases, she was again looking forward to the trip. Happily, she filled her tote bag with necessary toiletries, travel books, and as many gadgets as she could cram into it.

In the taxi on the way to the airport, Robert had been especially nice to her. He'd nuzzled her neck until she'd pushed him away in embarrassment when she saw the taxi driver watching.

"Have you guessed the surprise yet?" he asked.

"You won the lottery," Dougless answered, still playing the game and pretending ignorance.

"Better than that."

"Let's see . . . You've bought a castle and we'll live in it forever as lord and lady."

"*Much* better than that," Robert said seriously. "Do you have any idea what the upkeep on one of those places is? I'll bet you can't guess anything as good as this surprise."

Dougless had looked at him with love. She knew just what her wedding dress would look like, and she imagined all her relatives smiling at her in approval. Would their children have Robert's blue eyes or her green? His brown hair or her auburn? "I have no idea what the surprise is," she said, lying.

Leaning back against the seat, Robert smiled. "You'll soon find out," he'd said enigmatically.

At the airport Dougless dealt with checking the luggage while Robert kept looking about the terminal as though he were searching for something. As Dougless tipped the porter, Robert threw up his hand to wave to someone. At first Dougless was too busy to realize what was happening.

She looked up at the cry, "Daddy!" and saw Gloria running across the terminal, a porter trailing behind her pushing a hand truck loaded with six new suitcases.

What a coincidence, Dougless thought as she checked the tags the baggage handler gave her. Imagine meeting Gloria at the airport. Distractedly, Dougless watched as Gloria flung herself on her father. Moments later they broke apart, Robert keeping his arm tightly around his precious daughter's plump shoulders.

Once Dougless had finished with the bags, she gave her attention to Robert's daughter, and it was difficult to keep the frown off her face. Gloria was wearing a fringed jacket and cowboy boots, and a too-short leather skirt. She looked like an overweight stripper from the sixties.

Where was her mother and how could she allow the child to dress like that? Dougless thought as she glanced about the airport for Robert's ex-wife.

"Hello, Gloria," Dougless said. "Are you and your mother going somewhere too?"

Gloria and her father nearly collapsed with laughter at Dougless's words. "You haven't told her," Gloria squealed.

It took Robert a moment to sober himself. *"This* is the surprise," he said, pushing Gloria forward as though she were some huge trophy Dougless had just won. "Isn't this the *most* wonderful surprise you could imagine?"

Dougless still didn't understand—or maybe she was too horrified to want to understand. All she could do was stand there and stare at the two of them, speechless.

Robert put his other arm around Dougless and drew her close to him. "Both of my girls are going with me," he said with pride.

"Both?" Dougless whispered, her throat closing down on her.

"Yes," Robert said, his voice joyous. "Gloria is the surprise I've been hinting at for weeks. She's going with us to England. I knew you'd never guess! You didn't, did you?"

No, Dougless had not come close to guessing. And now that she was finally understanding that the beautiful, romantic trip she'd dreamed of wasn't going to happen, she wanted to scream, to yell, and to refuse to go. But she did none of those things. "All the hotel rooms are just for two people," she'd managed to say at last.

"So we'll have a rollaway bed brought in," Robert said in dismissal. "I'm sure we'll manage, because we have love going for us and that's all we need." He dropped his arm from Dougless's shoulder. "Now for business. Dougless, you won't mind getting Gloria's luggage checked in while I catch up with lambykins, will you?"

Dougless could only shake her head. Numbly she went off to the ticket counter, the porter and the suitcases following her. She had to pay two hundred and eighty dollars in overcharge for Gloria's four extra bags, and she had to tip the porter.

They didn't have much time to spare before the plane took off, and Robert and his daughter were absorbed in each other so, thankfully, Dougless wasn't asked to speak. If she had been asked anything, she wasn't sure she could have answered. With each passing minute, she saw one dream after another disappear. Champagne dinners gave way to fast food eaten in the car. Afternoons spent lazily strolling on wooded paths turned into visions of arguments about "finding something Gloria can enjoy, too"—a request that Dougless had already heard too many times.

And then there was the privacy issue. The three of them would share one room. When could she and Robert be alone?

It was when they boarded the plane that Dougless saw that Robert had put quite a bit of work into Gloria's trip. Her boarding pass said she was in the same row as they were, in the aisle seat.

But Robert set Gloria between them, so Dougless ended up on the aisle, which she hated because no matter where she put her arms or her legs, she was always told by the flight attendant that she was blocking the passage of the cart.

It was during the long flight that Robert, smiling, had handed Dougless Gloria's ticket. "Add this to our list of expenses, will you? And I'll need a penny by penny—or should I say shilling by shilling," he added, winking at Gloria, "accounting of all the money spent. My accountant thinks I can deduct this whole trip."

"But it's a pleasure trip, not business."

Robert frowned. "Dougless, please don't start on me already. Would you please just keep track of the money we spend so that when we get home, you and I can split the expenses in half?"

Dougless looked at Gloria's ticket she was holding. "You mean in thirds, don't you? Me one third, two thirds for you and Gloria."

Robert gave her a look of horror as he put his arm around Gloria protectively, as though Dougless had tried to hit the kid. "I *meant* in half. Gloria is for you to enjoy, too. Money spent is nothing compared to the joy you'll receive from her company."

Dougless turned away. She wasn't going to get into an argument now; they'd discuss this further later—when they were in private and Gloria wasn't watching them with interest.

For the rest of the long flight, she read while Gloria and Robert played cards and ignored her. Twice Dougless took a tranquilizer to keep her stomach from eating itself.

Now, in the car, Dougless rubbed her aching stomach. In the four days they'd been in England she'd tried to enjoy herself. She'd tried not to complain when the first night in their beautiful hotel room, Gloria had moaned so much about the trundle bed the hotel had put in the room—after the owner had crossly lectured Dougless about not having expected Gloria—that Robert had asked Gloria to get into their four poster with them. After nearly being pushed out of bed twice, Dougless had ended up sleeping on the trundle bed. Nor had Dougless complained when Gloria ordered three entrees at the expensive restaurant. "I just want my baby to have a taste of everything," Robert said. "And, Dougless, please stop being so stingy. I don't know what's come over you. I always thought you were a generous person," Robert said, then handed Dougless the enormous bill that Dougless was to pay half of.

Dougless managed to keep her mouth shut by constantly reminding herself that she was the adult and Gloria was just a child. And Dougless consoled herself with the knowledge that somewhere in Robert's baggage was a five-thousand-dollar engagement ring. The thought of that ring made her remember that he did love her. And she reminded herself that all the things he did for Gloria were done out of love, too.

But after last night, Dougless was finding it impossible to keep up her appearance of good humor. Last night at yet another hundred-and-fifty-dollar dinner, Robert had presented Gloria with a long blue velvet box. As Dougless watched Gloria open the box, she had a sinking feeling.

Gloria's eyes lit up when she saw what was inside. "But it's not my birthday, Daddy," she'd whispered.

"I know, Muffin," Robert said softly. "It's just to say, 'I love you.'"

Slowly, Gloria withdrew from the box a wide bracelet made of twisted wires of gold and silver, from which dripped diamonds and emeralds.

Dougless couldn't prevent the gasp that escaped her, for she knew that her engagement ring was being fastened about Gloria's chubby wrist.

Gloria held her arm up triumphantly. "See?"

"Yes, I see," Dougless said coolly.

After dinner, in the hall outside their room, Robert had been furious with her. "You didn't show much enthusiasm about the bracelet I gave my daughter. Gloria was trying to show it to you. She was *trying* to make overtures of friendship to you, but you snubbed her. You've hurt her deeply."

"Is that what you paid five thousand dollars for? A diamond bracelet for a *child?*"

"Gloria happens to be a young woman, a very beautiful young woman, and she deserves beautiful things. And besides, it's my money. It's not as though you and I were married and you had any legal rights to my money."

It was the first time they'd been alone in days, and Dougless wanted to keep her pride, wanted to tell herself that it didn't matter that Robert bought his young daughter diamonds but gave the woman he lived with half his bills. But Dougless had never been able to conceal her true feelings. With her eyes filling with unshed tears, Dougless put her hands on his arms. *"Are* we going to get married?" she whispered. "Is it ever going to happen?"

Angrily, he jerked away from her touch. "Not if you don't start showing a little love and generosity to both my daughter and me." He gave her a cold look. "You know, I thought you were different, but now I'm beginning to think that you're as cold as my ex-wife. Now, if you'll please excuse me, I have to go comfort my daughter. She's probably crying her little eyes out after the way you treated her." After one last glare at Dougless, he turned and went into their room.

Dougless slumped against the wall. "Emerald earrings should dry her tears," she whispered to no one.

So now, in the car, she sat with her body twisted around Gloria's suitcases and knew that no marriage proposal, and certainly no engagement ring, was going to be given to her. Instead she knew that she was going to spend the month-long trip acting as a secretary and navigator for Robert, and being taunted by his daughter. At the moment Dougless wasn't sure what she was going to do, but the thought of taking the first plane home appealed to her.

Even as she thought of leaving, she looked at the back of Robert's head and her heart lurched. If she got on a plane in a rage, she knew she'd have to return to the U.S. and move out of Robert's house. She'd have to find an apartment; then she'd— What? Start dating again? As a schoolteacher, she didn't meet too many men. She could go to her family and— Admit that she'd had yet another relationship fail?

"Dougless," Robert said. "I think maybe we're lost. Where is this church? I thought you were going to watch the road maps. I can't drive *and* navigate." There was an edge to his voice that hadn't been there yesterday and Dougless knew he was still angry about her reaction to the bracelet.

Quickly, Dougless fumbled with the map, then looked around Gloria's head to try to see the road signs. "Here!" she said. "Take a right."

Robert turned down one of the narrow English lanes, bushes on either side nearly covering the road, and drove toward the remote village of Ashburton, a place that looked as though it hadn't changed in hundreds of years.

"There's a thirteenth-century church here containing the tomb of an Elizabethan earl." Dougless checked her notebook. "Lord Nicholas Stafford, died 1564."

"Do we have to see another church?" Gloria wailed. "I'm sick of churches. Couldn't she find something better to look at?"

"I was told to search out historic sights," Dougless snapped before she thought to modulate her tone.

Robert stopped the car in front of the church and looked back at Dougless. "Gloria's statement was valid, and I see no call for your bad temper. Dougless, you are making me begin to regret bringing you with us," he said, then got out of the car and walked away.

"*Bringing* me?" Dougless said, but he was already halfway to the church, his arm around Gloria. "But I'm paying my own way," she whispered.

Dougless didn't go inside the church with Robert and Gloria.

Instead she stayed outside, walking around the lumpy graveyard, absently looking at the ancient grave markers. She had some serious decisions to make and she wanted time to think. Should she stay and be miserable, or should she leave? If she left now, she knew Robert would never forgive her and all the time and effort she'd invested in him would have been for nothing.

"Hello."

Dougless jumped at the voice, then turned to see Gloria just behind her. Maybe it was Dougless's imagination, but the girl's diamond bracelet seemed to flash in the sun.

"What do you want?" Dougless asked suspiciously.

Gloria stuck her lower lip out. "You hate me, don't you?"

Dougless sighed. "No, I don't hate you. I just . . . It's a grown-up thing." She took a deep breath. She wanted to be alone so she could think. "Why aren't you inside looking at the church?"

"I got bored. That's a pretty blouse," Gloria said, her eyelids lowered in a sly way that Dougless had seen too many times before. "It looks expensive. Did your rich family buy it for you?"

Dougless wasn't about to take the bait and let the girl get to her. Instead, she gave her a quelling look, then turned and walked away.

"Wait!" Gloria cried out, then yelled, "Ow!"

Dougless turned back to see Gloria crumpled in a heap beside a rough-surfaced tombstone. Dougless doubted if the girl was actually hurt because Gloria loved drama. Sighing, Dougless went back to help her up, but as soon as she was upright, Gloria burst into tears. Dougless couldn't quite bring herself to hug Gloria, but she did manage to pat her shoulder. She even gave a little expression of sympathy because Gloria's arm was raw where she'd hit the stone. Gloria looked at her arm and began to cry louder.

"It couldn't hurt that much," Dougless said, trying to soothe the girl. "I know. Why don't you put your new bracelet on that arm? I'll bet the pain'll stop instantly."

"It's not that," Gloria said, sniffing. "I'm upset because you hate me. Daddy said you thought my bracelet was going to be an engagement ring."

Dougless dropped her hand from Gloria's arm and stiffened.

"What made him think such a ridiculous thing as that?"she asked, trying to sound convincing.

Gloria looked at Dougless out of the corner of her eye. "Oh, my daddy knows everything about you," she said, her voice sly. "He knows you thought his surprise was going to be a marriage proposal, and he knows that you thought the check to the jeweler was for an engagement ring." Gloria gave a little smile. "Daddy and I laugh all the time about you and how much you want to marry him. He says you'll do anything he tells you to if he makes you think he's going to ask you to marry him."

Dougless was standing so rigid that her body began to tremble.

Gloria's little smile turned malicious and her voice lowered. "Daddy says that if you weren't going to inherit so much money, he'd get rid of you."

At that remark, Dougless slapped Gloria's smug, fat face.

Robert appeared from inside the church just in time to see the slap, and Gloria went screaming into her father's arms.

"She hit me over and over," Gloria screamed, "and she scratched my arm. Look at it, Daddy, it's bleeding. She did this to me!"

"My God, Dougless," Robert said, his eyes wide in horror. "I can't believe this of you. To beat a child, to—"

"Child! I've had enough of that *child!* And I've had enough of the way you baby her. And I've had enough of the way you two treat *me!*"

Robert glared at her coldly. "We have been nothing but kind and thoughtful to you this entire trip, while you have been jealous and spiteful. We have gone out of our way to please you."

"You haven't made any effort to please me. Everything has been for Gloria." Tears came to Dougless's eyes and filled her throat until she almost choked. She kept hearing Gloria's words ringing in her head. "You two have laughed at me behind my back."

"Now you're fantasizing," Robert said, still glaring at her, still holding Gloria protectively under his arm as though Dougless might attack the girl at any moment. "But since we are so displeasing to you, perhaps you'd rather do without our company." Turning, Gloria huddled against his side, he started walking toward the car.

"I agree," Dougless said. "I'm ready to go home." Bending, she reached for her handbag where she'd set it down by a gravestone. But her bag wasn't there. Quickly, she looked behind a few tombstones, but there was no sign of her bag. She looked up when she heard a car start.

At first she couldn't believe what she was seeing. Robert was driving away and leaving her!

Dougless ran toward the gate, but the car had already pulled onto the road. Then, to Dougless's horror, she saw Gloria stick her arm out the window—and dangling from her fingertips was Dougless's handbag.

In a futile attempt to reach them, Dougless ran after the car, but it was soon out of sight. Dazed, numb, disbelieving, she walked back to the church. She was in a foreign country with no money, no credit cards, no passport. But, worst of all, the man she loved had just walked out on her.

The heavy oak door of the church was standing open, so Dougless went inside. It was cool and damp and dim inside the church, and the tall stone walls made the place feel calm and reverent.

She had to think about her situation and make some plans about what she should do. But, then, surely, Robert would return for her. Maybe even now he was turning around and driving back to get her. Maybe any minute he'd come running into the church, pull Dougless into his arms, and tell her he was sorry and he hoped she could forgive him.

But, somehow, Dougless didn't believe any of that was going to happen. No, Robert had been too angry—and Gloria was too much of a liar. Dougless was sure the girl would elaborate on how Dougless had injured her arm, and Robert's anger would be refueled.

No, it would be better if Dougless made some plans about how to get herself out of this mess. She'd have to call her father, collect, and have him send her money. And again she would have to tell him that his youngest daughter had failed at something. She'd have to tell him that his daughter couldn't so much as go on a holiday without getting herself into trouble.

Tears started in her eyes as she imagined hearing her oldest sister, Elizabeth, say, "What has our little scatterbrained Dougless done now?" Robert had been Dougless's attempt at making her family proud of her. Robert wasn't like the other stray-cat men Dougless had fallen for. Robert was *so* respectable, so very suitable, but she'd lost him. Maybe if she'd just held her temper with Gloria . . . Maybe . . .

Tears blurred Dougless's eyes as she looked around the church. Sun was streaming through the old windows high above her head, and sharp, clear rays lit the white marble tomb in the archway to the left. Dougless walked forward. Lying on top of the tomb was a full-length, white marble sculpture of a man wearing the top half of a suit of armor and an odd-looking pair of shorts, his ankles crossed, a helmet tucked under his arm. "'Nicholas Stafford,'" she read aloud, "'Earl of Thornwyck.'"

Dougless was congratulating herself for holding up so well under her current circumstances when, suddenly, everything that had happened hit her, and her knees collapsed. She fell to the floor, her hands on the tomb, her forehead resting against the cold marble.

She began to cry in earnest, to cry deeply from far down inside herself. She felt as though she were a failure, a complete and absolute failure. Her tears were not just for today, but it seemed that everything she'd ever touched in her life had failed. Since she'd reached puberty, her father had had to bail her out of what had to be hundreds of scrapes.

There was the "boy" she'd fallen madly in love with when she was sixteen. She had defied her entire family because they hadn't liked him. But her sister Elizabeth—wise, never-made-a-mistake-in-her-life Elizabeth—showed Dougless some papers. The boy she loved was twenty-five years old and had a prison record. Defiantly, Dougless declared that she loved him no matter what flaws he had. They broke up when he was arrested for grand theft.

Then there was the minister she'd fallen for when she was nineteen. A minister had seemed a safe person for her to love. She ended their relationship when his picture appeared on the front page of the newspapers. He was already married to three other women.

And then there was . . . Dougless was crying so hard that she couldn't remember all the others. But she knew that the list was endless. Robert had seemed so different, so ordinary, so respectable—but she hadn't been able to hold on to him.

"What is wrong with me?" she cried.

Through her tears, she looked at the marble face of the man on the tomb. In the Middle Ages they had arranged marriages. When she was twenty-two and had just found out that her latest love, a stockbroker, had been arrested for insider trading, she'd crawled onto her father's lap and asked him if he'd choose a man for her.

Adam Montgomery had laughed. "Your problem, sweetheart, is that you fall in love with men who need you too much. You ought to find a man who doesn't need you, but just wants you."

Dougless had sniffed. "That's exactly what I want: a Knight in Shining Armor to swoop down off his white horse and want me so much that he carries me back to his castle, where we live happily ever after."

"Something like that," her father had said, smiling. "Armor's okay but, Dougless, sweetheart, if he gets mysterious phone calls in the night, then jumps on his Harley and doesn't return for days at a time, get out, okay?"

Dougless cried harder as she remembered the many times she'd had to go to her family for help. And now she was going to have to ask for their help again. Once again she was going to have to admit that she'd made a fool of herself over a man. But this time was worse, because this man had been someone who had her family's approval. But somehow Dougless had lost him.

"Help me," she whispered, her hand on the marble hand of the sculpture. "Help me find my Knight in Shining Armor. Help me find a man who wants me."

Sitting back on her heels, with her hands covering her face, Dougless began to cry harder.

After a long while, she slowly came to realize that someone was near her. When she turned her head, a stream of sunlight coming from a high window hit metal and so blinded her that she sat back on the stone floor with a thud. She put her hand up to shield her eyes.

Standing before her was a man, a man who appeared to be wearing . . . armor.

He was standing so still, and glaring down at Dougless so fiercely, that at first she thought he wasn't real. She couldn't help staring up at him in openmouthed astonishment. He was an extraordinarily good

looking man, and he was wearing the most authentic-looking stage costume she'd ever seen. There was a small ruff about his neck, then armor
to his waist. But what armor! The shiny metal looked almost as though
it was silver. Down the front of the armor were many rows of etched
flower designs, each design filled with a gold-colored metal. From his
waist to mid-thigh he wore a type of shorts that ballooned out about his
body. Below the shorts, his legs—his big, muscular legs—were clad in
stockings that looked to be knitted of . . . there was only one fiber on
earth that reflected light in just that way: silk. Tied above his left knee
was a garter made of blue silk and beautifully embroidered. His feet
sported odd, soft shoes that had little cut-outs across the toes.

"Well, witch," the man said in a deep baritone, "you have conjured
me, so what now do you ask of me?"

"Witch?" Dougless asked, sniffing and wiping away tears.

From inside his ballooned shorts, the man pulled out a white linen
handkerchief and handed it to her. Dougless blew her nose noisily.

"Have my enemies hired you?" the man asked. "Do they plot
against me more? Is not my head enough for them? Stand, madam, and
explain yourself."

Gorgeous, but off his rocker, Dougless thought. "Listen, I don't
know what you're talking about." Slowly, she stood up. "Now, if you'll
excuse me—"

She didn't say any more because he drew a thin-bladed sword that
had to be a yard long, then held the sharp point against her throat.
"Reverse your spell, witch. I would return!"

It was all too much for Dougless. First Robert and his lying daughter, and now this mad Hamlet. She burst into tears again and slumped
against the cold stone wall.

"Damnation!" the man muttered, and the next thing Dougless
knew he had picked her up and was carrying her to a church pew.

He put her down to sit on the hard pew, then stood over her, still
glaring. Dougless couldn't seem to stop crying. "This has been the
worst day of my life," she wailed. The man was scowling down at her
like an actor out of an old Bette Davis movie. "I'm sorry," she managed
to say. "I don't usually cry so much, but to be abandoned by the man I
love and attacked—at sword point, no less—all in the same day, sets

me off." As she wiped her eyes, she glanced down at the handkerchief. It was a large linen square, and around the border was an inch and a half band of intricate silk embroidery of what looked to be flowers and dragons. "How pretty," she choked out.

"There is no time for trivialities. My soul is at stake—as is yours. I tell you again: Reverse your spell."

Dougless was recovering herself. "I don't know what you're talking about. I was having a good cry all alone, and you, wearing that absurd outfit, came in here and started yelling at me. I've a good mind to call the police—or the bobbies, or whatever they have in rural England. Is it legal for you to carry a sword like that?"

"Legal?" the man asked. He was looking at her arm. "Is that a clock on your arm? And what manner of dress is it that you wear?"

"Of course it's a clock, and these are my traveling-to-England clothes. Conservative. No jeans or T-shirts. Nice blouse, nice skirt. You know, Miss Marple–type clothes."

He was frowning at her, but there seemed to be less anger about him. "You talk uncommonly strangely. What manner of witch are you?"

Throwing up her hands in despair, Dougless stood up and faced him. He was quite a bit taller than she was, so she had to look up. His black, curling hair just reached the stiff little ruff he wore, and he had a black mustache above a trim, pointed, short beard. "I am not a witch, and I am not part of your Elizabethan drama," she said firmly. "And now I'm going to leave this church, and I can promise you that if you try anything fancy with that sword of yours, I'll scream the windows out. Here's your handkerchief. I'm sorry it's so wet, but I thank you for lending it to me. Good-bye, and I hope your play gets great reviews." Turning sharply, she walked out of the church.

"At least nothing more horrible than what I've already been through can happen to me today," Dougless murmured as she left the churchyard. There was a telephone booth beyond the gate, within sight of the church door, and Dougless used it to make a collect call to her parents' home in the U.S. It was early in the morning in Maine, and a sleepy Elizabeth answered the phone.

Anybody but her, Dougless thought, rolling her eyes skyward. She'd rather talk to anyone on earth than her perfect older sister.

"Dougless, is that you?" Elizabeth asked, waking up. "Are you all right? You're not in trouble again, are you?"

Dougless grit her teeth. "Of course I'm not in trouble. Is Dad there? Or Mom?" Or a stranger off the street, she thought. Anybody but Elizabeth.

Elizabeth yawned. "No, they went up to the mountains. I'm here house-sitting and working on a paper."

"Think it'll win a Nobel prize?" Dougless asked, trying to make a joke and sound carefree.

Elizabeth wasn't fooled. "All right, Dougless, what's wrong? Has that surgeon of yours stranded you somewhere?"

Dougless gave a little laugh. "Elizabeth, you do say the funniest things. Robert and Gloria and I are having a wonderful time. There are so many fantastic things to see and do here. Why, just this morning we saw a medieval play. The actors were so good. And you wouldn't believe how good the costumes are!"

Elizabeth paused. "Dougless, you're lying. I can hear it over the phone. What's wrong? Do you need money?"

Try as she might, Dougless could not make her lips form the word "yes." Her family loved to tell what they called Dougless-stories. They loved the one about the time Dougless got locked out of her hotel room when she was wearing only a towel. Then there was the time Dougless went to the bank to deposit a check and walked into a bank robbery. What they especially loved about this story was that when the police arrived, they discovered that the robbers were carrying toy guns.

Now she could imagine Elizabeth's laughter when she told all the Montgomery cousins how funny little Dougless had gone to England and been left at a church with no money, no passport, nothing. "And, oh, yes," Elizabeth would say over the howls of laughter, "she was attacked by a crazed Shakespearean actor."

"No, I don't need money," Dougless said at last. "I just wanted to say hello. I hope you get your paper done. See ya." She heard Elizabeth say, "Dougless" as she dropped the receiver into the cradle.

For a moment Dougless leaned back against the booth and closed her eyes. She could feel the tears starting again. She had the

Montgomery pride, but she'd never done anything to be proud of. She had three older sisters who were paragons of success: Elizabeth was a research chemist, Catherine was a professor of physics, and Anne was a criminal attorney. Dougless, with her lowly elementary school teaching job and her disastrous history with men, was the family jester. She was an endless source of material for laughter among the relatives.

As she was leaning against the telephone booth, her eyes blurred with tears, she saw the man in the armor leave the church and walk down the path. He glanced quickly at the ancient gravestones, but didn't seem to have much interest in them as he headed past the gate.

Coming down the lane was one of the little English buses, as usual doing about fifty miles an hour on the narrow street.

Suddenly, Dougless stood up straight. The bus was coming, the man was walking very fast, and, somehow, she instinctively knew he was going to walk in front of the bus. Without another thought, Dougless started to run. Just as she took flight, the vicar walked from behind the church in time to see the man and the fast-moving vehicle. He too started running.

Dougless reached the man first. She made her best flying tackle, the one she'd learned from playing football with her Colorado cousins, and landed on top of him. The two of them skidded across the graveled path on his armor as though it were a little rowboat as the bus flew past them. If Dougless had been only one second later, the man would have been hit by the bus.

"Are you all right?" the vicar asked, offering his hand to help Dougless up.

"I . . . I think so," she said as she stood up and dusted herself off. "You okay?" she asked the man on the ground.

"What manner of chariot was that?" he asked, sitting up, but not attempting to stand. He looked dazed. "I did not hear it coming." His voice lowered. "And there were no horses."

Dougless exchanged looks with the vicar.

"I'll get him a glass of water," the vicar said, giving a little smile to Dougless as though to say, *You saved him, so he's yours.*

"Wait!" the man said. "What year is this?"

"Nineteen eighty-eight," the vicar answered, and when the man lay back on the ground as if exhausted, the vicar looked at Dougless. "I'll get the water," he said, then went hurrying off, leaving them alone.

Dougless offered her hand to the man on the ground, but he refused it and stood up on his own.

"I think you ought to sit down," she said kindly as she motioned to an iron bench inside the low stone wall. He wouldn't go first but followed her through the open gate, then wouldn't sit until she had. But Dougless pushed him to sit down. He looked too pale and too bewildered to pay attention to courtesy.

"You're dangerous, you know that? Listen, you sit right here and I'm going to call a doctor. You are not well."

She turned away, but his words halted her.

"I think perhaps I am dead," he said softly.

She looked back at him in speculation. If he was suicidal, then she couldn't leave him alone. "Why don't you come with me?" she said quietly. "We'll go together to find you some help."

He didn't move from the bench. "What manner of conveyance was it that nearly struck me down?"

Dougless moved to sit beside him. If he was suicidal, maybe what he needed most was someone to talk to. "Where are you from? You sound English, but you have an accent I've never heard before."

"I am English. What was the chariot?"

"All right," she said with a sigh. She could play along with him. "That was what the English call a coach. In America, it's called a minibus. It was going entirely too fast, but it's my opinion that the only thing of the twentieth century the English have really accepted is the speed of the motor vehicle." She grimaced. "So what else don't you know about? Airplanes? Trains?"

It was one thing to offer help, but she had important things of her own to take care of. "Look, I really need to go. Let's go to the rectory and have the vicar call a doctor." She paused. "Or maybe we should call your mother." Surely the people of this village knew of this crazy man who ran about in armor and pretended he'd never seen a wristwatch or a bus.

"My mother," the man said, his lips forming a little smile. "I would imagine my mother is dead now."

Maybe grief had made him lose his memory. Dougless softened. "I'm sorry. Did she die recently?"

He looked up at the sky for a moment before answering. "About four hundred years ago."

At that Dougless started to rise. "I'm calling someone."

But he caught her hand and wouldn't let her leave. "I was sitting . . . in a room writing my mother a letter when I heard a woman weeping. The room darkened, my head swam; then I was standing over a woman—you." He looked up at her with pleading eyes.

Dougless thought that leaving this man alone would be so much easier if he weren't so utterly divine looking. "Maybe you blacked out and don't remember dressing up and going to the church. Why don't you tell me where you live so I can walk you home?"

"When I was in the room, it was the year of our Lord 1564."

Delusional, Dougless thought. Beautiful but crazy. My luck.

"Come with me," she said softly, as though speaking to a child about to step over a cliff. "We'll find someone to help you."

The man came off the bench quickly, his blue eyes blazing. The size of him, the anger of him, not to mention that he was steel-covered and carried a sword that looked to be razor sharp, made Dougless step back.

"I am not yet ready for Bedlam, mistress. I know not why I am here or how I came to be here, but I know who I am and from whence I came."

Suddenly, laughter began to rumble deep inside Dougless. "And you came from the sixteenth century. Queen Elizabeth's time, right? The *first* Elizabeth, of course. Oh, boy! This is going to be the best Dougless-story ever. I'm jilted in the morning and an hour later a ghost holds a sword to my throat." She stood up. "Thanks a lot, mister. You've cheered me up immensely. I am now going to call my sister and ask her to wire me ten pounds—no more, no less—then I'm catching a train to the hotel where Robert and I are staying. I'll get my plane ticket, then I'm going home. I'm sure that after today the rest of my life is going to be uneventful."

She turned away from him, but he blocked her path. From inside his balloon shorts he withdrew a leather pouch, looked in it, took out a few coins, and pressed them into Dougless's hand, closing her fingers over them.

"Take the ten pounds, woman, and be gone. It is worth that and more to be rid of your spiteful tongue. I will beseech God to reverse your wickedness."

She was tempted to throw the money at him, but her alternative was to call her sister again. "That's me, Wicked Witch Dougless. I don't know why I want a train when I have a perfectly good broomstick. I'll send your money back in care of the vicar. So long, and I hope we never meet again."

She turned and left the churchyard just as the vicar returned with the man's water. Let someone else deal with his fantasies, she thought. The man probably had a whole trunk full of costumes. Today he's an Elizabethan knight, tomorrow he's Abraham Lincoln—or Horatio Nelson, since he's English.

It was easy to find the train station in the little village, and she went to the window to purchase her ticket.

"That'll be three pounds six," the man behind the window said.

Dougless had never been able to figure out the English money. There seemed to be so many coins that had the same value, so she shoved the coins the man had given her under the cage window. "Is this enough?"

The man looked at the three coins one by one, slowly turning them over, examining them carefully. After a moment, he looked back at Dougless, then excused himself.

I'll probably be arrested for passing counterfeit money, Dougless thought as she waited for the man to return. Being arrested would be a fitting end to a perfect day.

After a few minutes a man with an official-looking hat came to the window. "We can't take these, miss. I think you ought to take them to Oliver Samuelson. He's just around the corner to your right."

"Will he give me train fare for the coins?"

"I 'spect he will that," the man said, seeming to be amused at some private joke.

"Thank you," Dougless murmured as she took the coins. Maybe she should call her sister and forget about the coins. She looked at them, but they looked as foreign as all foreign coins did. With a sigh, she turned right and came to a shop. "Oliver Samuelson, Coin Dealer" the painted window said.

Inside the shop, a bald-headed little man was sitting behind a desk, a jeweler's loupe about his shiny forehead. "Yes?" he asked when Dougless entered.

"The man in the train station sent me to you. He said you might give me train fare for these."

The man took the coins and looked at them under the jeweler's loupe. After a moment he began to softly chuckle. "Train fare, indeed."

He looked up. "All right, miss," he said. "I will give you five hundred pounds each for these, and this one is worth about, say, five thousand pounds. But I don't have that much money here. I'll have to call some people in London. Can you wait a few days for the money?"

Dougless couldn't speak for a moment. "Five *thousand* pounds?"

"All right, six thousand, but not a shilling more."

"I . . . I . . ."

"Do you want to sell them or not? They're not ill-gotten are they?"

"No, at least I don't think so," Dougless whispered. "But I have to talk to someone before I sell them. You're sure they're genuine?"

"As a rule medieval coins aren't so valuable, but these are rare and in mint condition. You don't by chance have more, do you?"

"Actually, I believe there are a few more." Maybe a whole bag full of them, she thought.

The man smiled at her as though she were the light of his life. "If you have a fifteen-shilling piece with a queen in a ship on it, let me see it. I can't afford it, but I'm sure I can find a buyer."

Dougless started backing toward the door.

"Or a double," he said. "I'd like to have an Edward the Sixth double."

Nodding at him, Dougless left his shop. In a daze, she walked back to the church. The man wasn't in the churchyard, so she hoped he hadn't left. She went into the church, and there he was, on his knees before the white tomb of the earl, his hands clasped, his head bowed in prayer.

The vicar stepped from the shadows to stand beside her. "He's been there since you left. I tried, but I couldn't get him to stand up.

Something is deeply troubling that poor man." He turned to her. "He's your friend?"

"No, actually, I just met him this morning. I thought he was from here."

The vicar smiled. "My parishioners seldom wear armor." He looked at his watch. "I must go, but you'll stay with him? For some reason, I hate to see him left alone."

Dougless said that she would stay by him, then the vicar left the church, and she was alone with the praying man. Quietly, she walked to stand behind him. "Who are you?" she whispered.

He didn't open his eyes, unclasp his hands, or even lift his head. "I am Nicholas Stafford, earl of Thornwyck."

It took Dougless a moment to remember where she'd heard that name before, then she looked at the marble tomb. Carved deeply in Gothic letters was the name, Nicholas Stafford, Earl of Thornwyck. And the full-length sculpture of the man on top of the tomb was wearing exactly what this man was wearing. And the face carved in the marble was this man's face.

The idea that this man really was from the past, really was a living, breathing ghost, was more than Dougless could comprehend. She took a deep breath. "You don't have any identification, do you?" she asked, trying to lighten the moment.

Lifting his head, the man opened his eyes and glared at her. "Do you doubt my word?" he asked angrily. "You, the witch who has done this to me, can doubt me? If I did not fear being accused of sorcery myself, I would denounce you and stay to watch you burn."

Standing there, silent, her thoughts in turmoil, Dougless watched as the man turned away and began to pray again.

TWO

When at last *Nicholas Stafford stood up,* he stared at the young woman before him. Her manner, her dress, and her speech were so strange to him that he could hardly keep his thoughts together. She looked to be the witch he knew her to be: she was as beautiful as any woman he'd ever seen, her uncased hair flowing to her shoulders, her eyes as green as emeralds, and her skin was white, flawless. But she was wearing an indecently short skirt, as though she were daring the contempt of man and God alike.

In spite of the fact that he felt dizzy and weak, he did not allow himself to waver from his firm stance. He returned her straightforward glare with one of his own.

He still could not believe what had happened to him. At the lowest point in his life, when there seemed to be no hope in his life, his mother had written him that at last she had discovered something that would give them the hope they had nearly abandoned. He had been writing her, questioning her, and revealing some information when he'd heard a woman weeping. The sound of tears in a place of confinement was not so unusual, but something about this woman's weeping had made him put down his pen.

When the woman's sobs had grown until they'd filled the little room, echoing off the stone walls and ceiling, Nicholas had put his hands over his ears to shut out the sound. But he had still heard her. Her weeping had grown louder, until he could no longer hear his own thoughts. Overwhelmed, he'd put his head down on the table and given himself over to the pull of the woman.

Then, it had been as though he were dreaming. He knew he was still sitting, his head still on the table, but at the same time, he was trying to stand up. When he was at last on his feet, the floor seemed to fall away from under him. He felt light, as though he were floating. Then he held out his hand and saw, to his horror, that his hand seemed to have lost substance. He could see through his hand. Staggering toward the door, he tried to call out, but no sound came from his mouth. As he watched, the door seemed to fall away, and with it went the room. For a moment Nicholas appeared to be standing on nothing. There was a void around him, his body naught but a shadow through which he could see the darkness of nothing.

He had no idea how long he drifted in the nothingness, feeling neither hot nor cold, hearing nothing but the woman's deep weeping.

One moment he was nowhere, was but a shadow, and the next moment he was standing in the sunlight in a church. He had on different clothes. Now he was wearing demi-armor, the armor he wore only for the most auspicious occasions, and he had on his emerald satin slops.

Before him, weeping next to a tomb was a girl or woman, he could not tell which, for her hair was hanging slovenly over her face. She was weeping so hard, so intent on her own misery, that she did not see him.

Nicholas's eyes moved from her to look up at the tomb she was clutching—and it was the sight of the tomb that made him step backward. On top of it was a white marble sculpture of . . . himself. Carved beneath was his name and today's date. They have buried me before I am dead? he wondered in horror.

Feeling sick from his experience and at seeing his own tomb, he looked about the church. There were burial plaques set in the walls. The dates read, 1734,1812,1902.

No, he thought, it could not be. But as he looked at the church he could see that everything was different. The church was so very *plain*. The beams were bare wood; the stone corbels were unpainted. The altar cloth looked as though it had been embroidered by a clumsy child.

He looked back down at the sobbing woman. A witch! he thought. She was the witch who had called him forth to another time and place. When she had at last stopped her sobbing long enough to become aware of his presence, he had immediately demanded that she return him—he *had* to return, he thought, for his honor and the future of his family depended upon his returning. But at his words, she had once again collapsed into helpless sobbing.

It did not take him long to discover that she was as vile-tempered and sharp-tongued as she was evil. She had even been bold enough to say she had no knowledge of how he came to be in this place, and that she knew nothing of why he was there.

At last she had left the church, and Nicholas had been relieved when she'd gone. He was feeling more steady, and he was beginning to believe that he had dreamed that flight through the void. Perhaps all that he was experiencing was merely a dream of remarkable reality.

By the time he left the church, he was feeling much stronger, and he was glad to see that the churchyard looked the same as all church-yards—but he did not pause to examine the gravestones' dates. One of those in the church had been 1982—a date he could not fathom.

He left through the church gate and walked into the silent road. Where were the people? he wondered. And the horses? Where were the carts carrying goods?

What happened next had happened too quickly for him to remember clearly. There was a sound to his left, a loud, fast sound such as he'd never heard before; then, to his right, came the witch, running faster than a woman should. Nicholas was unprepared when the woman leaped on him. He was weaker than he realized because the frail weight of the woman knocked him to the ground.

Seconds after they fell to the earth together, close by them roared an obscenly fast horseless chariot. Afterward, Nicholas had asked the woman and the vicar—who was properly dressed in an unadorned, long robe as befitted his station—questions, but they had seemed to believe that Nicholas was without sanity. He allowed the witch to lead him back inside the churchyard. Was this his fate? he wondered. Was he destined to die alone in a strange place . . . in a strange time?

He had tried to explain to the witch that she must return him to his own time. He told her of his need, but she persisted in pretending that she knew nothing of how or why he was in this place. He'd had difficulty understanding her speech, and that, combined with the ordinariness of her dress—no jewels, no gold, no silver—told him she was of peasant stock. Because of the strangeness of her speech, it had taken him a while to understand that she was begging money from him. She was demanding of him the outrageous sum of ten pounds! But he did not dare refuse her demand for fear of what other spells she might perform.

The instant she had the money, she left, and Nicholas went back inside the church. Slowly, he walked to the tomb, *his* tomb, and ran his fingers over the carving of the death date. Had he died when he'd traveled through the void? When the witch had conjured him forth to this time—the churchman had said it was now 1988, four hundred and twenty-four years later—did that mean she had killed him in 1564?

How could he make her understand that he *had* to return? If he had died on 6 September 1564, that meant he had proven nothing. It would mean he had left too much undone. What horror had befallen the people he'd left behind?

Nicholas had dropped to his knees on the cold stone floor and begun to pray. Perhaps if his prayers were as strong as the witch's magic, he could overrule her power and return himself.

But as he prayed, his mind raced. Phrases ran through his head: *The woman is the key. You need to know.* These words were what he heard over and over.

After a while he stopped reciting prayers and opened his mind to his thoughts. Witch or no, the woman had brought him forward, therefore only she had the power to return him to his own time.

Yet, for all that she had brought him forward, she did not seem to have a use for him. Perhaps, Nicholas thought, she had not meant to call him forth. Perhaps she had great power, but knew not how to use it.

But, again, perhaps he had been pulled across time for some reason neither of them knew.

So *why* had he come forward? he wondered. Was he to learn something? Was this witch to teach him something? Could it be possible that she was as innocent as she claimed to be? Had she been weeping over some base lovers' quarrel, and, for some reason neither of them knew, she had conjured him forward to this dangerous time when chariots drove at unimagined speeds? If he learned what he needed to know here, would he then return to his proper time?

The witch was the key. The phrase kept running through his mind. Whether she had brought him forth through malicious intent or by unhappy accident, he was sure that she held the power to return him. And if that were true, then, through her, he was to learn what he must in this time.

He *must* bind her to him, he thought. No matter what the cost to his peace, no matter if he had to lie, slander, blaspheme, he knew that he must bind the woman to him. He had to see to it that she did not leave him until he discovered what he needed to know from her.

He remained on his knees, praying for God's guidance, asking advice, and pleading with God to stay with him as he did what he must do and learned what he needed to know.

When the woman returned to the church, Nicholas was still praying, and while she was complaining about the money Nicholas had given her, he offered God his thanks for the woman's return.

THREE

W ho are you?" Dougless asked the man wearing the ridiculous costume. "And where did you get these coins?" She watched him get off his knees, and from the ease with which he moved in the heavy armor, she knew he must have been rehearsing with it for a long time. "Are the coins stolen?"

When she saw his eyes ignite, she stepped back. She didn't want him to press a sword against her throat again. But she saw him calm himself.

"Nay, madam, the coins are my own."

"I can't accept them," Dougless said firmly, holding out the coins. "They're quite valuable."

"They are not enough for your needs?" he asked softly, even giving a slight smile.

Dougless gave him a suspicious look. A few minutes ago he was attacking her with a sword, but now he was smiling at her as though he meant to . . . well, to seduce her. The sooner she got away from this crazy man the better off she would be, she thought.

When the man made no effort to take the coins, she put them on the edge of the tomb. "Thanks for offering them to me, but no thanks. I'll make do some other way." She turned to leave the church.

"Pause, madam!" he said loudly.

Dougless clenched her fists at her sides. This man's pseudo-Elizabethan grammar was getting on her nerves. She turned to face him. "Look, I know you have problems. I mean, maybe you cracked your head and can't remember who you are, but that's not my problem. I have problems of my own. I don't have a penny to my name, I'm hungry, I don't know anyone in this country, and I don't even know how I'm going to get a bed tonight, even if I could afford one."

"Nor do I," the man said softly, looking at her with sad, hopeful eyes.

Dougless sighed. Needy men, she thought, the bane of my life. But this time, she told herself, she wasn't going to fall for it. This time she wasn't going to help an insane man who, when angry, pulled a sword on her. "Go outside the church, take a right—be sure and watch out for cars—walk two blocks, then take a left. Three blocks past the train station is a coin dealer. He'll give you lots of modern money for your old coins. Then take the money, buy yourself some proper clothes, and check into a good hotel. Miss Marple says there are few problems in life that can't be solved by a week in a good hotel. If you take a long, hot bath, I'll bet your memory will return in no time."

Nicholas could only stare at her. Did this woman speak English? What was a "block"? Who was "Miss Marple"?

At his blank look, Dougless sighed again. She could no more leave him alone than she could leave an injured puppy in the middle of the highway. "All right," she said at last. "Come with me to the telephone and I'll point you on your way. But that's it. That's all I'm doing! You're on your own after that."

Quietly, Nicholas followed her out of the church, but he stopped in his tracks when they stepped outside the gate. What he was seeing was too horrifying to believe.

After only a few steps, Dougless realized the man wasn't behind her. Turning, she saw him gaping at a young girl on the opposite side of the road. She was dressed in the current English idea of chic: all in black. She wore tall black high heels, black hose, a tiny black leather skirt, and a huge black sweater that reached to the top of her thighs. Her short hair was sprayed purple and red, and stuck up like a porcupine's quills.

Dougless smiled. The punk rocker-influenced fashions were a shock to anyone, much less to a crazy man under the illusion that he was from the sixteenth century. "Come on," she said good-naturedly. "She's ordinary. You should see the people attending a rock concert."

They walked to the phone booth, and Dougless again gave him directions but, to her annoyance, he didn't leave, but stood outside the booth. "Please go away," she said, but he didn't move. I'll ignore him, she thought as she picked up the telephone, but she put it down quickly and turned to him. "I think we need to get some things straight between us. If this is an English pickup, I'm not interested. I already have a guy. Or did have one." Dougless took a breath. "I *do* have a man in my life. In fact I'm going to call him right now, and I'm sure he'll come and get me."

The man didn't reply to her little speech, but just stood there looking at her. With a sigh, Dougless called the operator to place a collect call to Robert at their hotel. After a moment's hesitation, the hotel clerk informed her that Robert and his daughter had checked out an hour ago.

Dougless hung up, then slumped against the telephone cubicle. Now what do I do? she thought.

"What is this?" the man asked, looking at the telephone with great interest. "You talked to this?"

"Give me a break, will you?" she half-yelled, taking her anger out on him. Turning back, she jerked the phone up, called the operator, and got information for the number of the hotel that was next on the itinerary she'd made for Robert and her. The clerk at the second hotel informed her that Robert Whitley had canceled his reservation only moments before.

Dougless leaned against the phone cubicle and, in spite of herself, tears came to her eyes. "So where's my Knight in Shining Armor?" she whispered. As she said the words, she looked at the man standing before her. A fading ray of sunlight struck his armor, a shadow fell across his blue-black hair, and a jewel in his sword hilt twinkled. This man had appeared the last time she'd cried and begged for a Knight in Shining Armor.

"You have had bad news?" he asked.

She straightened. "It looks as though I've been abandoned," she said softly, looking at him. No, it couldn't be, and she wasn't going to even consider it. It was a one in a million chance that this actor, who was so involved in his role that he believed it, should appear exactly at the moment she'd asked for a Knight in Shining Armor. The truth was that Dougless was a magnet for strange men. Men who had problems seemed to have radar for finding her.

"I, too, seem to have lost all," he said so softly she hardly heard him.

Oh, no! she thought. She was not going to fall for that line. "Someone around here must know who you are. Maybe if you ask at the post office, someone can tell you how to get home."

"Post office?"

He looked so genuinely lost that she could feel herself softening toward him. No, Dougless, no, she told herself, but the next moment she heard herself say, "Come on. I'll take you to the coin dealer so you can exchange your coins."

They walked together, and his erect, perfect carriage made Dougless straighten her shoulders. None of the English people they passed stared at them—as far as Dougless could tell, the English stared only at people wearing sunglasses—but then she and Nicholas passed a couple of American tourists with their two adolescent children. The man had two cameras about his neck.

"Lookit that, Myrt," the man said, the adults rudely gaping at Nicholas in his armor, and the children laughing and pointing.

"Ill-mannered louts," Nicholas said under his breath. "Someone should teach them how to behave in the presence of their betters."

Things happened very quickly after that. A bus stopped just a few feet from them, and out stepped fifty Japanese tourists, their cameras clicking as they photographed every inch of the quaint little English village. When they saw Nicholas, they advanced on him, cameras covering their faces.

At the sight of the approaching tourists, Nicholas drew his sword and stepped forward. Watching from the sidelines, the American woman tourist yelled in fear, but the Japanese kept moving closer, their cameras clicking like cicadas on a hot summer night.

To prevent the coming clash, Dougless did the only thing she knew worked: she flung herself against the armor-clad man and yelled, "No!" Unfortunately, when she hit him, the edge of his sword slashed the upper sleeve of her blouse and cut her arm. Startled by the pain, Dougless tripped and nearly fell, but the knight caught her, lifted her into his arms for the second time, and carried her back to the sidewalk. Behind them, the Japanese cameras were still clicking and the Americans applauded.

"Gee, Daddy, this is better than Warwick Castle," an American kid said.

"It's not in the guidebook, George," the woman said. "I think they should put things like this in the guidebook, or otherwise a body could think it was *real.*"

Nicholas set the woman down. Somehow, he did not know how, but he had made a fool of himself. Did this century allow a nobleman to be defamed? And what manner of weapon were the small black machines these people held before their faces? For that matter, what manner of little people were they who held the machines?

He did not ask his questions, as questions seemed to annoy the witch-woman. "Madam, you are injured," he said, and Dougless could tell by the way he stiffened that he was mortified that he'd injured her.

Her arm was bleeding and the wound hurt, but she decided to let him off the hook. "It's only a flesh wound," she said, parodying the TV westerns. But the man didn't smile at her joke. Instead, he continued to look embarrassed. "It's not anything," she said, looking at the bloody place on her arm. She took a tissue from her skirt pocket and pressed it over the cut. "The coin shop is down there. Let's go."

When Dougless entered the little shop, the dealer smiled at her in welcome. "I hoped to see you again. I—" He broke off when he saw Nicholas. Slowly, without a word, the man came forward and began to walk around Nicholas, examining his clothing. After one circuit, he dropped the jeweler's loupe down over his eye and looked at the armor, murmuring, *"Mmm hmm,"* over and over. While Nicholas stood stiffly erect, looking at the man in distaste, but also looking as though he didn't want to commit another faux pas, the coin dealer examined the jewels on Nicholas's sword hilt, the jewels of the ring on the hand that rested on the sword, and the jewels on the dagger in his belt—a weapon Dougless hadn't noticed before. Flipping up his loupe, the man went to his knees and examined the embroidery on the garter about Nicholas's knee, then looked at the knitting of his hose, and, last of all, at his soft slippers.

Finally, the coin dealer straightened and peered at Nicholas's face, examining his beard and hair.

Throughout this, Nicholas had been enduring the tradesman's scrutiny with ill-concealed distaste.

At last the coin dealer stepped back. "Remarkable," he said. "I have never seen anything like it. I must get the jeweler from next door to see this."

"You will do no such thing!" Nicholas snapped. "Do you think I wait all day here to be inspected like a hog at a fair? Will you do business, or do I go elsewhere?"

"Yes, sir," the coin dealer muttered, scurrying back behind his counter.

Nicholas dropped a sackful of coins onto the counter. "What do you trade me for these, and remember, man, I take care of those who cheat me."

At Nicholas's tone of voice, Dougless found herself cowering to one side. This armored man had a way of giving orders that could frighten one into doing his bidding. After he'd dropped the coins, Nicholas went to stand before the window while the dealer, with trembling hands, opened the bag.

Dougless moved to the counter. "Well?" she whispered. "What did you see when you examined him?"

The dealer glanced nervously at Nicholas's back, then leaned toward Dougless to whisper, "His armor is silver—remarkably pure—and it's etched with gold. Those emeralds on his sword are worth a fortune, as are the rubies and diamonds on his fingers." He glanced at her. "Whoever made his costume spent a great deal. Oh, my," he said, holding up a coin. "Here it is."

"A queen in a ship?"

"Just so," he said, holding the coin in a caressing way. "I can find a buyer, but it will take a few days." His voice was like that of a lover.

Dougless took the coin out of his hand, and slipped it and all but one of the others back into the bag. Before these were sold, she wanted to do a little research and compare prices. "You said you'd give me five hundred pounds for that one."

"And the others?" the dealer asked, his voice almost begging.

"I'll . . . I mean, *we* will think about it."

Sighing, the man went to the back of the store, then returned a few moments later and counted out five hundred pounds' worth of the large, pretty English money.

"I'll be here if you should change your mind," the dealer called as Nicholas and Dougless left the shop.

On the street, Dougless handed Nicholas the bag of coins plus the modern bills. "I sold one coin for five hundred pounds, but the rest of them are worth a fortune. In fact, it seems that everything you're wearing is worth a king's ransom."

"I am an earl, not a king," Nicholas said, puzzled as he looked at the paper money with interest.

She peered closely at his armor. "Is that really silver, and is the yellow metal actually gold?"

"I am not a pauper, madam."

"It wouldn't seem so." She stepped back from him. "I guess I better go now." Suddenly, she realized that she had wasted most of the day with this man, yet she still had no money nor any place to go. And there was no one in England she could call to get the immediate help she needed. Robert and his daughter had checked out of one hotel and had canceled the next one. Dougless grimaced. No doubt dear little Gloria had balked at staying at another historic hotel and spending the day looking at castles and other educational sights.

"You will help me choose?" the man said at the end of what she realized had been a rather long speech.

"I'm sorry, I didn't hear you."

The man seemed to be trying to say something that was very difficult for him. He swallowed as though his own words were poison. "You will help me choose clothes and find lodging for the night? I will pay you for your services."

It took Dougless a moment to understand what he meant. "Are you offering me a *job?*"

"Employment, yes."

"I don't need a job; I just need . . ." Trailing off, she turned away and blinked back tears. Her tear ducts seemed to be attached to Niagara Falls.

"Money?" he offered.

She sniffed. "No. Yes. I guess I do need money, but I also need to find Robert and explain." He thinks I hit his daughter, she thought. No wonder he's furious. But how does someone say, "Your daughter is a liar," in a nice way?

"I will pay you money if you will help me," the man said.

Dougless turned to look at him. There was something in his eyes, something lost and lonely that made her sway a little toward him. No! she told herself. You cannot hook up with a man who you are dead certain is crazy. There is absolutely no doubt with this one. He's undoubtedly rich, but he is insane. He's probably a rich eccentric who had his costume made by some medieval historian and he now wears it as he goes from village to village hitting on lone females.

But then there were his eyes. What if he *had* lost his memory?

And, besides, what were her alternatives? She could almost hear her sister Elizabeth's derisive laughter if Dougless called and asked for money. *Elizabeth* would certainly never consider taking a job from a man wearing armor. No doubt Elizabeth would know exactly what to do, and how to do it, in this situation, because Elizabeth was perfect. As were her other two sisters, Catherine and Anne. In fact, all the Montgomerys seemed to be perfect—except for Dougless. She'd often wondered if she'd been put in the wrong crib in the hospital.

"All right," Dougless said abruptly. "I might as well lose the rest of the day. I'll help you get some clothes and find a place to stay, but that's it. And I'll do it for, say . . . fifty dollars." That should be enough to get her a bed-and-breakfast for the night, she thought, and tomorrow she'd screw up her courage and call Elizabeth again.

Swallowing his rising anger, Nicholas gave the woman a curt nod.

He understood her meaning if not her words, but at least he had made her agree to stay with him for a few more hours. Later, he would have to find something else to keep her by his side until he discovered how to get back to his own time. And when he found what he needed to know, he would rejoice to leave this woman.

"Clothes," she was saying. "We'll get you clothes, then it'll be tea time."

"Tea? What is tea?"

Dougless stopped walking. An Englishman who pretended he didn't know about tea? This man was more than she could bear. She'd help him until she got him checked into a hotel, then she'd be glad to get rid of him.

FOUR

They walked together down the wide sidewalk in silence, the man looking in shop windows, at the people, and at the cars on the street. His handsome face wore such an expression of astonishment that Dougless could almost believe he had never seen the modern world before. He asked her no questions, but often halted for a moment to stare at a car or at a group of young girls in short skirts.

It was only a block to a small clothing store for men. "Here's where we can buy you something less conspicuous to wear," she said.

"Yes, I would see a tailor," he said, looking up over the door and frowning as though something were missing.

"It's not a tailor, just ready-made clothes."

When they were inside the little shop, Nicholas stood still, gaping at the shirts and trousers hanging from the racks. "These clothes have been made," he said, his eyes wide.

Dougless started to reply, but instead turned to the clerk who'd come forward to greet them. The man was small, thin, and had to be at least ninety years old. "We need clothing for him from the skin out.

And he'll have to be measured for size." Even if the man did remember his sizes, he'd no doubt pretend he didn't, she thought.

"Certainly," the clerk said, then looked at Nicholas. "If you'll step over here, sir, we can begin measuring."

When she saw that the man was leading the way to a semi-private area at the back of the store, Dougless stood where she was. But Nicholas insisted that she go with him into the curtained-off area.

Dougless sat on a chair off to one side, picked up a magazine, and pretended to read while the clerk began to undress Nicholas. The way he raised his arms for the clerk to unlatch his armor made it look as though he was used to other people undressing him. Carefully, almost reverently, the little man set Nicholas's armor on a cushioned bench. Dougless saw the man run a caressing hand down one side of the armor before turning back.

Under the armor, Nicholas wore a big-armed linen shirt that was plastered to his body with sweat.

And what a body he had! Dougless thought as she almost dropped her magazine. She'd seen armor in museums and had laughed at the way the metal had been molded into the shape of a muscular torso. She'd always thought that it had been done to hide a man's paunch. But this man, this Nicholas Stafford, was indeed as broad-shouldered and as muscled as the shape of the armor.

Dougless tried her best to keep her attention on the magazine she was holding, some treatise on the joys of salmon fishing, but she kept glancing up at the bare-chested Nicholas. The clerk brought one shirt after another for him to try on, but the earl liked none of them. After about the fifteenth shirt, the clerk looked with pleading eyes to Dougless.

She put down the magazine and walked to stand before him, her eyes determinedly on his face. "What's wrong?" she asked Nicholas.

He moved to one side, away from the clerk, who busied himself with folding clothes. "There is no beauty in this raiment," he said, frowning. "There is no color, no jewels, no needlework. Perhaps a woman could ply her needle to one of these and—"

Dougless smiled. "Women don't sew today. At least not like this," she said as she touched the cuff of his linen shirt that had been thrown across a clothing rack. The cuff was embroidered in black silk in a design of birds and flowers with a lovely hand-done trim of black cut-work on the edge.

Dougless caught herself. Of course women—some women, some-where—still sewed like that because someone in this century had sewn that shirt, hadn't she?

Dougless picked up a beautiful cotton shirt from the discarded heap. The English weren't like Americans in always wanting something new every five minutes, so the clothing in English stores tended to be of the best quality, made to last for years. If one could afford the outra-geous prices, the quality was worth the cost.

"Here, try this one on again," she said, finding herself coaxing him. She wondered if there was a woman alive who hadn't experienced shop-ping with a man and trying to persuade him to like something. "Look at this fabric; feel how soft it is."

As Dougless held the shirt for him, his reluctance evident, Nicholas slipped his arms into the sleeves, while she did her best to keep her eyes off the way his muscles played under his skin.

The shirt was beautiful. "Now," she said, "step over to the mirror and have a look."

She had seen the three full-length mirrors when they'd entered the curtained area, so it had not occurred to her that Nicholas had not noticed them. She wasn't prepared for his reaction to the three mirrors. At first he just stared at them; then, cautiously, he reached out to touch one.

"They are glass?" he whispered.

"Of course. What else are mirrors made of?"

From inside his balloon shorts, he withdrew a little round wooden object and handed it to her. On the other side of the wood was a metal mirror, and when Dougless looked into it, her image was distorted.

Glancing up at the man, she saw the way he was studying his reflection. Was it truly the first time he'd ever seen a clear full-length view of himself? Had he only seen his own reflection in distorted metal mirrors such as the one she was holding?

Of course not, she told herself. He just didn't remember the last time he'd seen a mirror. Or maybe he did remember and was pretend-ing he didn't.

Looking up, she caught sight of her own reflection in the mirror. What a mess she was! As a result of all her crying, her eye makeup was under her eyes instead of above them. Her blouse was hanging out of her belt, and there a long cut on the sleeve, and it was dotted with blood. Her navy blue tights were bagging at the ankle. And her hair, tangled and droopy, was too awful to contemplate.

Turning away from the unpleasant vision, she mumbled, "Trousers." This time, Dougless left the curtained area as the clerk measured Nicholas. When the door to the shop opened and more customers entered, the clerk ushered Nicholas to a dressing room, then handed him several pair of trousers through the door. All was quiet for a moment until Dougless saw the dressing room door open a crack and the man peeped out, looking at Dougless for help. She went to him.

"I cannot manage," he said softly, then opened the door wider so she could enter. "What manner of fastening is this?"

Dougless tried not to think of this situation. She was squashed into a dressing room with a strange man who couldn't figure out how to work the zipper on the front of his trousers. "Here, like . . ." She started to show him on the trousers he had on, but she thought better of that. Taking a pair hanging from a hook, she showed him the zipper, then the snaps; then she took a step back to watch while, childlike, he zipped and unzipped, snapped and unsnapped. When she was sure he'd caught on, she started to open the door.

"Wait. What is this wondrous substance?" He held up a pair of boxer shorts, stretching the waistband in and out.

"It's elastic," she said.

"Elastic," he said, mispronouncing the word as "elistic." But his face was so alight with discovery that she couldn't help feeling good also.

"That's nothing," she said, smiling. "Wait until you see velcro." She backed out of the dressing room. "You need any more help, let me know."

She was still smiling as she closed the door behind her. Standing with her back to the dressing room door, she looked at the clothes around her. How plain they must look to a man who was used to wearing silver armor, she thought.

While they had been inside the dressing room, the clerk had placed the armor, the sword, and the dagger in two large, doubled shopping bags and had set them to the left of the dressing room door. When Dougless went to pick up the bags, they were so heavy she almost dropped them.

After a while, Nicholas came out of the dressing room. He was wearing a soft white cotton shirt and slim gray cotton trousers. The shirt was of the current voluminous style, while the trousers were snug. He looked utterly divine.

As Dougless watched him, he walked to the mirror, then glowered at his image.

"These . . . these," he said, tugging at the ease of the trousers at the back of his leg.

"Trousers. Pants," she supplied, blinking at him. It was taking her a while to adjust to his good looks.

"They do not fit me. They do not show my legs, and I have a fine pair of legs."

Dougless laughed and her trance was broken. "Men don't wear stockings now, but, really, you look great."

"I am not sure," he said, frowning. "Perhaps a chain."

"No chain," she said firmly. "Trust me on this. *No chain.*"

She chose a leather belt for him, then socks. "We'll have to go to another store for shoes."

Feeling as though she'd done her good deed for the year, Dougless wasn't prepared for Nicholas's actions at the cash register. The little clerk totaled the tags he'd cut from the clothes, then told them the cost. Dougless was shocked speechless when Nicholas shouted, "I will have your head, thief!" then reached for his sword—which, thankfully, was in the shopping bags by Dougless's feet.

"He means to rob me!" Nicholas bellowed. "I can hire a dozen men for less than he asks for these unadorned clothes."

Dougless nearly leaped as she put herself between Nicholas and the counter while the poor little clerk huddled against the opposite wall. "Give me the money," she said firmly. "Everything costs more now than it used to. I mean," she said as she clenched her teeth, "you'll remember soon enough about how much things cost. Now, give me the money."

Still angry, he handed Dougless the leather bag full of coins. "No," she said, "the modern money." When Nicholas just stood there, not seeming to understand what she was talking about, she searched through the shopping bags until she found the English pounds.

"He will take paper for clothes?" the earl whispered as Dougless counted out the money; then he smiled. "I will give him all the paper he wants. He is a fool."

"It's paper *money,*" she said as they left the shop. "And you can exchange the paper for gold."

"Someone will give me gold for paper?" he asked, incredulous.

"Yes, there are gold dealers, and some banks sell gold."

"Then why do you not use gold to buy goods with?"

"Too heavy, I guess." She sighed. "You put your money in a bank. Money you aren't using, that is, and use the paper as a substitute for the gold. Where do you put *your* money?" she asked.

"In my houses," he answered, frowning as he considered what she'd told him.

"Oh, I see," she said, smiling. "I guess you dig a hole and hide it. Well, today money is put in a bank where it earns interest."

"What is interest?"

Dougless groaned. Enough was enough! "Here's a tea shop. Are you hungry?"

"Yes," he answered as he opened the door for her.

The English custom of afternoon tea was a tradition Dougless had taken to readily. It was heaven to sit down at four o'clock and sip delicious hot tea and eat a scone. Or five scones, as Gloria did, she thought with a grimace.

At the thought of Gloria, her fists clenched. Did Robert know his daughter had taken Dougless's handbag? Did he know he'd left Dougless completely stranded, alone at the mercy of crazy men? And *how* had Gloria known that Dougless had been expecting an engagement ring? For the life of her, Dougless couldn't believe that Robert had told Gloria such a thing. Had Dougless said something and Gloria had guessed from that?

Dougless couldn't believe that Robert had done what Gloria said and "laughed" about her. Robert wasn't a bad person. If he were, he wouldn't love his daughter so much. He wasn't one of those men who went off and left their children without a backward glance. No, Robert felt bad because he'd left his child when he'd divorced, and he desperately wanted to make it up to his daughter, so he took her with him when he went on vacation. And it was natural for Gloria to fight for her father's love, wasn't it? And wasn't it natural for the child to be jealous of the woman her father loved?

Dougless knew that if Robert walked into the tea shop at that moment, she would fall to her knees and beg his forgiveness.

"May I help you?" the woman behind the counter asked.

"Tea for two," Dougless said. "And two scones, please."

"We have clotted cream and strawberries also," the woman said.

Absently, Dougless nodded, and in moments the woman passed a tray holding a pot of strong tea, cups, and plates of food across the counter to her. She paid, then picked up the tray and looked at Nicholas. "Shall we eat outside?"

He followed her outside to a little garden that had vines growing over the old brick walls that enclosed it. Fat old-fashioned roses ran along the border and filled the area with their fragrance. Silently, Dougless set the tray down and began to pour the tea into two cups. On her previous trips to England, her mother had considered her too young to drink tea, but she'd tried the English custom of adding milk to tea the first day of this trip and had found it delicious. The milk made the tea the correct temperature and took the sharp tannin flavor out of the tea.

Nicholas was walking about the little garden, studying the walls and the plants. She called him to the picnic table and handed him his cup of tea and a scone.

He gave the tea a tentative look, then sipped cautiously. After two sips, he looked at Dougless with such naked joy on his face that she laughed as he drained the cup. She poured him another cup while he picked up the scone and looked at it. It was very much like a southern American biscuit, but it had sugar in the dough, and these were fruit scones, so they had raisins in them.

She took the scone from him, broke it in half and slathered it with the thick clotted cream. He bit into it and as he chewed he looked like a man who had fallen in love.

In minutes he had drunk all the tea and eaten all the scones. After a couple of remarks about his gluttony, Dougless went back into the shop and bought more of everything. When she returned, she ate while he leaned back in his chair, sipped tea, and studied her.

"What made you to weep in the church?" he asked.

"I . . . I really don't believe that's any of your business."

"If I am to return—and I must return—I need to know what brought me forth."

Dougless put her half-eaten scone down. "You aren't going to start that again, are you? You know what I think? I think you're a graduate student in Elizabethan history, probably Ph.D. level, and you got carried away with your research. My father said it used to happen to him, that he'd read so much medieval script that after a while he couldn't read modern handwriting."

Nicholas looked at her with distaste. "For all your wonders of horseless chariots, your marvelous glass, and the riches of goods to purchase, you have no faith in the mystery and magic of the world," he said softly. "But I do not doubt what has happened to me, and I know from whence I came," he said evenly. "And you, witch—"

At that, Dougless got up and left the table. But he caught her before she reached the door to the shop, his hand cutting into her arm.

"Why were you weeping when first I saw you? What could cause a woman to weep such as I heard?" he demanded.

She jerked out of his grip. "Because I'd just been left behind," she said angrily. Then, to her shame, tears began again.

Gently, he slipped her arm in his and led her back to the table. This time, he sat beside her, poured her another cup of tea, added milk, and handed her the pretty porcelain cup.

"Now, madam, you must tell me what plagues you so that tears pour forth from your eyes as from a waterfall."

Dougless didn't *want* to tell anyone what had happened to her. But her need to share was greater than her pride, and within minutes, she was pouring out her story to him.

"This man left you alone? Unattended?" Nicholas asked, aghast. "He left you at the mercy of ruffians and thieves?"

Nodding, Dougless blew her nose on a paper napkin. "And at the mercy of men who believe they're from the sixteenth century, too. Oh, sorry," she added.

But Nicholas didn't seem to hear her. He got up and began pacing the garden. There were four other tables but no other customers. "You but knelt by the tomb—my tomb—and asked for a . . ." He looked at her.

"A Knight in Shining Armor. It's an American saying. All women want a gorgeous . . . I mean, a . . . Well, a man to rescue her."

Smiling a bit, his lips hidden in his beard and mustache, he said, "I was not wearing armor when you called me forth."

"I *didn't* call you," she said fiercely. "It's customary to cry when you get left in a church. Especially when a fat brat of a girl steals your handbag. I don't even have a passport. Even if my family wired me money for a ticket home, I couldn't leave immediately. I'd have to apply for another passport."

"Nor can I get home," he said, beginning to pace again. "That we have in common. But if you brought me forth, you can send me back."

"I am *not* a witch," she practically shouted at him. "I do not practice black magic, and I certainly don't know how to send people back and forth in time. You've imagined *all* of this."

He raised an eyebrow at her. "No doubt your lover was justified in leaving you. With your vile temper, he would not want to remain with you."

"I was *never* 'vile-tempered' as you call it, with Robert. Maybe a little short-tempered now and then, but only normally so, because I loved him. *Love* him. And I shouldn't have complained so much about Gloria. It was just that her lying was beginning to get on my nerves."

"And you love this man who abandoned you, this man who allowed his daughter to steal from you?"

"I doubt if Robert knows Gloria took my bag and, besides, Gloria is just a kid. She probably doesn't even realize what she did. I just wish I could find them and get my passport back so I could go *home.*"

"It seems we have kindred goals," he said, his eyes boring into hers.

Suddenly, she knew where he was leading. He wanted her to help him on a permanent basis. But she was *not* going to saddle herself with a man with amnesia.

She set her empty cup down. "Our goals aren't alike enough that we should spend the next few months together until you remember that you live in New Jersey with your wife and three kids, and that every summer you come to England, put on fancy armor, and play some little sex game with an unsuspecting tourist. No, thank you. Now, if you don't mind, I believe we have an agreement. I'll find you a hotel room, then I'm free to leave."

When she finished speaking, she could see the flush of anger through his beard. "Are all the women of this century as you are?"

"No, just the ones who have been hurt over and over again," she shot back at him. "If you really have lost your memory, you should go to a doctor, not pick up a woman in a church. And if this is all an act, then you should definitely go to a doctor. Either way, you don't need *me*." She put the tea things on the tray to carry them back into the shop, but he stood between her and the door.

"What recourse have I if I tell the truth? Have you no belief that your tears could have called me from another time, another place?"

"Of course I don't believe that," she said. "There are a thousand explanations as to why you *think* you're from the sixteenth century, but not one of them has to do with my being a witch. Now, will you excuse me? I need to put these down so I can find you a hotel room."

He stepped aside so she could enter the tea room, then followed her to the street. All the while, he kept his head down as though he were considering some great problem.

Dougless had asked the woman in the tea shop where the nearest bed-and-breakfast was, and as she and Nicholas walked quietly along the street, it bothered her that he didn't speak. Nor did he look about him with the intense interest he'd shown earlier.

"Do you like your clothes?" she asked, trying to make conversation. He was carrying the shopping bags full of armor and his old clothes.

He didn't answer, but kept walking, his brow furrowed.

There was only one room available at the bed-and-breakfast, and Dougless started to sign the register. "Do you still insist that you're Nicholas Stafford?" she asked him.

The woman behind the little desk smiled. "Oh, like in the church." She took a postcard of the tomb in the church from a rack and looked at it. "You do look like him, only a bit more alive," she said, then laughed at her own joke. "First door on the right. Bath's down the hall." Smiling, she left them alone in the entrance hall.

When Dougless turned to look at the man, she suddenly felt as though she were a mother abandoning her child. "You'll remember soon," she said soothingly. "And this lady can tell you where to get dinner."

"Lady?" he asked. "And dinner at this hour?"

"All right," she said, frustrated. "She's a woman and a meal this late is supper. I'll bet that after a good night's sleep you'll remember everything."

"I have forgot naught, madam," he said stiffly, then seemed to relent. "And you cannot leave. Only you know how to return me to my own time."

"Cut me some slack, will you?" she snapped at him. Didn't he understand that she, too, had needs? She couldn't give up all that she needed to help this stranger, could she? "If you'll just give me the fifty dollars we agreed on, I'll leave. In pounds, that's . . ." To her horror, she realized that was only about thirty pounds. A room in this bed-and-breakfast had cost forty pounds. But a deal was a deal. "If you'll give me thirty pounds, I'll be on my way."

When he just stood there, she rummaged in the shopping bags until she found his paper money; then she removed thirty pounds and gave him the rest of it. "Tomorrow you can take your coins to the dealer and he'll give you more modern money," she said as she turned to go. "Good luck." She gave one last look to his blue eyes that looked so sorrowful, then turned and left.

But once she left the house, she didn't feel jubilant at finally having rid herself of the man. Instead, she felt as though she were missing something. But Dougless forced herself to put her shoulders back and her head up. It was getting late and she had to find a place to spend the night—a cheap place—and she had to decide where to go from here.

FIVE

*W*hen *Nicholas found* the upstairs room where he was to spend the night, he was appalled. The room was small, with two tiny, hard-looking beds with no cloth hangings enclosing them, and the walls were very bare. But upon closer examination he saw that the walls were painted with thousands of tiny blue flowers. On second thought, he decided that with a few borders and some order to the paintings they might look all right.

There was a window with that marvelous glass in it, and it had fabric side hangings of painted cloth. There were framed pictures on the walls, and when he touched one, he felt the glass—so clear he could hardly see it. One of the pictures was quite lewd, showing two naked women sitting on a cloth near two fully dressed men. It was not that Nicholas didn't like the picture, but he couldn't bear to see such a shameful thing displayed so openly. He turned it to face the wall.

There was a door that led to a press, but there were no shelves in it. There was only a round stick going from one side to the other, with the same steel shapes that he had seen in the clothes shop hanging from the stick. There was a cabinet in the room, but such as he'd never seen before. It was entirely full of drawers! He tried, but the top of the cabinet did not lift up. He pulled the drawers out one by one and they worked marvelously well.

After a while, Nicholas began to look for a chamber pot, but one was not to be found anywhere in the room. Finally, he went downstairs and out to the back garden to find a privy, but there was none.

"Have things changed *that* much in four hundred years?" he mumbled as he relieved himself in the rosebushes. He fumbled with the zipper and snaps, but managed rather well, he thought.

"I will do well without the witch," he said to himself as he went back into the house. Perhaps tomorrow he would wake and find this all to be a dream, a long, bad dream.

No one was about downstairs, so Nicholas looked into a room with an open door. There was furniture in the room that was fully covered with fine, woven fabric. There was a chair with not one inch of wood showing. When he sat on the chair, the softness enveloped him. For a moment he closed his eyes and thought of his mother and her old, frail bones. How she'd like a chair like this, covered in softness and fabric, he thought.

Against one wall was a tall wooden desk with a stool beneath it. Here was something that looked somewhat familiar. When he examined the cabinet, he saw the hinge and lifted the top. It was not a desk but a type of harpsichord, and when he touched the keys, the sound was different. There was written music in front of him and for once something looked familiar.

Nicholas sat down on the stool, ran his fingers over the keys to hear the tone of them, then, awkwardly at first, began to play the music before him.

"That was beautiful."

Turning, he saw the landlady standing behind him.

"'Moon River' always was one of my favorites. How do you do with ragtime?" She searched inside a drawer in a little table that had an extraordinary plant on top of it and withdrew another piece of music. "They're all American tunes," she said. "My husband was an American."

The most extraordinary piece of music, called "The Sting," was put before Nicholas. It took him some time before he played it to the woman's satisfaction, but once he understood the rhythm of the music, he played it with enjoyment.

"Oh, my, you are good," she said. "You could get a job in any pub."

"Ah, yes, a public house. I will consider the possibility," Nicholas said, smiling as he stood up. "The need of employment might yet arise." Suddenly, he felt dizzy and reached out to catch himself on a chair.

"Are you all right?"

"Merely tired," Nicholas murmured.

"Traveling always wears me out. Been far today?"

"Hundreds of years."

The woman smiled. "I feel that way too when I travel. You should go up to your room and have a bit of a lie-down before supper."

"Yes," Nicholas said softly as he started for the stairs. Perhaps tomorrow he would be able to think more clearly about how to get himself back to his own time. Or perhaps tomorrow he'd wake up in his own bed and find that all of it was over, not just this twentieth-century nightmare, but also the nightmare he'd been in when last he was home.

In his room he undressed slowly, and hung his clothes up as he had seen done in the clothes shop. Where was the witch now? he wondered. Was she back in the arms of her lover? She was powerful enough to have called him forward over four hundred years, so he had no doubt that she could conjure an errant lover back across mere miles.

Nude, Nicholas climbed into bed. The sheets were smooth beyond believing and they smelled clean and fresh. Over him, instead of multiple, heavy coverlets, was a fat, soft, light blanket.

Tomorrow, he thought as he closed his eyes in weariness. Tomorrow he would be home.

Instantly, he fell into a sleep that was deeper than any he'd ever experienced before, and he heard nothing when the sky opened and it began to rain.

Hours after he went to bed, reluctantly, he was awakened by his own thrashing about. Groggily, Nicholas sat up. The room was so dark that at first he didn't know where he was. As he listened to the rain pounding on the roof, his memory gradually returned. He fumbled at the table beside the bed for flint and candle so he could make a light, but there were none.

"What manner of place is this?" he exclaimed. "There are no chamber pots, no privies, and no lights."

As he was grumbling, his head turned sharply as he listened. Someone was calling him. The voice was not in words. He couldn't hear the actual sound of his name, but he could feel the urgency and the desperate need of a voice that was reaching out to him.

No doubt it was the witch-woman, he thought with a grimace. Was she bent over a cauldron of snakes' eyes, stirring and cackling and whispering his name?

As Nicholas felt the pull of the call, he knew there was no use fighting her. As he lived and breathed, he knew he had to go to her.

With great reluctance, he left the warm bed, then began the arduous task of trying to dress himself in the strange modern clothes. It was when he pulled up the zipper that he discovered the parts of his body that were most susceptible to being caught in the tiny metal teeth. Cursing, he put on the flimsy shirt and felt his way out of the dark room.

He was glad to see that there was light in the hall. On the wall was a glass-enclosed torch, but the flame was not fire, and whatever it was, it was encased in a round glass sphere. He wanted to examine this miracle further, but through a window came a flash of lightning, and a crack of thunder rattled the house—and the call came to him more forcefully.

He went down the stairs, across lush carpets, and out into the pouring rain. Shielding his face with his hands, Nicholas looked up to see that high above his head were more flames set on top of poles, yet the blowing rain did not extinguish their fire. Shivering, already wet through, Nicholas put his head down into his collar. These modern clothes had no substance! The modern people must be strong! he thought. How did they survive with no capes, or jerkins to protect them from the driving rain?

Struggling against the force of the rain, he went down streets that were unfamiliar to him. Several times he heard strange noises and reached for his sword, then cursed when he found that the weapon was not there. Tomorrow, he thought, he would sell more coins and hire guards to accompany him. And tomorrow he would force the woman to tell him the truth of what she had done to bring him to this strange land.

He struggled down street after street, making several wrong turns, but then he'd stop and listen until the call came again. After a while of following what he was hearing inside his mind, he left the streets that had the torches on poles and entered the darkness of the countryside. For several minutes, he walked along a road, then stopped and listened as he wiped rain from his face. Finally, he turned right and started across a field, and when he reached a fence, he climbed over it, then kept walking. At long last, he reached a small shed, and he knew that, at last, he had found her.

As he flung open the door, a flash of lightning showed her inside the shed. She was drenched and shivering, and curled into a ball on some dirty straw, trying her best to get warm. And, once again, she was weeping.

"Well, madam," he said, his teeth clenched in anger, "you have called me from a warm bed. What is it you want of me now?"

"Go away," she sobbed. "Leave me alone."

As he looked down at her, he had to admire her fortitude—as well as her pride. Her teeth were chattering so hard he could hear them over the rain; she was obviously freezing. With a sigh, he released his anger. If she were such a powerful witch, why had she not conjured herself a dry place for the night? Nicholas stepped into the leaking shed, bent, and lifted her into his arms. "I do not know who is the more helpless," he said, "you or I."

"Let me go," she said, as he picked her up, but she made no real struggle to get away from him. Instead, she put her head against his shoulder and began to sob harder. "I couldn't find any place to stay. Everything in England costs so much and I don't know where Robert is and I'll have to call Elizabeth and she'll laugh at me," she said all in one almost unintelligible sentence.

Nicholas had to adjust her in his arms as he swung over the fence, but he kept walking, and Dougless continued crying as her arms slipped around his neck. "I don't belong anywhere," she said. "My family is perfect, but I'm not. All the women in my family marry wonderful men, but I can't even *meet* any wonderful men. Robert was a great catch but I couldn't hold on to him. Oh, Nick, what am I going to do?"

They were out of the fields and back onto a paved road. "First, madam," he said, "you may not call me Nick. Nicholas, yes, Colin, perhaps, but not Nick. Now, since we seem destined to know one another, what is your name?"

"Dougless," she said, clinging to him. "It's Dougless Montgomery."

"Ah, a good, sensible name."

Dougless sniffed, her tears slowing down. "My father teaches medieval history so he named me after Dougless Sheffield. You know, the woman who bore the earl of Leicester's illegitimate child."

Nicholas halted. "She what?"

Dougless pulled away to look up at him in surprise. The rain was now just a soft drizzle and there was enough moonlight so she could see his expression. "She bore the earl of Leicester's child," she said in surprise.

Immediately, Nicholas set her on the ground and glared at her. The rain was dripping off both their faces. "And, pray tell, *who* is the earl of Leicester?"

His disguise is slipping, Dougless thought as she smiled up at him. "Shouldn't you pretend to know this?" When Nicholas didn't answer, Dougless said, "The earl of Leicester was Robert Dudley, the man who loved Queen Elizabeth so much."

At that, rage filled Nicholas's face; then he turned and stomped away. "The Dudleys are traitors, executed every one of them," he said over his shoulder. "And Queen Elizabeth is to marry the king of Spain. She will not marry a Dudley, I can assure you of that!"

"You're right, she won't marry a Dudley, but she won't marry the king of Spain, either," Dougless shouted as she ran after him. But she let out a yelp of pain when she twisted her ankle and fell onto the asphalt, scraping her hands and knees.

Angrily, Nicholas turned back to her. "Woman, you are a bloody great trouble," he said as he again lifted her into his arms.

Dougless started to speak, but when he told her to be quiet, she put her head back against his shoulder and said nothing.

He carried her all the way back to the B and B where he was staying, and when he pushed open the door, he found the landlady sitting on a chair and waiting for him.

"There you are," the landlady said, relief in her voice. "I heard you leave, and I knew in my heart that something was wrong. Oh, you poor dears, you both look done in. Why don't you take her upstairs and while she's having a nice, hot soak I'll make you both some tea and sandwiches." She looked at Nicholas. "I took your dinner up earlier, but you didn't answer my knock. You must have been asleep."

Nicholas nodded at the woman, then followed her up the stairs, still carrying Dougless, but also managing to ignore her. The landlady led them to a room Nicholas had not seen before. It had strange, large pottery vessels in it, one of which he recognized as a bathtub. But he saw no buckets of water, and he'd seen no maids about. Who filled this large tub?

He nearly dropped the woman he was holding when the landlady turned a knob above the tub and out poured water. A fountain *inside* the house! Nicholas thought, his eyes wide in disbelief.

"It'll be hot in a minute," the landlady said. "You should get her undressed and put her in the tub while I get fresh towels. And you look like you could use a soak too," she said as she left the room.

Nicholas had understood enough of what the landlady said to consider the idea. He looked down at Dougless with interest.

"Don't even think about it," Dougless warned. "You're to leave this room while I take a bath."

Smiling, he set her down and looked about. "What manner of room is this?"

"It's the bathroom."

"I see the bathing pot, but what is this object? And this?"

Dougless stood there in her cold, wet clothes, and looked at him. She'd thought he'd made a major slip up in his disguise when he'd pretended to know so little about Robert Dudley, but as he'd said more, Dougless knew he'd been right. She'd have to call her father for the dates, but she knew without asking that in 1564, the year this man said he'd last been in, Robert Dudley had not yet been made the earl of Leicester.

So now this man was standing there in wet clothes that clung to his beautiful body, and he was asking her what a toilet and sink were. She had to restrain herself from asking what he'd been using if he didn't know what a toilet was. But of course he knew, she told herself. However, he must have been studying very, very hard to have forgotten something so basic. She demonstrated the basin; then, with a face red with embarrassment, she explained the toilet. She demonstrated seat up and seat down. "And you never, *never* leave the seat up," she said, feeling as though she were doing her part for womankind in teaching one man this simple thing.

They were interrupted when the landlady returned with more towels and a flowered cotton robe. "I noticed you didn't have much luggage," she said, her tone hinting that she wanted to know why. "Usually, Americans show up with so much luggage."

"The airlines lost it all," Dougless said quickly, and wondered if she thought Nicholas was also American. Was his accent odd to an English person?

"I thought it was something like that," the landlady said. "I'll get your tea and leave it on the table in the hall, if that's all right with you. So, good night."

"Yes, thank you," Dougless said as the door closed, leaving her alone with Nicholas, whom she dismissed quickly. "You can go now. I won't be long." Smiling as though he was enjoying Dougless's nervousness, he left the bathroom. When she was alone, Dougless slipped into the hot water, lay back, and closed her eyes. The water stung her scraped knees and elbows, but already the hot water was beginning to warm her.

How had he found her? she wondered. After she'd left him at the B and B, she'd wandered all over the village trying to find a place to stay for thirty pounds, but there was nothing. All the less expensive places were full. She'd spent six pounds on a meal in a pub, then started walking. She thought perhaps she could make it to another village before night and find shelter there. But the rain had started, it'd grown dark, and all Dougless could find was a leaky shed set in the middle of a field. At first she'd curled up on some dirty straw and gone to sleep, but she awoke sometime during the night to find herself crying—but then, crying seemed to be her normal state over the last twenty-four hours.

While she'd been crying, he had appeared—and, the truth was, she hadn't been surprised to see him. In fact, it had seemed perfectly natural that he'd known where to find her and that he'd come out into the rain for her. It had also seemed natural when he'd picked her up in his strong arms.

When the water grew cold, Dougless got out of the tub, dried herself off, then put on the flowered robe. A glance in the mirror showed her to have on no makeup and her hair . . . The less thought about that the better. There was nothing she could do about her appearance as she didn't have so much as a comb.

Shyly, she knocked on the half-open bedroom door. Nicholas, wearing only his still-wet trousers, flung it open. "The bathroom is yours," she said, trying to smile and trying to act as though the situation was normal.

But now there was no softness in his face. "Get into that bed and stay there," he ordered. "I do not intend to go bat-fowling again."

She only nodded at him as he passed her on the way to the bathroom. On the table was a tray of food and a pot of tea. "Bet he didn't leave me any," she muttered at the same time she was thinking that she didn't deserve any more kindness from him. She *had* been a pest to him. But he'd left enough in the pot for her to have a cup of tea and he'd left a chicken sandwich for her. Gratefully, Dougless ate and drank it all; then, wearing the thin robe, she slipped under the comforter of the second bed. When he returned, they would talk, she thought. She would ask him how he found out where she was. How had he found her in the dark in the pouring rain?

She meant to talk to him when he returned, but she closed her eyes for a moment, and the next thing she knew it was morning. Warm sunlight was hitting her full in the face, and slowly, groggily, she opened her eyes.

There was a man standing before the window, his back to her, and he was wearing only a small white towel fastened about his hips. As though in a dream, Dougless noticed that he had a muscular back that tapered down to a small slim waist, and his legs were heavy with muscle.

Slowly, Dougless came awake enough to remember who this man was. She remembered everything, their first meeting in the church when he'd drawn a sword on her, to last night when he'd found her and carried her through the rain.

When she sat up, he turned to look at her.

"You are awake," he said flatly. "Come, get up, as there is much we must do."

As she got out of bed, she saw that he, too, meant to get dressed . . . in front of her. Grabbing her own wrinkled clothing, she went to the bathroom to dress. When she had her clothes on, she looked into the mirror and nearly started crying again. She looked awful! Her eyes were still red, and her hair was a tangled, frizzy mess—and she knew she had no way to repair the damage. As she looked into the mirror, she thought that if all women had to confront the world with the face God gave them, there would be a great increase in female suicides.

Putting her shoulders back, she left the bathroom, where she almost ran into Nicholas, as he was waiting for her in the hall.

"First we eat; then, madam, we talk," he said as though his words were a dare.

Dougless merely nodded as she went ahead of him down the stairs to the little dining room.

Dougless smiled when they entered the room, and she remembered something she'd read in a guidebook. It had stated that there are two meals that should be eaten in England: breakfast and tea. When she and Nicholas were seated at a small table, the landlady began bringing in platters full of food. There were fluffy scrambled eggs, three types of bread, bacon that was like the best American ham, grilled tomatoes, fried potatoes, golden kippers, cream, butter, and marmalade. And in the middle of the table was a large, pretty porcelain pot of brewed tea that the landlady kept filled throughout the meal.

Ravenous, Dougless ate until she could hold no more, but she couldn't come close to competing with Nicholas. He ate nearly all the food that was set on the table. When Dougless finished eating, she caught the landlady watching Nicholas curiously. He ate everything with his spoon or his fingers. He used his knife to cut the bacon while holding it in place with his fingers, but he never once touched his fork.

When he had finally finished eating, he thanked the landlady, then took Dougless's arm in his and ushered her outside.

"Where are we going?" she asked as she ran her tongue over her teeth. She hadn't brushed them in twenty-four hours, and they felt fuzzy. Also, her scalp itched.

"To the church," he said. "There we will conceive of a plan."

They walked quickly to the church, with Nicholas stopping only once to gawk at a small pickup truck. Dougless started to tell him about eighteen-wheelers and cattle trucks, but thought better of participating in his game.

The old church was open and empty, and Nicholas led her to sit on a pew that was at a right angle to the tomb. In silence, she watched him as he looked at the marble sculpture for a while, then ran his hands over the date and name.

At last he turned away, clasped his hands behind his back, and began to pace. "As I see it, Mistress Montgomery," he said, "we need each the other. It is my belief that God has put us together for a reason."

"I thought I did it with a spell," she said, meaning it as a joke, but, actually, she was glad that he at last seemed to realize that she was not a witch.

"It is true that I believed that at first, but I have not slept since you called me into the rain and I have now had time to consider more thoroughly."

"I *called* you?" she said in disbelief. "I never even thought about you, much less called you. And I can assure you that there weren't any telephones in that field, and I certainly couldn't shout loud enough for you to hear me."

"Nonetheless, you did call me. You woke me with your need."

"Oh, I see," she said, starting to get angry. "We're going back to your belief that I somehow, through some sort of hocus-pocus, brought you here from your grave. I can't take this anymore. I'm leaving," she said as she started to stand up.

But before she could move, he was in front of her, one hand on the high arm of the pew, the other on the back, his big body pinning her to her seat. "It matters not to me whether you believe or not," he said, his face near hers, his eyebrows drawn together. "Yesterday morn when I woke it was the year of our Lord 1564, and this morn it was . . ."

"Nineteen eighty-eight," she whispered up at him.

"Aye," he said, "over four hundred years later. And you, witch, are the key to my being here and to my returning."

"Believe me, I'd send you back if I could," she said, her mouth a hard line. "I have enough problems of my own without having to take care of—"

He leaned so close to her face that his nose nearly touched hers, and she could feel the heat of his anger. "You could not dare to say that you must care for me. It is I who must pull you from fields in the dead of night."

"It was just the one time only," Dougless said weakly, then sat back against the pew. "Okay," she said with a sigh, "how did you hear my . . . need, as you call it?"

He dropped his arms from the pew, then went back to look down at the tomb. "There is a bond between us," he said quietly. "Mayhap it is an unholy bond, but it is there. I was awakened during the night with your calling of me. I did not hear words, but nonetheless, I heard you calling me. The . . . feel of the call woke me, so I followed it to find you."

Dougless was silent for a moment. She knew that what he said had to be true because there was no other explanation for how he'd found her. "Are you saying that you think there's some kind of mental telepathy between us?"

Turning back to her, he gave her a puzzled look.

"Mental telepathy is thought transference. People can read each other's thoughts."

"Perhaps," he said, looking back at the tomb. "I am not sure it is thoughts as much as it is . . ." He trailed off for a moment. "Need. I seem to hear your need of me."

"I don't need anyone," Dougless said stubbornly.

Turning back, he glared at her. "I do not understand why you are not still in your father's house. I have yet to see a woman who needs care more than you."

Again, Dougless started to stand up, but a look from Nicholas made her sit back down. "All right, you heard me 'call,' as you say. So what do you think that means?"

Again, Nicholas put his hands behind his back and began to pace. "I have come to this time and this fast, strange place for a reason, and I believe you are to help me find the answer as to why I am here."

"I can't," Dougless said quickly. "I have to find Robert and get my passport so I can go home. The truth is that I've had all the vacation I can stand. Another twenty-four hours like the last ones, and somebody better start carving *my* tombstone."

"My life and death are a jest to you, but they are not so to me," Nicholas said quietly.

Dougless lifted her hands in frustration. "You want me to feel sorry for you because you're dead? But you aren't dead. You're here; you're alive."

"No, madam, there am I," he said, pointing at the tomb.

For a moment, Dougless put her head back against the pew and closed her eyes. Right now, she should leave. Actually, she should probably ask someone for help. But the truth was, she couldn't do either of those things. Whatever this man's real story was, even if she didn't believe he was from another time period, he certainly seemed to believe it. And after he'd rescued her last night, she owed him. She looked at him. "What do you plan?" she asked softly.

"I will help you find your lover, but in return, you must help me find the reason I am here."

"How can you help me find Robert?" she asked.

"I can feed, clothe, and shelter you until he is found," he shot back instantly.

"Ah, yes. Those things. How about eyeshadow too? Okay, only kidding. So, supposing 'we' do find Robert, what do you want me to do to help you find your, ah, way back?"

"Last night you talked to me of Robert Dudley and Queen Elizabeth. You seemed to know who our young queen will marry."

"Elizabeth doesn't marry anyone, and she becomes known as the Virgin Queen. In America there're a couple of states named for her: Virginia and West Virginia."

"Nay! This cannot be true. No woman can rule alone."

"She not only rules alone but does a damn fine job of it. *Did* a great job of it. She made England the ruling power of all Europe."

"This is so?"

"You don't have to believe me; it's history."

For a moment, Nicholas was thoughtful. "History, yes. All that has happened to me, to my family, is now history, so perhaps all of it is recorded somewhere?"

"I see," Dougless said, smiling. "You think maybe you were sent forward to find out something? How intriguing," she said, then frowned. "I mean if it were possible for a person to have been sent forward, it would be intriguing. But since it isn't possible, it's not."

His look of puzzlement was beginning to become familiar to her. When he couldn't seem to figure out what she'd just said, he continued. "Perhaps there is something you know that I must find from you." He moved to stand over her. "What do people of your time know of the Queen's decree against me? Who has told her I raise an army to overthrow her? This would be recorded?"

"Oh, yes. My father used to get angry whenever he read something that said Elizabeth the First had an illegitimate child. My father said that every day of her life is documented, so it wasn't possible that she could have sneaked away and had a baby in secret." As she was saying this, Nicholas was looking at her with such intensity that she smiled. "I have an idea. Why don't you stay here in this time period? Why go back at all? I'm sure you could get a job. You'd be great as an Elizabethan teacher. Or you could research and write. I'm sure you'd have enough to live on after the sale of your coins. If you invested carefully, that is. My father could help you invest, or my uncle J.T. could. Both of them know a lot about money."

"No!" Nicholas said fiercely, his right fist clasped in his left hand. "I *must* return to my own time. My honor is at risk. The future of the Staffords is at stake. If I do not go back, all will be forfeit."

"Forfeit?" Dougless asked, and a little shiver went up her spine. She knew enough about medieval history to have some idea what he was talking about. Her voice lowered. "Usually a nobleman forfeited his estates to the king, or queen, when he was accused of . . ." For a moment, she just looked up at him. "Treason," she whispered. "In medieval times, people forfeited estates due to treason. And treason was paid for . . . in other ways." She took a deep breath. "How . . . how did you die?"

"I assume I was executed."

SIX

*D*ougless *forgot about the question* of whether he was or was not from the sixteenth century. "Tell me what happened," she whispered.

He paced a moment longer; then, after another look at the tomb, he went to sit by her. "I have lands in Wales," he said softly. "When I learned my lands were under attack, I raised an army. But in my haste to protect what was mine, I did not petition the queen for permission to raise this army. She was . . ."

For a moment he looked into the distance, his eyes angry and hard. "The queen was told by someone . . ." Pausing, he took a breath. "She was told that the army I was gathering was to join forces with the young Scots queen."

"Mary Queen of Scots," Dougless said, and he nodded.

"I was given a hasty trial and condemned to be beheaded. I had but three days left before I was to be executed when you . . . when you called me here."

"Then you're lucky!" Dougless said. "Beheading. Disgusting. We don't do that now."

"You have no treason that you do not need to behead people?" Nicholas asked. "Or perhaps you punish the nobility in another way." He put up his hand when she started to answer. "Nay, we will discuss this later. My mother is a powerful woman and she has friends. From the moment I was taken, she has worked without rest to prove my innocence—and she has made progress. She believes she is close to finding who betrayed me. I must return and prove that I am not guilty. If I do not, she will lose all. She will be a pauper."

"The queen would take everything you own?"

"All. It would be as though I truly were a traitor."

Dougless thought about what he'd told her. Of course none of what he was saying was real, but if it were, perhaps there was something to be learned today from the history books. "Do you have any idea who told the queen your army was going to be used to take her throne?"

"I am not sure, but when I came forward, I was writing a letter to my mother. At last I had remembered a man from some ten years ago who may have had a grudge against me. I had been told that he was now at court. Perhaps he . . ." Trailing off, Nicholas put his head in his hands in despair.

Dougless almost reached out to him to touch his hair, perhaps to rub his neck, but she withdrew. She reminded herself that this man's problems were not her own, and there was no reason on earth she should spend her time trying to help him find out why he—or maybe one of his ancestors—had been unjustly accused of treason.

On the other hand, the idea of injustice made Dougless's skin crawl. Maybe it was in her blood. Her grandfather, Hank Montgomery, had been a union organizer before he returned home to Maine to run the family business, Warbrooke Shipping. To this day, her grandfather hated any type of injustice and would risk his life to stop it.

"As I told you, my father is a professor of medieval history," Dougless said softly, "and I've helped him do some research. Maybe I could help you find what you're looking for. And, besides, how many people are you going to find who are in such a situation that they'd even consider helping a man wearing a sword and balloon shorts?"

Nicholas stood up. "You refer to my slops? You jest at my clothing? These . . . these . . ."

"Trousers."

"Aye, these trousers. They bind a man's legs so that I cannot bend. And these," he said as he put his hands in his pockets. "They are so small that I can carry nothing. And last night I was cold in the rain and—"

"But you're cool today," she said, smiling.

"And this." He pulled back the fly to show the zipper. "This can hurt a man."

Dougless began to laugh. "If you *wore* your underwear instead of leaving it on the bed, maybe the zipper wouldn't hurt."

"Underwear? What is that?"

"Elastic, remember?"

"Ah, yes," he said, and began to smile.

Dougless suddenly thought, What else do I have to do? Cry some more? Six of her women friends had taken her out to dinner before she left for England to wish her bon voyage. There had been a lot of laughter about her romantic holiday. Yet here she was wanting to go home after just five days.

Looking up at this smiling man, Dougless wondered, if she were honest with herself, would she rather spend four and a half weeks with Robert and Gloria, or would she rather help this man research what may or may not be his previous life? Smiling back at Nicholas, she thought that the whole thing reminded her of a ghost story where the heroine goes to the library and reads about the curse on the house she's rented for the summer.

"Yes," she heard herself say. "I will help you."

Nicholas sat down by her, took her hand in his, and fervently kissed the back of it. "You are a lady at heart."

She was smiling at the top of his head, but his words made her smile disappear. "At heart? Are you saying that I'm not a lady elsewhere?"

He gave a little shrug. "Who can fathom why God has joined me with a commoner?"

"Why you—" she began. It was on the tip of her tongue to tell him that her uncle was the king of Lanconia and she often spent summers playing with her six cousins, the princes and princesses. But something stopped her. Let him think what he wanted. "Should I address you as 'your lordship'?" she asked archly.

Nicholas frowned thoughtfully. "I have considered that question. Now, when no one knows of my titles, I can move about unharmed. And these clothes, they are the clothes of all the people. I cannot understand your sumptuary laws. I am sure I should hire retainers, yet in this time a shirt costs a man's yearly wage. Try as I might, I cannot understand your ways. Often I . . ." He looked away. "Often, I make a fool of myself."

"Oh, well, I do that and I've grown up in this century," Dougless said lightly.

"But you are a woman," he said, looking back at her.

"First of all, let's get one thing straight: in this century women aren't men's slaves. We women today say what we want to say and do what we want to do. We know we weren't put on this earth only to entertain men."

Nicholas's mouth dropped open in astonishment. "Is this what is believed today of women of my time? You believe that our women were for pleasure only?"

"Obedient, docile, locked away in a castle somewhere, kept pregnant, and never allowed to go to school."

Emotions ran across Nicholas's face: astonishment, anger, disbelief. At last, his face relaxed and he smiled, his eyes full of merriment. "When I return, I will tell my mother what is believed about her. My mother has buried three husbands." Laughter made his lips twitch. "King Henry said my mother's husbands wished themselves into the grave because they weren't half the man she is. Docile? Nay, lady, not docile. No schooling? My mother speaks four languages and argues philosophy."

"Then your mother is an exception. I'm sure most women are— were—downtrodden and brutalized. They had to be. They were the property of the men. Chattel."

He gave her a piercing stare. "And in your day men are noble? They do not abandon women? They do not leave them to the mercy of the elements, with no means of support, no protection, no funds to so much as find a night's lodging?"

Dougless turned away, blushing. So maybe she wasn't in a good position to argue about this. "Okay, you've made your point." She looked back at him. "All right, let's get down to business. First we go to a drugstore, or chemist, as it's called here in England, and we buy toiletries." She sighed. "I need eyeshadow, base, blush, and I'd kill for a tube of lipstick right now. And we need toothbrushes, toothpaste, and floss." Halting, she looked at him. "Let me see your teeth."

"Madam!"

"Let me see your teeth," she repeated in a no-nonsense voice. If he were an overworked graduate student, he'd have fillings, but if he were from the sixteenth century no dentist would have touched his mouth.

After a moment, Nicholas obediently opened his mouth, and Dougless moved his head this way and that to look inside. He had three molars missing and there looked to be a cavity in another tooth, but there was no sign of modern dental work. "We need to get you to a dentist and take care of that cavity."

Instantly, Nicholas pulled away from her. "The tooth does not pain me enough to have it pulled," he said stiffly.

"Is that why you have three teeth missing? They were pulled?"

He seemed to think this was obvious, so Dougless opened her mouth, showed him her fillings, and tried to explain what a dentist was.

"Ah, there you are," said the vicar from the back of the church. "So you two have become friends." His eyes were twinkling.

"We haven't . . ." Dougless began, intending to explain that they hadn't become the friends that the vicar's tone was implying. But she stopped. The truth would take too much explanation. She stood up. "We have to go, as we have a great deal to do. Nicholas, are you ready?"

Smiling at her, Nicholas offered her his arm, and they left the church together. Outside, Dougless paused for a moment and looked at the enclosed graveyard. It had been just yesterday that Robert had left her here.

"What shines there?" Nicholas asked, looking at one of the grave markers.

It was the gravestone Gloria had fallen against, then lied to Robert about her scrapes, saying Dougless had hurt her. Curious, Dougless went to the stone. At the bottom, hidden by grass and dirt, was Gloria's five-thousand-dollar diamond and emerald bracelet. Picking it up, Douglass held it up to the sunlight.

"The quality of the diamonds is good, not excellent," Nicholas said as he peered over her shoulder. "The emeralds are but cheap."

Smiling, Dougless clasped the bracelet tightly in her hand. "I'll find him now," she said. "Now he'll come back for sure." Quickly, she went into the church and told the vicar that should Robert Whitley call and ask about a lost bracelet, he was to say that Dougless had it; then she gave him the name of the bed-and-breakfast where she and Nicholas were staying.

As Dougless left the church, she felt jubilant. Everything was going to work out now. Robert would be so grateful that she'd found the bracelet that . . . Her mind flooded with visions of Robert's protestations of undying love and endless apologies. "I didn't know I could miss anyone as much as I missed you," ran through her head in Robert's tearful voice. "How can you forgive me?" and "I wanted to teach you a lesson, but *I* was the one who learned from you. Oh, Dougless, can you—?"

"What?" she asked, looking up at Nicholas blankly.

He was frowning. "You said we must see an alchemist. Do you prepare new spells?"

She didn't bother to defend herself; she was too happy to allow anything he said to bother her. "Not 'alchemist,' a chemist's," she said happily. "Let's go shopping."

As they walked, she made a mental list of the things she'd need to be looking her best when she saw Robert again. She needed products for her face and hair, and she'd need a new blouse that didn't have a cut sleeve.

First they went to the coin dealer and sold another coin, this one for fifteen hundred pounds. There Dougless called the B and B to reserve their room for three more nights because the dealer had said he needed time to find a buyer for Nicholas's rarer coins. And to give Robert time to find me, Dougless thought.

Then they went to a chemist's shop. As the doors to a magnificent

English drugstore, a Boots, opened, even Dougless looked about in awe. The English didn't fill their shelves with gaudily packaged over-the-counter medicines—even cough syrup was kept behind the counter—but, instead, the shelves were full of products that smelled good. Within minutes, Dougless, a canvas shopping basket at her feet, was trying to decide between mango shampoo or jasmine. And should she get the aloe face pack or the cucumber? she wondered as she tossed a bottle of lavender-scented conditioner into the basket.

"What is this?" Nicholas whispered, looking at the many rows of gaily wrapped packages.

"Shampoo, deodorant, toothpaste, all the usual stuff," Dougless said distractedly. She had lemon verbena body lotion in one hand and evening primrose in the other. Which?

"I know not those words."

Dougless's head was full of the decisions she was trying to make, but then she looked at the products as an Elizabethan man must see them—if Nicholas were from the past, which of course he wasn't, she reminded herself. Her father had said that until recently, people had made all their toiletries at home.

"This is shampoo to wash your hair," she said as she opened a bottle of papaya-scented shampoo. "Smell."

At first whiff, Nicholas smiled at her in delight, then he nodded toward the other bottles, and Douglass began opening them. With each product, Nicholas's face showed his wonder. "This is marvelous. These are heaven. How I'd like to send one of these to my queen."

She recapped a bottle of hyacinth-scented conditioner. "Is this the same queen who cut off your head?"

"She had been lied to," Nicholas said stiffly, making Dougless shake her head. An American had a difficult time understanding such loyalty to the monarchy.

"I have heard that she is especially fond of what smells good," Nicholas said, picking up a bottle of men's aftershave. "Mayhap they have washed gloves here," he said, looking about.

"Washed? You mean clean gloves?"

"Scented."

"Scented skin but no scented gloves," Dougless said, smiling.

"Ah, well," he said slowly, then looked at her in a way that threatened to make her blush. "I needs must make do with scented skin."

Quickly, Dougless looked down at the rows of shaving products. "You wouldn't consider shaving that beard of yours, would you?"

Nicholas ran his hand over his beard, seeming to consider her words. "I have seen no man with a beard now."

"Some men still wear beards, but, on the whole, they're not fashionable."

"Then I will find a barber and shave it," he said finally, then paused. "You have barbers now?"

"We still have barbers."

"And this barber is the one you will have put silver in my sore tooth?"

Dougless laughed. "Not quite. Barbers and dentists are separate professions now. Why don't you pick out a shaving lotion while I get foam and razors?" Picking up the portable shopping basket, she saw that she had nearly filled it with shampoo, cream rinse, combs, toothbrushes, toothpaste, floss, and a small electric travel set of hair rollers. Minutes later, she was happily looking over the makeup when she heard a noise from the other side of the shelves. Nicholas was trying to get her attention.

When she went around the corner, she saw that he'd opened a tube of toothpaste and the white cream had squirted down the front of the racks.

"I but meant to smell it," he said rigidly, and Dougless could feel his deep embarrassment.

Grabbing a box of tissues from a shelf, she opened it, took out a handful, and began to clean the counter.

At the wonder of the tissues, Nicholas lost his embarrassment. "This is paper," he said, feeling the soft tissues, wonder in his voice. "Here, stop that!" he said. "You cannot waste paper. It is too valuable, and this paper has not been used before."

Dougless didn't understand what he was talking about. "You use a tissue once, then throw it away."

"Is your century so rich as this?" he asked, then ran his hand over his face as though to clear his mind. "I do not understand this. Paper is so valuable it is used in place of gold, yet paper is so worthless, it can be used for cleaning, then thrown away."

Smiling, Dougless thought of how all paper in the sixteenth century was handmade. "I guess we are rich in goods," she said. "Maybe richer than we should be." She put the opened tissue box in her basket, then continued choosing items they needed. She bought shaving cream, razors, and deodorant, washcloths for both of them (because the English hotels didn't supply them), and a full set of cosmetics for herself.

When she went to checkout, once again, she took charge of Nicholas's modern money. And once again he was nearly sick when he heard the total. "I can buy a horse for what this bottle costs," he mumbled when she read a price to him. After she paid, she lugged the two shopping bags full of goods out of the store. Nicholas did not offer to take the bags from her, so she guessed that only bags full of armor were masculine enough for him to carry.

"Let's take these back to the hotel," she said. "Then we can—" She broke off because Nicholas had stopped in front of a shop window. Yesterday he'd had eyes only for the street, for gaping at cars, for feeling the surface of the pavement, and for staring at the people. Today he was more interested in the other side of the street, as he kept noticing the shops, marveling at the plate-glass windows, and frequently touching the lettering of the signs.

He had halted in front of a bookstore window. On prominent display was a big, beautiful coffee table edition of a book on medieval armor. Beside it were books on Henry the Eighth and Elizabeth the First. Nicholas's eyes were as wide as dinner plates. Turning, he pointed at the books, then opened his mouth to speak, but no words came out.

"Come on," she said, smiling, as she pulled him inside. Whatever troubles of her own that Dougless had, she soon forgot them when she saw the wonder and joy on Nicholas's face as he reverently touched the books. After dropping off the shopping bags at the counter, she walked about the store with Nicholas. Some big, expensive books were lying faceup on a table just inside the door, and he ran his fingertips slowly over the glossy photos.

"They are magnificent," he whispered. "I have never imagined such as these could exist."

"Here's your Queen Elizabeth," Dougless said, lifting a large color volume.

As though he were almost afraid to touch it, Nicholas gingerly took the book from Dougless.

Watching him, Dougless could almost believe that he'd never seen a modern color photo before. She knew that in Elizabethan times books were precious and rare, prized possessions owned by only the richest of people. If the books had pictures, they were woodcuts or hand-colored illuminations.

She watched as Nicholas reverently opened the book he held and ran his hand over the glossy photos. "Who has painted these? Do you have so many painters now?"

"All the books were printed by a machine."

Nicholas looked at a picture of Queen Elizabeth the First. "What is it she wears? Is the shape of this sleeve the new fashion? My mother would know of this."

Dougless looked at the date: 1582. She took the book from him. "I'm not sure you should look at the future." *What* was she saying?! 1582 the *future?* "Why don't you look at this book?" she said as she handed him *Birds of the World.* Her reaction was, of course, absurd, because any moment now, this man was going to regain his memory. However, just to be safe, she didn't want to tamper with changing history because a medieval man had seen the future. Except of course what history they changed if they saved his life. But that—

Dougless's attention was taken from her thoughts when Nicholas almost dropped the book because the music system, which had been silent until then, suddenly began to play. Twisting about, Nicholas looked around the store. "I see no musicians. And what is that music? Is it ragtime?"

Dougless laughed. "Where'd you hear of ragtime? No," she corrected herself, "I mean, your memory must be returning if you're remembering ragtime."

"Mrs. Beasley," he said, referring to the woman who ran the bed-and-breakfast. "I played for her from her music, but it was not like this music."

"Played for her on what?"

"It is like a large harpsichord, but it sounded most different."

"Probably a piano."

"You have not told me what is the source of the music."

"It's classical music. Beethoven, I think, and it comes from a cassette in a machine."

"Machines," he whispered. "Again machines."

As Dougless watched him, she had an idea. Perhaps she could use music to help bring his memory back.

Along one wall of the store was a selection of cassette tapes. She chose Beethoven, excerpts from La Traviata, and some Irish folk music. She started to choose the Rolling Stones, but then thought she ought to get something more modern, but her thought made her laugh at herself. "Mozart is new to him," she said as she took the Stones tape off the shelf. "Maybe." On the bottom shelf were some inexpensive cassette players for sale, so she bought one that included earphones.

When she went back to Nicholas, he had moved to the stationery section of the store and was gingerly touching the wide selection of papers. Dougless picked up a spiral notebook and began demonstrating felt-tip pens, ballpoints, and mechanical pencils. Nicholas made a few squiggles on the testing paper, but she noticed that he didn't write words. For all that, according to him, his mother was a scholar of great magnitude, Dougless wondered if he could read and write, but she didn't ask him.

They left the store with another shopping bag, this one full of spiral notebooks, felt-tips of every color imaginable, cassettes and a player, plus six travel books. Three of the travel books were on England, one about America, and two were about the world. On impulse she'd also purchased a set of Winsor and Newton watercolors and a block of watercolor paper for Nicholas. She somehow felt that he might like to paint. She also tucked in an Agatha Christie.

"Could we take these bags back to the hotel now?" Dougless asked. Her arms felt as if they were lengthening from carrying the heavy bags.

But Nicholas had stopped again, this time in front of a women's clothing store. "You will purchase yourself new clothing," he said, and it was an order.

Dougless didn't like his tone. "I have my own clothes, and when I get them, I will—"

"I will travel with no beldame," he said stiffly.

Dougless wasn't sure what the word meant, but she could guess. She looked at her reflection in the glass. If she thought she had looked bad yesterday, she had surpassed herself today. There was a time for pride and a time for being sensible. Without another word, she handed him the bag with the books. "Wait for me over there," she said in the same tone of command that he had used on her, as she pointed to a wooden bench under a tree.

After taking the bag with the cosmetics, Dougless straightened her shoulders and entered the shop.

It took over an hour, but when Dougless returned to him, she didn't look like the same person. Her auburn hair, wildly unkempt from days without care, was now pulled back off her face and, neatly combed, it fell back in soft waves to the silk scarf she'd used to tie it at the nape of her neck. Softly applied cosmetics brought out the beauty of her face. She was not a beauty of the type that looked fragile and overbred, but Dougless was healthy and wholesome-looking, as though she'd grown up on a horse ranch in Kentucky or on a sailboat in Maine—which she had.

She'd chosen clothes that were simple, but exquisitely made: a teal Austrian jacket; a paisley skirt of teal, plum, and navy; a plum silk blouse; and boots of soft navy leather. On impulse she'd also purchased navy kid gloves and a navy leather handbag, as well as a full set of lingerie and a nightgown.

Carrying her shopping bags, she crossed the road toward Nicholas, and when he saw her, she was pleased by his incredulous expression. "Well?" she asked.

"Beauty knows no time," he said softly, rising, then kissing her hand.

There were advantages to Elizabethan men, she thought.

"Is it time for tea yet?" he asked.

Dougless groaned. Men were timeless, she thought. It was always: You-look-great-what's-for-dinner?

"We are now going to experience one of the worst aspects of

England, and that is lunch. Breakfast is great; tea is great. Dinner is great if you like butter and cream, but lunch is . . . indescribable."

He was listening to her with concentration, as one does when hearing a foreign language. "What is this 'lunch'?"

"You'll see," Dougless said as she led the way to a nearby pub. Pubs were one of the things Dougless liked best about England, as they were family oriented, but you could still have a drink. After they'd settled into a booth, Dougless ordered two cheese salad sandwiches, a pint of beer for him, a lemonade for her; then she proceeded to tell Nicholas the difference between a bar in America and a pub in England.

"There are more unescorted women?" he asked in amazement.

"More than just me?" she asked, smiling. "There are lots of independent women today. We have our own jobs, our own credit cards. We don't have, or need, men to take care of us."

"But what of cousins and uncles? Do these women have no sons to look after them?"

"It's not like that now. It's—" She stopped talking when the waitress put their sandwiches before them. But they were not sandwiches as Americans know them. An English cheese sandwich was a piece of cheese on two pieces of buttered white bread. A cheese salad sandwich had a small piece of lettuce on it. The sandwich was small, dry, tasteless.

Nicholas watched her as she picked up the strange-looking food and began to eat it; then he followed her lead.

"Do you like it?" she asked.

"It has no flavor," he said, then took a drink of his beer. "Nor does the beer."

Dougless looked about the pub and asked if it was anything like the public houses in the sixteenth century. Not that she believed he was . . . The heck with it, she thought.

"Nay," he answered. "There is gloom and quiet here. There is no danger here."

"But that's good. Peace and safety are good."

Nicholas shrugged as he ate the rest of the sandwich in two bites. "I prefer flavor in my food and flavor in my public houses."

She smiled as she started to stand up. "Are you ready to go? We still have lots to do."

"Leave? But where is dinner?"

"You just ate it."

He raised one eyebrow at her. "Where is the landlord?"

"The man behind the bar seems to be in charge, and I saw a woman behind the counter. Maybe she cooks. Wait a minute, Nicholas, don't make a fuss. The English don't like for people to cause problems. If you'll wait a minute, I'll go and—"

But Nicholas was already halfway to the counter. "Food is food, no matter what the year. No, madam, stay where you are and I will procure us a proper dinner."

As Dougless watched, Nicholas talked earnestly to the bartender for a few moments; then the woman was called over and she, too, listened to Nicholas. When Dougless saw the man and woman scurrying away to do whatever they'd been told, it occurred to her that if Nicholas learned his way around the twentieth century, he might be a bit of a problem.

Moments later he returned to the booth, and minutes afterward, dishes of food began to be placed on the table. There was chicken, beef, a big pork pie, bowls of vegetables, one of salad, and a nasty looking dark beer was set before Nicholas.

"Now, Mistress Montgomery," he said when the table was loaded with food, "how do you propose to find my way home?"

When she looked up at him, his eyes were twinkling and she knew that, for once, she had been the one wearing the incredulous expression. It was his turn to be the one who knew how to do something she didn't.

"Chalk one up for you," she said, laughing as she speared a chicken leg. "Why don't you ask the cook if she knows any good witches' spells?"

"Perhaps if we mix all those bottles you bought . . ." Nicholas said, his mouth full of English beef. "Ow!" he said when he nearly pierced his tongue with the fork he was trying to learn to use.

"Forget the witchcraft," she said as she withdrew a spiral notebook and a pen from a bag. "I have to know all about you before we can start research." Perhaps now, with dates and places, she'd trip him up.

But nothing she asked him even slowed him down as he ate plateful after plateful of food. He was born the sixth of June, 1537.

"And what's your full name, or, I guess, in your case, what's your title?" She was eating mashed parsnips with her left hand, writing with her right.

"Nicholas Stafford, earl of Thornwyck, Buckshire, and Southeaton, lord of Farlane."

Dougless blinked. "Anything else?"

"A few baronetcies, but none of great importance."

"So much for barons," she said as she had him repeat what he'd said so she could write it down. Next, she began to list the properties he owned. There were estates from East Yorkshire to South Wales, plus more land in France and Ireland.

When her head was beginning to whirl with all the names, she closed her notebook. "I think that with all that we should be able to find something about you—him," she said, her tone showing her understatement.

After "lunch" they stopped in a barbershop so Nicholas could be shaved. When he sat up in the chair, clean shaven at last, Dougless took a moment to catch her breath. Hidden under the beard and mustache had been a full-lipped mouth of great sensitivity.

"I will do, madam?" he asked, softly chuckling at her expression.

"Passable," she said, trying to sound as though she'd seen better. But as she walked ahead of him, his laugh filled her ears. Vain! she thought. He was much too vain!

When they returned to the bed-and-breakfast, the landlady said a room with a private bath had come vacant. A sane, sensible part of Dougless knew she should ask for a room of her own, but she didn't open her mouth when the landlady looked at her in question. Besides, Dougless told herself, when Robert came for her, it might be good for him to see her with this divine-looking man.

After she and Nicholas had moved what little they had into the new room, they went to the church and spoke to the vicar, but there was no word from Robert for her, nor any inquiries about the bracelet. They went to a grocery and bought cheese and fruit; to a butcher for meat pies; to a baker for bread, scones, and pastries; then to a winery, where they purchased two bottles of wine.

By teatime, Dougless was exhausted.

"My purse bearer looks sinking-ripe," Nicholas said, smiling at her.

Dougless felt exactly like sinking-ripe sounded. Together they walked back to their little hotel, where they took the bag containing the new books to the garden. Mrs. Beasley served them tea and scones, and gave them a blanket to spread on the grass. Nicholas and Dougless sat on the blanket, drank tea, ate the scones, and looked at the books. It was heavenly English weather, cool yet warm, sunny but not brilliant. The garden was green and lush, the roses fragrant. Dougless was sitting up; Nicholas stretched before her on his stomach as he ate scones with one hand and carefully turned pages with the other.

The cotton shirt he wore was stretched across his back muscles, and the trousers clung to his thighs. Black curls brushed his collar. Dougless found herself looking at him more than at the travel book she was thumbing through.

"It is here!" Nicholas said, rolling over and sitting up so abruptly Dougless's tea splashed out. "My newest house is here." He shoved the book at her as she put down her cup.

"'Thornwyck Castle,'" she read beside the full page photo, "'begun in 1563 by Nicholas Stafford, earl of Thornwyck . . .'" She glanced at him. He was lying on his back, his hands behind his head, and smiling angelically, as though he'd at last found some proof of his existence. "'. . . was confiscated by Queen Elizabeth the First in 1564 when . . .'" She trailed off.

"Go on," Nicholas said softly, but he was no longer smiling.

"'. . . when the earl was found guilty of treason and sentenced to be beheaded. There was some doubt of Stafford's guilt, but all investigation stopped when'"—Dougless's voice lowered—"'when three days before his execution the earl was found dead in his cell. He had been writing a letter to his mother when he apparently died of a heart attack. He was found with his head face down on a table, the letter to his mother'"—she looked up and whispered—"'unfinished.'"

Nicholas watched the clouds overhead and was silent for a while. "Does it say what became of my mother?" he asked at last.

"No. The rest of the article describes the castle and says it was never finished. 'What had been completed fell into disrepair after the Civil War'—your Civil War, not mine—'then was renovated in 1824, for the James family, and—'" She stopped. "'And now it's an exclusive hotel with a two-star restaurant!'"

"My house is a public house?" Nicholas asked, obviously appalled. "My house was to be a center of learning and intelligence. It was—"

"Nicholas, that was hundreds of years ago. I mean, maybe it was. Don't you see? Maybe we can get reservations to stay at this hotel. We can possibly stay at your house."

"I am to pay to stay in my own house?" he asked, his upper lip curled in disgust.

She threw up her hands in despair. "Okay, don't go. We'll just stay here and go shopping for the next twenty years, and you can spend all your time badgering pub owners into serving you medieval banquets every day."

"You have a sharp tongue on you."

"I can see the truth, if that's what you mean."

"Except about men who abandon you."

She started to get up, but he caught her hand.

"I will pay," he said, looking up at her, but he began caressing the fingers of the hand he held. "You will remain with me?"

She pulled her hand out of his grasp. "A bargain's a bargain. I'll help you find out what you need to know so maybe you can clear your ancestor's name."

Nicholas smiled. "So now I am my own ancestor?"

With a look at him that said she could do without his sarcasm, she went into the house to call Thornwyck Castle. At first the reservations clerk haughtily told her that reservations needed to be made a year in advance, but there was a commotion and a moment later the clerk returned to say that, unexpectedly, their best suite was currently available. Dougless said, "Yes!" without asking the price.

As she hung up, Dougless realized she wasn't surprised by the co-incidence of a room becoming available. It was beginning to seem as though a kind of wish therapy was at work. Every time she wished for something, she got it. She'd wished for a Knight in Shining Armor and he had appeared. Maybe her wish had been more of a metaphor than a desire for a man who believed he was from the sixteenth century and wore silver armor, but, still, she had received her wish. She'd wished for money and a bag of coins worth hundreds of thousands of pounds had shown up. She needed a place to spend the night and that had appeared too. Now she needed a reservation to an exclusive hotel and of course the hotel had "unexpectedly" had a vacancy.

Dougless took Gloria's bracelet from her pocket and looked at it. It looked like something some rich, fat old man would give his twenty-years-younger mistress. What could Dougless wish for with Robert? That he'd come to realize that his own daughter was a lying thief? She didn't want any parent to despise his own child. So where did that leave her? She wanted Robert, but his daughter and his love for his daughter came with him. How was she going to deal with that? Was she destined to be cast as the proverbial wicked stepmother no matter what she did?

Before Dougless went back to the garden, she called the vicarage and was again told that no one had called about the bracelet. She asked the vicar for a recommendation for a dentist, and when she was able to make an appointment, again due to a cancellation, for the next morning, Dougless almost laughed aloud. As she started back outside, she saw several American magazines on a table. There was *Vogue, Harper's Bazaar,* and *Gentleman's Quarterly.* Scooping them up, she took them outside and handed them to Nicholas.

Right away, there were some exclamations on his part when she explained that these beautiful "books" were actually disposable goods. Once he conquered his amazement, he started looking through the magazines, studying the ads and the clothes on the models with the intensity of a general studying battle campaigns. At first he hated the clothes, but by the end of the first magazine he was nodding his head as though he were beginning to understand.

Dougless picked up her Agatha Christie and began to read.

"You will read aloud to me?" he asked.

From the way he merely looked at the pictures of the books and magazines, she again thought that perhaps he didn't know how to read, so she read aloud as he looked at the photos in *Gentleman's Quarterly.*

At seven, they opened a bottle of wine, and ate cheese and bread and fruit. Nicholas insisted she read more of the mystery while they ate.

When it grew dark, they went upstairs to their room and the reality of the intimacy of sharing a room began to dawn on Dougless. But as the hours passed, it seemed more and more natural to spend all her time with this gentle man. Watching him look at the world through wonder-filled eyes was becoming a joy to her. And with each passing hour, her memory of Robert was becoming less distinct.

When they were alone in the room, Nicholas didn't allow her to feel awkward. After examining their private bathroom, he demanded to know where the tub was. To Dougless's American delight, there was a shower stall in the bathroom. But before she could explain how to use the shower, Nicholas had turned on the taps and sprayed himself with cold water. Then, both of them laughing, he bent over while she toweled his hair dry.

She showed him how to use shampoo and cream rinse, then how to brush his teeth. "Tomorrow I'll show you how to shave," she said, smiling at him with his mouth full of toothpaste lather.

After she'd showered and washed her hair, she put on the plain white nightgown she'd bought and slipped into one of the twin beds. She and Nicholas had had a somewhat heated "discussion" about his bathing every day. The idea seemed to appall him. He'd argued against chills and talked of how body oils protected a person. Dougless had countered by showing him a jar of cold cream. Nicholas said that washing off oils, then buying oil to replace what came for free, was absurd. Dougless had replied that if he didn't take a bath *every day,* people on the street and in the restaurants would start talking about how bad he smelled. At that horrible prospect, Nicholas went into the bathroom, shut the door, and she soon heard the water running.

He must have enjoyed himself, because he stayed in the shower so long that steam came rolling out from under the door. When he finally emerged, he was wearing only a towel about his hips and rubbing his wet hair with another towel.

There was an awkward moment when he looked up at her as she sat in bed, fresh-faced, wet hair slicked back, and Dougless's heart jumped into her throat.

But then Nicholas saw the table lamp beside her, and Dougless spent the next fifteen minutes answering questions about electric lights. Nicholas nearly drove her crazy with turning every switch in the room on and off until, to make him go to bed, she promised to read more to him. She looked away as he dropped his towel and climbed into his own bed wearing absolutely nothing. "Pajamas," she murmured. "Tomorrow we buy pajamas."

She read for only about thirty minutes before she realized that he was asleep, and, turning off the light, she snuggled down under the covers. She was just dozing off when Nicholas's thrashing made her sit up in alarm. The room was just light enough that she could see him flailing at the covers, rolling back and forth, as he moaned in the grips of a nightmare. Reaching across to his bed, she put her hand on his shoulder. "Nicholas," she whispered, but he didn't respond, and his thrashing increased. She shook his shoulder, but he still didn't wake.

Throwing back the covers, she sat on the edge of the bed, and leaned over him. "Nicholas, wake up," she said. "You're having a nightmare."

Immediately, his strong arms reached out, and he pulled her to him.

"Let me go!" she said, struggling against his grip, but he didn't release her. Instead, he calmed his thrashing and seemed to be perfectly content to hold her to him as though she were a life-size stuffed toy.

Using all her strength, Dougless pried his arms from around her, then went back to her own bed. But she was no more under the covers than he began moving about and moaning again. Getting out of bed, she went back to stand over his bed. "Nicholas, you have to wake up," she said loudly, but her voice had no effect on him. He was kicking at the covers, his arms were flailing about, and judging from the expression on his face, he was reliving some truly horrible experience.

Sighing in resignation, Dougless pulled back the covers and slipped in beside him. Immediately, he clasped her to him as though he were a scared child and she his doll and, instantly, he settled back into a peaceful sleep. Dougless told herself she was a true martyr, and that she was doing this for him. But somewhere inside herself, she knew she was as lonely and as scared as he probably was. Putting her cheek in the hollow of his warm shoulder, she went to sleep in his arms.

She awoke before dawn, smiling even before she was fully aware that it was Nicholas's warm, big body next to hers that was making her feel so good. Her impulse was to turn in his arms and kiss that warm skin.

But as soon as she was fully aware of where she was, she opened her eyes, then eased out of bed and went to her own bed. For a while, she lay there alone, looking across the beds at him. He was sleeping so quietly, his black curls such a contrast to the white of the pillowcase. Was he her own Knight in Shining Armor? she wondered. Or would he eventually get his memory back and realize that he had a home somewhere in England?

Feeling a bit devilish, Dougless tiptoed out of bed, quietly pulled the new tape player from where she'd hidden it on the windowsill—she had been waiting for the right moment to show it to him—then put in the Stones tape. Putting the player by Nicholas's head, she turned the volume up, then pressed *play*.

When "I Can't Get No Satisfaction" blasted out, Nicholas came bolt upright in bed. Laughing at the expression of shock on his face, Dougless turned the music off before she woke the other guests.

Nicholas sat up in bed with a dazed look on his face. "What chaos was that?"

"Music," Dougless said, laughing; but as he continued to look shocked, she said, "It was a joke. It's time to get up, so I thought—"

Dougless quit smiling when he didn't smile back. She guessed Elizabethan men didn't like practical jokes. Correction: Modern men who thought they were Elizabethan men didn't like practical jokes.

It was twenty minutes later when Dougless came sputtering out of the bathroom. "You put shampoo on my toothbrush!" she said, wiping her tongue on a towel.

"I, madam?" Nicholas asked, an exaggerated look of innocence on his face.

"Why, you—" she said as she grabbed a pillow and tossed it at him. "I'll get you for this."

"More of your 'music' at dawn, mayhap?" he said, fending off the pillow.

Dougless laughed. "All right, I guess I deserved it. Are you ready for breakfast?"

At breakfast, Dougless told him of his dental appointment. She saw his grimace, but paid no attention to it. Everyone grimaced at the thought of going to the dentist. While he was eating, she got him to give her the names of some of his other estates besides Thornwyck, so, while he was at the dentist, she could go to the local library and see what she could find out.

Nicholas was quiet as they walked to the dentist, and in the waiting room he didn't examine the plastic-covered chairs. Dougless knew he was really worried when he wouldn't even look at the plastic plant she pointed out to him. When the receptionist called him, Dougless squeezed his hand. "You'll be all right. Afterward I'll . . . I'll take you out and buy you ice cream. That's something to look forward to." But she knew he had no idea what ice cream was—didn't remember what ice cream was, she corrected herself.

Since she'd booked him for a checkup, at least one filling and a cleaning, she knew he'd be in the chair for a while, so she asked the receptionist to call her at the library when he was nearly finished.

As she walked to the library, she felt as a mother must feel at having left her child behind. "It's only the dentist," she told herself.

The Ashburton library was very small, oriented toward children's books and novels for adults. Dougless sat on a stool in the British travel section and began searching for any mention of the eleven estates Nicholas said he'd owned. Four were now ruins, two had been torn down in the 1950s (it made her sick to think they'd survived so long and been torn down so recently), one was Thornwyck Castle, one she couldn't find, two were private residences, and one was open to the public. She copied down the pertinent information about the estate open to the public—hours, days open—then looked at her watch. Nicholas had been in the dentist's an hour and a half now.

She searched through the card catalog, but could find nothing on the Stafford family. Another forty-five minutes went by.

When the telephone on the checkout desk rang, she jumped. The librarian told Dougless it was the dentist calling and that Nicholas was nearly finished. Dougless practically ran back to the dentist's office.

The dentist came out to greet her and asked her to come to his office. "Mr. Stafford puzzles me," the doctor said, as he put Nicholas's X-rays on a wall-lit machine. "I usually make it a policy to never give an opinion about another doctor's work, but as you can see here," he said, pointing at the X-ray, "Mr. Stafford's previous dental work has been . . . Well, I can only describe it as brutal. The three teeth that have been extracted look as though they were literally torn from his mouth. See, here and here the bone was cracked and grew back crooked. The extractions must have been extremely painful afterward as the bone healed. And, too, I know it's impossible, but I don't believe Mr. Stafford has ever seen a hypodermic before. Perhaps he was put under when he had those teeth removed."

The doctor turned off the light. "Of course he *had* to have been put under. In this day and age we can't imagine the pain that extractions such as these must have caused him."

"This day and age," Dougless said softly. "But four hundred years ago teeth were, as you said, 'torn' from a person's mouth?"

The doctor smiled. "Four hundred years ago I imagine that every-one had extractions like his—but without anesthetic or painkillers afterward. And, yes, I imagine a lot of people went away with cracked jawbones."

Dougless took a deep breath. "How were his teeth otherwise? How was he as a patient?"

"Excellent on both counts. He was very relaxed in the chair, and laughed when the hygienist asked if she'd hurt him when she'd cleaned his teeth. I filled one cavity and checked his other teeth." The doctor looked puzzled for a moment. "He has some slight ridging on his teeth. I've only seen that in school textbooks, and it usually means hunger for a year or so as a child. I wonder what could have caused such ridging in him? He doesn't strike me as a man whose family couldn't afford food."

Drought, Dougless almost said. Or flooding. Something to make the crops fail in a time of no refrigeration or frozen food or fresh food flown in from around the world.

"I didn't mean to keep you," the doctor said when Dougless said nothing. "It was just that I was concerned about his previous dental work. He . . ." The doctor chuckled. "He certainly asked a lot of ques-tions. He isn't by chance thinking of going to dental school?"

Dougless smiled. "He's just curious. Thank you so much for your time and your concern."

"I'm glad I had the cancellations. He has a most interesting set of teeth."

Dougless thanked him again, then went into the reception room to see Nicholas leaning across the counter flirting with the pretty receptionist.

"Come on," she snapped at him after she'd paid the bill. She hadn't meant to be so short-tempered, but it seemed that circumstances were trying to force her to believe that this man actually was from the sixteenth century.

"That is not the barber I have been to," Nicholas said, smiling, rubbing his still-numb lip. "I should like to take that man and his machines back with me."

"All the machines are electric," Dougless said gloomily. "I doubt that Elizabethan houses were wired for the two-twenty they have in this country."

Catching her arm, Nicholas turned her to face him. "What ails you?"

"Who are you?" she cried, looking up at him. "Why do you have ridges on your teeth? How did your jawbone get cracked when your other teeth were pulled?"

Nicholas smiled at her because he could see that, at last, she was truly beginning to believe him. "I am Nicholas Stafford, earl of Thornwyck, Buckshire, and Southeaton. Two days ago I was in a cell awaiting my execution and the year was 1564."

"I cannot believe it," Dougless said, looking away from his face. "I will not believe it. Time travel cannot happen."

"What would make you believe?" he asked softly.

SEVEN

*A*s *Dougless walked with him* toward the ice cream shop, she pondered the question. What *would* make her believe? she asked herself. But she could think of nothing. There seemed to be explanations for everything. He could be a fabulous actor and merely pretending that everything was new to him. His teeth could have been wrenched out while playing rugby in school. Since she could verify nearly everything he'd told her, that meant he could have found the information previously, then used it in his charade.

Was there anything he could do to prove to her that he was from the past?

In the ice cream parlor she absently ordered herself a single cone of mocha ice cream, but for Nicholas, she ordered a double cone of French vanilla and chocolate fudge. She was considering her question so hard that she didn't see his face when he took his first licks, so she was startled when he leaned over and kissed her quickly, but firmly, on the mouth.

Blinking, she looked up at him and saw the sublime happiness on his face as he ate his ice cream. Dougless couldn't help laughing.

"Buried treasure," she said, and startled herself with the words.

"*Mmm?*" Nicholas asked, his attention one hundred percent on his ice cream.

"To prove to me that you're from the past, you have to know something no one else does. You have to show me something that isn't in a book."

"Such as who the father of Lady Arabella Sydney's last child was?" He was down to the chocolate scoop and looked as though he might melt from happiness. Placing her hand under his elbow, she ushered him to a table.

Sitting across from him, looking at those blue eyes and thick lashes as he licked his cone, she wondered if he looked at a woman like that when he made love to her.

"You gaze at me most hard," he said, then looked at her through his lashes.

Turning away, Dougless cleared her throat. "I do not want to know who fathered Lady Arabella's kid." She didn't look back when she heard Nicholas's laugh.

"'Buried treasure,'" he said as he crunched the cone. "Some valuable trinket that was hidden, but is still there after four hundred and twenty-four years?"

He can add and subtract, Dougless thought as she looked back at him. "Forget about it. It was just an idea." She opened her notebook. "Let me tell you what I found out at the library," she said as she began to read her notes about the houses.

When she looked up, Nicholas was wiping his hands on a paper napkin and frowning. "A man builds so that something of himself lives on. It pleases me not to hear that what was mine is gone."

"I thought children were supposed to carry on a person's name."

"I left no children," he said. "I had a son, but he died in a fall the week after my brother drowned. First his mother, then the child."

Dougless watched pain shoot across his face and suddenly felt how easy and safe the twentieth century was. Sure, America had rapists and mass murderers and drunk drivers, but Elizabethans had plague and leprosy and smallpox. "I'm sorry," she said. "Sorry both for you and for them." She paused a moment. "Have you had smallpox?" she asked softly.

"Neither small nor large," he said with some pride.

"*Large* pox?"

He glanced about the room, then whispered, "The French disease."

"Oh," she said, understanding. Venereal disease. For some reason she was glad to hear that he'd never had "large pox"—not that it mattered, but they did share a bathroom.

"What is this 'open to the public'?" he asked.

"Usually the owners couldn't afford the houses, so they gave them to the National Trust, so now you pay money and a guide takes you through the house. They're great tours. This particular house has a tea shop and a gift shop and—"

Nicholas suddenly sat up straight. "It is Bellwood that is open?"

She checked her notes. "Yes, Bellwood. Just south of Bath."

Nicholas seemed to be calculating. "With fast horses we can be to Bath in about seven hours."

"With a good English train we could make it in two hours. Would you like to see your house again?"

"See my house sold to a company, with tallow-faced apron-men marching through it?"

Dougless smiled. "If you put it like that . . ."

"Can we go on this . . ."

"Train."

"Train to Bellwood now?"

Dougless looked at her watch. "Sure. If we leave right now, we can have tea there and see Bellwood. But if you don't want to see the tallow-faced . . ."

"Apron-men," he said, smiling.

"Marching through the house, then why go?"

"There is a chance, a small chance, that I could, mayhap, find your buried treasure. When my estates were confiscated by your"—he looked at her mockingly—"your Virgin Queen"—he let Dougless know what he thought of the absurdity of that idea—"I do not know if my family was given permission to clear the estates. Perhaps there is a chance . . ."

The idea of an afternoon spent looking for buried treasure excited Dougless. "What are we waiting for?" she asked as she picked up her new handbag. This time, she'd packed it full of travel-size toiletries, and she wasn't going anywhere without it.

The train system was another thing Dougless loved about England. Nearly every village had a station, and, unlike American trains, they were clean, with no graffiti, and well kept. When Dougless bought their tickets, she was told that a connecting train to Bath was just about to leave the station, which was not an unusual occurrence since the English trains were wonderfully frequent.

Once seated on the train and it started to move, Nicholas's eyes bulged at the speed. But, after a few nervous moments, like a true Englishman, he adjusted to the speed and began to walk around. He studied the ads high up on the walls, smiling in delight at one for Colgate, recognizing the toothpaste she'd purchased. If he could recognize words, perhaps it wouldn't be so difficult to teach him to read, she thought.

In Bristol, they changed trains. Nicholas was aghast at the number of hurrying people in the station, and he was fascinated with the ornate Victorian ironwork. She purchased a fat guidebook to the great houses of southern England at the newsstand, and on the ride to Bath, she started to read to Nicholas about his houses that were now in ruins. But when she saw that hearing of such waste and destruction made him sad, she stopped reading.

He looked out the big windows and now and then would say, "There's William's house," or "Robin lives there," when he saw one of the enormous houses that dotted the English countryside almost as frequently as did the cows and sheep.

Bath, beautiful, beautiful Bath, was a wonder to Nicholas. To Dougless it was old, since the architecture was all eighteenth century, but to him it was very modern. Dougless thought that New York or Dallas with its steel and glass buildings would look like outer space to him. He would *act* as though they looked weird, she corrected herself, then noticed that she was correcting herself less often with each hour she spent with him.

They had lunch at an American-type sandwich shop, and Dougless ordered club sandwiches, potato salad, and iced tea for both of them. He thought the meal was tasty but lacking in quantity. It took some fast talking, but Dougless managed to drag him out of the restaurant before he started demanding a boar's head or whatever.

He was so fascinated with the crescent-shaped rows of houses in Bath that Dougless hated to get a taxi and take him out of town. But getting into an automobile took Nicholas's mind off the buildings. The taxi drivers in England are a different breed from those in America. English drivers don't yell when someone takes "too long" to get into a car, so Nicholas was given time to look at the vehicle. He examined the door and the door lock, opening and closing it three times before getting in, and once in, after examining the backseat, he leaned forward and watched the driver steer and shift gears.

When they arrived at Bellwood, the next tour didn't start for half an hour, so they had time to walk around the gardens. Dougless thought they were beautiful, but Nicholas curled his lip and barely looked at the flowering plants and the ancient shade trees. When he walked around the big, sprawling house, he told her what had been added to the house and what had been changed. He thought the additions were architecturally dreadful and minced no words in telling her so.

"Is the treasure buried in the garden?" she asked, annoyed at herself for asking; she sounded like an excited child.

"Ruin a garden by putting gold at the roots of my plants?" he asked in mock horror.

"By the way, where *did* you put your money? Where did they put their money, I mean?"

Nicholas clearly didn't understand her question—or didn't want to—so she dropped it. Since the gardens seemed to be making him angry, she led him to the gift shop, and for a while, he was happy in the shop. He played with the pens and some plastic change purses, and he laughed aloud when he first saw a tiny flashlight with "Bellwood" stamped on it. But he didn't like the postcards, and Dougless couldn't figure out what had so upset him about them.

He removed a tote bag with a silk-screened photo of Bellwood on the front from a rack. "You will need one of these," he said, smiling; then he leaned forward and whispered, "For the treasure."

Dougless did her best not to look thrilled at his words. As calmly as she could, she carried the tote bag and the flashlight to the register, where she paid for them and tickets for the next tour. She tried again to look at the postcards, but Nicholas would not let her. Every time she got near the rack, he forcibly clamped his strong fingers on her arm and pulled her away.

When the next tour was called, Dougless and Nicholas followed a dozen other tourists into the house. To Dougless's eyes, the interior of the house looked like a set for a play about Elizabeth the First. The walls were paneled in dark oak, there were Jacobean chairs scattered about as well as carved chests, and armor was hanging on the wall.

"Is this more like what you're used to?" Dougless whispered up to Nicholas.

There was an expression of disgust on his handsome face; his upper lip curled upward. "This is not my house," he said in distaste. "That what I did should come to this is most unpleasing."

Dougless thought the place was beautiful, but didn't say so because the guide had started her lecture. It was her experience that English tour guides were excellent and knew their subject thoroughly. The woman was telling the history of the house, built as a castle in 1302, by the first Stafford.

Nicholas was quiet as she spoke—until she came to Henry the Eighth's time.

"A medieval woman was the chattel of her husband," their guide said, "to be used as her husband saw fit. Women had no power."

Nicholas snorted loudly. "My father told my mother she was his property—once."

"Sssh," Dougless hissed, not wanting to be embarrassed by him.

They moved to a small, oak-paneled room where the darkness was oppressive. "Candles were very expensive," the guide was saying, "so medieval man lived his life in gloom."

Nicholas again started to speak, but Dougless frowned at him to be quiet. "Stop complaining, and, by the way, where's your treasure?" she asked.

"I cannot seek treasure now. I must hear how your world thinks of mine," he said. "Pray tell me why your people think we had no mirth?"

"With all the plague and big pox and small, plus trips to the barber to have your teeth torn out, we think you didn't have time for fun."

"We made use of the time we had," he said as the group moved into another room. As soon as they entered, Nicholas opened a door concealed in the paneling, and as soon as he did, a loud buzzer went off. Dougless slammed the door shut, then gave a weak smile of apology to the tour guide, whose quelling look made her feel like a child caught with her hand in a cookie jar.

"Behave!" Dougless hissed at him. "If you want to leave, I'm ready." His actions were embarrassing, and she feared that he just might start telling the guide that *he* had built this house, and he had lived here.

But Nicholas didn't want to leave. He followed the guide through room after room, snorting now and then in derision, but saying nothing.

"We now come to our most popular room," the guide said, and by the little smile she gave, her audience knew something amusing was coming up.

Nicholas, being taller, saw into the room before Dougless did. "We will leave now," he said stiffly, but he said it in a way that made Dougless very much want to see what was in the room.

The guide began to speak. "This was Lord Nicholas Stafford's private chamber, and, to put it politely, Lord Nicholas was what is known as a rake. As you can see, he was a very handsome man."

When she heard that, Dougless pushed her way through the group to the front. There, hanging over the mantel, was a portrait of Lord Nicholas Stafford—her Nicholas. He was dressed just as she'd first seen him, wearing the beard and mustache she'd first seen, and he was just as handsome then as he was now.

Of course he wasn't the same man, Dougless told herself, but she was willing to admit that the man she knew had to be a descendant.

The guide, smiling at what she felt was an amusing story, began to tell of Lord Nicholas's exploits with various ladies. "It was said that no woman could withstand his charm once he set his mind to have her, so his enemies were concerned that if he went to court, he might seduce the young and beautiful Queen Elizabeth."

Dougless felt Nicholas's fingers biting into her shoulder. "I will take you to the treasure now," he whispered into her ear.

She put her fingers to her lips for him to be quiet.

"In 1560," the guide said, "there was a great scandal concerning Lady Arabella Sydney." The guide paused.

"I wish to go now," Nicholas said emphatically into her ear.

Dougless waved him away.

The guide continued. "It was said at the time that Lady Sydney's fourth child was fathered by Lord Nicholas, who was some years younger than she. It was also said"—the guide's voice lowered conspiratorily—"that the child was fathered on *that* table."

There was a combined intake of breath as everyone looked at an oak trestle table standing against the wall.

"Furthermore," the guide said, "Lord Nicholas—"

From the back of the room came a very loud buzzer. It went on then off, on then off, making it impossible for the guide to continue speaking.

"Would you mind!" the guide said, but the buzzer kept going on and off.

Dougless didn't have to look to see who was opening and closing the alarmed door—or why he was doing it. Quickly, she began to make her way to the back of the group.

"I'm going to have to ask you to leave," the guide said sternly, looking over the heads of the tourists to the back of the group. "You may go out the way you came."

Grabbing Nicholas's arm, Dougless pulled him away from the buzzing door and back through two rooms.

"What trivial knowledge is remembered through these hundreds of years," Nicholas said in anger.

She looked up at him with interest. "Is it *true?*" she asked. "About Lady Arabella? About the *table?*"

He frowned at her. "Nay, madam, such did not happen on that table." Turning, he walked away.

Smiling, Dougless was relieved that the story wasn't true—not that it mattered, but still . . .

"I gave the true table to Arabella," he said over his shoulder.

Dougless gasped as she watched him walk away, but she hurriedly followed him. "You impregnated—" she began, but when he halted and looked down his nose at her, she stopped speaking. He had a way of looking at a person that could make you believe he was an aristocrat.

"We will see if these sottish people have violated my cabinet," he said, again turning away from her.

Dougless had to run to cover the distance his long legs were eating up. "You can't go in there," she said as he put his hand on a door that had a NO ADMITTANCE sign on it. Ignoring her, Nicholas pulled on the latch. For a moment, Dougless closed her eyes and held her breath, waiting for a buzzer to go off. When there was no sound, tentatively, she opened her eyes and saw that Nicholas had disappeared behind the door. With a quick look around to see if anyone was watching, she followed him, expecting to walk into a room full of secretaries.

But there were no secretaries in the room, nor any people at all. There were just boxes stacked to the ceiling, and from what was printed on the sides, they looked to be full of paper napkins and other items for the tearoom. Behind the boxes was beautiful paneling that Dougless thought was a shame to hide.

She caught sight of Nicholas as he opened another door, so she ran after him. She followed him through three more rooms and got to see the difference between restored and unrestored. The rooms not open to the public had broken fireplaces, missing paneling, and painted ceilings spoiled by a leaky roof. In one room some Victorian had put wallpaper over the carved oak panels, and Dougless could see where workmen were painstakingly removing it.

At last Nicholas led her to a small room off a larger one. Here the ceiling had leaked until the plaster was a dirty brown, and the wide floorboards looked to be dangerously rotten. Standing in the doorway, she saw Nicholas looking about the room, sadness in his eyes.

"This was my brother's chamber, and I was here but a fortnight ago," he said softly, then shrugged as though to block the regret from his mind. He walked across the rotten boards, went to a section of the paneling, and pushed at it. Nothing happened.

"The lock has rusted," he said, "or someone has sealed it shut."

Suddenly, he seemed to become enraged and began hammering on the paneling with both fists.

Mindless of the disintegrating floor, Dougless ran to him, and not knowing what else to do, she put her arms around him, pulled his head to her shoulder, and stroked his hair. *"Sssh,"* she whispered as she would to a child. "Quiet."

He clung to her, held her so tightly she could barely breathe. "It was my intent to be remembered for my learning," he said against her neck, and there were tears in his voice. "I commissioned monks to copy hundreds of books. I began building Thornwyck. I have . . . Had. It is done now."

"Sssh," Dougless soothed, holding his broad shoulders.

He pushed away from her and turned his back, but Dougless saw him wipe away tears. "They remember a moment on a table with Arabella," he said.

When he looked back at her, his face was fierce. "If I had lived . . ." he said. "If I had but lived, I would have changed all. I must find out what my mother knew. She believed she had knowledge that would clear my name and save me from execution. And once I know this, I *must* return. I must change what is now said about me and about my family."

As Dougless looked at him, it was at that moment that she knew he was telling the truth. It was the way she, too, felt about her family. She didn't want to be remembered for all the idiot things she'd done. She wanted to be remembered for her good deeds. Last summer, she'd volunteered to help children who couldn't read. For four summers in a row she'd spent three days a week at a shelter where she worked with children who, for the most part, had had very little kindness in their lives.

"We'll find out," she said softly. "If the information still exists today, we'll find it, and when we have the information, I'm sure you'll be sent back."

"You know how to do this?" he asked.

"No, I don't. But maybe it'll just happen once you know what you were sent here to find out."

He was frowning, but, slowly, his frown changed to a smile. "You have changed. You are looking at me in a different way. Do you not tell me I am lying?"

"No," she said slowly. "No one could act this well." She didn't want to think about what she was saying. A sixteenth-century man could not come forward in time, but . . . but it had happened.

"Look at this," she said as she touched the section of paneling he had been pounding. A little door stood open about an inch.

Nicholas pulled the door open. "My father told only my brother of this hidden cabinet, and Kit showed me but a week before he died. I told no one. The secret of its existence died with me."

As she watched, he stuck his hand in the hole and pulled out a roll of yellowed, brittle papers.

Nicholas looked at the papers in disbelief. "I but put these in here a few days ago. They were new-made then."

Taking the papers from him, she unrolled them a bit. They were covered top to bottom, side to side, no margins, with writing that was incomprehensible to her.

"Ah, here is your treasure." He showed Dougless a small yellow-white box, beautifully carved with figures of people and animals.

"This is ivory?" she asked in wonder as she handed him the papers, then took the box. She had seen boxes like this one in museums, but she'd never touched one. "It's beautiful, and it's a wonderful treasure."

Nicholas laughed. "The box is not the treasure. That lies inside. But wait," he said as Dougless began to open the lid. "I find I am greatly in need of sustenance." He shoved the papers back into the cabinet as though he never wanted to see them again. Then he took the box from her, opened the tote bag she'd purchased, and slipped the box inside.

"You're going to make me *wait* until after you've eaten before I can see what's inside that box?" She was incredulous.

Nicholas laughed. "It pleases me to see that the nature of woman has not changed these four hundred years."

She gave him a smug look. "Don't get too smart, or did you forget that I have your return train ticket?"

She thought she had bested him, but as she watched, his face changed to softness, and he looked at her through his lashes in a way that made Dougless's heart beat a little faster. He stepped forward; she stepped back.

"You have heard," he said, his voice low, "that no woman can withstand me."

Dougless was backed against the wall, her heart pounding in her ears as he looked down at her. Putting his fingertips under her chin, he gently lifted her face upward. Was he going to kiss her? she wondered, half in outrage and half in anticipation. Anticipation won out; she closed her eyes.

"I shall seduce my way back to the hotel," he said in a different tone that made Dougless know he'd been teasing her—and he'd known exactly how his warm looks would affect her.

When her eyes flew open and she straightened up, he chucked her under the chin as a father might do—or as the gorgeous private eye might do to his soppy secretary.

"Ah, but mayhap I could not seduce a woman of today. You have told me that women now are not as they were in my day," he said, shutting the little secret door. "Alas, this is the day of women's . . ."

"Lib," she answered. "Liberation." She was thinking about Lady Arabella on the table.

He looked back at her. "I am sure I would not be able to charm a woman such as you. You have told me that you love . . . ?"

"Robert. Yes, I do," Dougless said firmly. "Maybe when I get back to the States, he and I can work things out. Or maybe when he gets my message about the bracelet, he'll come for me." She wanted to remember Robert. Compared to this man, Robert seemed safe.

"Ah," Nicholas said, starting for the door, Dougless inches behind him.

"Just what is that supposed to mean?"

"No more, no less."

She blocked him from leaving the room. "If you want to say something, say it."

"This Robert will come for jewels but not for the woman he loves?"

"Of course he's coming for me!" she snapped. "The bracelet is . . . It's just that Gloria is a brat and she lied, but she's his daughter so of course Robert believed her. And stop looking at me like that! Robert is a fine man. At least he'll be remembered for what he did on an operating table instead of on a—" She stopped at the look on Nicholas's face.

Turning, he strode ahead of her.

"Nicholas, I'm sorry," she said, running after him. "I didn't mean it.

I was just angry, that's all. It's not your fault you're remembered for Arabella; it's *our* fault. We see too much TV, read too much *National Enquirer.* Our lives are filled with too much sensationalism. Colin, please." She stopped where she was. Was he going to walk away and leave her too?

Her head was down, so she wasn't aware that he'd walked back to her. Companionably, he put his arm around her shoulders. "Do they sell ice cream in this place?"

When she smiled at that, he tipped her chin up and wiped away a single tear. "Are you onion-eyed again?" he asked softly.

She shook her head, afraid to trust her voice.

"Then come," he said. "If I remember rightly, there is a pearl in that box as big as my thumb."

"Really?" she asked. She had forgotten all about the box. "Anything else?"

"Tea first," he said. "Tea and scones and ice cream. Then I shall show you the box."

They walked together out of the unrestored rooms, past the next tour, and out the In, which the guides did not like at all.

In the tea shop, this time, Nicholas took over. Dougless sat at a table and waited for him as he talked to a woman behind the counter. The woman was shaking her head about something Nicholas was asking, but Dougless had an idea that he'd get whatever it was that he wanted.

Minutes later, he motioned for her to come with him. He led her outside, then down stone stairs, across an acre of garden, to at last stop under the dappled shade of a yew tree with bright red berries. When Dougless turned around, she saw a woman and a man carrying two large trays filled with tea, pastries, little sandwiches with no crusts, and Nicholas's beloved scones.

Nicholas ignored the two people as they spread a cloth on the ground and set out the tea things. "There was my knot garden," he said, pointing, his voice heavy with sadness. "And there was a mound."

After the people left, Nicholas held out his hand to help her sit on the cloth. She poured his tea, added milk, filled a plate full of food for him, then said, "Now?"

He smiled. "Now."

Dougless dove into the tote bag and pulled out the old, fragile ivory box, then slowly, with breath held, opened it.

Inside were two rings of exquisite loveliness, one an emerald, one a ruby, the gold mountings cast into intricate forms of dragons and snakes. Nicholas took the rings and, smiling at her, slipped them onto his fingers, where, she wasn't surprised to see, they fit perfectly.

On the bottom of the box was a bit of old, cracked velvet, and she could see that it was wrapped around something. Gingerly, Dougless removed the velvet and slowly opened it.

In her hand lay a brooch, oval, with little gold figures of . . . She looked up at Nicholas. "What are they doing?"

"It's the martyrdom of Saint Barbara," he said, his tone implying that she knew nothing.

Dougless had guessed it was a martyrdom because it looked as if the gold man was about to cut off the head of the tiny gold woman. Encircling the figures was an abstract enamel design, and around the edges were tiny pearls and diamonds. Hanging from a loop below the brooch was indeed a pearl as large as a man's thumb. It was a baroque pearl, indented, even lumpy, but with a luster that no years could dim.

"It's lovely," she whispered.

"It is yours," Nicholas said.

A wave of avarice shot through Dougless. "I cannot," she said, even as her hand closed over the jewel.

Nicholas laughed. "It is a woman's bauble. You may keep it."

"I can't. It's too valuable. This pin is worth too much and it's too old. It should be in a museum. It should—"

Taking the jewel from her hand, he pinned it between the collar points of her blouse.

Dougless took her compact from her purse, opened the mirror, and looked at the brooch. She also looked at her face. "I have to go to the rest room," she said, making Nicholas laugh as she rose.

Alone in the rest room, she had some time to really look at the pin, and only left when someone else entered. On her way back to Nicholas, she couldn't resist slipping into the gift shop to look at the postcards. It took her a moment to see what Nicholas had not wanted her to see.

There, on the bottom of a rack, was a postcard of a portrait of the notorious Lady Arabella. Dougless took one.

As she was paying, Dougless asked the cashier if there was anything in any of the books for sale about Nicholas Stafford.

The woman smiled in a patronizing way. "All the young ladies ask after him. We usually have cards of his portrait, but we're out right now."

"There's nothing written about him? About his accomplishments other than . . . than with women?" Dougless asked.

Again there was that little smirk. "I don't believe Lord Nicholas accomplished anything. The only thing of importance that he did was to raise an army against the queen, and he was sentenced to be executed for that. If he hadn't died beforehand, he would have been beheaded. He was quite a scoundrel of a young man."

Dougless took the single postcard and started to leave, but she turned back. "What happened to Lord Nicholas's mother after he died?"

The woman brightened. "Lady Margaret? Now there was a grand lady. Let me see, I believe she married again. What was his name? Oh, yes, Harewood. She married Lord Richard Harewood."

"Do you know if she left any papers behind?"

"Oh, my, no, I have no idea of that."

"All the Stafford papers are at Goshawk Hall," came a voice from the door. It was the guide whose tour she and Nicholas had so rudely interrupted.

"Where is Goshawk Hall?" Dougless asked, feeling embarrassed.

"Near the village of Thornwyck," the woman said.

"Thornwyck," Dougless said, and nearly gave a whoop of joy, but caught herself. It was all she could do to thank the women before she ran from the shop into the garden. Nicholas lay stretched out on the cloth, sipping tea and finishing the scones.

"Your mother married Richard, ah . . . Harewood," she said breathlessly, "and all the papers are at . . ." She couldn't remember the name.

"Goshawk Hall?" he asked.

"Yes, that's it! It's near Thornwyck."

He turned away from her. "My mother married Harewood?"

Dougless watched the back of him. If he'd died accused of treason, had his mother, in her poverty, been forced to marry some despicable despot? Had his old, frail mother been forced to endure some man who treated her as no more than property?

When Nicholas's shoulders began to shake, Dougless put her hand on his arm. "Nicholas, it's not your fault. You were dead, you couldn't help her." *What* am I saying? she thought.

But when Nicholas turned around, she saw that he was . . . laughing. "I should have known she would land on her feet," he said. "Harewood! She married Dickie Harewood." He could hardly speak for laughing so hard.

"Tell me everything," Dougless urged, eyes alight.

"Dickie Harewood is a tardy-gaited, unhaired pajock."

Dougless frowned, not understanding.

"An ass, madam," Nicholas explained. "But a rich one. Aye, he's very rich." He leaned back, smiling. "It is good to know she was not left one-trunk-inheriting."

Still smiling, he poured Dougless a cup of tea, and as she took it, he picked up her little paper bag and opened it.

"No" she began, but he was already looking at the postcard of Lady Arabella's portrait.

He looked up at her with such a knowing look that she wanted to dump the tea over his head. "Did they not have a picture of the table too?" he mocked.

"I have no idea what you mean," she said haughtily, not looking at his face as she snatched the card out of his hands and put it back into the bag. "The picture is for research. It might help us . . ." For the life of her, she couldn't think what a picture of the mother of Nicholas's illegitimate child could possibly help them find out. "Did you eat all the scones? You really can be a pig sometimes."

Nicholas gave a snort of laughter.

After a moment he said, "What say you we stay in this town this night? On the morrow I shall purchase Armant and Rafe."

It took Dougless a moment to understand what he meant, but then she remembered the American magazines he'd seen. "Georgio Armani and Ralph Lauren?" she asked.

"Aye," he said. "Clothing of your time. When I return to my house in Thornwyck, I will not be one-trunk-inheriting either."

Dougless bit into a little sandwich. Unless she found Robert and got her suitcases back soon, she was going to have to buy more clothes too.

She looked at Nicholas, his hands behind his head. Tomorrow they'd go shopping, then the next day they'd go to Thornwyck, where they'd try to find out who had betrayed him to the queen.

But tonight, she thought. Tonight they'd once again spend alone in a hotel room.

EIGHT

*D*ougless sat in the back of the big black taxi, luggage all around her. This is where I came in, she thought, remembering being in the back of Robert's rental car and trying to get comfortable around Gloria's luggage. But now, sprawled beside her, his long legs stretched out, was Nicholas. He was absorbed in a battery-powered video game that they'd purchased this morning.

Putting her head back, Dougless closed her eyes and thought about the last several hours. After tea at Bellwood yesterday, she had called a taxi and asked to be taken to a nice hotel in Bath. The driver had taken them to a lovely eighteenth-century building where she was able to get a double room for the night. Neither she nor Nicholas mentioned asking for separate rooms. It was a beautiful room done in yellow chintz and flowered wallpaper, with white bedspreads piped in yellow on the two beds. Nicholas ran his hand over the wallpaper and vowed that when he got home, he was going to have someone paint the walls of his house with lilies and roses.

After they checked in, they went walking to look in the windows of the wonderful shops in Bath. It was near dinnertime when Dougless saw a movie house called the American Cinema.

"We could always go to a movie and eat hot dogs and popcorn for dinner," she said, making a joke.

But Nicholas had been so intrigued that he'd started asking questions, so Dougless bought tickets. She thought it was a bit ironic that an "American" Cinema was playing an English movie—*Room With a View*—but they did have American hot dogs, popcorn, Cokes, and Reese's peanut butter cups. Knowing Nicholas's appetite, Dougless bought so much of everything that they could hardly waddle down the aisle for the load they were carrying.

Nicholas loved the popcorn, choked on the Coke, thought the hot dog had possibilities, and nearly cried in delight over the peanut butter and chocolate. Before the movie started, Dougless tried to explain what a movie was, and how very large the people would look. But Nicholas was too interested in what was going on in his mouth to listen very carefully.

He was fascinated when the lights went down, then nearly jumped out of his seat when the music came on. At the first sight of the enormous people, the expression on his face was so horrified that Dougless nearly dropped her popcorn.

Throughout the film, watching Nicholas was much more interesting than watching the movie—which Dougless had already seen twice before anyway.

As they walked back to the hotel after the film was over, he was full of questions. He'd been so enamored with the technical aspect of the movie that he could hardly follow the story. Also, he couldn't understand the clothes. It took some explaining to make him understand that Edwardian was "old."

In the hotel, they shared the toiletries Dougless had in her handbag, and what was in the little basket in the hotel. Dougless meant to sleep in her underwear so, after a shower, she wrapped herself in the robe supplied by the hotel. She'd planned to go straight to bed, but Nicholas wanted her to read to him, so she took her Agatha Christie from her bag, sat on a chair by him, and read until he fell asleep.

Before she turned out the light, she stood over him for a moment, looking down at his soft black hair against the crisp white sheets. On impulse, she lightly kissed his forehead. "Good night, my prince," she whispered.

Without opening his eyes, Nicholas clasped her fingers. "I am but a mere earl," he said softly, not opening his eyes, "but my thankings for the tribute."

Embarrassed but smiling, she pulled away from him and went to her own bed. But, tired as she was, she lay awake for a long while, listening carefully for any sounds from him, wondering if he'd have bad dreams as he had the night before. But when he was silent, she at last drifted off. When she awoke, it was morning and he was already up and in the bathroom. Her first feeling was one of disappointment that she'd not slept cuddled in his arms, but she reprimanded herself. She was in love with Robert, wasn't she? She couldn't be so frivolous as to have fallen out of love in just a few days, could she? Not over one argument?

And she couldn't possibly imagine herself to be in love with a man who was not and never could be hers, could she? She could never love a man who at any minute could go up in a puff of smoke and leave as quickly as he had arrived. Could she?

Nicholas came out of the bathroom, barefoot and barechested, wearing only his trousers, and toweling his wet hair. There were much worse sights in the morning than the broad, nude chest of a beautiful man, she thought. Dougless lay back against the pillows and sighed.

At her sigh, Nicholas looked at her and frowned. "Do you waste the day? We must find me a barber to shave this," he said as he ran his hand over the growing whiskers.

"It's quite fashionable now to have black stubble. Movie stars go to formal ceremonies with five o'clock shadow," she said. But Nicholas didn't like that idea. He said it was a beard or bare and "naught between." In the end, she used the razor and tiny can of lather furnished by the hotel to show him how to shave. Unfortunately, before she could stop him, he ran his fingertips over the blade of the razor and sliced them. He laughed at Dougless for the to-do she made over such a little cut.

Later, dressed, fortified with a hearty English breakfast, they went shopping. Dougless was becoming accustomed to helping Nicholas do the most ordinary of things, but, this time, when he shopped for clothes, he knew exactly what he wanted. Dougless was amazed at how much he'd learned from an evening of looking at fashion magazines.

This time in an exclusive shop, Nicholas the earl took over, while Dougless merely stood in the background and watched. The English clerks seemed to recognize that they were dealing with aristocracy because it was "Yes, sir" and "No, sir" to him right and left.

Now, in the taxi, around Dougless's feet were piled shopping bags filled with shirts, trousers, socks, belts, a marvelous coat of waxed cloth, caps, two Italian silk jackets, a luscious leather jacket, ties, and even a full set of evening clothes. It was as they were leaving the fifth store that Dougless had begun making moans of fatigue, especially now that they had several heavy bags to carry. Nicholas had given her a look of disdain, as though she were a real wimp. A moment later he gave a piercing whistle and a taxi stopped. He learns quickly, Dougless thought. Without her help, Nicholas arranged for the taxi to follow them for the rest of the morning as he purchased more clothes. Dougless paid for them while the driver hauled the bags out to the taxi.

At one o'clock she was wilted and ready to suggest lunch when he stopped before a lovely window display of women's clothes. He looked at the display, then at Dougless, then half-shoved her into the shop, ahead of him. It was truly amazing how her energy revived! Nicholas was as generous as he was good at choosing clothing. He sent three young women clerks scurrying as he demanded that he be shown the best they had to offer. Dougless spent an hour and a half in the dressing room in her underwear, pulling clothes on and off. When they left, three bags full of new clothes for her were added to what Nicholas had bought for himself.

Finally, the only clothing he still needed was shoes. Nicholas had come to enjoy the comfort of modern clothes, but he hated the hard leather of modern shoes. The shoes he liked best were soft leather bedroom slippers. After three stores Dougless persuaded him to purchase two pairs of Italian shoes that were frightfully expensive. He told Dougless she must buy new shoes also, but when he pulled four pair—dress boots, pumps, walking shoes, and loafers—off the shelves, she said he'd already spent too much on her. Nicholas threatened to wear the terry cloth bedroom slippers from the hotel unless she purchased all four. Laughing, she agreed.

They made one last stop to buy luggage to pack everything into. Nicholas wanted leather luggage, but as there was little money left, Dougless talked him into some blue canvas bags with belting leather trim.

By the time they were done shopping, it was three P.M. and all the lunch shops were closed. They purchased bread and cheese, meat pies, and a bottle of wine, then ate in the back of the taxi as it drove them back to the bed-and-breakfast in Ashburton. And since eating while traveling went against Nicholas's aristocratic ideas of etiquette, she'd had to talk him into it. But she couldn't move him about the train. Dougless had said they should take the train back, as it was much cheaper than a taxi. But Nicholas had scoffed at her idea that he handle luggage, so they were being driven all the way back to the hotel.

On the return trip Nicholas got his first sight of the six-lane English motorways. She didn't know how he felt about the speed of the cars around him, but it terrified her. The slow lane traveled at seventy miles per hour, so she couldn't imagine what the fast, outside lane was doing.

After a while, Nicholas stopped staring at the trucks and asking questions about everything he saw, and settled back against the seat to play with the little video game she'd run into Boots and bought for him. As she watched him, she thought of all the many things in the world there were for him to see and do yet. There were VCRs, TVs, Ferris wheels, airplanes, space rockets. There was all of America: Maine with its boats; the South, which would have to be experienced to be believed; the Southwest with its cowboy heritage and the Native Americans; and there was California with . . . Smiling, she thought of Hollywood and Venice Beach. She could take him to the Pacific Northwest for salmon, to ski in Colorado, to a roundup in Texas. She could—

They arrived back at their little bed-and-breakfast before she could think of all the things she'd like to show him, and before she reminded herself that he was only temporarily with her. But if he really was *her* Knight in Shining Armor, maybe he wouldn't return.

Nicholas directed the taxi driver in removing the many bags from the vehicle and setting them in the entryway, while Dougless started to pay the driver with the last of the money from the sale of the coins. While she was figuring out the tip, the landlady came hurrying down the steps.

"He's been here all day, miss," Mrs. Beasley said excitedly. "He came this morning and hasn't left since. He's in an awful mood, and he's said some terrible things. I thought you and Mr. Stafford were married," she said, reproach in her voice.

Dougless knew, of course, who "he" was. Besides Nicholas, there was only one "he" in England who knew where she was—or where she'd been left, that is. So now was her chance to sort out things with Robert. This is what she'd wanted. Why, then, was her stomach starting to hurt? She suddenly remembered the pills the doctor had prescribed for her stomach. She hadn't needed any in days. "Who is here?" she asked softly, biding for time.

"Robert Whitley," the landlady said.

"Alone?"

"No, there's a young lady with him."

Dougless nodded and, with her stomach hurting more with each step, she went up the stairs to the entryway. Nicholas was busy ordering the taxi driver about, but he stopped when he saw Dougless's face. Calmly, she paid the driver, saying not a word; then she went into the parlor, where Robert and Gloria were waiting for her.

Gloria was seated on a chair, her face angry, but Dougless ignored the girl. Instead, she looked at Robert, who was standing in front of the window. She couldn't see any remorse on his face.

"At last," Robert said when Dougless entered. "We have been waiting the entire day. Where is it?"

She knew what he meant, but she refused to let him know she did. Hadn't he missed her at all? "Where is what?"

"The bracelet you stole!" Gloria said. "That's why you pushed me down in that graveyard, so you could take my bracelet."

"I did no such thing," Dougless said. "You fell against the—"

Moving to stand beside her, Robert put his arm around Dougless. "Look," he said as he smiled at her, "we didn't come here to quarrel.

Gloria and I have missed you." He gave a little laugh. "Oh, you should see us. We get lost every few minutes. Neither one of us is good with a road map and we can't figure out the hotels at all. You were always so good at figuring out schedules and whether a hotel had room service or not."

Dougless wasn't sure whether to feel elated or dejected. He wanted her, but only to read the road maps and to order room service for the two of them.

Robert gave her a quick kiss on the cheek. "I know you didn't steal the bracelet. That was something that was said in the heat of the moment. But it was certainly lucky that you found it."

When Gloria started to speak, Robert gave her a look to be quiet, and that look made Dougless feel better. Maybe he was going to force his daughter to show her some respect. Maybe—

"Please, Lessa," Robert said, nuzzling her ear, "please come back with us. You can sit in the front half the time, and Gloria half the time. That's fair, isn't it?"

She wasn't sure what to do. Robert was being so nice, and it was wonderful to hear his apology, and to think that he needed her.

"Well, madam," Nicholas said, striding into the room, "do you mean to unkiss our bargain?"

Robert jumped away from Dougless, and immediately she was aware of hatred coming from him—a hatred that was directed toward Nicholas. Was Robert jealous? she wondered. Never before had he shown any signs of jealousy. And, as for Nicholas, he was staring at Robert with wide eyes, as though he were staring at an apparition. It took both men a few minutes to recover themselves.

"Who *is* this?" Robert asked.

"Well, madam?" Nicholas asked.

As Dougless looked from one man to the other, she felt like running from the room and never seeing either of them again.

"Who *is* this?" Robert demanded. "Have you obtained a . . . a lover in the few days since you left us?"

"Left *you?*" Dougless said. "You left *me,* and you took my handbag with you! You left me without money or credit cards or—"

Robert waved his hand in dismissal. "That was all a mistake. Gloria picked up your bag for you. She thought she was helping you. Neither of us had any idea that you'd decide to remain here, or that you'd refuse to travel with us. Isn't that right, sweetheart?"

"Helping me?" Dougless gasped, so overwhelmed with his twisting of the truth that she could hardly speak. "I decided to remain here?"

"Dougless," Robert said, "do we have to discuss our private problems in front of this stranger? We have your luggage in the car, so I suggest that we leave here now." Firmly taking her arm, he started to lead her away.

But Nicholas stood in the doorway, blocking their way. "Do you mean to leave me?" he asked as he looked down at Dougless, anger in his voice. "Do you mean to go with this man who wants you for the service you do him?"

"I . . . I . . ." Dougless said, feeling confused. On the one hand, Robert was being a jerk, but at least he was *real*. For all the romance that surrounded this Nicholas Stafford, if he found what he was looking for, he'd be gone in a second. Besides, both men wanted her for what she could *do* for them. Robert wanted her to read road maps; Nicholas wanted her to help him research.

Dougless didn't know what she should do.

Nicholas decided for her. "This woman has been hired by me," he said. "Until I have done with her services, she will remain with me." At that he clamped his hand on Robert's shoulder and pushed him toward the door.

"Get your hands off of me!" Robert shouted. "You can't treat me like this, I'll have the police on you. Gloria, call the police! Dougless, either you come with me *now* or you'll never get a marriage proposal out of me. You'll never—" His last words were cut off as Nicholas shut the door behind him.

Dougless sat on the nearest chair, her head down.

When Nicholas returned, he took one look at Gloria and said, "Out!"

Gloria ran for the doorway, then pounded down the front stairs.

Nicholas went to the window and looked out. "They are gone now, but they have left your capcases on the ground. We are well rid of them."

Dougless didn't look up. How did she get herself in these messes? She couldn't even go away on a vacation without something awful happening to her. Why couldn't she have a normal, ordinary relationship with a man? She'd meet a man in a classroom somewhere, he'd ask her out, then they'd go on simple dates to movies or to play miniature golf. After a few dates, he'd propose marriage over a bottle of wine. They'd have a nice wedding, a nice house, two nice kids. Her whole life would be simple and ordinary.

Instead, she met guys who had been in jail or were about to be taken off to jail, guys who were ruled by their obnoxious daughters, or men who were from the sixteenth century. Honestly, she didn't know any other woman who'd ever had as much trouble with men as she'd had.

"What is wrong with me?" she whispered, burying her face in her hands.

Kneeling before her, Nicholas pulled her hands away from her face. "I find I am most tired. Mayhap you will come upstairs and read to me so I may rest."

Like a dumb animal, she let Nicholas take her hand and lead her upstairs. But once upstairs, he didn't expect her to read to him. Instead he told her to stretch out on the bed, which she did, while he sat beside her on the bed and began to sing to her. He sang a soft, sweet lullaby that she doubted anyone else in this century had ever heard before. Gradually, she drifted off into sleep.

NINE

When she was asleep, Nicholas leaned back against the headboard and stroked her hair. God, but how much he wanted to touch her! He wanted to put his hands in her thick hair of that glorious dark red. He wanted to run his hands over her pale skin, wanted to feel those legs of hers wrapped around him. He wanted to kiss away her tears, then kiss her mouth. He wanted to kiss her all over until she smiled and laughed and was happy.

She slept bonelessly, like a child, but there was a catch in her breathing as though she'd been weeping. He'd never seen a woman cry as often as she did, he thought. But then, he'd never seen any woman who was like her. She wanted love so very much.

He had asked her about marriage in this strange new world, and the answers did not please him. In his mind, marriage should be a contract, something made as an alliance, made to breed a suitable heir. But it seemed that in this new century marriage partners chose each other for love.

Love! Nicholas thought. The emotion was a waste of a man's

energy. Too many times he had seen men who'd lost all because of the "love" of some woman.

He touched Dougless's temple, stroked the soft hair there, and looked down at her beautiful body of full breasts and slim legs. Look what this girl had suffered for "love," he thought. With a smile, Nicholas thought of what his mother would have said to the idea of marrying for love. Lady Margaret Stafford had had four husbands, and she'd never considered loving any of them.

But as Nicholas looked down at this modern woman, he felt a softness inside him that he'd never felt before. She wore her heart on the outside of her body, ready to give it to anyone who was kind to her. As far as he could tell, she had no ulterior motives for the help she gave, for the warmth she gave. She didn't ask for money. Nor did she try to take advantage of his constant confusion in this century. No, she gave help because someone needed her help.

He put his hand to her cheek, and in her sleep, she snuggled her face against his hand.

What bond had brought them together? And what bond held them? He had not told her, as she did not seem to experience it, but he could feel her pain. From the first day, when she felt pain, so did he. That first day, outside the church, she had made what he now knew was a telephone call to her sister. He'd had no idea what she was doing, but he'd sensed that she was hurt.

Today, he'd been directing the driver with the bags when, suddenly, he had sensed a feeling of great despair, and he knew it was coming from her. His first sight of the lover who had abandoned her was such a shock to him that he'd had difficulty understanding the words.

At first his only thought had been that Dougless was going to leave him. How would he find the key to returning if she left him? But more than that, what would he do without *her?* Without her smiles and teasings? Without her innocence and her laughter?

It was still difficult for him to understand the modern speech, but he understood that her ex-lover wanted her to go with him, and he could see that Dougless was having difficulty deciding what to do. When Nicholas threw the man out, he had reacted out of a primitive instinct. How could Dougless consider leaving with a man who gave his daughter precedence over a woman? If for no other reason, Dougless deserved respect because she was older. What manner of country was this that worshiped children to the extent that they were treated as royalty?

Now, as she lay beside him, Nicholas touched her shoulder, then ran his hand down Dougless's arm. Three days, he thought. Three days ago he had never seen her before, but now he found himself doing whatever he could to make her smile. She was so easy to please. All it took was a kind word, a gift, or even a smile.

Leaning over her, he softly kissed her hair. The woman needed caring for, he thought. She needed someone to watch over her. She was like a rosebud that needed a little sunshine to make it open into a full blossom. She needed . . .

Abruptly, Nicholas pulled away from her, then got off the bed and went to stand by the window. Her needs were not his concern, he told himself. Even if he could somehow take her back with him, he could do no more than make her his mistress. He gave a one-sided smile. He did not think the soft Dougless would make a very good mistress. She would never ask her master for a thing, and what she had she'd give to any child who had no shoes.

Nicholas ran his hand over his eyes as though to clear his vision. There was more in this twentieth century that he did not understand than machines that produced light and pictures. He did not understand their philosophy. Yesterday he had seen an outrageous thing called a movie. It had taken him some time to be able to see it, as the people were so large, and the concept of flat giants who looked so round was difficult for him to understand. Dougless had told him the people were normal size, but, like a person could be drawn small, one could be photographed large. After he got over his horror of the pictures themselves, he found that he did not understand the story. A young girl was to marry a perfectly suitable man of means, but she had thrown him over for a penniless young man who had nothing more than a fine pair of legs.

Afterward, Dougless had told him she thought the story "wonderful" and "romantic." He did not understand this philosophy. If his mother had had a daughter and that daughter had refused to honor a good marriage contract, Lady Margaret would have beaten the girl until her arm grew tired; then his mother would have directed the strongest groom to beat the girl some more. But in this age it seemed that disobedience in children was to be encouraged.

He looked back at her, asleep on the bed, her knees tucked up, her hand under her face.

If he remained in this age, he thought, then perhaps he could remain with her. It would be pleasant to live with such a soft female, a woman who put his needs before her own, a woman who held him when his dreams were bad. A woman who did not want him because he was an earl or because he had money. Yes, life with her could be pleasant.

No! he thought, then turned away from her to look out the window. He thought back to that hideous beldame at Bellwood, that hag who had laughed at the memory of Nicholas Stafford. If he remained in this time with Dougless, he would never change how he was remembered. The woman at Bellwood had said that after Nicholas's death, Queen Elizabeth had taken the Stafford estates, and later most of them had been destroyed in the Civil War. Only four of his many estates now remained—and none of them belonged to a Stafford.

Honor, Nicholas thought. People of this age seemed to think little of honor. Dougless did not really understand what he meant by honor. She thought the story of Lady Arabella was amusing. Even the idea of what a man's execution for treason did to his family did not bother her. "It was so long ago," she'd said. "Who rememberers what happened so many years ago?"

But it wasn't long ago to Nicholas. To him, just three days ago he had been in the White Tower, trying to save his family's honor, and his own head as well.

This changing of time had happened to him for a reason. He was sure that God was giving him a second chance. He was convinced that somewhere in this century was the answer to who had hated him enough to want him killed. Who had benefitted by his death? And who so had the queen's ear that she would believe this person completely?

Nothing had come out at his trial. The facts were that he had raised an army, but he had not sought the queen's permission. Men had come from his estates in Wales to swear that they had requested the troops, but the judges would not listen to the men. The judges swore they had "secret" evidence. They said that they "knew" that Nicholas Stafford had been planning to overthrow the young Queen Elizabeth and return England to the Catholic religion.

When Nicholas had been condemned to death, he had believed that would be his fate. But his mother had sent a message saying that she had found new evidence and soon the truth would be known. Soon Nicholas would be a free man.

But before he could find out what the evidence was, he'd "died." At least that is what history wrote of him. An ignoble death to be sure, he thought. He'd been found slumped over an unfinished letter.

Why hadn't his mother brought the evidence forth after his death and cleared his name? Instead, she had relinquished all control over the Stafford estates and married a fat-brain like Dickie Harewood. Why? For money? Had she been left without even the estates she had inherited from her mother?

There were so many questions to be answered and so much injustice to correct. And there was so much honor at stake.

All Nicholas felt he knew for sure was that he had been called forward to this time to discover what he needed to know. And, for some fortuitous reason, he had been given this lovely young woman to assist him. Looking back at her, he smiled. Would he have been as generous as she if she had come to him and told him she was from the future? He thought not. He might have ordered the lighting of the fires that burned her as a witch.

But she had devoted all her time to him, reluctantly at first, but he had soon discovered that it was not in her nature to be ungenerous.

And now, he thought with a sigh, she was falling in love with him. He could see it in her eyes. In his time, when a woman started to love him, he left her. Women who loved you were an annoyance. He much preferred women like Arabella who liked jewels or a fine piece of silk. He and Arabella understood each other. There was only sex between them.

But that was not the way with this Dougless. She would be one to

give love, and to love with all her being. That man Robert had had
some of her love, but, obviously, he was too stupid to know what to do
with it. Nicholas could see that the man used Dougless, played with
her love, and enjoyed his control over her.

Nicholas took a step toward her. If he, Nicholas, had her love, he
would know what to do with it. He would—

No! he told himself, then looked away. No, he could not let her
love him. When he left this modern world, she would be overcome
with grief. Nicholas would not like to return and think of her here
alone, think of her loving a man who'd been dead over four hundred
years.

Therefore, he had to find a way to make her stop loving him. He
couldn't feign anger and send her away because he needed her knowledge of this foreign world. But, at the same time, he couldn't bear to
think of leaving her behind in misery. He had to find a way to stop her
love, and it had to be a way she could understand, a way that related to
her world, not his.

Smiling at the absurdity of the idea, Nicholas thought that perhaps
he could tell her he was in love with another woman. That usually set
women off in any century. But who? Arabella? He almost laughed
aloud when he thought of the postcard Dougless had bought. Perhaps
a woman she'd not heard of would be better. Alice? Elizabeth? Jane?
Ah, dear little Jane.

He stopped smiling. What about Lettice?

In love with his *wife?*

Nicholas hadn't thought of that cold-eyed bitch in weeks. When he
had been arrested for treason, Lettice had started looking for a new
husband.

Could he make Dougless believe he was in love with his wife? That
movie had shown people marrying for love. Perhaps if he told Dougless
he wanted to go back because he loved his wife so much . . . He could
not believe Dougless would consider love more important than honor,
but this age was very strange to him.

Now all he had to do was find a place and time to tell her.

He had made his decision, but it didn't make him feel better.
Quietly, he left the room. He'd go to the coin dealer and see about sell-

ing more of the coins. Tomorrow, they would go to Thornwyck Castle and start finding the answers to his questions.

With one last look at Dougless, he left the room.

Dougless awoke with a start, and when she saw she was alone, a sense of panic gripped her, but she calmed herself. Then the scene with Robert came back to her. Had she done the right thing? Should she have gone with him? After all, Robert did apologize—sort of. He'd explained why he'd left her: he thought she was refusing to travel with him, and maybe Gloria *had* picked up her handbag innocently.

Dougless put her hands to her head. Everything was so confusing. What did she mean to Robert? To Nicholas? What did these men mean to her? Why had Nicholas come to her? Why not to someone else? Why not to someone who wasn't confused about everything in her life?

The door opened and Nicholas came in smiling. "I have sold but a few of the coins and we are rich!" he said.

Smiling back at him, she remembered the way he'd pushed Robert out the door. Was this man her Knight in Shining Armor? Had he been sent to her because she just plain *needed* him so much?

Her look seemed to annoy Nicholas, for he turned away, frowning. "Shall we have supper?" he asked.

As they walked through the village on their way to an Indian restaurant their landlady had recommended, they were both quiet, each thinking hard on their own thoughts. Once they were at the restaurant, Nicholas gave himself over to the food. He loved the flavors of the cumin, coriander, garam masala, and cinnamon all mixed together. As he ate, Dougless saw envious looks directed toward them from several women at nearby tables. Out of interest, and partly to keep him from looking at the women, she asked him what food they ate in 1564, and was it very different from food in the twentieth century?

He talked, but Dougless didn't really listen. Instead, she looked at his eyes and his hair, and watched the way his hands moved. He wasn't going to leave this century, she thought. She'd wished him forward and he'd come to her. She knew enough about him to know that he was the man she'd always wanted: kind, thoughtful, funny, strong, a man who knew what he wanted.

By the end of dinner, Nicholas had grown quiet and something seemed to be worrying him. They were silent as they walked back to the bed-and-breakfast. Nor did he want to talk once they were in their room. He didn't even want Dougless to read to him. When he went to bed, he turned away from her without so much as a good night.

Dougless lay awake for a long time, trying to puzzle out what had happened to her in the last few days. She had cried and begged for a Knight in Shining Armor and Nicholas had come to her. That one fact seemed to prove that he was hers and she was meant to keep him.

Near midnight, just as she was finally dozing, she was startled by sounds from Nicholas. She smiled, knowing he was again having a bad dream. Still smiling, she went to him and climbed into bed beside him. At once he clasped her in his arms and immediately fell into a peaceful sleep. Dougless snuggled close, her cheek on his furred chest, and contentedly went to sleep. Let what is to be, happen, she thought.

When Nicholas awoke it was daylight, and when he realized Dougless was in his arms, he knew his dreams had come true. She fit his body as though they were carved from one piece of earth. What was the word she used? Telepathy. There was a feeling between them, a deep bond that he'd never come close to feeling with another woman.

Putting his face in her hair, he breathed deeply, and his hands began to caress her. He'd never felt such lust as he felt for her, never even known such lust existed.

"Give me strength," he prayed, "strength to do what I must. And forgive me," he whispered.

He hoped he could do what he had to, but first he wanted to taste her, just this once, this one and only time; then never again would he allow himself to touch her.

He kissed her hair, her neck, his tongue on her smooth skin. His hand ran up her arm, then covered her breast. Nicholas's heart was in his ears.

Waking, Dougless turned in his arms to kiss him—a kiss such as she'd never experienced before. The other half of me, she thought. What I have been missing all my life is this man. He's the other half of me.

"Lettice," Nicholas murmured near her ear.

Their legs were entwined, their arms clasping one another. Dougless smiled, her head back as Nicholas placed hot kisses on her neck and throat. "I've been called . . . Carrots," she said, breathless, "for my hair, but never lettuce."

"Lettice is . . ." He was kissing down her throat, lower and lower. "Lettice is my wife."

"Mmm," Dougless murmured as his hand caressed her breast and his lips went lower.

What he'd said hit her suddenly. She pushed away to look at him. "Wife?" she asked.

Nicholas pulled her back to him. "We care naught for her now."

She pushed away from him again. "You seem to care about her enough to say her name when you're kissing *me."*

"A mere slip," he said, pulling her toward him.

Dougless shoved at him hard, then got out of bed and straightened her unbuttoned gown. "Why don't you explain to me about this *wife* of yours?" she demanded angrily. "And why haven't I heard of her before? I know you had a child, but you said the mother had died."

Nicholas sat up in bed, the sheet to his waist. "There was no reason to tell of my wife. Her beauty, her talents, and my love for her are private to me." He picked up Dougless's watch off the table. "Perhaps today we will purchase me such as this."

"Put that down!" Dougless snapped. "This is serious. I think you owe me an explanation."

"Explain to *you?"* Nicholas said, getting out of bed, wearing only a pair of tiny briefs. He pulled on his trousers, then turned to her as he fastened them. "Pray, madam, who are you? Are you a duke's daughter? An earl's? Even a baron's? I am the earl of Thornwyck, and you are my servant. You work for me. In return, I feed you and clothe you, and perhaps, if you are worth it, I will mayhap give you a small stipend. I have no obligation to tell you of my own life."

Dougless sat down hard on the bed. "But you never mentioned a wife," she said softly. "Not once have you referred to her."

"I would be a poor husband to profane my beloved's name to my servant."

"Servant," Dougless whispered. "Do you love her very much?"

Nicholas snorted. "She is the true reason I must return. I must find the truth, then return to my loving wife's arms."

Dougless was having difficulty understanding what she was hearing. Robert yesterday and today finding that Nicholas had a wife—a wife he loved madly—was more than she could handle. "I don't understand," she said, burying her face in her hands. "I wished you here. I prayed for you. Why did you come to me if you love someone else?"

"You prayed on my tomb. Perhaps if anyone had done that—man or woman—I would have come forth. Perhaps God knew I would need a servant and you needed work. I do not know. All I do know is that I must return."

"To your wife?"

"Aye, to my wife."

She turned to look at him. "And what of this?" she asked, motioning to the bed.

"Madam, you placed yourself in my bed. I am but a man, therefore I am weak."

As understanding came to Dougless, she began to feel deeply embarrassed. Was there any woman on earth who was a bigger fool than she was? Was there any man on earth she *hadn't* fallen in love with? Let her spend three days with a man and she began to imagine a life together. If Attila the Hun or Jack the Ripper had come forward, she'd no doubt have fallen in love with him. With her luck, she'd be in love with Genghis Khan in *two* days.

She stood up. "Look, I'm sorry for the misunderstanding. Of course you have a wife. A beautiful wife and three lovely kids. I don't know what I was thinking of. You were on death row *and* married. I'm used to guys with only one major strike against them. I just seem to get luckier and luckier. I'll get my things and get out of here. You go back to Mrs. Stafford and have a swell life."

He blocked the entrance to the bathroom. "You mean to unkiss the bargain?"

"'Unkiss'?" she asked, voice rising. "Again with the 'unkiss.' Yes, I mean to unkiss, unhug, un-whatever else it needs. You don't need me, not when you have lovely Lettice and Arabella-on-the-table."

When Nicholas moved toward her, his voice lowered seductively. "If our interrupted love play annoys you, we may return to the bed."

"Not on your life, buster," she said, eyes blazing. "Put one hand on me and you draw back a bloody nub."

Nicholas put his hand over his jaw to hide a smile. "I see no cause for your anger. I have represented myself truly. I need help in searching for the person who betrayed me. I want to find the information and return to my home. I have never been false with you."

Dougless turned away. He was right. He'd never been secretive in any way. She was the one who'd imagined castles in the sky and their living happily ever after. Idiot, idiot, idiot, she told herself.

She turned back to him. "I'm sorry about all this. Maybe you should get someone else to help you. I've got my passport now, and my plane ticket, so I think I'd better go home."

"Ah, yes," he said. "I see. You are a coward."

"I am no such thing. It's just . . ."

"You have fallen in love with me," he said with a sigh of resignation. "All the women do. It is a curse that plagues me much. I cannot spend three days with a woman and not have her come to my bed. Think not on it. I do not blame you."

"You don't blame me?" Anger was beginning to replace Dougless's self-pity. "Listen, mister! You overrate your charms by a long shot. You don't know what women are like today. Any liberated women could live in the same house with you and not fall for you. We don't like conceited, puffed-up peacocks like you."

"Oh?" he said, one eyebrow raised. "It is just you who is different? In just three days' time you are in my bed."

"For your information, I was trying to settle you down after a nightmare. I thought I was comforting you. Like a mother and child."

Nicholas smiled. "Comfort? You may comfort me any morn you wish."

"Save it for your wife. Now, will you get out of the way? I need to get dressed and get out of here."

He put his hand on her arm. "You are angry at me that I kissed you?"

"I'm angry at you because . . ." She turned away. Why was she angry at him? He'd awakened and found her in his bed and he'd started kissing her. Before today, he hadn't made a pass at her; he hadn't been anything but a gentleman. Never once had he even hinted that they were more than employer and employee.

It was she who'd made everything up. Out of his teasings, out of the laughter they'd shared and, especially, out of her hurt over Robert, she'd imagined more between them than there was.

"I'm not angry at you at all," she said. "I'm mad at myself. I guess I was on the rebound."

"'Rebound'?"

"Sometimes when you get jilted, or abandoned as I was, you want to jump right back on the train." He still looked puzzled. "I thought maybe you could replace Robert. Or maybe I just wanted to go home with a ring on my finger. If I went home engaged, maybe I wouldn't have too many questions asked about the man I left America with and what happened to him."

She looked up at him. "I'm sorry for what I thought. Maybe you better get someone else to help you."

"I understand. You could not resist me. It is as the guide said. No woman can withstand me."

Dougless groaned. "I could withstand you all right. Now that I know the true extent of your enormous ego, I could *live* with you and not fall for you."

"You could not."

"I could, and I'll prove it. I'll find your secret for you, and even if it takes years, I won't even be tempted by you." She narrowed her eyes. "You have any more bad dreams and wake me up, I'll throw a pillow at you. *Now* will you let me in the bathroom?"

Nicholas stepped aside, and she angrily closed the door behind her, but he couldn't help grinning at the door. Ah, Dougless, he thought, my sweet, sweet Dougless. You may be able to resist me, but how will I resist you? A year together? A year without touching you? I will go mad.

He turned away to finish dressing.

TEN

*T*he long black car made its way south through the beautiful English countryside. In the backseat Nicholas looked across at Dougless. She was sitting stiffly upright. Her lovely, thick auburn hair was pulled tightly back to the nape of her neck and put in what she told him was called a bun. Since this morning she had not smiled or laughed or made any comment except, "Yes, sir," or "No, sir."

"Dougless," he said. "I—"

She cut him off. "I believe, Lord Stafford, we have already discussed this. I am Miss Montgomery—not Mistress Montgomery—your secretary, no more, no less. If you will remember that, sir, it will prevent people from thinking that I am more to you than I am."

Turning away, he sighed. He could think of nothing to say to her, and actually, he knew this attitude was the better way, but already, he missed her.

Moments later his attention was caught by the tower of Thornwyck Castle, and he found his heart beginning to beat a little faster. He had designed this place. He had taken what he knew and loved of every house he'd ever seen, improved on every idea, and created this beautiful house. It had taken four years to cut the stone and to ship the marble from Italy. Among his many ideas, in the inner courtyard he had built towers with curved glass in them.

Thornwyck Castle had been only half finished when he was arrested, but the half that was completed had been as beautiful as any building in the land.

Nicholas frowned as the driver turned into the drive. Now, his house looked so old. Just a month ago he had been here, and then it had been new and perfect. Now the chimney pots were crumbling, there were broken places along the roof, and some of his windows had been bricked in.

"It's beautiful," Dougless whispered, then straightened, "sir."

"It is crumbling," Nicholas said in anger. "And were the western towers never completed? I drew the plans. Did no one see them?"

When the car stopped, Nicholas got out and looked around. To his mind, it was a sad place, the unfinished half in ruins, the other half looking hundreds of years old—which it was, he thought with dismay.

When he turned back, Dougless had already entered the hotel lobby, two boys behind her carrying their luggage. "Lord Stafford will want early tea at eight A.M.," she was telling the desk clerk. "And he takes luncheon promptly at noon, but I must be given a menu beforehand." She turned to him. "Would you like to sign the register, my lord, or should I?"

Nicholas gave her a quelling look, warning her with his eyes to stop her pompous behavior. He'd seen enough of the modern world to know that she was acting strangely. But Dougless turned away, acting as though she hadn't seen his look. Nicholas quickly signed the guest book in an unreadable scrawl; then the clerk led them to their suite.

The room was beautiful, with dark rose-colored wallpaper and a four-poster bed hung with rose and yellow chintz. A little couch in yellow and pale green sat at the foot of the bed on a rose-colored carpet. Through an arched-top doorway was a small sitting room decorated in shades of rose and pale green.

"I will need a cot put in here," Dougless said, indicating the sitting room.

"A cot?" the clerk asked.

"Of course. For me to sleep on. You did not think that I would sleep in his lordship's chamber, did you?"

Nicholas rolled his eyes. Even in his own time this behavior would be strange.

"Yes, miss," the clerk said. "I will have a cot sent up." He left them alone.

"Dougless," Nicholas began.

"Miss Montgomery," she said in a cold voice.

"Miss Montgomery," he said just as coolly, "see that my capcases are sent up. I plan to look at my house."

"Shall I accompany you?"

"Nay, I want no hellkite with me," he said angrily, then left the room.

Dougless saw that the suitcases were brought up, then asked the clerk where the local library was. Feeling very efficient, she set off through the little village, notebook and pens in hand, but as she neared the library, her steps slowed.

Don't think about your life, she told herself. Being dropped by one man and immediately finding another one—a good one—was all a dream, an impossible, unreachable dream. Cold, she thought, I have to remain cold. Think of Antarctica. Siberia. Do your job and remain cool to him. He belongs to another woman and to another time.

It was easy finding what the librarian called the "Stafford Collection." "Many of the visitors to our village ask after the Staffords, especially the guests staying at Thornwyck Castle," the librarian said.

"I'm especially interested in the last earl, Nicholas Stafford."

"Oh, yes, poor man, condemned to be beheaded, then dying before the execution. It's believed he was poisoned."

"Poisoned by whom?" Dougless asked eagerly as she followed the woman into the stacks.

"By the person who accused him of treason, of course," she said, looking at Dougless as though she didn't understand even simple things. "It's believed that Lord Nicholas built Thornwyck Castle. A local historian says that he believes Lord Nicholas may have even designed it, but no one can prove it. No one has found drawings with his name on them. Well, here we are, all the books on this shelf have something in them about the Staffords."

After the librarian left, Dougless took out each book, searched the index for any mention of Nicholas or his mother, and began reading.

One of the first things she did was look for the name Nicholas had given her of the man he said had had a grudge against him. It was the name he had been writing to his mother when he'd heard Dougless crying. "Land disputes," Nicholas had said, by way of explaining the grudge. But after only ten minutes of searching, Dougless had found the man's name. He had died six months before Nicholas had been arrested, so he couldn't have been the one who told the queen Nicholas was raising an army.

What little she could find on Nicholas was told in a derogatory way.

His older brother, Christopher, had been made earl when he was twenty-two, and the books raved about how Christopher had taken the failing Stafford fortunes and rebuilt them. Nicholas, only a year younger, was portrayed as frivolous, spending vast amounts on horses and women. He had been the earl for only four years before he was tried for treason.

"He hasn't changed," Dougless said aloud, opening another book. This one was even more unflattering. It told at length the story of Lady Arabella and the table. It seems that two servants were in the room when Nicholas and Arabella entered, and they ducked into a closet when they heard the lord and lady. Later the servants told everyone what they'd seen, and a clerk by the name of John Wilfred had put the whole story down in his diary—a diary that had survived until the present.

The third book was more serious. It told of Christopher's great accomplishments, then added that his wastrel of a younger brother had squandered everything on a foolhardy attempt to put Mary Queen of Scots on Elizabeth's throne.

Dougless slammed the book shut and looked at her watch. It was time for tea. She left the library and made her way to a pretty little tea shop. After she had been served tea and a plate of scones, she began reading her notes.

"I have sought you most earnestly."

She looked up to see Nicholas standing over her. "Should I rise until you are seated, my lord?"

"No, Miss Montgomery, a mere kiss of my toes will be sufficient."

Dougless almost smiled, but she didn't. He got himself a tray of tea, but Dougless had to pay for it, as he still carried no money.

"What is it you read?"

Coolly, she told him what she had found out, sparing him no details of what history had recorded about him. Except for a slight flush around his collar, he didn't seem to react.

"There is no mention in your history books that I was chamberlain to my brother?"

"None. It says you bought horses and fooled around with women." And she'd thought she could love such a man! But then, it seemed that a lot of women had thought so.

Nicholas ate a scone and drank his tea. "When I return, I will change your history books."

"You can't change history. History is fact; it's already made. And you certainly can't change what the history books say. They're already printed."

He didn't answer her. "What did your book say of my family after my death?"

"I didn't look that far. I only read about your brother and you."

He gave her a cool look. "You read only of the bad about me?"

"That's all there *was*."

"What of my design of Thornwyck? When the queen saw my plan, she hailed it as a monument of greatness."

"There is no record that you designed it. The librarian said some people believed you did, but there was no proof."

Nicholas put down his half-eaten scone. "Come," he said angrily. "I will show you what I did. I will show you the great work I left behind me."

As he strode out of the tea room, the unfinished scone was testimony to how upset he was. He walked ahead of her with long, angry strides, and Dougless had difficulty keeping up with him as they went back to the hotel.

To Dougless the hotel was beautiful, but to Nicholas it was mostly ruins. To the left of the entrance were what she'd assumed were stone fences, but he showed her that they were walls to what would have been nearly half of the house. Now there was grass underfoot and vines growing down the walls. He told her of the beauty of these rooms if they had been built as he designed them: paneling, stained glass, carved marble fireplaces. He pointed high on one wall to a stone face, worn by rain and time. "My brother," he said. "I had the likeness carved of him."

As they walked down long avenues of roofless rooms and Nicholas talked, Dougless began to see what he had planned. She could almost hear the lutes in the music room.

"And now it is this," he said at last. "A place for cows and goats and . . . yeomen."

"And their daughters," Dougless said, including herself in his derogatory description.

Turning, he looked at her with cool contempt. "You believe what these fools have written about me," he said. "You believe my life was naught but horses and women."

"I didn't say that, the books did, my lord," she answered him in the same tone.

"On the morrow we will begin to find what the books do *not* say."

ELEVEN

*I*n *the morning they were both* at the library when the door was unlocked. After spending twenty minutes explaining the free library system to Nicholas, Dougless got five of the books on the Staffords from the shelves and began to read. Nicholas sat across from her, staring at the pages of a book, and frowning in consternation. After thirty minutes of watching him struggle, Dougless took pity on him.

"Perhaps, sir," she said softly, "in the evenings I might teach you to read."

"Teach me to read?" he asked.

"In America I teach school, and I've had quite a bit of experience teaching children to read. I'm sure you could learn," she said gently.

"Could I?" he asked, one eyebrow raised. He didn't say any more, but got up, went to the librarian, and asked her a few questions, which Dougless couldn't hear. Smiling, the librarian nodded, left the desk for a moment, then returned and handed him several books.

Nicholas put the books on the table in front of Dougless and opened the top one. "There, Miss Montgomery, read that to me."

On the page was an incomprehensible type-face of oddly-shaped letters and strangely-spelled words. She looked up at him.

"*This* is my printing." Picking the book up, he looked at the title page. "It is a play by a man named William Shakespeare."

"You haven't heard of him? I thought Shakespeare was as Elizabethan as any man ever was."

Nicholas, starting to read, took a seat across from her. "Nay, I have no knowledge of him." Quickly, he became absorbed in his reading as Dougless dug more into the history books.

She could find very little about what happened after Nicholas's death. The estates had been taken over by the queen. Neither Christopher nor Nicholas had children, so the Stafford title and line had died with them. Again and again, she read of what a wastrel Nicholas had been and how he'd betrayed his entire family.

At noon they went to a pub for lunch. After their first visit, Nicholas had not insisted upon a heavy midday meal. He was beginning to get used to the light lunches, but he continued to grumble.

"Foolish children," he said, moving his food about on his plate. "If they had listened to their parents, they would have lived. Your world fosters such disobedience."

"What children?"

"In the play. Juliet and . . ." He paused, trying to remember.

"*Romeo and Juliet?* You've been reading *Romeo and Juliet?*"

"Aye, and a more disobedient lot I have never seen. That play is a good lesson to children everywhere. I hope children today read it and learn from it."

Dougless nearly screeched at him. "*Romeo and Juliet* is about *romance,* and if the parents hadn't been so narrow-minded and uptight, they—"

"Narrow-minded? They were good parents. They knew such a liaison could only end in tragedy—and it *did!*" he said fiercely.

Dougless's ideas of being cool fled her mind. "The tragedy came because the parents—" They argued throughout the meal.

Later, as they walked back to the library, Dougless asked him how his brother Christopher had died.

Nicholas stopped walking and looked away. "I was to go hunting

with him that day, but I had cut my arm during sword practice."
Dougless saw him rubbing his left forearm. "I still bear the scar." After
a moment Nicholas turned to her, and she could see the pain in his
eyes. Whatever she thought of Nicholas Stafford, she had no doubt of
his love for his brother. "He drowned. I was not the only brother who
liked women. Kit saw a pretty girl swimming in a lake, and he told his
men to leave him alone with her. After a few hours the men returned to
find my brother floating in the lake."

"And no one saw what happened?"

"Nay. Perhaps the girl did, but we never found her."

Dougless was thoughtful for a moment. "How odd that your
brother drowned with no witnesses to attest to what happened; then a
few years later you were tried for treason. It's almost as though someone planned to take the Stafford estates."

Nicholas's face changed. He looked at her with that expression
men have when a woman says something they've not thought of—as
though the impossible has happened.

"Who stood to inherit? Your dear, darling Lettice?" Dougless
snapped her lips together, wishing she'd kept the jealousy out of her
voice.

Nicholas didn't seem to notice. "Lettice had her marriage property,
but she lost all at my death. I inherited from Kit, but I can assure you I
did not wish for his death."

"Too much responsibility?" Dougless asked. "Being the boss carries
a burden to it."

He gave her a look of anger. "You believe your history books.
Come," he said, "you must read more. You must discover who betrayed
me."

Dougless read all afternoon while Nicholas laughed over *The
Merchant of Venice,* but she could find out nothing more.

In the evening Nicholas wanted her to dine with him, but she
refused. She knew she had to spend less time with him. Her heart was
too newly broken and she had come too close to caring more for him
than was good for her. Looking like a sad little boy, he stuck his hands
in his pockets and went downstairs to dinner, while Dougless asked for
a bowl of soup and some bread to be brought up to her room. As she

ate, she went over her notes, but could come up with no new ideas. No one seemed to gain anything by the deaths of Christopher and Nicholas.

About ten P.M., Nicholas had still not returned from dinner so, curious, she went downstairs to look for him. He was in the beautiful stone-walled drawing room laughing with half a dozen guests. Dougless stood in the shadow of the doorway and watched—and anger, unreasonable, unjust anger, flooded her body. *She* had called him forward, but now two other women were drooling over him.

Turning away, she left the hallway. He was exactly as the books said, she thought. No wonder someone had so easily betrayed him. When he should have been taking care of business, he was probably in bed with some woman.

She went upstairs, put on her nightgown, and got into the little bed the hotel had brought up for her. But she didn't sleep. Instead, she lay there feeling angry and foolish. Maybe she should have left with Robert. Robert had a bit of a problem about sharing money and he did love his daughter excessively, but he'd always been faithful to her.

At about eleven she heard Nicholas open the bedroom door, and she saw light under the door between their rooms. When she heard him open her door, she tightly closed her eyes.

"Dougless," he whispered, but she didn't answer. "I know you do not sleep, so answer me."

She opened her eyes. "Should I get my pad and paper? I'm afraid I don't take shorthand."

Sighing, Nicholas took a step toward her. "I felt something from you tonight. Anger? Dougless, I do not want us to be enemies."

"We're not enemies," she said sternly. "We are employer and employee. You are an earl and I am a commoner."

"Dougless," he said, his voice pleading and all too seductive. "You are not common. I meant . . ."

"Yes?"

He backed away. "Forgive me. I have had too much to drink, and my tongue runs away from me. I meant what I said. On the morrow you must discover more about my family. Good night, Miss Montgomery."

"Aye, aye, Captain," she said mockingly.

In the morning, she refused to eat breakfast with him. This is better, she told herself. Do not relax for even a moment. Remind yourself that he is as much a scoundrel now as he was then. She walked to the library alone, and when she looked out its windows, she saw Nicholas laughing with a pretty young woman. Dougless buried her nose in the book.

Nicholas was still smiling when he came to sit across from her. "A new friend?" she asked, and immediately wished she hadn't.

"She is an American and she was telling me about baseball. And football."

"You *told* her that you've never heard of those sports because last week you were in Elizabethan England?" Dougless was aghast.

Nicholas smiled. "She believes me to be a man of learning, so I have had not time for such tilly-fally."

"Learning, ha!" Dougless muttered.

Nicholas continued to smile. "You are jealous?"

"Jealous? Most certainly not. I am your employee. I have no right to be jealous. Did you tell her about your wife?"

Nicholas picked up one of the books of Shakespeare's plays the librarian had left out for him. "You are frampold this morning," he said, but he was smiling as though he was pleased.

Dougless had no idea what he meant, so she wrote the word down and looked it up later. *Disagreeable.* So, he thought she was disagreeable, did he? She went back to her research.

At three o'clock she nearly jumped out of her chair. "Look! It's here." Excitedly, she went around the table to take the chair next to Nicholas. "This paragraph, see?" He did, but he could read only phrases of it. She was holding a two-month-old copy of a magazine on English history.

"This article is on Goshawk Hall that we heard about at Bellwood. It says that there's been a recent find at Goshawk of papers of the Stafford family—and the papers date from the sixteenth century. The papers are now being studied by Dr. Hamilton J. Nolman, a young man with . . . There's an impressive list of his credentials, then . . . it says that Dr. Nolman 'hopes to prove that Nicholas Stafford, who was accused of treason at the beginning of Elizabeth the First's reign, was actually innocent.'"

When Dougless looked at Nicholas, the expression in his eyes was almost embarrassing.

"This is why I have been sent here," he said softly. "Nothing could be proved until these papers were found. We must go to Goshawk."

"We can't just *go*. First, we'll have to petition the owners to look at the papers." She closed the magazine. "What size of house must it be to have misplaced a trunkload of papers for four hundred years?"

"Goshawk Hall is not so large as four of my houses," Nicholas said as though he were offended.

Dougless leaned back in the chair and felt that at last they were getting somewhere. She had no doubt that these papers had belonged to Nicholas's mother, and they contained the information Nicholas needed to prove himself innocent.

"Well, hello."

They looked up to see the pretty young woman who had explained baseball to Nicholas. "I thought that was you," she said, then gave Dougless the once-over. "Is this your friend?"

"I'm merely his secretary," Dougless said, rising. "Will there be anything else, my lord?"

"Lord?!" the young woman gasped. "You're a *lord?*"

Nicholas started to leave with Dougless, but the overexcited American, thrilled at meeting a lord, would not allow him to go.

As Dougless went back to the hotel, she was trying her best to think of her letter to Goshawk Hall, but, actually, she was thinking mostly of Nicholas flirting with the pretty American. It didn't matter to her, of course. This was just a job. Soon she'd be home, teaching her fifth graders, dating now and then, visiting her family and telling them all about England—and explaining how she was ditched by one man and half fell in love with a man who was married and about four hundred and fifty-one years old.

The best Dougless-story yet, she thought.

By the time she got to the hotel, she was slamming things about. Damn all men, she thought. Damn the good ones as well as the bad. They broke your heart over and over again.

"I see your temper has not improved," Nicholas said from behind her.

"My temper is not your concern," she snapped. "I was hired to do a job, and I'm doing it. I'm going to write Goshawk Hall and see when we can look at the papers."

Nicholas was beginning to get angry himself. "The animosity you be-mete to me has not foundation."

"I have no animosity toward you," she said with fury. "I'm doing my best to help you so you can get back to your loving wife and to your own time." Her head came up. "I just realized that there's no need for you to be here. I can do the research alone. You can't read modern books anyway. Why don't you go to . . . to the French Riviera or somewhere? I can do this by myself."

"You would that I leave?" he asked softly.

"Sure, why not? You could go to London and party. You could meet all the beautiful women of this century. We have lots of tables nowadays."

Nicholas stiffened. "You want away from me?"

"Yes, yes, and yes," she said. "My research would go much better without you. You're . . . you're just getting in my way. You know nothing about my world, so you can't help me. You can barely dress yourself, you still eat with your hands half the time, you can't read or write our language, and I have to explain the simplest things to you. It would be a thousand times better if you left me alone." Her hands were gripping the chair back so hard her knuckles appeared to be about to come through the skin.

When she glanced up at him, the naked pain on his face was more than she could bear. He *had* to leave, she thought. He had to let her piece her mind and body back together. Before she yet again humiliated herself with tears, she turned and left the room. Once she was in her own sleeping alcove, she leaned against the door and cried deeply.

Just to get this over, she thought, to send him away, to go back home and never even look at another man again, that's what she needed.

She fell down on her bed, buried her face in her pillow, and cried silently. She cried for a long time, until the worst of it was over and she began to feel better. And once her tears were shed, she began to think more clearly.

How stupid she'd been acting! What had Nicholas done wrong? She visualized him sitting in a dungeon awaiting execution for a crime he didn't commit, then the next minute he's floating through the air and he's in the twentieth century.

She sat up and blew her nose. And how well he'd handled everything! He'd adjusted to automobiles, paper money, a strange language, strange food, and . . . And a weepy woman suffering from the rejection of another man. Yet, through it all, Nicholas had been generous with his money, his laughter, and his knowledge.

And what had Dougless done? She'd been furious with him because he'd dared marry another woman some four hundred years ago.

When she looked at it that way, it was almost humorous. She glanced up at the door. Her room was dark, but there was light coming under the door. The things she'd said to him! Awful, terrible things.

She practically ran to the door and flung it open. "Nicholas, I—" The room was empty. She opened the door into the hall and looked out, but the hallway was also empty. When she turned back into the room, she saw the note on the floor, where he must have slipped it under her door. Quickly she looked at the note.

Dougless had no idea what the words said, but to her eyes the paper looked like an Elizabethan runaway note. His clothes were still in the closet and so were his capcases—suitcases, she corrected herself.

She had to find him and apologize, tell him he shouldn't leave, tell him that she did need his help. Her head seemed to ring with all the rotten, terrible things she'd said to him in the last two days. He *could* read. And he had lovely table manners. He— Damn, damn, damn, she thought as she tore down the stairs and ran out of the hotel into the rain.

She clasped her hands about her upper arms, put her head down, and started running. She had to find him. He probably had no idea what an umbrella was or a raincoat. He'd catch his death. Or he'd be fighting the rain so hard he'd walk in front of a bus—or a train. Would he know a train track from a sidewalk? What if he got on a train by himself? He wouldn't know where to get off—or how to get back to her if he did get off.

She ran to the train station, but it was closed. Good, she thought, pushing cold, wet hair out of her face so she could see. She tried to read the dial on her watch, but the rain was hitting her in the face too hard to see clearly. It looked to be after eleven, so she must have been crying for hours. She shivered, thinking what could have happened to him in all those hours.

There was a shadow in a gutter, and Dougless ran to it, knowing it was Nicholas lying dead in a heap. But it was only a shadow. Blinking, trying to keep her eyes open against the rain, sneezing twice, she looked at the dark windows of the village.

Maybe he had just started walking. How far could a person walk in . . . ? She didn't even know how long he'd been gone. Which direction had he gone?

She started running toward the end of the street, cold water splashing up the back of her legs and under her skirt. There seemed to be no lights on anywhere; then, as she rounded a corner, she saw a light in a window. A pub, she thought. She'd ask there and see if anyone had seen him.

When she walked in, the warmth and light of the pub hit her so strongly that for a moment she couldn't see.

Freezing, shivering, dripping, she stood still to allow her eyes to adjust to the light; then she heard a laugh that had become familiar to her. Nicholas! she thought, as she ran through the smoke-filled room.

What she saw was like a painting advertising the seven sins.

Nicholas, his shirt unbuttoned to the waist, a cigar clamped between his strong teeth, sat behind a table that looked as though it might break under the weight of the food on it. There was a pretty woman on either side of him, and there was lipstick on his cheeks and his shirt.

"Dougless," he said in delight. "Come join us."

She stood there feeling like a wet cat, her hair plastered against her head, her clothes sticking to her, a gallon of water in each shoe, a puddle at her feet that could sail a three-masted schooner.

"Get up from there and come with me," she said in the voice she used to settle down unruly schoolchildren.

"Aye, aye, Captain," Nicholas said, smiling and mocking her at the same time.

He's drunk, she thought.

He kissed each woman on the mouth, then leaped onto the seat, bounded over the table, and swooped Dougless into his arms. "Put me down," she hissed, but he carried her through the pub and outside.

"It's raining," she said, her lips tight and her arms folded over her chest.

"Nay, madam, it is a clear night." Still holding her, he began to nuzzle her neck.

"Oh, no, you don't," she said. "You're not going to start *that* again. Put me down at once."

He put her down, but he did so in such a way that her body slid down his.

"You're drunk," she said, pushing him away.

"Oh, aye, I am that," he said happily. "The ale here pleases me. And the women please me," he said as he caught her about the waist.

Dougless again pushed him away. "I was worried about you and here you were boozing it up with a couple of floozies and—"

"Too fast," he cried. "Too many words. Here, my pretty Dougless, look at the stars."

"In case you haven't noticed, I happen to be very wet and I'm also freezing." As though to emphasize the fact, she sneezed.

Once again, he lifted her into his arms. "Put me down!"

"You are cold; I am warm," he said, as though that settled the matter. "You feared for me?"

Was it possible to stay angry at this man for very long? She was willing to admit defeat as she snuggled against him. He was indeed warm. "I said some awful things to you, and I'm very sorry. You aren't really a burden."

He smiled down at her. "Is this the cause of your fear? That perhaps I was angered?"

"No. When you were gone, I thought maybe you'd walked in front of a bus or a train. I was afraid of your being hurt."

"Do I appear to have no *pia mater?*"

"Huh?"

"Brain. Do I seem stupid to you?"

"No, of course not. You just don't know how our modern world works, that's all."

"Oh? Who is wet and who is dry?"

"Both of us are wet, since you continue carrying me," she said smugly.

"For all your knowledge, I have found what we need to know, and tomorrow we ride to Goshawk."

"How did you find out anything and from whom? Those women in there? Did you kiss it out of them?"

"Are you jealous, Montgomery?"

"No, Stafford, I am not." That statement proved that the Pinocchio theory was false. Her nose didn't grow at all. (She checked to make sure.) "What did you find out?"

"Dickie Harewood owns Goshawk."

"But didn't he marry your mother? Is he as old as *you?*"

"Beware, or I will show you how old I am." He shifted her in his arms. "Am I feeding you too much?"

"It's more likely you're weak from flirting with all the women. It saps a man's strength, you know."

"Mine has not been impaired. Now, I was telling you?"

"That Dickie Harewood still owns Goshawk."

"Yes, on the morrow I shall see him. What is a weekend?"

"It's the end of the workweek when everyone gets off. And you can't just go riding up to some lord's house. I hope you're not thinking of inviting yourself for the weekend."

"The workers get off? But no one seems to work at all. I see no farmers in the fields, no one plowing. People now shop and drive cars."

"We have a forty-hour workweek and tractors. Nicholas, you're not answering me. What are you planning to do? You really can't tell this man Harewood you're from the sixteenth century. You can't tell anyone that, even women in bars." She tugged at his collar. "You've ruined that shirt. Lipstick never comes out."

Grinning, he shifted her again. "You have on none of this lipstick."

She moved her head away from him. "Don't start that again. Now, tell me about Goshawk Hall."

"The Harewood family owns it still. They come for the end . . ."

"Weekend."

"Aye, the weekend, and—" He gave Dougless a sideways look. "Arabella is there."

"Arabella? What does the twentieth-century Arabella have to do with anything?"

"*My* Arabella was Dickie Harewood's daughter, and there seems to be a Dickie Harewood again at Goshawk hall, and he again has a daughter named Arabella who is the same age as my Arabella was when we—"

"Spare me," Dougless said, then looked at him in silence for a moment. The papers recently found, another Arabella, and another Dickie. It was almost as though history were repeating itself. How odd, she thought.

TWELVE

*D*ougless *watched Nicholas atop the stallion* and held her breath. She'd heard of people riding horses like this one, but she'd never seen it. Every employee and every visitor at the riding stables had stopped to watch as Nicholas brought the high-strung, angry, mean-tempered animal under control.

Last night they'd stayed up until after one A.M. while Dougless made him tell her all about his relationship to the Harewoods. They'd had estates near one another. Dickie was old enough to be Nicholas's father and he'd had a daughter, Arabella, who'd married Lord Robert Sydney. She and her husband had hated each other, so after she'd given him an heir, they'd lived apart, although Arabella had given birth to three more children.

"One of them yours," Dougless had said, taking notes.

Nicholas's face softened. "There is no reason to think ill of her. She and the child died in that childbirth."

"I'm sorry," Dougless said with a grimace, and knew that the woman could easily have died from something as simple as the midwife's not washing her hands.

Dougless tried to think of a way to get invited to the Harewood estates as quickly as possible, but she had no credentials as a scholar, and although Nicholas was an earl, his title had been taken from him when he was condemned for treason. He couldn't even claim to be his own aristocratic descendant. She thought until she couldn't stay awake any longer; then she'd bid Nicholas good night and gone to her own bed.

"This is better," she thought as she drifted into sleep. She had her emotions under control. She was getting over Robert and she was no longer thinking she was falling for a married man. She'd help Nicholas get back to his wife, help him clear his name; then she'd go home feeling good about herself. For once in her life she was *not* going to fall for an unsuitable man.

Nicholas woke her early the next morning by throwing open the sitting room door. "Can you ride a horse? Can anyone today ride a horse?"

Dougless assured him she could ride, courtesy of her Colorado cousins; then after breakfast she'd found a nearby riding stables. It was four miles to the stables and Nicholas insisted they walk. "Your machines have made you lazy," he said, slapping her on the back as he set off at a brisk pace. At the stables, as Dougless sat on a bench fanning herself, Nicholas had turned up his nose at all the horses for rent, but his eyes had lit up at the sight of an enormous black horse in a field. The animal was prancing about and tossing its head as though it dared anyone to come near it. As though in a trance, Nicholas had walked toward the creature. When the horse ran toward him, Dougless sat up and bit her knuckles in fear.

"This one," Nicholas said to the stableman.

Dougless hurried to him. "You can't really think of riding *that* horse. There are lots of horses here; why don't you pick one of them?"

But nothing anyone could say would change Nicholas's mind. The owner of the stables came into the yard, and he seemed to think it would be a great joke to see Nicholas break his neck. Dougless knew that in America there'd be talk of insurance, but not in England. A groom got a rope around the stallion's neck, then led it into a stall, where another groom saddled it. Finally, the horse was led into a cobbled courtyard and the reins were gleefully handed to Nicholas.

"I never seen nobody ride like that," one of the grooms said as soon as Nicholas had mounted and pulled the horse under control. "He ride a lot?"

"Always," Dougless answered. "He'll get on a horse before he'll get in a car. In fact, he's spent much more of his life on a horse than in a car."

"Must have," the groom mumbled, watching Nicholas with awe.

"You are ready?" Nicholas asked Dougless.

She mounted her sedate mare and followed him as he took off. Never had she seen a happier man, and it struck Dougless afresh how different the modern world must be from what he knew. He and the horse fit together as one being, as though he'd become a centaur.

Rural England is full of footpaths and horse trails, and Nicholas went galloping down one of them as though he'd been down it a thousand times—which he probably had, Dougless thought. She called out to him that maybe he should ask directions, but then she doubted if someone had moved Goshawk Hall in the last few hundred years.

She had trouble keeping up with him, lost him repeatedly, and once he returned for her. She had stopped at a crossroads and was looking at the ground for his tracks. When he saw her, he was very interested in what she was doing. Dougless, trying her best to control her mare, who was reacting to the aggressive nearness of Nicholas's stallion, told him she'd buy him some Louis L'Amour books and read to him about tracking. Laughing, he pointed the way to her, then left in a flurry of mud and leaves.

At last she reached an open gate with a small brass plaque that said, "Goshawk Hall." She rode down the drive to see an enormous, rectangular fortress of a house set amid acres of beautiful, rolling gardens.

Dougless felt a bit embarrassed to be riding up to this house uninvited, but Nicholas was there, already off his horse and walking toward a tall, grubby-looking man on his hands and knees in a bed of petunias.

Gratefully dismounting, Dougless took her horse's reins and ran after him. "Don't you think we should knock on the front door first?" Dougless asked when she reached him. "Why don't you ask for Mr. Harewood and tell him we'd like to see the papers."

"You are on my ground now," he said over his shoulder as he walked toward the gardener.

"Nicholas!" she hissed at him.

"Harewood?" Nicholas said to the man on his knees in the flower bed.

Turning, the tall man looked up at Nicholas. He had blue eyes and blond hair that was now turning gray, and his face had the smooth, pink complexion of a baby's. He also didn't look especially intelligent. "Ah, yes. Do I know you?"

"Nicholas Stafford of Thornwyck."

"Hmmm," the man said as he stood up, not bothering to dust off his dirty old trousers. "Not the Staffords with that rogue son who got himself tried for treason?"

Dougless thought the man could have been speaking of something that happened last year.

"The same," Nicholas said, his back straight.

Harewood looked from him to his horse. Nicholas was wearing a very expensive riding outfit with tall, shiny black boots, and Dougless suddenly felt grubby in her Levi's, cotton shirt, and Nikes. "You ride that?" Harewood asked.

"I did. I hear you have some papers on my family."

"Oh, yes, we found them when a wall fell down," he said, smiling. "Looks like somebody hid them. Come in and we'll have some tea and see if we can find the papers. I think Arabella has them."

Dougless started to follow them, but Nicholas, without looking at her, dropped the reins of his horse into her hand, then calmly strode off with Lord Harewood.

"Just a minute," she said as she started after the men, leading the horses behind her. But when Nicholas's stallion started prancing, Dougless looked back at the animal. It was looking at her with a wild-eyed expression, as though it meant to do something bad. Dougless had had enough of men—any kind of man! "Just try it," she warned, and the horse stopped prancing.

Now what do I do, she wondered. If she was supposed to be Nicholas's secretary and she was supposed to find out what secrets may or may not be in the papers, why was she standing here holding the horses?

"Should I rub them down, your lordship?" she muttered as she started walking toward the back of the house. Maybe there was a stables where she could get rid of the animals.

There were half a dozen buildings in the back of the house, so Dougless headed toward one that looked as though it might be a stables. She was nearly there when a horse and rider came tearing past her. The horse was as large and as mean-looking as Nicholas's stallion (it was probably a stallion too, but Dougless always thought it was rude to look) and on top of it was a stunning woman. She looked like what all women wanted to grow up to look like: tall, slim-hipped, long, long legs, an aristocratic face, big breasts, a straight-backed carriage that would make a piece of steel envious. She had on English riding breeches that could have been painted on, and her dark hair was pulled back in a severe bun, but that only emphasized the striking features of her beautiful face.

The woman halted her horse, then jerked on the reins and turned it around. "Whose horse is that?" she demanded in a voice that Dougless knew men would love: deep, throaty, husky, and powerful. Let me guess, Dougless thought, this is the great-great-great-etcetera-granddaughter of Arabella-on-the-table. Just my luck.

"Nicholas Stafford's," Dougless said.

The woman's face turned pale—which made her lips redder, and her eyes even darker. "Was that meant to amuse me?" she asked, glaring down at Dougless.

"He's a descendant of *the* Nicholas Stafford, if that's what you mean," Dougless answered. Dougless tried to imagine how an American family would react if someone mentioned the name of an Elizabethan-era ancestor. They'd have no idea whom she was talking about, but these people acted as though Nicholas had been gone only a couple of years.

The woman dismounted beautifully, then tossed Dougless the reins. "Rub him down," she said as she started toward the house.

"I wouldn't hold my breath," Dougless muttered. She now held three horses, two of whom looked as though they liked to kill small females before breakfast. She didn't dare look at the horses but kept walking toward the stables.

An older man, sitting in the sun, drinking a mug of tea and reading a newspaper, did a double take when he saw her.

Slowly, cautiously, he rose. "Just be quiet, miss," he said. "Stand very still and I'll take both of 'em."

Dougless didn't dare move, as the man was moving toward her with the stealth that one would use when approaching a wounded tiger. Slowly, he stuck out his hand, not wanting to get too near, and took the reins to one of the stallions. Cautiously, he led the horse away from her and toward the stables. Moments later he repeated his performance as he took Nicholas's stallion away.

When the man returned, he removed his cap and wiped the sweat from his brow. "How did you get Lady Arabella's horse and Sugar together?"

"Sugar?"

"The stud from the Dennison's stables."

"Sugar. Great joke. He should be named Enemy of the People. So that was Lady Arabella?" she asked as she looked back at the house and pretended she hadn't guessed who the woman was. "So how do I get into the house? I'm supposed to be . . . helping."

When the man looked Dougless up and down, she knew her American clothes and her accent were about four strikes against her.

"That door there's the kitchen entrance."

Dougless handed him the reins to her docile mare, thanked him, and went off muttering. "The kitchen entrance. Should I bob a curtsey to the cook and ask for employment as a scullery maid? Wait until I see Nicholas! We'll settle a few things right away. I am *not* his horse tender."

When she knocked on the back door, a man answered, and when she asked for Nicholas, he led her into the kitchen. It was an enormous room, fitted out with new appliances, but in the center of the room was a vast table that had probably been there since William the Conqueror arrived. All five of the people in the kitchen stopped working and stared at her. "Just passing through," she said. "My, ah . . . employer, he, ah, needs me." She smiled weakly. Too bad I'm going to kill him, she thought, and imagined the lecture she was going to give him on modern equality.

The man she was following—who didn't speak to her—led her through several storage rooms for the kitchen, with everyone she saw stopping and staring at her. Nicholas is going to look forward to his execution when I finish with him, Dougless thought.

The man didn't stop until they were at the entrance hall, a big round room with magnificent staircases going up both sides, portraits hanging everywhere. Lord Harewood, Nicholas, and the dashing Lady Arabella were standing close together, looking as though they were old friends. Arabella, if possible, looked even better now than she had when Dougless had first seen her, and her beautiful eyes were practically eating up Nicholas.

"You have joined us," Nicholas said when he saw Dougless, acting as though she'd been out taking the air. "My secretary must stay with me."

"With you?" Arabella said as she looked down her nose at Dougless. Dougless knew how a grape must feel when it was being made into a raisin.

"A place must be made for her," Nicholas clarified, smiling.

"I think we can find room," Arabella said.

"Where? In the trash compactor?" Dougless said under her breath.

Nicholas clamped down on her shoulder painfully. "American," he said, as though that explained everything. "We will be here for tea," he said; then before Dougless could say another word, he pushed her out the front door before him. He seemed to know exactly where the stables were because he headed toward them.

Dougless had to hurry to keep up with his long strides. There were sometimes disadvantages to being five feet three inches tall. "What have you done now?" she asked. "Are we staying here for the weekend? You didn't tell them you were from the sixteenth century, did you? And where do get off calling me an American in that tone?"

He stopped on the gravel path. "What do you have to wear to dinner? They dress for dinner."

"What's wrong with what I have on?" she said with a smirk.

Turning, he started walking again.

"Think Arabella will dress? Something with a cleavage to the floor, I'll bet."

Nicholas glanced over his shoulder, a smile on his face. "What is a trash com . . . ?"

"Compactor," she filled in, then explained it to him. His laugh floated back to her.

At the stables two grooms stayed well back while Nicholas mounted Sugar. "Had I grooms that cowardly, I would have flogged them," Nicholas mumbled.

Dougless couldn't get a word of information out of Nicholas as they rode back to the rental stables. Thankfully, a man at the stables gave them a ride back to Thornwyck Castle, but he and Nicholas talked nonstop about horses, so Dougless couldn't ask about what Nicholas had found out.

It was lunchtime at the hotel when they returned, and Nicholas, still sweaty, went straight into the dining room, where he ordered three entrees and a bottle of wine.

Only when the wine had been poured did he speak. "What would you know of me?" he asked, his eyes twinkling. Obviously, he'd been well aware that she was drowning in curiosity.

Her first thought was to not give him the satisfaction of asking him anything. Instead, she'd blast him about the way he'd treated her. But, in the end, her curiosity won. "Who? How? What? When?"

He laughed. "A woman without guile."

As the food began to arrive, he told her how Dickie Harewood was the same, not too bright, wanting only to hunt and tend to his gardens. "His gardens are not near as good as mine," Nicholas said.

"Stop bragging and go on." She dug into her plate of roast beef. English beef was one of the great wonders of the earth: tender, succulent, cooked perfectly.

Two months ago workmen were repairing the roof of Goshawk Hall and it seemed their hammering had knocked out a piece of a wall. "They do not build today as well as they should," Nicholas said. "In my houses—"

He broke off at a look from Dougless. Inside the wall was a trunk full of papers, and when they were examined, they were found to be the letters of Lady Margaret Stafford.

Dougless leaned back against her chair. "That's wonderful! And now we're invited to their house to read them. Oh, Colin, you are beautiful."

Nicholas's eyes widened at the name she'd called him, but he did not comment. "There are problems."

"What sort of problems? No, let me guess. In exchange, Lady Arabella wants you served on a platter to her every morning with her orange juice."

Nicholas nearly choked on his wine. "Your language, madam," he said primly.

"Am I right or wrong?"

"Incorrect. Lady Arabella is authoring a book on . . ." When he turned away, Dougless wasn't sure, but she thought his face was turning pink.

"On you?" she gasped.

He looked back at his food but not at her. "It concerns the man she believes to be my ancestor. She has, ah, heard the stories of . . ."

"Of you two on the table." Dougless grimaced. "Great, now she wants to repeat history. Is she going to let you see the documents or not?"

"She cannot. She has signed a contract with a physician."

Dougless had to figure that one out. A physician? Was she ill? No, a *doctor*. "Not the doctor in the magazine? What was his name? Dr. Something Hamilton. No, Hamilton something. That guy?"

Nicholas nodded. "He arrived but yesterday. He hopes to gain something by clearing my name, but I do not know what. Arabella says the book will take years. I do not believe I can wait that long. Your world costs too much."

Dougless knew from her father's career how important it was to get published. To the outside world it might not seem important to solve an Elizabethan mystery, but to a scholar, especially a young man just starting out, a book with new information could mean the difference between tenure or not, or between getting a teaching position at a large, well-paid school or at a small community college.

"So," she said, "Dr. Whatever is there, and he's sworn your Arabella to secrecy, so you're not going to be given access to the papers. Yet it seems that we're invited as houseguests anyway."

Nicholas smiled over his wineglass. "I have persuaded Arabella to tell me what she knows of me. I hope I can persuade her to tell me all. And you"—he fixed Dougless with a look—"you are to talk to this physician."

"He's a Ph.D., not a physician and . . . What! Wait a minute, are you saying what I think you are? I am not, under any circumstances, going to play up to some history nut to help you out. I signed on as a secretary, not as a . . . What are you doing?"

Nicholas had taken her hand in both of his and was kissing her fingertips one by one.

"Stop that! People are looking." Dougless's shoes came off her feet. Nicholas's lips traveled up her arm until they reached the sensitive little spot on her inner elbow. Dougless was sinking down in the chair.

"All right!" she said. "You win! Stop that!"

He looked up at her through his lashes. "You will help me?"

"Yes," she said as he kissed her arm again.

"Good," he said, then dropped her arm so that it landed in her dirty plate. "Now we must pack."

Dougless, grimacing, mopped up her arm and ran after him. "Is that how you're going to persuade Arabella?" she called after him, then stopped as she saw the other diners staring at her. Dougless gave a crooked smile of apology and ran from the room.

In their suite, Dougless saw a different Nicholas. He was very concerned that his clothes weren't correct. He held up a gorgeous linen shirt and said, "It needs pluming up."

Dougless looked at her own meager wardrobe and felt like crying. A weekend at an English lord's estate, where they dress for dinner, and she had nothing but serviceable wool. She wished she had her mother's white gown, the one with the pearls, or the red one with—

Halting, she thought for a moment. Then she smiled. And the next minute she was on the phone to her sister Elizabeth in Maine.

"You want me to send you two of Mother's best gowns?" Elizabeth said. "She will kill both of us."

"Elizabeth," Dougless said firmly. "I take full responsibility. Just send them NOW. Overnight mail. Got a pencil?" She gave Elizabeth the address at Goshawk Hall.

"Dougless, what's going on? First I get a frantic-sounding call from you where you won't tell me anything, and now you want me to ransack Mother's closet."

"Nothing much. How's your paper coming?"

"It's making me crazy. And if that weren't bad enough, I have stopped up drains. A plumber is coming today. Dougless, are you sure you're all right?"

"I'm fine. Good luck with your paper and your plumber. Bye."

Dougless packed her suitcase, then Nicholas's—it was one of those things he wouldn't consider doing for himself—then she called a taxi. There was no suitcase large enough to hold his armor, so it was put into the biggest shopping bag.

When they arrived at Goshawk Hall, Arabella literally met Nicholas with open arms. "Come inside, darling," she purred, her hands all over him. "I feel we already know one another. After all, our ancestors were *very* friendly. Who are we to be any different?" She ushered him inside, leaving Dougless with a half-dozen or so suitcases at her feet.

"Who are we to be any different?" she mocked in a falsetto voice as she paid the cab driver.

It didn't take Dougless five minutes to learn that she was not considered a houseguest but a servant, and not a very welcome one at that. A man ushered her—Dougless carrying her own suitcases—to a small, barren, cold room not far from the kitchen. Feeling like a governess in a gothic, neither servant nor family, she unpacked and hung her clothes in a grubby little wardrobe. Looking about the ugly little room, she felt martyred. Here she was doing this to help some guy save his life and his family name and she was never even going to be able to tell anyone about it.

She left the room and went into the kitchen to find the big room empty, but tea for two had been set up at one end of the worktable.

"There you are," said a large woman with graying hair.

Minutes later, Dougless was sitting at the table having tea with the woman. Mrs. Anderson was the cook and the most wonderful gossip Dougless had ever met. There wasn't a thing the woman didn't know or was unwilling to tell. She wanted to know why Dougless was there and who Lord Stafford was, and in return she wanted to tell Dougless *everything*. Dougless obliged with a complicated web of lies that she prayed she'd be able to remember.

An hour later the other servants began filtering back into the kitchen, and Dougless could see they wanted her to leave so Mrs. Anderson could tell them all the juicy news.

Upon leaving the kitchen, Dougless went in search of Nicholas. She found him outside with Arabella under a grape arbor, the two of them cozied up like nesting birds.

"My lord," Dougless said loudly, "you wanted to dictate letters?"

"His lordship is busy at the moment," Arabella said, glaring. "He will attend to business on Monday. In the library are notes of mine that you may type."

"His lordship is—" Dougless had intended to say "my employer, not you," but Nicholas interrupted her.

"Yes, Miss Montgomery, perhaps you can help Lady Arabella."

Dougless started to tell him what she thought of him, but his eyes were pleading with her to be obedient. In spite of what she knew she should do, that is, tell them both what she thought of them, she turned and went back into the house. It wasn't any of her business, she thought. It didn't matter to her what he did with other women. Of course she might point out to him that his foolishness with Arabella in the past had left generations of people laughing at him, and now it looked as though he was about to repeat himself. Yes, she might bring herself to point out that one small fact to him. And, also, if he was so madly in love with his wife, why was he snuggling up with the overendowed Arabella?

It took Dougless a while to find the library, and when she did, she was pleased to see that it looked just as she thought a library in one of these big, grand houses should look: leather-bound books, leather chairs, dark green walls, oak doors. She was looking around the room so intently that she didn't at first see the man standing in front of the bookcases, reading a book. She saw him before he saw her, and instantly, she knew who he was. Only a man like her father, a man who had dedicated his life to learning, could be so absorbed in a book that he was oblivious of all else. He was young, blond, broad-shouldered, slim-hipped, and he looked as though he worked out often. Even with his face tipped down, Dougless could see that he was very good looking, not divine, as Nicholas was, but good enough to set a few hearts to beating quickly. She also took in the fact that he was only about five feet six inches tall. However, it had been Dougless's experience that short, handsome men were as vain as bantam roosters, and they loved short, pretty females such as Dougless.

"Hello," she said.

The man glanced up from his book, down, then up again, and ended by staring at her with unabashed interest. He put his book away and came forward with his hand outstretched. "Hi, I'm Hamilton Nolman."

Dougless took his hand. Blue eyes, perfect teeth. What a very interesting man, she thought. "I'm Dougless Montgomery, and you are an American."

"The same as you," he said, and there was an immediate bond between them. He stepped closer. "Can you believe this place?" he said as he glanced around the room.

"Never. Or the people. Lady Arabella sent me in here to type and I don't even work for her."

Hamilton laughed. "She'll have you scrubbing toilets before long. She doesn't allow pretty women near her. All the maids working here are dogs."

"I hadn't noticed." She looked at him. "Aren't you the doctor who's working on the Stafford papers? The ones that fell out of the wall?"

"That I am."

"That must have been exciting," Dougless said, wide-eyed, trying to look as young and innocent, and as dumb, as possible. "I heard the papers contained secret information. Is that true, Dr. Nolman?"

He chuckled in a fatherly way. "Please, call me Lee. It has been rather exciting, although I'm just now getting into the papers."

"They're all about some man who was about to be beheaded, aren't they? I . . ." She lowered her eyes and her voice. "You wouldn't possibly tell me about the papers, would you?"

She watched him puff out his chest in pride; then the next minute they were seated and he was telling her about how he'd come to have the job and what had happened since he'd arrived. In spite of the fact that he seemed a tiny bit too full of himself, she found herself liking him. Wouldn't her father love having a son-in-law who was interested in medieval history?

Wait a minute, Dougless, she cautioned herself. You're swearing off men, remember? She was listening so intently to Lee that she didn't hear Nicholas enter the room.

"Miss Montgomery!" Nicholas said so loudly that her arm fell out from under her chin and she nearly fell off the chair. "Are my letters typed?"

"Typing?" she asked. "Oh, Ni . . . Ah, your lordship, I'd like you to meet Dr. Hamilton Nolman, he's—"

Arrogantly, Nicholas walked past Dr. Nolman, ignoring the doctor's outstretched hand, as he went to the window. "Leave us," Nicholas said over his shoulder.

Lee wiggled his eyebrows at Dougless, picked up his books, and left the room, shutting the heavy doors behind him.

"Just who do you think you are?" Dougless asked. "You're no longer some sixteenth-century lord and master now. You can't just dismiss people like that. And, besides, what do you know about typing?"

When Nicholas turned to look at her, she could tell by his expression that he had no idea what she was talking about. "You were very close to that small man."

"I was . . . ?" Dougless trailed off. Was that jealousy in his voice? She walked over to the big oak desk. "He's very good looking, isn't he? And a scholar at his age, imagine. How's Arabella doing? Told her about your wife yet?"

"What conversation did you have with that man?"

"The usual," she said, running her finger along the desk. "He told me I was pretty, that sort of thing."

When she looked back at Nicholas, she saw his face had an expression of controlled rage. Her heart swelled with happiness. Revenge, she thought, *can* be sweet. "I did find out some things though. Lee—that's Dr. Nolman—hasn't really read much of the papers yet. It seems that your Arabella took her time in choosing from the many scholars who asked to look at the papers. From what I gather, she chose the best-looking man from the photographs she insisted that the applicants send. Sort of a male beauty contest. I hear she threw away the women's photos. Pure heterosexual, our lovely Arabella is. Lee said she was awfully disappointed that he turned out to be shorter than she is. He said Arabella took one look at him and said, 'I thought all Americans were tall.' Lee, thankfully, seems to have his ego intact, because he just laughed. He pretty much thinks Arabella is a jerk. Oh, sorry, I'm forgetting how much you adore her."

Nicholas's face was still enraged, and Dougless gave him her biggest smile. "How *is* Arabella?" she asked sweetly.

Nicholas glared at her for a moment, then his eyes changed. Turning, he pointed at an old oak table standing against a wall. "That, madam, is the *true* table." With a smug little smile, he left the room.

With her fists clenched, Dougless went over to the table and gave it a good, hard kick. Hobbling about, holding her toe, she cursed all men.

THIRTEEN

D*inner was to be served* at *eight,* and as Dougless dressed in her
museum-visiting clothes, she hoped Elizabeth would send the gowns to
her as soon as possible. But as eight drew near and no one summoned
her to dinner, she wondered what was going on. She knew the servants
had eaten earlier and she hadn't been invited to eat with them, so she
assumed she was to eat with the family. Sitting in her room, she waited.

At eight-fifteen, a man came to her and told her to follow him. She
was led through the maze of rooms to a narrow dining room with a big
fireplace and a table long enough to use for skateboarding. Arabella,
her father, Nicholas, and Lee were already seated. Arabella, as Dougless
had expected, was wearing a dress so low cut it pretty much left her
bare from the waist up. She was showing more than Dougless even possessed.

As unobtrusively as possible, Dougless slipped into a chair next to
Lee that a servant held out for her.

"Your boss wouldn't eat until you were here," Lee whispered as the
first course was served. "What's going on between you two? Is he a

descendant of *the* Nicholas Stafford, the one that was almost beheaded?"

Dougless gave Lee the same story she had given the cook, a story she was sure that by now every servant probably knew, that Nicholas was indeed a descendant, and he very much wanted to clear his ancestor's name.

"I'm glad I had ol' Arabella sign a contract," Lee said, "because if he'd asked first, I think she would have given him exclusive access to the papers. Look at the two of them. With the way she's looking at him, they just might go to it on the table—again."

Dougless choked on her salmon so badly, she had to drink half a glass of water to clear her throat.

"What is this boss to you? You two aren't . . . ? You know."

"No, of course not," Dougless said as she watched Nicholas lean over Arabella, his eyes looking down her dress. Looking down to see what? Dougless thought. There weren't but a couple of inches that she wasn't exposing for everyone in the house to see.

When Nicholas glanced up at her, Dougless moved a little nearer Lee. "I was thinking, Lee, since my boss seems to be so busy, maybe you need a secretary for the weekend. My father is a professor of medieval history, so I've had some experience with helping him research."

"Montgomery," Lee said slowly; then his eyes lit up. "Not Adam Montgomery?"

"That's my dad."

"I once heard him present a brilliant paper on thirteenth-century economics. So, he's your father. Maybe I could use a little help."

Dougless could almost read his mind. Adam Montgomery would be in a position to help a struggling young professor. But Dougless didn't mind. Wasn't ambition good? Besides, she would let Lee believe whatever he wanted if it helped her find out what secret Nicholas's mother knew.

"The trunk is in my room," Lee was saying, and his glances were decidedly warmer since finding out who her father was. "Maybe after dinner you'd like to, ah . . . visit."

"Sure," Dougless said as she envisioned an evening spent running around a table trying to escape his advances. At the thought of a table, she glanced at Nicholas and saw he was glaring at her. Smiling, she lifted her wineglass to him in salute, then took a deep drink. Nicholas turned away, glowering.

After dinner, Dougless went back to her room to get her notebook and a few supplies as well as her handbag. She thought she might as well be prepared for a long night spent rummaging through four-hundred-year-old documents.

Twice she got lost in the house as she turned wrong corners in her search for Lee's room. She halted outside an open door when she heard Arabella's seductive voice coming from inside. "But, darling, I get so frightened when I'm alone at night."

"Truly," Dougless heard Nicholas say, "I would have thought you past such childish fears."

Dougless rolled her eyes skyward.

"Here, let me refill your glass," Arabella said. "And then I'd like to show you something." Her voice lowered. "In my room."

Dougless grimaced. Stupid man! According to the cook, Arabella showed everything in her room to every male who visited Goshawk Hall. With a malicious little smile, Dougless began looking through her handbag. Smiling brightly, she walked into the parlor. Every light except one dim one was off, Arabella was pouring a water glass full of bourbon, and Nicholas sat on the sofa with his shirt half open.

"Oh, your lordship," Dougless said briskly as she began going about the room turning on every light. "Here's the calculator you wanted, but I'm afraid the only one I have is solar. It will only work in a brightly lit room."

Nicholas stared with interest at the small calculator she handed him, and when she began to demonstrate it, his eyes turned to saucers. "One may add?"

"And subtract and multiply and divide. See, here's your answer. Say you wanted to subtract this year, 1988, from 1564, the year your ancestor was accused of treason and lost his family's fortune forever, you'd get a minus four hundred and twenty-four years. Four hundred and twenty-four years in which to right a wrong and keep your descendants from laughing at you—at him, I mean."

"You," Arabella said, so angry she could barely speak, "leave this room at once."

"Uh-oh," Dougless said innocently. "Was I disturbing the two of you? I'm so awfully sorry. I didn't mean to. I was just doing my job." She started backing toward the door. "Please carry on with what you were doing."

Dougless left the room, walked down the hall a few feet, then tiptoed back to stand outside the door. She saw the shadows from the room darken.

"I need light," Nicholas said. "The machine does not work without light."

"Nicholas, for God's sake, it's only a calculator. Put it away."

"It is a most wondrous machine. What is this mark?"

"It's a percent sign but I can't see what it matters now."

"Demonstrate its function."

Dougless could hear Arabella's sigh through the walls. Smiling, quite pleased with herself, Dougless continued her search for Lee's room. He greeted her wearing, of all things, a silk smoking jacket. Dougless refrained from giggling. One look at his face and at the martini glass he held, and Dougless knew that he had no intention of talking to her about anything except why she should jump into bed with him. She took the martini he offered her, sipped it, then grimaced. She hated martinis, dry or otherwise.

Lee started by telling her how beautiful her hair was, how surprised he was to find such a stunning woman in this moldy old house, what a great dresser she was, and how little her feet were. Dougless could have yawned. Instead, when he refilled her glass, she surreptitiously took two of her stomach tranquilizers from her bag, opened the capsules, and poured them into Lee's drink. "Bottoms up," she said cheerfully.

While she was waiting for the pills to take effect, she showed Lee the note Nicholas had slipped under her door the night before. "What does this say?"

He glanced at it. "I think I should write the translation." He took a pen and paper and wrote:

> *I think my selfe moch*
> *bownden unto yow.*
> *I am Desyrynge yo*
> *assystance no further.*

"Desyrynge?"

"Deserving."

She had come close to guessing what Nicholas had written last night when he'd left her, before she'd found him in a tavern.

Yawning, Lee rubbed his hand over his eyes. "I feel a little—" He yawned again.

With many apologies, he stood up, then went to the bed and stretched out "for just a minute." He was asleep instantly, and Dougless quickly went to the little wooden chest on the table near the fireplace.

The papers inside were old, yellow, and brittle, but the writing was clear, the ink not faded as modern inks faded in a mere year or two. Dougless eagerly grabbed the papers, but her heart sank as she looked at them. They were in the same kind of handwriting as the note Nicholas had slipped under her door, and she couldn't read a word.

She was bent over the papers, trying to decipher a word here and there, when suddenly the door burst open.

"Ah ha!" Nicholas said, his sword in his hand, as he charged into the room.

When Dougless's heart settled back in place from the fright he'd given her, she smiled at him. "Arabella finish with you?"

Nicholas looked from Lee asleep on the bed to Dougless bending over the papers, and began to look embarrassed. "She was off to bed," he said.

"Alone?"

Nicholas walked to the table and picked up a letter. "My mother's hand," he said.

At the tone in his voice, Dougless forgot her jealousy. "I can't read them."

"Oh?" he said, lifting one eyebrow. "I might teach you to read. In the evenings. I believe you could learn."

Dougless laughed. "Okay, you've made your point. Now sit down and read."

"And him?" Nicholas pointed with his sword at the sleeping Lee.

"He's out of it for the night."

Nicholas put his sword across the table and began to read the letter. Since Dougless could be of no help, she sat quietly and watched him. If he was so in love with his wife, why was he jealous when another man looked at her, Dougless? And why was he fooling around with Arabella?

"Nicholas?" she said softly. "Have you ever considered what would happen if you didn't return to your time?"

"No," he answered, scanning a letter. "I *must* return."

"But what if you don't? What if you stay here forever?"

"I have been sent here to find answers. A wrong has been done my family as well as me. I have been sent here to right that wrong."

Dougless was playing with the hilt of his sword, rolling it so the jewels reflected in the table lamp. "But what if you were sent here for another reason? A reason that had nothing to do with your being accused of treason?"

"And what would be that reason?"

"I don't know," she said, but she thought, love.

He looked at her. "For this love you speak of?" he asked, almost reading her mind. "Perhaps God thinks as a woman and cares more for love than for honor." He was making fun of her.

"For your information, there are many people who believe God is a woman."

Nicholas gave her a look that let her know how absurd he thought that idea was.

"No, really," Dougless said. "What if you don't go back? What if you find out what you need to know, but you still stay here? Like say for a year or more?"

"I will not," Nicholas said, but he looked up at Dougless. Four hundred years had not changed Arabella, he thought. She was the same. She still wanted one man after another in her bed, still had a heart of stone. But this girl who made him laugh, who helped him, who looked at him with big eyes that showed everything she felt, this woman could almost make him want to stay. "I *must* return," he said sternly, then looked back at the letters.

"I know that what happened to your family is fiercely important, but then it did happen a long time ago, and, all in all, everything seems to have worked out all right. Your mother married a rich man and lived out her days in luxury. It wasn't as though she were tossed out in the snow. And I know your family lost the Stafford estates, but, really, who was left to inherit them? You said you had no children, and your brother died childless, so who did you deprive? The estates went to Queen Elizabeth and she built England into a great country, so maybe your money helped your country. Maybe—"

"Cease!" Nicholas said angrily. "You do not understand honor. My memory is ridiculed. Arabella says she has read about me, and your world remembers only what a clerk recorded. I know that man. He was ugly and no woman would have him."

"So he wrote about you. Nicholas, I'm sorry, but it really is done. It's over. Maybe history can't be changed. I was just wondering what you'd do if you had to stay, if you weren't called back."

Nicholas didn't want to think about that. Would he tell Dougless that he'd marry her and run with her to bed? He didn't want to tell her that Arabella, once so very, very appealing, was now a bore to him.

"Montgomery, do you fall in love with me again?" he asked, smiling at her. "Come, we will take these letters to my bedchamber. I will let you make love to me."

"Drop dead," Dougless said, rising. "Stay here and read. I don't care what happens to you, whether you stay in the twentieth century or go back to the sixteenth century, or to the eighth, for all I care." She left the room, shutting the door so hard Lee stirred on the bed.

Falling in love with him, indeed, she thought as she made her way back to her dreadful little room. She might as well fall in love with a ghost. He had about as much substance as a ghost. And, besides, if he did stay in the twentieth century, he'd be a great nuisance. Always, she'd have to explain things to him. Imagine trying to teach him to drive a car! Horrendous thought. And if he did stay, what would he do? What could he do? All he seemed capable of was riding mean horses, handling a sword, and . . .

And making love to women, she thought. He seemed to be awfully good at that.

As she made her way downstairs to her dreary little room, she told herself she'd be quite glad to get rid of him. His poor wife. She had a great deal to put up with. Arabella was the only one of his women Dougless knew about. There were probably hundreds of women the poor ugly little clerk had known nothing about, so the twentieth century knew nothing about all those women.

Yes, Dougless thought as she put on her nightgown, she would be well rid of him when the time came. But as she climbed into bed, she couldn't imagine not seeing Nicholas every day, not watching his delight over things she took for granted. She couldn't imagine not seeing his smile or having him tease her.

It took her a long time before she slept and when she did, she slept fitfully.

In the morning, feeling absolutely rotten, Dougless went into the kitchen and found Mrs. Anderson and another woman staring at the worktable. It was covered with opened tin cans, somewhere between twenty and thirty of them.

"What happened?" Dougless asked.

"I'm not sure," the cook said. "I opened a tin of pineapple, then left the room for a moment. When I returned, someone had opened all these tins."

Dougless stood frowning for a moment, then looked at Mrs. Anderson. "Did anyone see you open the can of pineapple?"

"Now that you mention it, there was someone here. Lord Nicholas came through to go to the stables. He stopped and spoke to me. Very nice man, that."

Dougless tried to hide her smile. Nicholas had no doubt seen the marvel of a can opener and decided to try it out. At that moment a maid came running into the kitchen carrying a vacuum cleaner hose.

"I need a broom handle," the maid said, sounding as though she were about to cry. "Lord Nicholas asked me to show him how the Hoover worked, and he sucked up all of Lady Arabella's jewelry. I'll be discharged when she finds out."

Dougless left the kitchen feeling a great deal better than she had when she got up that morning.

She didn't know where she was supposed to eat breakfast, but she wandered into the empty dining room and found a sideboard covered with silver chafing dishes. Feeling a little defiant, she filled a plate and sat down.

"Good morning," Lee said, entering the room. He filled a plate and sat across from her. "Ah . . . sorry about last night," he said. "I guess I sort of passed out. Did you see the letters?"

"I did, but I couldn't read them," she said honestly, then leaned forward. "Have you read enough to find out who betrayed Nicholas Stafford to the queen?"

"Oh, heavens, yes. I found that out the first time I opened the trunk, and I have *that* letter hidden."

"Who?" she asked under her breath.

Lee opened his mouth to speak, but then Nicholas entered the room, and Lee shut up.

"Montgomery," Nicholas said sternly. "I would see you in the library." He turned and left the room.

Lee grunted. "What's wrong with him? Get out on the wrong side of Arabella's bed?"

Dougless threw down her napkin, glared at Lee, then went to the library. She closed the door behind her. "Do you know what you just did? Lee was about to tell me who betrayed you when you walked in and stopped him."

Nicholas had circles under his eyes, but instead of making him look bad, they made him look even more darkly romantic, rather like Heathcliff. "I read the letters," he said as he sat down in a leather-upholstered chair and stared out the window. "There is no naming of who betrayed me."

Something was making him sad. Dougless went to him and put her hand on his shoulder. "What is it? Did the letters upset you?"

"The letters tell," he said softly, "of what my mother suffered after my death. She tells of . . ." He stopped, took her hand, and held on to her fingers. "She tells of the ridicule of the Stafford name."

Dougless couldn't bear the pain in his voice. Moving to the front of the chair, she knelt before him and put her hands on his knees. "We'll find out who lied about you," Dougless said. "If Lee knows, I'll find out. And when we do find out, you can return and change things. Your being here means you're being given a second chance."

He looked at her for a long moment, then cupped her face in his big hands. "Do you always give hope? Do you never believe there is no hope?"

She smiled. "I'm almost always optimistic. That's why I keep falling in love with thugs and hoping one of them will turn into my Knight in Shining—Oh, Colin," she said, and started to pull away.

But Nicholas pulled her up from the floor and into his arms; then he kissed her. He'd kissed her before, but then he'd merely desired her, now he wanted more from her. Now he wanted her sweetness and her loving heart. He wanted the way she looked at him, the way she was so eager to please.

"Dougless," he whispered, holding her, kissing her neck.

It was when the thought crossed his mind that he didn't want to leave that he shoved her from him. "Go," he murmured in the tone of a man under great stress.

Dougless stood up, but anger filled her. "I don't understand you. You kiss any woman who can reach your face, you never push any of them away, but with me you act like I have some contagious disease. What is it? Do I have terminal bad breath? I'm too short for you? My hair isn't the right color?"

When Nicholas looked at her, all his desire for her, all his longing, was flaming in his eyes.

Dougless stepped back from him, as a person might step back from a fire that was too hot. She put her hand to her throat, and for a long moment they just looked at each other.

The door flew open and Arabella burst into the room. She was wearing what was obviously a designer-made English outdoor outfit. "Nicholas, where have you been?" She looked from Nicholas to Dougless and back again, and she didn't seem to like what she saw.

Dougless turned away, for she could no longer bear to look in Nicholas's eyes.

"Nicholas," Arabella demanded. "We are waiting. The guns are loaded."

"Guns?" Dougless asked, turning around, trying to compose herself.

Arabella looked Dougless up and down, and obviously found her wanting. Tall women often seemed to feel like that about small women, Dougless thought, and was awfully glad men didn't feel the same way.

"We hunt duck," Nicholas said, but he wasn't looking at Dougless. "Dickie has promised to show me what a shotgun is."

"Great," Dougless said, "go shoot pretty little ducks. I'll manage." Hurrying past Arabella, she ran out the door. Later, from an upstairs window, she looked down on the courtyard as Nicholas got into a Land Rover and Arabella drove him away.

Turning away, Dougless realized that she had nothing to do. She didn't feel free to explore Arabella's house, and she didn't want to walk in Arabella's gardens. She asked a passing servant where Lee was, but was told that he was locked in his room with the letters and had left instructions that he was not to be disturbed.

"But he left a book for you in the library," the servant said.

Dougless went back to the library and there on the desk was a small volume with a note attached. "Thought you might enjoy this. Lee," the note read. She picked up the book.

At first sight she knew what it was: it was the diary of John Wilfred, the ugly little clerk who wrote of Nicholas and Arabella-on-the table. The forward said the book had been found hidden in a cubbyhole behind a wall when one of Nicholas's houses had been torn down in the nineteen fifties.

Dougless took the book and settled down on a big sofa to read it. Within twenty pages she knew it was the diary of a lovesick young man—and he loved Nicholas's wife, Lettice. According to John Wilfred, his mistress could do no wrong and his master no right. Pages that listed Nicholas's shortcomings were followed by pages listing Lettice's glories. According to this drooling clerk, Lettice was beautiful beyond pearls, wise, virtuous, kind, talented . . . On and on he went, until Dougless wanted to throw up.

The clerk had nothing good to say about Nicholas. According to the book, Nicholas spent his time fornicating, blaspheming, and making the lives of everyone around him hell. Other than the snide, spiteful story about Arabella and the table, there were no specific stories about what Nicholas had done to deserve the animosity of all (if Wilfred was to be believed) his household.

When Dougless finished the book, she slammed it shut. Because of the false accusation of treason against Nicholas, his estates had been destroyed, and with them the true story of his life. Lost to the future was the true story of how he'd managed the estates owned by his brother and how he'd designed a beautiful mansion. All that was left of him were the spiteful yearnings of a whining man. Yet people today *believed* this.

She stood up, her anger making her fists clench. Nicholas was right: he had to return to his own time to right the wrong done him. She'd tell him about the book, and when he returned to the sixteenth century, he could kick ol' John Wilfred out of his house. Or, Dougless thought, smiling, he could send the ugly little clerk off with the perfect Lettice.

Taking the book, Dougless left the library and asked a servant where Lord Nicholas's room was. She thought she'd leave the book for him to see. He was beginning to be able to read modern print now, and she was sure he'd have enough interest to read this book.

His room was next to one that a maid said was Lady Arabella's. It would be, Dougless thought angrily.

Once in his room, her anger left her. It was done in shades of blue, with a four-poster bed draped with rich blue silk. In the bathroom were Nicholas's toiletries, all the things she'd chosen for him. Putting out her hand, she touched the shaving cream, the toothpaste, and his razor.

Quite suddenly, it hit her how much she missed him. Since he'd appeared they'd been together almost constantly. They'd shared a bedroom and a bathroom; they'd shared meals and jokes. Turning, she looked at the tub, saw that there was no showerhead above it, and wondered how he was dealing with the lack of a shower. Were there other things in his room that he didn't understand yet had no one to ask about?

As she walked back into the bedroom, she smiled as she remembered the way he would come out of the bathroom wearing nothing but a towel, his hair clean and wet. Before they'd come to Goshawk Hall, they'd been intimate in such a pleasant way. She'd shared meals with him, kissed him on the forehead goodnight, and even washed out his underwear in the basin. They'd laughed together, talked together, shared together.

There was a *Time* magazine on the bedside table, and on impulse she pulled open the table drawer. Inside was a little pencil sharpener and three pencils, two of which were now only an inch long, and a stapler and two pieces of paper with about fifty staples in them. There was a toy friction car on top of a colored brochure for Aston Martin cars, and beneath that was the current issue of *Playboy* magazine. Smiling, she closed the drawer.

She walked toward the window and looked out across the rolling lawns to the trees beyond. It was odd how she had lived with Robert for over a year and had believed herself to be madly in love with him, but when she thought of her life with him, she wondered if she'd ever been as intimate with Robert as she had with Nicholas. She'd spent a lot of her time making an effort to please Robert. But Nicholas was so easy to be with. He never complained when she squeezed the toothpaste tube in the middle. He never whined about how she hadn't made everything absolutely perfect.

In fact, Nicholas seemed to like her just as she was. In fact, he seemed to accept what was, whether in people or things, and he found joy in them. Dougless thought of all the dates she'd been on with modern men and how they'd complained about everything: the wine wasn't right, the service was slow, the movie had no deeper meaning. But Nicholas, faced with insurmountable problems, found joy in things like a can opener.

She wondered how Robert would react if he'd suddenly found himself in the sixteenth century. No doubt he'd start demanding this and demanding that, and whining when it wasn't given to him. She wondered if Elizabethan men were like the cowboys of old and hanged men who were particularly bothersome.

She leaned her head against the cool glass. When would Nicholas leave this century? When he found out who had betrayed him? If Lee mentioned the name at dinner, would Nicholas instantly disappear in a puff of smoke?

It's almost over, she thought, and suddenly felt her heart yearning for him. How would she deal with never seeing him again? She could barely stand not seeing him for one whole day, so how was she to live the rest of her life without him?

Please come back, she thought. We have so little time left. Tomorrow you might be gone, and I don't want to miss this time with you. Don't spend this little bit of time we have left with Arabella.

Closing her eyes, she tightened her whole body as she wished for him to return.

"If you'll come back," she whispered, "I'll make you an American lunch: fried chicken, potato salad, deviled eggs and a chocolate cake. While I'm cooking, you can . . ." She thought. "You can look at plastic wrap and aluminum foil and Tupperware—if they have it in England. Please, please, please return, Nicholas."

FOURTEEN

Nicholas's head came up. Arabella's arms were about his neck, her abundant breasts pressed against his bare chest. They were in a private glade where he and a past Arabella had spent an energetic afternoon. But today Nicholas had little interest in the woman. She had told him she wanted to discuss what she'd found out about his ancestor. She'd said she had new information, facts that had never been published before.

Her words were a lure to him, and to find out what she knew, he'd pay any price, so he'd followed her to the secluded spot.

Arabella pulled Nicholas's head back down.

"Do you hear it?" Nicholas asked.

"There's nothing, darling," Arabella whispered. "I hear only you."

Nicholas pulled away from her. "I must go."

Seeing anger flood her haughty face, Nicholas knew he did not want to enrage her. "Someone comes," he said, "and you are too lovely to share with the prying eyes of anyone. I would keep your beauties to myself."

This seemed to mollify her enough that she began fastening her clothes. "I've never met a man who was more of a gentleman than you. Tonight then?"

"Tonight," he said, then left her.

For the most part the hunters had driven Land Rovers, but there were a half dozen horses tied near the cars. Nicholas took the best one, rode it back to the house, then mounted the stairs two at a time. He flung open the door to his bedroom.

Dougless wasn't surprised, really, when Nicholas appeared in the doorway.

For a moment, he stood there staring at her. Her face and her body showed her wanting of him. It was the most difficult thing Nicholas had ever done, but he looked away. He could not, would not, touch her. If he did . . . If he did, he was not sure he would want to return to his own time.

"What do you want of me?" he asked harshly.

"*I* want you?" she asked, angry. She'd seen the way he'd turned away from her. "It looks as though someone else wanted you, not me."

Nicholas looked up at the mirror in the wardrobe door and saw that his shirt was buttoned wrong. "The guns are good," he said, refastening his shirt. "With those we could beat the Spanish."

"England beats everyone and without modern guns. Next thing, you'll be telling me you want bombs to take back with you. Did the guns unbutton your shirt?"

He looked at her in the mirror. "Your jealousy brightens your eyes."

Dougless's anger dissolved. "Cad!" she said. "Did it ever occur to you that you're making a fool of yourself a second time around? History has loved the story of you and Arabella, and now here you are doing it again."

"She knows what I do not."

"I'll bet she does," Dougless muttered. "Probably more experienced."

Nicholas chucked her under the chin. "I doubt so. Is that food I smell? I am hungry."

Dougless smiled. "I promised you an American lunch. Come on, let's go see Mrs. Anderson."

They walked arm in arm to the kitchen. The hunters had taken lunch with them in baskets, so the kitchen was not being used now except for a pudding steaming on the back burner of the Aga.

After getting Mrs. Anderson's permission, Dougless set to work, putting potatoes and eggs on to boil, then starting on the cake, but she decided on chewy, pecan-filled brownies instead. Nicholas sat at the big table and experimented with plastic wrap and aluminum foil and opened and closed plastic containers until Dougless said the "whooshing" sound was driving her crazy, so she gave him eggs and potatoes to peel. He wouldn't chop onions, though.

"Did you help Lettice cook?" she asked, trying to sound innocent.

Nicholas's laugh was the only answer he would give.

When the food was ready, Dougless cleaned the kitchen—Nicholas refused to help—and packed everything in a big basket along with a thermos of lemonade. Nicholas carried it for her out to a little walled garden, where they sat under elm trees and ate.

She told him about reading the diary that morning, and as he ate his fifth piece of chicken, she asked him about his wife. "You never mention her. You talk about your mother and your brother who died. You've even mentioned your favorite horse, but you never say anything about your *wife*."

"You would have me tell of her?" he said in a tone that was almost warning.

"Is she as beautiful as Arabella?"

Nicholas thought of Lettice. She seemed farther away than a mere four hundred years. Arabella was stupid—a man could never have a moment's conversation with her—but she had passion. Lettice had no passion, but she had brains—brains enough to always determine what was best for her. "No, she is not like Arabella."

"Is she like me?" Dougless asked.

Nicholas looked at her and thought of Lettice cooking a meal. "She is not like you. What is this?"

"Sliced tomatoes," she said absently, then started to ask Nicholas more questions, but he interrupted her.

"The man who abandoned you, you said you loved him. Why?" he asked.

Dougless immediately felt defensive and started to say that Robert was great husband material, but before she spoke, her shoulders slumped. "Ego," she said. "My own overblown sense of how powerful I was. Robert told me no one had ever loved him very much. He said his mother was cold to him and his wife had been frigid. I don't know why I thought this, but I truly believed that I could give him all the love he'd ever need. So I tried. I gave to him and gave to him, and when that wasn't enough, I gave some more. I honestly tried to do everything he wanted me to do, but . . ."

Halting, she looked up at the sky for a moment. "I guess I thought that someday he'd be like those men in the movies, and turn to me and say, 'You're the best woman in the world. You give me all that I ask for.' But he didn't. Robert kept saying, 'You never give me anything.' So, dumb me, I'd try even harder to give him more. But . . ."

"Yes?" Nicholas asked softly.

Dougless tried to smile. "But in the end, he gave his daughter a diamond bracelet and me half of the bills."

She looked away from him, but then she saw he was holding out a ring to her. He'd stopped wearing his big rings when he astutely saw that no other men wore such rings. This ring had an emerald the size of a beach pebble.

"What is this for?"

"Had I access to what is mine, I would shower you with jewels."

She smiled at him. "You've already given me the pin." She held her hand to her heart. She wore the pin inside her bra, afraid to wear it outside because its age and uniqueness might cause questions. "You've given me too much already. You've bought me clothes, you've . . . You've been kind to me." She smiled. "Nicholas, the time since I met you has been the happiest of my life. I hope you never go back."

She clamped her hand over her mouth. "I didn't mean that. Of course you need to go back. You need to go back to your beautiful wife. You need to . . . need to make some heirs to inherit those wonderful estates you'll not have to forfeit to the queen. But, did you realize that if Dr. Nolman tells us who betrayed you, you might return at that moment? Immediately. Lee says the name and you disappear. Pouf! Gone, just like that."

Nicholas, who had been rummaging in the basket, stopped. "I will know tomorrow. Whether he wishes to tell me or no, on the morrow I will find out."

"Tomorrow," Dougless said, and looked at him as though trying to memorize his features. She looked down at his body, at the shirt stretched across his wide shoulders, at his flat belly and his muscular legs. Fine legs, he'd said, and she remembered him wrapped in a towel.

"Nicholas," she whispered, leaning toward him.

"What is this?" he asked sharply, holding up a big square of chocolate between their faces.

"A brownie," she said, feeling like a fool. Who was she kidding? He'd kissed her a few times, but only when she'd thrown herself at him. Yet he'd returned from a morning with Arabella with his shirt misbuttoned. "Food," she muttered. She seemed able to please him only with food and plastic wrap. She so much wanted to touch him that her fingertips ached, but he seemed to have no such feeling toward her.

"I guess we better go," she said flatly. "Arabella will be back soon and she'll want you." She started to get up, but Nicholas caught her arm.

"I would rather an hour with you than a life with Arabella."

Swallowing, Dougless didn't dare look at him, but she sat back down. Was he telling the truth or just trying to make her feel better?

"Sing me a song while I eat these," he said.

"I can't sing and I don't know any songs. How about a story?"

"Mmm," was all he said, his mouth full of chocolate.

Dougless realized how many stories were new to him, stories that were part of her culture but he knew nothing of. She told him of Dr. Jekyll and Mr. Hyde.

"I have a cousin like that," he said. He finished off the plate of brownies, then, to her surprise, turned and put his head on her lap.

"You're going to get fat if you keep eating like you do."

"You think me fat?" he asked, looking up at her in a way that made Dougless's heart beat faster. He seemed to know exactly what he did to her and laughed at her for it, but he remained unaffected by her. Only when she was near another man did he show any interest in her.

"Close your eyes and behave," she said, then stroked his hair, that thick soft, curling mass, while she told him story after story, until he fell asleep.

It was nearly sundown when he opened his eyes again. Lying still, he looked up at her for a long while. "We must go."

"Yes," she said softly. "Tonight I will try to find out from Lee who betrayed you."

He moved so that he was kneeling before her, and he put one hand on her cheek. Dougless held her breath, as she thought he was going to kiss her again. "When I return to my time," he said, "I will think of you."

"And I, you," she said, putting her hand on his.

Moving away, he picked up the emerald ring from where it was sitting on the basket lid and put it in her hand, then closed her fingers over the ring.

"Nicholas, I can't take this. You've given me so much already."

When his eyes locked with hers, there was a faraway sadness in them. "I would give more than this to . . ."

"To . . ." she encouraged.

"To take you back with me."

Dougless drew her breath in sharply.

Nicholas cursed himself. He should not have said that. He should not make her hope. He did not want to hurt her, but the thought of leaving her behind was becoming an almost unbearable pain. Soon he would find out what he needed to know; then he knew he'd go back. One night more, he thought. At the most he'd have one more night with her.

Perhaps tonight he'd take her to his bed. Their last night spent in love and ecstasy.

No! he told himself, looking into her eyes, falling into them. He could not do that to her. He could not leave her behind weeping harder than when he'd first seen her. Hell, he thought, he could not do it to himself. To go back to his cold wife, to the emptiness of women like Arabella. No, it was better to leave her untouched.

"Aye," he said, grinning, "to cook for me."

"Cook?" Dougless asked stupidly. "You want me to *cook* for you? Why you overbearing, insufferable, vain—"

"Pillicock?" he asked.

"That sounds perfect. You pillicock! If you think I'm going back to a time of no running water, no doctors, where the dentists yank out your teeth and break your jaw doing it, just to *cook* for you, then—"

He leaned forward, nuzzled his face under her hair, then licked her earlobe. "I will let you visit my bed."

Pushing him away, Dougless started to describe his vanity, but, abruptly, her expression changed. She could give it out too. "Okay, I'll do it. I'll go back with you and cook for you, and Sunday afternoons we'll stay in bed together. Or on the tables. Whichever."

Nicholas rocked back on his heels, and his face seemed to drain of color. He began tossing scraps into the basket. It horrified him to think of her in his age. If she were his lover, Lettice would chop her into little pieces.

"Nicholas," Dougless said, "I was just teasing." He didn't look at her. "Here, I'll take the ring if it will make you happy."

He stopped shoving things into the basket and looked at her. "You do not know what you say. Do not wish for what should not be. When last I was home, I was to face the blade. If I went back, and you came with me, you would be alone. My age is not like yours. Lone women do not fare well. If I were not there to fend for you, you—"

She put her hand on his arm. "I was only teasing. I won't go back. I have no secrets to find out. You came here to find out something, remember?"

"You are right," he said, then lifted her hand and kissed it. He stood, and Dougless could see he planned to leave the basket where it was. He'd probably cleaned up only because he was upset. But what in the world had upset him? she wondered.

She carried the basket back to the house, following behind him, neither of them speaking.

FIFTEEN

W*hen they got back to the house,* Nicholas barely nodded to her as he went through the kitchen and up to his room. Dougless, more puzzled than anything else, went to her room. On her bed was a large box, bearing the name of an express company. Dougless tore into it, throwing tape and paper everywhere.

Inside were two of her mother's beautiful designer gowns.

"Thank you, thank you, Elizabeth," she breathed, holding a gown up to her body. Maybe tonight Nicholas would notice someone besides the stately Arabella, she thought, smiling broadly.

When Dougless walked into the sitting room where the Harewood family was serving cocktails, she knew the two and a half hours she'd taken to dress had been worth it. Lee paused with his drink halfway to his mouth, and Lady Arabella, for once, looked away from Nicholas. Lord Harewood even stopped talking about guns and dogs and his roses. But Nicholas, Dougless thought, ah . . . his reaction made all the effort worthwhile. When he first saw her, his eyes lit up, then they grew hot as he stepped toward her. But he halted before he reached her and stood there scowling at her.

Her mother's white dress was one piece of clingy fabric that had one long sleeve, but left her other shoulder and arm bare. It was covered with tiny beads, and when she moved, they showed off every curve she had. She had fastened Gloria's diamond bracelet about her bare left wrist.

"Good evening," she said.

"Wow," Lee said, looking her up and down. "Wow."

Dougless smiled at him rather regally. "Is that a drink? Could you possibly get me a gin and tonic?"

Lee went off as obediently as a schoolboy.

It was amazing what clothes could do for a woman, Dougless thought. Last night she'd wanted to cower under the table in Arabella's presence, but tonight Arabella's red, low cut gown looked cheap and tasteless.

"What do you do?" Nicholas asked, hovering over her.

"I have no idea what you're talking about," she said, blinking innocently up at him.

"You are exposed." He sounded shocked.

"A lot less than your Arabella is," she snapped, then smiled. "Do you like this dress? I had my sister ship it to me."

Nicholas's back was straighter than usual. "Do you mean to see that physician after supper?"

"Of course," she said sweetly. "Remember that you told me you wanted me to find out what he knew."

"Nicholas," Arabella called. "Dinner."

"You must not wear that gown."

"I'll wear anything I please, and you better go. Arabella is rattling your table legs."

"You—"

"Here you are," Lee said, handing Dougless a drink. "Good evening, your lordship."

Dinner was a wonderful experience for Dougless. Nicholas couldn't keep his eyes off her—much to the lovely Lady Arabella's fury. Lee hovered over her so closely that at one point his coat sleeve dangled in Dougless's soup bowl.

After dinner they went to the drawing room, and, like a scene out of a Jane Austen novel, Nicholas played the piano and sang. He had a rich, deep voice that she loved. He invited Dougless to sing with him, but she knew she had no voice. But she had to sit on a hard little chair and watch jealously as Arabella and Nicholas sang a duet, their heads together, their voices entwined.

At ten o'clock, Dougless excused herself and went to her room. She had no desire to spend the evening with Lee alone in his room. The secret of who betrayed Nicholas would have to wait another day.

But at midnight, Dougless knew she wasn't going to be able to sleep. She kept seeing Nicholas singing with Arabella, kept remembering the way he'd returned from the fields with his shirt misbuttoned. She got out of bed, put on her robe, fluffed up her hair, and made her way through the big house to Nicholas's room. There was no light from under his door, but there was light and the sound of glasses clinking and Arabella's seductive laugh coming from under *her* door.

Dougless didn't think about what she was doing. She gave a brisk single knock and at the same time, she put her hand on the doorknob, turned it, and walked into Arabella's bedroom. "Hi. I was wondering if I could borrow a pin. I seem to have broken a strap. A very important strap, if you know what I mean."

Nicholas was stretched out on Arabella's bed, his shirt open and hanging out of his trousers. Arabella was wearing a filmy black peignoir that didn't cover much of her skin, and what little fabric there was, was transparent.

"You . . . you . . ." Arabella sputtered.

"Oh hello, my lord. Did I interrupt something?"

Nicholas was looking at her with great amusement.

"Look at this," Dougless said, "a Bang and Olufsen TV. I've never seen one before. I hope you don't mind, but I really wanted to see the late news. Ah, here's the remote control." She sat on the edge of the bed, turned on the big color TV, then began flipping channels. Behind her she felt Nicholas sit up.

"A movie," he whispered.

"Naw, just TV." She handed him the remote control. "See, here's the on and off. This is volume, and these are channels. Look at that! It's an old movie about Queen Elizabeth." She flipped off the TV, put the remote control on the bedside table near Nicholas, yawned, then stood up. "I just remembered that I do have some pins after all. Thanks, though, Lady Arabella. Hope I didn't disturb you too much."

Dougless had to run to the door because Arabella was coming after her, her hands made into claws. Dougless barely made it out the door before it slammed on her heels. Standing outside, she listened to what went on inside the room. After a moment she heard the unmistakable sounds of a TV western; then Arabella screeched, "Turn that off!" But the next sound was Bette Davis's voice in her role as Queen Elizabeth the First. Clever man, Dougless thought, smiling; he had found the channel. Still smiling, Dougless went back to her room, and this time, she had no trouble going to sleep.

In the morning, Lee met her for breakfast. "I thought you were going to come by my room last night," he said. "I was going to read the letters to you."

"Planning to tell me who betrayed Nicholas Stafford?"

"Mmm," was all Lee would say; so after breakfast Dougless followed him up the stairs. If he told her the name, would Nicholas immediately return to the sixteenth century?

But she saw right away that getting Lee to tell her anything was going to be a problem.

"I was trying to remember. Wasn't your father on the board of directors at Yale? Maybe he'd be interested in reading my findings."

"I'd sure be glad to tell him about them. I'd especially like to tell him who betrayed Lord Nicholas," she said.

Lee stepped very close to her. "I'd tell you if perhaps you made a little call."

"My father's staying in the wilds of Maine right now and can't be reached."

"Oh," he said, turning away. "I guess I can't tell you then."

"You little extortionist," Dougless seethed before she thought. "You're playing with a career, but the name of this traitor means a man's life!"

He turned to her with a look of astonishment. "How can some sixteenth-century papers mean someone's life?"

There was no way she could explain to him. "I'll talk to my father. In fact, I'll write him a letter today. I'll even let you see the letter, and I'll make sure that he gets it the minute he returns home."

Lee looked at her, frowning. "Why do you want this name so much? There's something fishy about all this. Who is Lord Stafford anyway? You two don't act much like secretary and boss. You act more like—"

It was at that moment that the door flew open and Nicholas entered the dining room. He was wearing his Elizabethan clothes, his legs showing all their muscularity in the tight hose, his silver and gold armor flashing in the sunlight. He held his sword straight out and pointed it at Lee's throat.

"Just what is this?" Lee demanded. He pushed the sword away, then gasped when the sharp blade cut the side of his hand.

Nicholas advanced on him, the tip of the lethal weapon at Lee's throat.

"Dougless, go get some help," Lee said, backing up. "He's gone mad."

When Lee was pinned against the wall, Nicholas spoke. "Who betrayed me to the queen?"

"Betrayed *you?* You're crazy. Dougless, get some help before this lunatic does something we'll both regret."

"Say his name," Nicholas said, pushing the sword tip deeper into Lee's throat.

"All right," Lee said, exasperated. "It was a man named—"

"Wait!" Dougless cried as she looked at Nicholas. "If he tells, you might go. Oh, Nicholas, I might never see you again."

Still holding the sword at Lee's throat, Nicholas held his arm out to Dougless, and she ran to him, her mouth to his before their bodies touched. She kissed him with all the longing, all the pent-up desire she felt. Her hands clutched his hair, pulling his head down as she kissed him. For all that Dougless thought he didn't desire her, the passion she felt coming from Nicholas made her feet come off the floor as he lifted her with one arm.

He broke away first. "Go," he ordered her.

Tears were blurring Dougless's eyes, but she could swear there were tears forming in Nicholas's eyes too.

"Go," he said again. "Stand away from me."

Obediently, too limp to disobey, Dougless walked a few feet away, then stood in silence looking at him. Never to see him again, she thought. Never to hold him, never to hear him laugh, never—

"The name!" Nicholas demanded, his eyes never leaving Dougless's. When he left this world, he wanted his last sight to be of her.

Lee was bewildered by all that was going on. "The man was named—"

Everything happened at once. Dougless, unable to bear the thought of Nicholas's leaving, made a flying leap at him. If he was going, she was going too.

"Robert Sydney," Lee said as Nicholas and Dougless went sprawling on the floor at his feet. He looked down at them. *"Both* of you are crazy," he said, then stepped over them as he left the room.

Dougless kept her head buried against the silver-coated steel of Nicholas's armor, her eyes tightly shut.

When Nicholas recovered himself, he looked down at her, amused. "We have arrived," he said.

"Where? Are there cars outside or donkey carts?"

Chuckling, he lifted her face in his hands. "We remain in your time. I said you were to stand to one side."

"Well, I . . . ah, I . . ." She rolled off him to sit up. "I just thought it might be a wonderful experience to see Elizabethan England firsthand. I could write a book, and you know, answer all the questions that people *really* want to know, like was Elizabeth bald or not? How did you men *really* treat the women? What did—"

Nicholas sat up and kissed her mouth most sweetly. "You cannot return with me." He put his hand to his back. "You are hard on my armor. There are scratches from when you last struck me down."

"You were about to step in front of a bus."

Standing, he held out his hands to lift her, but when Dougless stood up, she wouldn't release his hands. "You're still here." She breathed at last. "You know the traitor's name and yet you're still here. Robert Sydney. Sydney? But wasn't it Arabella *Sydney* that you . . . That you and she . . ."

Nicholas put his arm about her shoulders and walked to the window. "He was Arabella's husband," he said softly. "But it is not easy to believe he would lie to the queen about me. I always thought of him as a good man."

"Damn you and that table!" Dougless said fiercely. "If you hadn't been so . . . so overzealous and had Arabella on the table, her husband might not have hated you. And what about your wife? She must have been pretty upset too."

"I was unmarried on that occasion when I took Arabella."

"On that occasion," Dougless muttered. "Maybe Sydney got mad for all the other times too." She turned to look at him. "If I went back with you, maybe I could keep you out of trouble."

He pushed her head down on his armored chest. "You cannot return with me."

"Maybe you won't return. Maybe you're going to stay here forever."

"We must go to Ashburton, where my tomb lies. Now that I know what I came to find, I needs must go there and pray."

She wanted to say more, wanted to say something that would make him give up the idea of returning, but she knew there were no words that could change his mind. His family, his name, and his honor were very important to him. "We'll leave today," Dougless said softly. "I can't see that you need to see any more of Arabella."

"Have you no more calculators or televisions to distract me?" he asked, smiling.

"I was saving the stereo for tonight."

He turned her around to face him, his hands on her shoulders. "I will pray alone," he said. "If I return, I go alone. You understand me?"

She nodded. Borrowed time, she thought. We are now on borrowed time.

SIXTEEN

*D*ougless sat on the twin bed in the bed-and-breakfast and looked across at Nicholas in the other bed. The early morning light made his face above the light cover dim and indistinct, but it was enough for her to see him. They'd known the name of the traitor for three days now, and every minute of those three days Dougless was sure he was going to disappear. Every morning he went to the church and spent two hours on his knees praying before his tomb. He spent another two hours in the afternoon praying.

And each time he went inside the church, Dougless stayed outside and held her breath. She was sure that each time he stepped inside it would be the last time she ever saw him again. At ten A.M. and four P.M. she would tiptoe into the church, and when she saw that he was still there, sharp tears of relief and joy came to her eyes. She would run to him, and her heart went out to him when she saw the sweat on his face and body. He prayed so hard each day that afterward he was limp with exhaustion. Dougless would help him stand, as his knees would be painful and stiff from two hours of kneeling on the cold stone floor. The vicar, feeling pity for Nicholas, had put out a cushion for him, but Nicholas refused to use it, saying he needed the pain of his body to make him remember what must be done.

Dougless didn't ask why he needed a reminder of his duty because she didn't want to jinx the growing seed of hope that she was beginning to cherish. Every day when she went to him in the church and she saw that he was still with her, there seemed to be a light in his eyes. Maybe he wouldn't return, Dougless was beginning to think. She knew she, too, should pray for his return. She knew that honor and a family name and the future of many people were more important than her selfish wants, but every time she saw him still kneeling in the church, sunlight on his big body, she whispered, "Thank You, God."

Three days, she thought, three heavenly days. When Nicholas wasn't in church, they spent every moment together. She rented bicycles, then had a hilarious time teaching him to ride. Whenever Nicholas fell, he pulled her with him, so that they went tumbling together across the sweet English grasses. Across sweet English grasses filled with cow manure.

Laughing at how awful they smelled, they ran back to the B and B to shower and shampoo. Dougless had rented a VCR machine and a tape, so they spent the rest of the afternoon in their room watching a movie.

As Nicholas was insatiable for knowledge, they purchased a lending card from the little local library and went through hundreds of books. Nicholas wanted to see everything that had happened since 1564, and he wanted to hear every piece of music. He wanted to smell, taste, touch everything.

"Were I to remain here," he said one afternoon, "I would make houses."

It took Dougless a moment to realize that he meant he would like to design them. The beauty of Thornwyck Castle showed he had talent. Before she could stop herself, a flood of words came from her mouth. "You could go to architecture school. You'd have to learn a lot about modern building materials, but I could help you. I could teach you how to read modern print better and my uncle J.T. could get you a passport. He's the king of Lanconia, so we'd just say you're a Lanconian;

that way, I could take you back to the U.S. My father could help you get into a school to study architecture, and in the summer we could go to my hometown of Warbrooke on the coast of Maine—it's beautiful there—and we could go sailing and—"

He turned away. "I must return."

Yes, return, she thought. To go back to his wife, the woman he loved so much. How could Dougless care so much for him and he feel nothing for her? The other men in her life had wanted something from her. Robert had wanted her submission; do it my way or don't do it, was his philosophy. A couple of men had dated her because of her family's money. A couple of men had wanted her because she was so gullible, so easy to fool. But Nicholas was different. He wasn't trying to take anything from her.

There were times when Dougless looked at him and such lust filled her that she wanted to leap on him in the library, or in the pub, or on the street. She kept having fantasies about tearing his clothes off and ravishing him.

But every time she got too close, he stepped away. It seemed that he was interested in tasting, smelling, touching everything in the world except her.

She tried to interest him. Heavens! but she tried. She paid—on her credit card—two hundred pounds for a red silk peignoir set that was guaranteed to drive a man wild. When she came out of the bathroom wearing it, Nicholas had barely glanced at her. She'd bought a tiny bottle of perfume called Tigress that set her back seventy-five pounds; then she'd leaned over Nicholas so that her shirt fell away from her breasts and asked if he liked the smell. He'd barely mumbled a reply.

She put her jeans in scalding hot water in the bathtub to shrink them, and when they were dry, they were so tight she had to put a big safety pin on the zipper and lie on the floor to pull it up. She wore them with a thin silk blouse and no bra. Nicholas didn't look.

She would have thought he was gay if he hadn't looked at every other female who passed them.

Dougless bought black hose, black high heels, and a teeny, tiny black skirt and wore it with the red silk blouse. She felt ridiculous riding a bicycle wearing high heels, but she did it anyway. She rode in front of Nicholas for four miles, but he never once looked. Two cars ran into ditches looking at her, but Nicholas paid no attention whatever.

The videotape she rented was *Body Heat*.

By the fourth day she was desperate, and with their landlady's help, she devised an elaborate scheme to get Nicholas in bed with her. The landlady told Nicholas she needed their room, so Dougless made reservations at a nearby lovely country house hotel. She told Nicholas the only room she could get had one large four-poster bed, but that they'd have to make do. He'd given her an odd look that she couldn't fathom, then walked away.

So now Dougless was in the bathroom of the hotel, where she'd been for thirty minutes. She felt as nervous as a virgin bride on her wedding night. With trembling hands, she doused herself in perfume and loosened the ties down the front of her peignoir.

Ready at last, she fluffed her hair and left the bathroom. The room was dark, but she could see the outline of the bed—the bed she was to share with Nicholas.

Slowly, she walked toward the bed. She could see the long shape of his body under the covers, and she reached out her hand to touch him. "Nicholas," she whispered.

But her hand didn't touch him. Instead, she touched . . . Pillows!

When she turned on the bedside lamp, she saw that Nicholas had made a barricade of all the pillows down the middle of the bed. They reached from the head to the foot of the bed. On the far side Nicholas lay with his back to her, and his broad back was like another barricade.

Biting her lip to keep tears from coming, she climbed into bed, staying on the edge, not touching the hated pillows. She didn't turn out the light because suddenly all strength left her body. Tears, hot, hot tears began rolling down her cheeks.

"Why?" she whispered. "Why?"

"Dougless," Nicholas said softly, turning toward her, but not reaching over the pillows to touch her.

"Why am I so undesirable to you?" she asked, and hated herself for doing so, but she had no pride left. "I see you look at other women who I know aren't built as well as I am. And I know they aren't . . . aren't as pretty as I am, but you never look at me. Sometimes you kiss me but nothing more. You had your hands all over Arabella and you've made love to so many women, but you refuse me. Why? Am I too short? Too fat? You hate redheads?"

When Nicholas spoke, she could tell that the words were from deep inside him. "I have never desired a woman as much as I have you," he said. "My body aches with the wanting of you, but I must leave. I cannot return and know I leave you grieving. When I first saw you, you were weeping so that I heard you across four hundred years. I cannot leave you to such grief again."

"You won't touch me because you don't want me to grieve for you?"

"Aye," he whispered.

Dougless's tears began to be replaced by laughter. She got out of bed and, standing, she looked down at him. "You idiot," she said. "Don't you realize that when you leave, I'm going to grieve for you every day for the rest of my life? I'm going to cry so long and loud and hard that I will be heard to the beginning of time. Oh, Nicholas, you fool, don't you know how much I love you? Whether you touch me or not, you won't be able to stop my tears."

Pausing, she smiled at him in a cocky way. "While I'm grieving, why don't you let me have a memory that will knock Arabella off her table?"

As Dougless stood and watched, Nicholas just lay there, not moving, just looking at her across the pillows. One second he was in bed, the next he was on her and they were on the floor. Dougless never saw him move, she just felt his body against hers, felt his mouth on her skin, his hands holding her shoulders, then moving quickly and firmly out to her hands.

"Nicholas," she whispered, "Nicholas."

He was on her, his mouth and hands everywhere, as she kissed whatever part of him came near her mouth. His hands tore at her gown and Dougless heard it ripping away. When his hot, wet mouth fastened onto her breast, she moaned in ecstasy.

This was Nicholas, the man she'd wanted, desired, and craved for hundreds of hours. His big, hard hands moved down the side of her, his thumb toying with her navel as his lips and tongue played with her breasts.

Her fingers buried into his hair. "Let me," she whispered. She had always chosen men who needed her, men who thought no one could give them enough. Dougless's experience with sex had been with men who expected her to give to them.

"Nicholas?" she said as his lips began moving down her belly. "Nicholas, I don't think—" His hands caressed her thighs, his thumb kneading the soft white flesh there; then he moved downward, downward.

Dougless arched her body against the carpet. No man had ever done this to her before. Passion built in her as his tongue . . . Oh, God, his tongue.

"Nicholas," she moaned, and began to pull his hair as her body moved under him. He nibbled at the inside of her thighs, caressing the back of her knees, until she didn't think she could stand it any more.

Taking her left leg in his hand, he bent it up as he moved on top of her and entered her so hard and big she tried to push him away. But her body closed around him, her free leg wrapping about his leg, as he pounded into her with hard, deep thrusts that pushed her across the carpet. She put up her hands to brace herself against the wall.

When Nicholas released her bent leg, she clasped him about the waist, and her hips rose to meet his thrusts as his hands cupped her buttocks and lifted her to him. Higher, higher.

When at last she felt him arch into her for a final blinding thrust, Dougless felt her own body shuddering in answer.

It was a while before she came to herself to remember where she was, or even who she was. Her head was almost against the wall; the bedside table and lamp loomed over her.

"Nicholas," she murmured, touching his sweaty hair. "No wonder Arabella risked all for you."

Lifting himself on one elbow, he looked down at her. "Do you sleep?" he asked, chuckling.

"Nicholas, that was wonderful," she whispered. "No man—"

He didn't allow her to finish, but took her hand and lifted her to stand by him. Gently, sweetly, deeply, he kissed her, then took her hand and led her into the bathroom. He got the shower water hot, then pulled her in with him. Pinning her to the wall, he kissed her, his big, hard body pressing against hers.

"I have dreamed of this," he murmured. "This water fountain was made for love."

Dougless was too absorbed in the way he was moving down to her breasts to be able to answer him. With the hot water beating on them, Nicholas began kissing her body, his mouth on her breasts, on her stomach and her neck. Dougless had her head back, her hands on his shoulders, shoulders so broad they nearly reached from one side to the other of the shower stall.

He came up to face her. When Dougless opened her eyes, she saw he was smiling at her. "Perhaps some things in this modern world do not change," he said. "I seem to be your teacher now."

"Oh?" she said as she began kissing his neck, then across his shoulder and down his muscular chest, her hands kneading his back muscles. Fat, she thought. She'd said he was going to get fat, but all of him was muscle, thick, hard, sculptured muscle.

The hot water beat down on her head, and she went lower, her hands on his buttocks. When her mouth closed over him, it was his turn to gasp. His hands buried themselves in her wet hair as she heard his soft moans of pleasure.

He nearly pulled her up by her hair as he slammed her against the slick wall, pulled her legs about his waist, and rammed into her almost brutally. Dougless held on to his passion, fastening herself to him as his mouth took hers, his tongue thrusting just as his body did.

When the final moment came, Dougless would have screamed except that Nicholas covered her mouth with his.

She clung to him, trembling, her body limp. She was sure that if Nicholas hadn't been holding her, she would have gone down the drain.

He kissed her neck. "Now I will wash you," he said softly as he set her on her own feet, then caught her when she nearly fell.

As though he had an electric switch in his body, he seemed to turn his passion off as he turned her to face the showerhead and began to shampoo her hair. His big, strong hands and his big body made her feel small and fragile—and protected. When he was done with her hair, he lathered his hands and began soaping her body.

Dougless leaned back against the wall as Nicholas's hands slid over her, up and down, around, in and out. Before she forgot herself, she took the soap and began to caress him with her soapy hands. He had the most beautiful body she'd ever seen on a human. Heavens! she thought, even his feet were beautiful.

She turned off the water and soaped him. She loved looking at him, touching him. There was a birthmark on his left hip, shaped like a figure eight. There was a scar on his right calf. "Fell off a horse," he murmured, eyes closed. There was a long scar on his left forearm. "Sword practice the day . . ." Dougless knew that the rest of the sentence was, "the day Kit died." There was an odd oval scar on his shoulder. Nicholas smiled, his eyes closed. "A fight with Kit. I won," he said.

She came back to his head. "I'm glad to see no woman has left a mark on you."

"Only you, Montgomery, have marked me," he whispered.

Dougless wanted to ask him about his wife. Did he care for her, Dougless, as much as he loved his beautiful wife? But she didn't ask, as she was too afraid of the answer she'd hear.

Nicholas turned her around, turned the water back on, then rinsed them both. When they were clean, he pulled her out of the shower and began gently combing her hair. Dougless wanted to put on her robe, but Nicholas wouldn't allow it.

"I have dreamed of you this way," he said, looking at her in the mirror. "You have fair driven me mad. The smell of you." He stopped combing and slid his hands down her arms. "The clothes you wear . . ."

Dougless smiled, her head back against his. He had noticed, she thought. He had.

When her hair was combed, he toweled it dry, then held up the white terry robe the hotel furnished. "Come," he said, putting on the other robe.

He led her downstairs, through the darkened hotel lobby, and into the kitchen.

"Nicholas," she said, "we shouldn't be here."

He kissed her to silence. "I am hungry," he said as though that were excuse enough.

Being in the hotel kitchen when she knew they shouldn't be added excitement to this most wonderful night. She looked at the back of Nicholas as he opened a refrigerator door (and felt a little pang that he had learned of refrigerators from someone other than her). Now he was truly hers, she thought, hers to touch whenever she wanted. Holding his hand, she pressed her body against his and put her head in the crook of his shoulder.

"Nicholas," she whispered. "I love you so much. Don't leave me."

Turning, he looked into her eyes, and his face was full of longing. He looked back in the refrigerator. "Where's the ice cream?"

She laughed. "In the freezer. Try that door," she said, pointing.

He wouldn't let her out of his sight or touch as he pulled her toward the freezer. There were big cardboard vats of ice cream inside. Clinging together like Siamese twins, they went about the kitchen and found bowls, spoons, and a steel ladle. Nicholas scooped out an enormous amount from one vat into each bowl, then slipped the vat back into the freezer. He dribbled vanilla ice cream down the front of her, then licked it off, the ice cream traveling lower, just below his tongue. He licked the last just as it reached her red-gold curls.

"Strawberry," he said, making Dougless laugh.

They sat facing each other, legs crossed, on the eight-foot-long butcher-block cutting table ("Unsanitary," Dougless said), but she didn't get down. They ate quietly for a moment, but then Nicholas dropped ice cream on Dougless's foot and licked it off. Dougless leaned forward to kiss Nicholas and "accidently" dropped ice cream on his inner thigh.

"I'll bet that's awfully cold," she said against his lips.

"I cannot bear it," he whispered.

She slowly, so that her breasts raked along his bare body, made her way to the splat of ice cream on his thigh, licked it off, and when it was gone, she continued licking. The ice cream was forgotten as Nicholas leaned back against the table and pulled her up to him. As though she weighed nothing, his biceps bulging, he picked her up and set her down on top of him, his hands moving up her body to clutch her breasts as Dougless moved slowly up and down.

It was a long time before they arched together, Nicholas pulling her down to him to kiss her hungrily and fiercely.

"I believe, madam," he whispered in her ear, "that you have melted my ice cream."

Laughing, Dougless snuggled against him. "I've wanted to touch you for so long," she said, her hand caressing his chest and shoulders inside the sleeve of the robe that he still wore. "I've never met a man like you."

She lifted on one elbow and looked down at him. "Were you an unusual man in the sixteenth century, or were they all like you?"

Nicholas grinned at her. "I am unique, which is why the women—"

She kissed him to silence. "Say no more. I'd as soon hear nothing more about your women—or your wife." She put her head down. "I'd like to think I'm special to you, not just one of hundreds."

He lifted her chin to look at her. "You called me across centuries, and I answered. Is that not enough to make you 'special'?"

"Then you do care for me? At least somewhat?"

"There are no words," he said, then kissed her lightly and pushed her head back down, but as he stroked her damp hair, he felt her relax against him and knew she was falling asleep. Closing her robe, he bundled her into his arms and carried her out of the kitchen and up to their room. Once they were inside their room, he removed both their robes, put her into bed, then climbed in beside her. She was already asleep as he snuggled her to him.

But Nicholas wasn't sleepy at all. He tried to pull her closer to him, her bare bottom up against his half-swollen maleness, his leg over hers, but she was as close as could be.

She asked if he cared for her, he thought. Cared for her? She was becoming all to him, his reason for living. He cared what she thought, what she felt, what she needed. He couldn't bear more than minutes away from her.

Each morning and afternoon he went to pray for God to return him to his own time, but part of his mind thought constantly of what it would be like to never see her again, to never hear her laugh, to never see her cry again, to never hold her in his arms.

He ran his hand over her shoulder and tucked the cover closer about her. Never had he met a woman like her. She had no guile, no sense of taking what she wanted, no sense of self-preservation. Smiling, he remembered her protests when he'd first met her. She'd said she would not help him, but he'd seen in her eyes how she couldn't bear leaving him alone in a strange land. He thought of the women of his own time and knew of no woman who would help some poor madman.

But Dougless had, he thought. She'd helped him and taught him and . . . loved him. She'd given her love freely and completely.

Completely, he thought, smiling in memory of this night. No woman had ever responded to him with such complete abandonment as Dougless had tonight. Arabella used to demand. "Here! Now!" she'd say. Other women thought they were granting him a favor. Lettice . . . He didn't like to think of his cold wife. She lay in bed stiff-limbed, her eyes open, as though challenging him to do his husbandly duties. In four years of marriage he'd not been able to get her with child.

As he caressed Dougless's bare arm, in her sleep she tried to move closer to him. He kissed her temple. How could he leave her? he asked himself. How could he go back to his other life, to his other women, and leave her alone and unprotected? She was so soft that it was no wonder she was at the mercy of men like the one he'd pushed out the door.

Nicholas thought of his mother and his wife. Those two women would be able to take care of themselves no matter what befell them. But not Dougless. He feared that a week after he left, she'd be back with that odious man whom she believed she loved.

He stroked her hair. How could he leave her alone with no one to protect her? He did not understand the modern world. It was her father's duty to choose a husband for her, yet the man left his daughter to her own devices. Smiling, Nicholas thought of how Dougless would fare with a man of his time who a father might choose for her. All her childish talk of love would mean nothing against the joining of estates.

But as Nicholas looked down at Dougless, he knew he was beginning to understand what she meant. Love. Dougless had said that perhaps he'd been sent to the modern world not for honor but for love. At the time, Nicholas had scoffed at the idea. This cataclysmic thing had happened for love and not for honor? Not possible! But they'd found the name of the traitor and Nicholas had not left her world.

He remembered Dougless saying that everything in the past had turned out all right. All right to her, perhaps. He was remembered as a fool, but then, perhaps he had been a fool. There had been many other women besides Arabella, all of whom he needed when he had a wife like Lettice. It was true that perhaps cuckolding Robert Sydney had been foolish enough to cause his own death, but if he could return, he would right the wrongs.

If he returned . . .

What then? He'd still be married to Lettice, and there would be women like Arabella to tempt him. Even if he could free himself from the accusation of treason, would his life change?

He turned on his back, holding Dougless tightly to him. What if he remained in this century? What if he had misjudged God's purpose? What if he had been sent forward in time, not to return and change what had happened then, but to do something in *this* time?

He remembered the books he and Dougless had looked at. There were books of houses from around the world, and they had intrigued him. Dougless had talked about something called architecture school where he could learn to design houses. To learn to be a tradesman? he thought in wonder. But, truthfully, "having a profession," as she called it, did not seem to be something bad in this century. Instead, men like Harewood who were mere landowners were looked down on—by Americans anyway, Dougless had explained.

America, he thought, this place that Dougless talked about constantly. She said they could go to America and "set up housekeeping" and he could go to school. School at his age? he'd asked disdainfully, not letting her see how the idea intrigued him. To live with Dougless in this modern world and design buildings? Was this the reason he had been brought forward? Perhaps God saw Thornwyck, liked it, and so had decided to give him another chance, Nicholas thought with a smile, laughing at the idea of God being so frivolous.

But what did he know of God's purpose? Obviously, he hadn't been sent forward in time to find out who betrayed him. He'd found that out days ago, yet he was still here. So why had he been sent to the modern world?

"Nicholas!" Dougless cried out, sitting up with a jolt.

As he pulled her back into his arms, she clung to him. "I dreamed you were gone, that you weren't here, that you'd left me," she said, blinking back tears and holding him so tightly his ribs were close to cracking.

He stroked her hair. "I will not leave you," he said softly. "I will remain with you for always."

It took a moment for his words to reach Dougless. She lifted up to look at him. "Nicholas," she said slowly, questioning.

"I . . ." He took a breath. The words were hard for him. "I do not wish to return. I will remain here." He looked at her. "With you."

Dougless buried her face in his shoulder and began to weep softly.

As he stroked her body, he couldn't keep from laughing. "Are you sad that I do not leave you so that you may return to this Robert who gives diamonds to children?"

"I'm just so happy."

He took a tissue from a box beside the bed. "Here, stop your weeping and tell me more of America." He gave her a sideways look. "And tell me of your uncle who is king."

Dougless blew her nose, then smiled at him. "I didn't think you heard that."

"What is a cowboy? What is a passport? What is the Grand Canon? And do not move so far from me."

"It's canyon," she said, moving back into his arms as she began to tell him of America, of her family, and of her uncle who'd married a princess and was now king of Lanconia.

As the dawn light came into the room, they began to make plans. Dougless would call her uncle J.T. and explain as best she could that she needed a passport for Nicholas so he could go to America with her. "Knowing Uncle J.T., he'll want you to go to Lanconia so he can inspect you first. But he'll like you."

"And his queen?"

"Aunt Aria? Well, she can be a little intimidating at times, but she used to play baseball with us kids. They have six kids of their own." She smiled. "And she has this weird friend named Dolly who runs around the castle wearing blue jeans and a crown." She looked at Nicholas, at his black hair and blue eyes, and thought of the way he walked, the way he sometimes had of looking at people that made them shrivel. "You'll fit in in Lanconia," she said.

They had breakfast served in their room, and over the table, Nicholas said, "I'd rather have strawberry ice cream."

In another moment they were on the floor, rolling about exuberantly as they tore at each other while they made love. Afterward they filled the tub and sat at opposite ends as they planned more of their future life together.

"We'll go to Scotland," Dougless said. "While we're waiting for the passport, we'll stay in Scotland. It's a beautiful country."

Nicholas had his foot on her stomach, kneading her flesh. "Will you wear the heeled shoes to ride a bicycle?" he asked.

Dougless laughed. "Don't make fun of me. Those shoes got me what I wanted."

"And I too," he said, looking at her from beneath his lashes.

After the bath they dressed, and Dougless said she'd call her uncle J.T. right away.

Nicholas turned away. "I must return to the church for one last time," he said quietly.

Dougless felt her entire body stiffen. "No," she whispered, then ran to face him, her hands gripping his arms.

"I must," he said, smiling down at her. "I have been often and naught has happened. Dougless, look at me."

She lifted her head, and he smiled. "Are you onion-eyed yet again?"

"I'm just frightened."

"I must pray for forgiveness for not wanting to return to save my name and my honor. Do you understand?"

She nodded mutely. "But I'm going with you and I don't let go of you. Got that? I don't wait outside for you this time."

He kissed her. "I mean to never again release you. Now we will go to the church for my prayers, then you will call your uncle. Does Scotland have trains?"

"Of course."

"Ah, then it has changed. In my time it was a wild place." Putting his arm about her shoulders, he left the hotel with her.

SEVENTEEN

*A*t the church, Dougless wouldn't release Nicholas. He knelt to pray, and she knelt beside him, both her arms tightly locked around his shoulders. When he didn't push her away as she feared he might, she knew that, in spite of his pretended amusement, he was as frightened as she was.

They knelt together on the cold floor for over an hour. Dougless's knees hurt from the stones, and her arms ached from holding on to Nicholas, but she never considered relaxing her grip. Twice, the vicar came in and stood for a while watching them, then silently walked away.

As hard as Nicholas prayed for forgiveness, Dougless prayed twice as hard for God not to take him away but to let him stay with her forever.

At long last, Nicholas opened his eyes and turned to her. "I remain," he said, smiling. Laughing, he stood up, and Dougless, almost crippled, also tried to stand, her arms still tight around him.

"My arms have no blood in them," he said, chiding her gently.

"I'm not letting you go until we're out of this place."

He laughed. "It is finished. Can you not see that? I am still here. I have not turned into marble."

"Nicholas, stop teasing me and let's get out of here. I never want to see your tomb again."

Still smiling at her, he started to take a step, but his body didn't move. Puzzled, he looked down at his feet. From his knees down, there was nothing, merely space. There was floor where his feet should have been.

Quickly, he pulled Dougless into his arms and held her as though to crush her. "I love you," he whispered. "With all my soul I love you. Across time I will love you."

"Nicholas," she said, her voice betraying her fear at his words. "Let's get out of here."

He held her face in his hands. "Only you have I loved, my Dougless. No other woman. Only you."

She felt it then. She felt that his body was no longer solid in her arms. "Nicholas," she yelled in fear.

He kissed her again, kissed her softly, but with all the yearning and wanting and desire and need he felt for her.

"I'm going with you," she said. "Take me with you. God!" she screamed. "Let me go with him!"

"Dougless," Nicholas said, and his voice was far away, "Dougless, my love."

He was no longer in her arms but standing before his tomb wearing his armor. He was faded, indistinct, like a movie seen in a bright room. "Come to me," he said, holding out his hand. "Come to me."

Dougless ran to him, but she couldn't reach him.

A streak of sunlight came through the windows and flashed off his armor.

And then there was nothing.

For one hideous moment, Dougless stood and stared at the tomb; then she put her hands to her ears and screamed, a scream such as no human had ever uttered before. The old stone walls vibrated with the sound, the windows quivered, and the tomb . . . The tomb just lay there, silent and cold.

Dougless collapsed to the floor.

EIGHTEEN

D*rink this,"* someone was saying.

Dougless caught the hand that held the cup to her lips. "Nicholas," she said, a faint smile on her lips. Her eyes flew open and she sat up. She was stretched out on a pew in the church, just a few feet from the tomb. She swung her legs to the side, placing her feet on the floor, but she felt too dizzy to take a step.

"Are you feeling better?"

She turned to see the vicar, his kindly face full of concern, a cup of water in his hand.

"Where is Nicholas?" she whispered.

"I didn't see anyone else. Should I call someone for you? I heard you . . . scream," he said, knowing it wasn't a scream. Just remembering that sound made the hair on his body stand on end. "When I got here, you were lying on the floor. Could I call someone for you?" he asked again.

On weak legs, Dougless made her way to the tomb. Slowly, memory was coming back to her, yet still she couldn't believe it. She looked at the vicar. "You didn't see him leave, did you?" she asked hoarsely. Her throat was raw.

"I saw no one leave. I just saw you praying. Not many people pray with such . . . intensity today."

She looked back at the tomb. She wanted to touch it, but she knew the marble would be cold, so unlike Nicholas. "You mean you saw *us* praying," she corrected.

"Just you," the vicar said.

Slowly, Dougless turned to look at him. "Nicholas and I were praying together. You came in and saw us. You've watched him for days."

The vicar gave her a sad look. "I'll take you to a doctor."

She moved away from his outstretched hand. "Nicholas. The man who prayed here every morning and every afternoon for the last four days. He was the man in the Elizabethan armor. Remember? He nearly walked in front of a bus."

"More than a week ago I saw you nearly step in front of a coach. Later, you asked me the date."

"I . . . ?" Dougless asked. "But that was Nicholas. You told me this week you were amazed at how devout he was. I waited for him outside while he prayed. Remember?" Her voice was urgent as she stepped toward him. "Remember? Nicholas! You waved to us as we rode by on bicycles."

The vicar backed away from her. "I saw you on a bicycle but no man."

"No . . ." Dougless whispered, then stepped back from him, her eyes wide with horror.

Turning, she ran out of the church, through the churchyard, down three streets, to the left, then the right, and into the hotel. Ignoring the greeting of the woman at the desk, she ran up the stairs.

"Nicholas," she cried as she looked about the empty room. The bathroom door was closed, and she ran to it, flung it open. Empty. She turned back to the room, but stopped in the doorway, then looked back into the bathroom. She stared at the shelf below the mirror. Her toiletries were there, but his were gone. She touched the empty half of the shelf. No razor, no shaving cream, no aftershave lotion. In the shower, his shampoo was gone.

In their room, she flung open the closet door. Nicholas's clothes were gone. Only hers hung there, her suitcases and her carry-on below on the floor. In the dresser his socks and handkerchiefs were missing.

"No," she whispered, then sat down on the side of the bed. It almost made sense that Nicholas was gone, but not his clothes, not the things he had given her. For a moment she put her hand to her heart, then snatched open her blouse. The pin, the beautiful gold pin with the pearl hanging from it, was gone.

Dougless didn't try to think after that. She tore the room apart looking for something, anything, of his that had been left behind. The emerald ring he'd given her was gone; the note he'd left under her door was gone. She opened her notebooks. Nicholas had written in them in his bizarre handwriting, but now the pages were blank.

"Think, Dougless, think," she said. There had to be some mark left by him. In the closet were the books they'd purchased; Nicholas had written his name inside them. They were blank now.

There was nothing, nothing of him. She even looked on her clothes for any dark hairs. Clean.

It was when she saw her red silk nightgown that Nicholas had torn from her body and saw that it was now whole that she became angry. "No!" she said, teeth clenched. "You can't take him away from me so completely. You cannot!"

People, she thought. Even if there was no physical evidence of him there were an awful lot of people who would remember him. Just because a daffy old vicar couldn't remember him didn't mean other people didn't.

Grabbing her handbag, she left the hotel.

NINETEEN

D*ougless opened the door to the hotel room slowly,* dreading the empty room. Her body was exhausted, but unfortunately, her mind was still working.

She sat on the edge of the bed, then wearily turned and lay down. It was late and her body was empty of food, but she didn't consider eating. Her eyes were wide open, sandy-feeling, dry, as she stared up at the underside of the bed canopy.

No one remembered Nicholas.

The coin merchant had no medieval coins, and he didn't remember seeing Nicholas. Vaguely, he remembered that Dougless had come into his shop to browse. He didn't remember examining Nicholas's clothes, and he said he'd never seen silver and gold armor outside a museum. The clerk in the clothing store didn't remember Nicholas pulling a sword on him. The librarian said Dougless had checked out books, but she'd always been alone. The dentist said he'd never seen a man with ridges on his teeth and a cracked jaw. He had no X-rays for a Nicholas Stafford. No one at the pubs remembered him or at the tea shops. They all remembered Dougless coming in alone. The bicycle shop showed her the receipt, which indicated she'd rented only one bike. Their sweet landlady at the bed-and-breakfast didn't remember Nicholas, and she said no one had played her piano since her husband had died.

Like a woman possessed, Dougless went wherever she and Nicholas had been and asked anyone who might have seen him. She asked tourists in tea shops, residents on the street, clerks in stores.

Nothing, nothing, nothing.

Weary, numb with the dawning realization of what had happened, she went back to the hotel and now lay on the bed. She didn't dare go to sleep. Last night she'd awakened from a dream that Nicholas was lost to her. Nicholas had cradled her in his arms, gently laughed at her, and told her she was dreaming, that he was with her and always would be.

Last night, last night, she thought. He had touched her and loved her, and today he was gone. More than gone. His body, his clothes, even other people's memory of him was gone.

And it was her fault. He had stayed as long as they hadn't made love, but once he'd touched her, he'd been taken away. It didn't help to know she'd been right. He'd come to her for love, not for righting a wrong. He'd stayed when he'd found out who had betrayed him, but he'd slipped away through her arms once he'd admitted he loved her.

She clasped her arms about her chest. He was gone as irreversibly as death. Only she had no comfort of other people who remembered and loved him.

When the telephone on the bedside table rang, she didn't at first hear it. On the fifth ring, dully, she picked it up. "Hello?"

"Dougless," said Robert's voice, stern and angry. "Are you over your hysterics yet?"

She felt too numb, too empty to fight. "What do you want?"

"The bracelet, of course. If you aren't too wrapped up in Lover-boy to find it."

"What?" Dougless said, slowly at first, then, "What! Did you see him? Did you see Nicholas? Of course you did. He pushed you out the door."

"Dougless, are you out of your mind? No one has *ever* pushed me through any door, and they better not try it either." He sighed. "Now you've got *me* acting crazy. I want that bracelet."

"Yes, of course," she said hurriedly, "but what did you mean when you referred to 'Lover-boy'?"

"I don't have time to repeat every—"

"Robert," Dougless said calmly, "you either tell me, or I flush the bracelet down the toilet, and I don't believe you have insurance on it yet."

There was a pause on the other end. "I was right to ditch you. You're crazy. No wonder your family won't let you have the dough until you're thirty-five. I can't put up with you that long."

"I'm on my way to the bathroom now."

"All right! But it's hard to remember what you said that night. You were hysterical. You said something about having a job helping some guy rewrite history. That's all I remember."

"Rewrite history," Dougless said under her breath. Yes, that's what Nicholas had wanted to do in this century: change history.

"Dougless! Dougless!" Robert was shouting, but she had put down the telephone.

When Nicholas had come to her, he had been facing an execution. But what they had found out had saved him from that. Grabbing her big carry-on satchel from the closet, she stuffed some clothing and toiletries into it. As she closed a drawer, she glanced into the mirror and put her hand to her throat. Beheading. Today, she thought, we read about it, read that some person walked up a platform and another person struck them with an ax. But we don't think of what it really means.

"We saved you from that," she whispered.

Once she was packed, she sat down on a chair to wait for morning. Tomorrow she'd go to Nicholas's houses and hear how they had changed history. Perhaps hearing that Nicholas had lived to be an old man and had accomplished great things would help her feel better. She leaned back on the chair and stared at the bed. She didn't dare close her eyes for fear she'd dream.

Dougless was on the first train out of Ashburton and arrived at Bellwood before they opened the gates. She sat outside on the grass and waited for them to open—and tried not to think.

When the gates opened, she bought a ticket for the first tour. Some of her misery was beginning to leave her as she thought of how much Nicholas's name had meant to him. He'd so hated being a laughing-stock, and now she was going to have the comfort of hearing how he'd changed history.

The tour guide was the same woman who'd led her and Nicholas the first time, and Dougless smiled at the memory of Nicholas opening and closing the alarmed door.

Dougless didn't pay much attention to the first part of the tour or listen to the guide. She just looked at the walls and furniture, and wondered what part of the design Nicholas had contributed.

"And now we come to our most popular room," the guide said, and there was that same little smirk in her voice as before.

The guide had Dougless's full attention now, but something in her tone puzzled Dougless. Shouldn't the guide be more respectful now?

"This was Lord Nicholas Stafford's private chamber and, to put it politely, he was what is known as a rake."

The crowd moved forward, eager to hear of this notorious earl, but Dougless stood where she was. Things should have changed. When Nicholas went back, he meant to change history. Dougless had once said that history couldn't be changed. Had she been terribly, horribly right?

With several firm "excuse me's," Dougless pushed to the front of the group. The guide's talk was word for word as it had been the first time. She talked of Nicholas's devastating charm with the ladies, and she again told the awful story of Arabella and the table.

Dougless felt as though she wanted to put her hands over her ears. Between the people in Ashburton not remembering Nicholas and now history being the same, it almost made her doubt whether any of what she remembered had happened. Was she crazy, just as Robert said? When she'd so frantically asked the people of Ashburton if they'd seen Nicholas, they had looked at her as though she were insane.

"Alas," the guide was saying, "poor, charming Nick was executed for treason on the ninth of September, 1564. Now, if you'll step through here, we'll see the south drawing room."

Dougless's head shot up. Executed? No, Nicholas was found dead, slumped over his mother's letter.

Dougless made her way to the guide, who looked down her nose at Dougless. "Ah, the door opener," she said.

"I didn't open the door, Ni . . ." She halted. There was no use in explaining if this woman remembered her, not Nicholas, opening and closing the alarmed door. "You said that Lord Nicholas Stafford was executed. I heard that three days before the execution was to take place, he was found dead, slumped over a letter he was writing to his mother."

"He was *not,*" the woman said emphatically. "He was sentenced to death, and the sentence was carried out on schedule. Now, if you'll excuse me, I have a tour to conduct."

Dougless stood where she was for a moment, staring up at the portrait of Nicholas hanging over the fireplace. Executed? Beheaded? Something was deeply, sincerely wrong.

Turning, she started to leave, but on her way out she stopped at the door with the NO ADMITTANCE sign on it. Behind that door, down a few corridors, was the room that held the secret cabinet and in it the ivory box. Could she find the room and the cupboard door? She put out her hand to the knob.

"I wouldn't if I were you," someone behind her said.

Dougless turned to see one of the guides, an unfriendly look on her face.

"A few days ago some tourists went in there. We've had to put a lock and an alarm on the door since then."

"Oh," Dougless murmured. "I thought it was a rest room." Turning away, she made her way out of the house, the guides outside frowning because she once again went out the entrance door.

She went to the gift shop and asked to buy anything they had on Nicholas Stafford.

"There's a bit on him in the tour book but nowhere else. He didn't live long enough to accomplish much," the cashier said.

She asked if they'd yet received postcards of his portrait, but they hadn't. Dougless bought the tour book, then went outside to the gardens. Finding the place where she and Nicholas had sat down to tea, that heavenly day when he'd given her the pin, she began to read.

In the fat, beautifully illustrated book, Nicholas rated only a short paragraph, and that was about the women and how he'd raised an army against the queen and been executed for it.

Dougless leaned back against the tree. Even knowing the name of the man who'd betrayed him hadn't helped. Nicholas still hadn't been able to persuade the queen of his innocence. And he hadn't even been able to destroy the diary written by that nasty little clerk that had left Nicholas's name blotted for all time. And, too, it seemed that now no one doubted Nicholas's guilt. The guidebook description, as brief as it was, portrayed Nicholas as a power-mad womanizer. And the tour group had chuckled when they'd been told of Nicholas's execution.

Dougless closed her eyes and thought of her beautiful, proud, sweet Nicholas mounting the steps to a wide platform. Would it have been like in the movies, with a muscular man dressed in black leather holding a hideous-looking ax?

Her eyes flew open. She could *not* think of that. Could not think of Nicholas's beautiful head rolling across a wooden floor.

She stood up, picked up her heavy tote bag, left the grounds, and walked the two miles to the train station, where she bought a ticket to Thornwyck. Perhaps there, in the library, in their collection of books on the Stafford family, she'd find some answers.

The librarian in Thornwyck welcomed her back, and in answer to Dougless's question, said she'd never seen Dougless with a man. Dispirited, Dougless went to the Stafford books and began to read. Each and every book told of Nicholas's execution. No more did they tell of his dying before the execution and poison being suspected. And every book was as disdainful of Nicholas as it had been before. The notorious earl. The wastrel. The man who had everything and threw it away.

The librarian came to tell her the library was closing, so Dougless shut the last book and stood. She felt dizzy and swayed, catching herself against the table.

"Are you all right?" the librarian asked.

Dougless looked at the woman. The man she loved had just had his head cut off. No, she was far from all right. "Yes, I'm fine," Dougless murmured. "I'm just tired and maybe a little hungry." She gave the woman a weak smile; then went outside.

Dougless stood in front of the library for a moment. She knew she should get a room somewhere, and she should eat something, but it didn't seem to matter. Over and over and over, she kept seeing Nicholas climbing the stairs to meet an executioner. Would his hands be tied behind his back? Would he have a priest with him? No, 1564 was after Henry the Eighth had abolished Catholicism. *Who* would have been with him?

She sat down on an iron bench and put her head in her hands. He had come to her and loved her and left her. For what? He had returned to a scaffolding and a bloody ax.

"Dougless? Is that you?"

She looked up to see Lee Nolman standing over her.

"I thought that was you. Nobody else has hair that color. I thought you left town."

When she stood up, she swayed against the bench.

"Are you all right? You look terrible."

"Just a little tired."

He looked at her closely, at the circles under her eyes and the gray tinge to her skin. "And hungry, too, is my guess." Taking her arm firmly in his, he shouldered her bag. "There's a pub around the corner. Let's get something to eat."

Dougless allowed him to lead her down the street. What did she care what happened to her?

Inside the pub, he escorted her to a booth and ordered a couple of beers and some food. One sip of her beer and it went to her head, and Dougless realized she hadn't eaten since yesterday, when she'd had breakfast with Nicholas—and they'd made love on the floor.

"So what have you been doing since you left Thornwyck last week?" Lee asked.

"Nicholas and I went to Ashburton," she said, watching him.

"He somebody you met?"

"Yes," she whispered. "And what about you?"

He smiled in a Cheshire cat way, as though he knew something very important. "The day after you left, Lord Harewood had the wall in Lady Margaret Stafford's room repaired, and guess what we found?"

"Rats," Dougless said, not caring about anything.

Lee leaned across the table conspiratorily. "A little iron box, and in it Lady Margaret's story of the truth of why Lord Nicholas was executed. I tell you, Dougless, what was in that box is going to establish my reputation forever. It'll be like solving a four-hundred-year-old murder mystery."

It took a while for his words to penetrate Dougless's misery. "Tell me," she whispered.

Lee leaned back against the booth. "Oh, no, you don't. You coaxed Robert Sydney's name out of me, but not this story. If you want to know the whole story, you'll have to wait for the book."

Dougless started to speak, but the waitress appeared with their food. She didn't look at her cottage pie, but when she and Lee were again alone, she leaned across the table toward him. With an intensity Lee had never seen before in human eyes, Dougless said softly, "I don't know if you know about my family, but the Montgomerys are one of the richest families in the world. On my thirty-fifth birthday I will inherit millions. If you will tell me what Lady Margaret wrote, I will this minute sign one million dollars over to you."

Lee was too stunned to speak. He hadn't known about the wealth of her family, but he believed her. Nobody could have the look on her face that she did and be lying. He knew she wanted this information—look how she'd pestered him for Robert Sydney's name—but he didn't feel like asking her why. If she was willing to offer a million dollars for the story, and if her family had as much money and power as she said, then it was rather like having a genie offer you one wish.

"I want a chair in the history department of an Ivy League school," he said quietly.

"Done," Dougless answered, sounding like an auctioneer. She'd donate a wing or a building to a college if she had to.

"All right," Lee said, "settle back and eat. This is a *great* story. I may be able to sell it to the movies. The story starts years before poor ol' Nick was executed. He—"

"Nicholas," Dougless said. "He doesn't like to be called Nick."

"Sure, okay, Nicholas then. What I'd never read in any book—I guess no historian thought it important—was that the Stafford family had an obscure claim to the throne through Henry the Sixth. They were descended directly through the male line, while Queen Elizabeth was considered by some to be a bastard and, being a woman as well, therefore unfit to rule. You know that for years her throne was not exactly secure?"

Dougless nodded.

"If the historians forgot that the Staffords were related to kings, there was someone who didn't. A woman named Lettice Culpin."

"Nicholas's wife?"

"You do know your history," Lee said. "Yes, the beautiful Lettice. It seems that her family also had some claim to the throne of England, a claim even more obscure than the Staffords'. Lady Margaret believed that Lettice was a very ambitious young woman. Her plan was to marry a Stafford, produce an heir, and put the child on the throne."

Dougless considered this. "But why Nicholas? Why not the older brother? It seems like she'd want to marry the man who was earl."

Lee smiled. "I have to keep on my toes with you, don't I? You're going to have to tell me where you learned so much about the Staffords. The eldest brother . . . ah . . ."

"Christopher."

"Yes, Christopher was engaged to marry a very rich French heiress who happened to be only twelve years old. I guess he decided he'd rather have the money from the heiress than have Lettice, no matter how beautiful she was."

"But Kit died and Nicholas became the earl," Dougless said softly.

"Lady Margaret hinted that her eldest son's death might not have been an accident. He drowned, but Lady Margaret said he was a strong swimmer. Anyway, she never knew for sure, she just guessed."

"So Lettice married the man who was to become the earl."

"Yes," Lee said, "but things didn't go the way Lettice planned. It seems Nicholas wasn't interested in furthering himself at court, or in talking conspiracy and trying to find someone who'd back him if he tried for the throne. Nicholas was mostly interested in women."

"And learning," Dougless shot at him. "He commissioned monks to copy books. He designed Thornwyck Castle. He—" She stopped.

Lee's eyes widened. "That's true. Lady Margaret wrote all that, but how did you know?"

"It doesn't matter. What happened after Nicholas married . . . her?"

"You sound as though you're jealous. Okay, okay. After they were married—and Lettice seems to have quickly realized Nicholas wasn't going to do what she wanted him to—she began to look around for some way to get rid of him."

"As she had Christopher."

"That was never proven. It may have been a fortunate accident—fortunate for Lettice anyway. Lady Margaret admitted that most of this was speculation, but after Lettice married Nicholas, he had some very close calls. A stirrup broke, a—"

"And he cut his calf," Dougless whispered, "when he fell from the horse."

"I don't know where he was hurt, Lady Margaret didn't say. Dougless, are you sure you're all right?"

She glared at him.

"Anyway, Nicholas proved much harder to kill than Christopher had been, so Lettice began to look for someone to help her."

"And she found Robert Sydney."

Lee smiled. "I bet you're great with detective novels, always figuring out the ending.

"Yes, Lettice found Robert Sydney. He was Arabella Harewood's husband, and he must have been pretty mad about all of England laughing about Stafford and his wife on the table. To make matters worse, nine months later, Arabella presented him with a black-haired son."

"And the child and Arabella died."

"Right. Lady Margaret thinks Sydney had a hand in those deaths."

Dougless took a breath. "So Lettice and Robert Sydney contrived to get Nicholas accused and executed for treason."

"Yes. Lady Margaret thinks Lettice just waited for an opportunity to get Nicholas for something, so when Stafford started gathering men to protect his Welsh estates, she informed Sydney, who rode hell-bent-for-leather to the queen. In a way, it's understandable that Elizabeth believed Sydney. Just months before, Mary Queen of Scots had declared herself queen of England as well as Scotland, and here was the earl of

Thornwyck raising an army. Elizabeth just clapped Stafford in chains, had a mock trial with "secret" evidence, then whacked off Stafford's head."

Dougless winced. "So Lettice and Robert Sydney went free."

Lee smiled. "Sort of. Actually, what happened after Stafford's execution was one of the great ironies of life. It seems that Lettice, who had planned everything so carefully, hadn't considered Robert Sydney's ambition. Lady Margaret thought Lettice planned to marry some English duke who was Elizabeth's cousin and start all over again, but Sydney had other plans. He threatened to tell the queen everything if Lettice didn't marry *him*. He wanted to put his *kid* on the throne."

"Blackmail," Dougless whispered.

"Right. Blackmail. I told you this was like a movie. Or a best-seller. Maybe I should fictionalize this. Anyway, she was forced to marry Sydney." Lee gave a snort of laughter. "What's *really* ironic about this whole story is that Lettice was barren. She never conceived at all, not even to miscarry. So she sent her first husband to the blade because of what she wanted for the child she planned to have; then she couldn't have children. Unbelievable, isn't it?"

"Yes," Dougless said through a closed throat. "Unbelievable." She paused. "What of Lady Margaret?"

"Neither Lettice nor Sydney had any idea the old woman knew what they'd done. No doubt they'd have killed her if they'd known, but she was a clever old broad and kept her mouth shut. Maybe she realized she couldn't prove anything. The queen confiscated everything she owned, so Sydney stepped in and offered her a choice between the pauper's farm or marrying his ex-father-in-law, Lord Harewood. Of course Sydney had an ulterior motive. Since he had three kids of Arabella's still alive, Lady Margaret's marriage made them obscurely related. It isn't much of a relationship by our standards today, but back then it was enough that Queen Elizabeth gave Sydney two of the Stafford estates."

He took a sip of his beer. "After Lady Margaret married Harewood, she wrote everything down, put it in an iron chest, had some faithful old servant knock out part of a wall, and hid the box in there. As an afterthought, she put her letters in a chest and hid them too. Then the wall was sealed up."

He paused. "It was a good thing she did it when she did. According to a letter that's survived that was written by a friend of hers, two weeks later Lady Margaret was found dead at the bottom of a staircase, her neck broken. I guess after Mr. and Mrs. Sydney got the two Stafford estates, they had all they needed from her."

Dougless leaned back against the booth and was silent for a while. "What happened to them? To . . . Lettice and Robert Sydney?" She could hardly bear to say the names.

"Roasted in hell, I imagine. But actually, I don't know. I know that since they never had any kids, their estates passed into the hands of his nephew, who was a dissolute little bastard. In one generation the little creep managed to bankrupt the Sydney estates. It'll take more research to find out specifically what happened to Lettice and her husband. Historians haven't been too interested in them." He smiled. "Up to now, that is. History will change after I write my book."

"To change history," Dougless whispered. That's what Nicholas had wanted to do, but all they'd managed was to make his execution happen. "I have to go," she said abruptly.

"Where are you staying? I'll walk you there."

"I don't have reservations." Her head came up. "But I plan to stay at Thornwyck Castle."

"Yeah, don't we all? You have to book a year in advance to get into that place. Wait a minute, don't look so sad. I'll call." He walked away and minutes later returned, grinning. "You are one lucky devil. They had a cancellation, so you can check in now. I'll walk you there."

"No," Dougless said. "I need to be alone. Thanks for dinner, and thanks for telling me. And I'll see that you get your chair at an Ivy League school." She put out her hand to shake his, then turned and left the pub.

TWENTY

*A*t *Thornwyck no one remembered Nicholas.* Dougless looked back through the guest register, and where Nicholas had signed the book, an unfamiliar hand had written "Miss Dougless Montgomery." Listlessly, she put her tote bag in the single room, then went outside to look at the unfinished part of the castle. This time, it had never been finished because Nicholas had been executed.

As she looked at the roofless walls, at the vines hanging down them, she remembered every word of what Nicholas had told her about what he'd planned for this place. A center of learning, he'd said. Yet all his plans had come to nothing.

When he'd left her yesterday, had he gone back to his cell? she wondered. Had he gone back to the time when he'd been writing his mother and trying to find out who had betrayed him? What had he done in those three days before his execution? Would no one listen to him when he told them of Robert Sydney's lies?

Wearily, she leaned back against a wall. Whom had he told about Robert Sydney? Lettice? Had his beloved wife come to visit him? Had he told her what he knew and asked for her help?

Irony, Dougless thought. Lee had said all of it was ironic. The true irony was that Nicholas had died because he was *good*. He'd refused to commit treason with his wife, refused to even consider it—and he'd died for it. Not a quick, honorable death, but a death that was public and meant to ridicule him. He'd lost his life, his honor, his name, his estates, and the respect of future generations, all because he'd refused to conspire with a power-mad woman.

"It is wrong!" Dougless said aloud. "What happened was *wrong.*"

Slowly, she walked back to the hotel, and as though in a trance, she showered, put on her nightgown, then went to bed. She lay awake for a long time, anger not allowing her to sleep. *Irony*, she thought. *Treason. Betrayal. Blackmail.* The words tumbled about in her head.

Toward dawn she fell into a fitful sleep, and when she awoke, she felt worse than she had before she went to bed. Feeling a thousand pounds heavier and very old, she dressed and went downstairs to breakfast.

Nicholas had been given a second chance, and he had asked her, Dougless, for help, but she had failed him. She had been so jealous of Arabella that she'd lost sight of the true purpose of why they'd been at the Harewoods. When she should have been searching for information, she had been worrying about whether Nicholas and Arabella were touching each other. Well, no one was going to touch Nicholas now— not in the twentieth century or in the sixteenth.

She ate, she checked out, and she walked to the train station and boarded a train going back to Ashburton. Somewhere during that train ride her failures stopped plaguing her and she began to ask herself what could be done now. Would the publication of Lee's book help to clear Nicholas's name? Perhaps if she volunteered her services as his secretary and helped him research, she could somewhat make up for how she'd failed to help Nicholas when he was in the twentieth century.

She leaned her head against the train window. If only she had it to do over again, she wouldn't be jealous and she wouldn't waste their precious time together. When she was at Goshawk Hall, why hadn't she asked Lee if there were any other secrets hidden behind the wall? Why hadn't she looked? Why hadn't she torn down that wall with her own bare hands?!! Why hadn't she—

When the sign for Ashburton appeared out the window, she got off the train. As she walked, she realized that there was nothing she could do. The

time to help was past. Lee could write his book himself and she was sure
he'd do a great job of it. Robert had his daughter, so he didn't need
Dougless. Nicholas had been the one who needed her, but she'd failed him.

There was nothing more for her to do but go home.

Leaving the train station, she started toward the hotel. She would
call the airlines and see if she could get a flight home immediately.
Perhaps if she returned to familiar surroundings, she could begin to forgive herself.

As she walked, she went past the church that contained Nicholas's
tomb and her feet seemed to turn toward the gate of their own accord.
The church was empty inside, the sunlight streaming down through
the stained-glass windows to gently touch Nicholas's tomb. The pale
white of the marble looked cold and dead.

Slowly, Dougless walked toward the tomb. Perhaps if she prayed,
Nicholas would return. Perhaps if she begged God, He'd let
Nicholas come back to her. If she could just see him for five minutes,
she thought. That's all she'd need to tell Nicholas of his wife's
treachery.

But as she touched the cold marble cheek, she knew it wouldn't
work. What had happened was a once-in-a-century happening. She'd
been given a chance to save a man's life and she'd failed.

"Nicholas," she whispered, and for the first time since he'd gone,
tears came to her eyes. They were hot, thick tears that blurred her
vision.

"I am onion-eyed again," she said, almost smiling. "I am so sorry
for failing you, my darling Nicholas. But I don't seem to be much good
at anything. But before now I never had anyone *die* because of my
shortcomings."

"Oh, God," she whispered, then turned around to sit on the edge of
the tomb. "How do I live with your blood on my hands?"

She unzipped her bag that was still hanging from her shoulder and
rummaged inside for a tissue. She pulled out a soft travel pack, then
took out a tissue. As she blew her nose, she saw a piece of paper fall from
the tissue pack to the floor. Bending, she picked it up and looked at it.

It was the note Nicholas had written and slipped under her door.

"The note," she said, standing up straight. It was the note written in Nicholas's own hand! It was something that he had touched, something that was . . . that was *proof,* she thought.

"Oh, Nicholas," she said, and the tears began in earnest then, real tears, deep, deep tears of grief. Her legs gave way beneath her and she slid slowly to the stone floor, the note held to her cheek. "I am sorry, Nicholas," she cried. "Very, very sorry that I failed you."

She leaned her forehead against the cold marble tomb, her body huddled in a knot. "Dear God," she whispered, "please help me to forgive myself."

Dougless, in her grief, was unaware of the way the light came in through the stained glass and touched her hair. The window depicted an angel kneeling and praying, and the light came through the angel's halo to touch Dougless's hair, and as a cloud moved, the sunlight touched Nicholas's marble hand.

"Please," Dougless whispered, "please."

It was at that moment that Dougless heard laughter. Not just any laughter, but Nicholas's laughter.

"Nicholas?" she whispered, then lifted her head, blinking to clear her vision. There was no one in the church.

Awkwardly, she rose. "Nicholas?" she said louder, then turned abruptly when she heard the laughter again, this time behind her. She reached out her hand, but there was no one, nothing, there.

"Yes," she said, standing up straight; then louder, "Yes." She raised her face to the sunlight and to the angel in the window. Closing her eyes, she put her head back. "Yes," she whispered.

Suddenly, Dougless felt as though someone had punched her in the stomach. Doubled over in pain, she fell forward onto her knees on the stone floor. When she tried to get up, she felt dizzy and as though she were going to throw up. She had to get to a rest room, she thought. She couldn't befoul the church.

But when she tried to move, nothing happened. It was as though her body were no longer obeying her brain. "Nicholas," she whispered, then reached out her hand toward his tomb, but the next moment everything went black and she collapsed to the floor.

TWENTY-ONE

When she awoke, she felt dizzy and weak and wasn't sure where she was. She opened her eyes to see blue sky overhead and a leafy tree nearby.

"Now what?" she whispered. Had she wandered out of the church? But the sight of the sky and the tree had calmed her. For the first time in days she didn't feel frantic.

She closed her eyes again. She was so weak she felt like staying where she was and taking a nap. She would figure out where she was later.

As she began to doze, she was vaguely aware of a feminine giggle nearby. Kids, she thought. Children playing.

But at the sound of a male's responding laughter, her eyes opened. "Nicholas?" Slowly, still feeling disoriented, she sat up and looked around. She was sitting on the grass under a tree in a pretty part of the English countryside. Turning about, she tried to get her bearings. When had she left the church?

Dougless stopped turning when she saw a man in a field. He was far away and difficult to distinguish, but he seemed to be wearing a sort of short brown robe and he was plowing a field with an ox. Dougless blinked her eyes, but the vision didn't change. Rural England was indeed rural.

Behind her came the woman's giggle again. "Sir Nicholas," the woman said in a dreamy sort of way.

Dougless didn't think about what she did; she merely reacted. Leaping to her feet, she went to the bushes behind her and shoved her way through them.

There on the ground, rolling about was Nicholas. *Her* Nicholas. His shirt was half off, and his strong arms were about a plump girl whose top half was coming out of an odd-looking dress.

"Nicholas," Dougless said loudly, "how could you? How could you do this to me?" Tears were starting again. "I've been crazy with worry about you, and here you are with . . . with this . . . Oh, Nicholas, how could you?" She took a tissue from her pocket and blew her nose loudly.

On the ground, Nicholas and the girl stopped moving. The girl, with frightened movements, hastily tied the front of her dress, scurried out from under Nicholas, then ran off through the hedges.

Nicholas, a scowl on his handsome face, turned over, leaned back on one elbow, and looked up at Dougless. "What mean you by this?" he demanded.

Dougless's first reaction of anger left her. For a moment she stood staring down at him. Nicholas was here with her. Here!

She leaped on him, her arms fastening about his neck as she began kissing his face. His arms went around her as they fell back against the ground.

"Nicholas, it *is* you. It is. Oh, my darling, it was awful after you left. No one remembered you. Nobody remembered us together." She kissed his neck. "You've grown your beard back, but that's okay, I kinda like it."

He was kissing her neck. His hand was on her shirt front, and her blouse easily parted as his lips moved down her throat.

"Nicholas, I have so much to tell you. I saw Lee after you left, and he told me all about Lettice and Robert Sydney . . . and . . . Oh, that's nice, that's very nice."

"No!" she said abruptly, then pushed him to arm's length. "We mustn't do this. You remember what happened the last time, don't you? We have to talk. I have so many things to tell you. Did you know that you were executed after all?"

Nicholas stopped trying to pull her back into his arms. "I? Executed? Pray, madam, for what?"

"For treason, of course, and for raising the army. For—Nicholas, don't you lose your memory too. I've had all the amnesia I can take lately. Listen to me. I don't know how long you'll stay here before you go back. Your wife planned everything. I know you love her, but she only married you because you're related to Queen Elizabeth—or is it the queen's father? Anyway, Lettice wants you out of the picture because you won't play along with her and put her kid on the throne. Of course she can't have any kids, but she doesn't know that."

She paused. "Why are you looking at me like that? Where are you going?"

"I make for my home, away from your Colley-westonward talk." He stood up, then began to tuck his shirt into his balloon shorts.

Dougless rose too. "'Colley-westonward.' That's a new one on me. Nicholas, wait, you can't leave."

He turned back to face her. "If you desire to finish what you began"—he nodded toward the ground—"I will remain and I will pay you well, but I cannot abide this deboshed manner of speaking."

Dougless stood there blinking at him, trying to understand what he was saying. "Pay me?" she whispered. "Nicholas, what's wrong with you? You act as though you've never seen me before."

"Nay, madam, I have not," he said, then turned his back to her and left the clearing.

Dougless was too stunned to move. Never seen her before? What was he talking about? She pushed through the bushes. Nicholas was dressed in the most extraordinary clothes. His black satin jacket seemed to be decorated with . . .

"Are those diamonds?" she gasped.

Nicholas narrowed his eyes at her. "I do not deal kindly with thieves."

"I wasn't planning to rob you; it's just that I've never seen anyone who had diamonds on his clothes before." Stepping back, she looked at him, really looked at him, and she saw that he was different. It wasn't just the clothes or that he was again wearing his beard and mustache, but there was a seriousness missing from his face. This was Nicholas, but he somehow seemed younger.

How could he have grown his beard back so soon?

"Nicholas?" she asked. "When you were last home, not the first time you came to me, but this time, what year was it?"

Nicholas slipped a short cloak of black satin that was trimmed in ermine about his shoulders, and from behind the bushes he pulled a horse, an animal as wild-looking as the rented Sugar had been. Easily, he vaulted into a saddle that was as big as an American cowboy's saddle, but it had tall wooden uprights in front of and in back of the seat. "When last I was home this morn, it was the year of our Lord 1560. Now, you, witch, get from my sight."

Dougless had to step back against the bushes to keep from being run down by the horse. "Nicholas, wait!" she called, but he was gone.

Disbelieving, Dougless stared after him until he was little more than a speck on the horizon; then she sat down on a big rock, her head in her hands. Now what? she thought. Did she have to start all over again and explain to him yet again all about the twentieth century? The last time she'd seen him, he'd come from 1564, but this time it was four years earlier. What had happened hadn't happened yet.

Her head came up. Of course! That was it. When he'd found out about Robert Sydney, he'd been in jail—or the medieval equivalent thereof—and he couldn't do much about saving himself. But this time he'd come forward four years earlier. Now there was time to *prevent* what had caused his execution.

Feeling a great deal more cheerful, she stood up. She had to go find him before he did something dumb, like walk in front of a bus again. Picking up her heavy tote bag from the ground, she slung it over her shoulder, then started walking in the direction Nicholas had gone.

The road was the worst she'd ever seen: deep ruts, rocks sticking up, narrow and weed-choked. The roads in rural America weren't this bad, and she'd never seen anything like this before in England.

She stepped to the side of the road when she heard a vehicle coming around a corner. A tired-looking donkey was pulling a cart that had two big wooden wheels. Beside the cart walked a man wearing a short dress that looked as though it'd been made from a burlap bag. His legs, bare from mid-calf down, had great ugly sores on them. Dougless stared at him in openmouthed astonishment, and the man turned and gaped at her in the same way. His face was like leather, and when he opened his mouth, Dougless could see rotten teeth. He looked her up and down, his eyes fastening on her stocking-clad legs; then he leered at her, grinning and showing off his hideous teeth.

Quickly, Dougless turned away and started walking rapidly. The road got worse, the ruts deeper, and there was manure everywhere. "England's using manure to fill the ruts now?" she muttered.

At the top of a little hill she stopped and looked down. Below her were three little houses, tiny places with thatched roofs and bare ground in front of them where chickens and ducks and children scratched about. A woman wearing a long skirt came out the front door of one hut and emptied a round container beside the door.

Dougless started down the hill. Perhaps she could ask directions of the woman. But as she neared the houses, she slowed. She could smell the place. Animals, people, rotting food, piles of manure, all of it reeked. Dougless put her hand to her nose and breathed through her mouth. Really! she thought, the English government should do something about this place. People shouldn't live like this.

She went to the first house, trying to keep her shoes clean but not succeeding very well. A child, about three, wearing a filthy nightgown, looked up at her. The poor thing looked as though it hadn't been washed in a year, and it obviously wasn't wearing a diaper. Dougless vowed that when she got Nicholas straightened out, she was going to complain about this place to the English government. It was a health hazard.

"Excuse me," she called into the dark interior of the house. It didn't seem to smell much better inside than out. "Hello? Is anybody home?"

No one answered, but Dougless felt as though she were being watched. When she turned, she saw three women and a couple of children behind her. The women weren't any cleaner than the child she'd seen, their long dresses encrusted with food and no telling what else.

Dougless tried smiling. "Excuse me, but I'm looking for the Ashburton church. I seem to have lost my way."

The women didn't speak, but one woman stepped toward Dougless. It was difficult to keep smiling, for the woman reeked of body odor.

"Do you know the way to Ashburton?" Dougless repeated.

The woman just walked around Dougless, staring at her, looking at her clothes, her hair, her face.

"A bunch of looney tunes," Dougless muttered. Living in filth as they did, they probably weren't too bright. She stepped away from the stinking woman and unzipped her tote bag. The woman jumped back at the sound. Dougless took out her map of southern England and looked at it, but it didn't help any because she didn't know where she was, so she couldn't figure out how to get where she was going.

She lowered the map when she realized one of the women was very near, her head almost inside Dougless's bag. "I beg your pardon," she said sharply. The woman's head was covered with a cloth that was caked with dirt and grease.

The woman jumped away but not before she'd snatched Dougless's sunglasses from her bag. She ran back to the other women, and the three of them examined the glasses.

"This is too much." Dougless strode toward the women, her foot slipping in something, but she didn't look down. "May I have those back?"

The women looked at her with hard faces. One of them had deep, pitted scars on her neck, and she held the sunglasses behind her back.

Dougless put her hands to her sides. "Would you please return my property?"

"Be gone with you," one of the women said, and Dougless saw that three upper teeth were missing and two others were rotten.

It was then that she began to understand. She looked at the house before her, saw the firewood stacked outside, saw the onions hanging from the roof. The dirt, the carts, the people who had never heard of a dentist.

"Who is your queen?" she whispered.

"Elizabeth," one woman said in an odd accent.

"Right," Dougless whispered, "and who was her mother?"

"The witch Anne Bullen."

The women were gathering around her now, but Dougless was too stunned to notice. Nicholas had said that this morning it had been 1560; then he'd ridden off on a horse with a funny saddle. He hadn't seemed disoriented or unsure of where he was going. He hadn't acted as he had when he'd first arrived in the twentieth century. Instead, he'd acted as though he were right at home.

"Ow!" Dougless said, for one of the women had pulled her hair.

"Be ye a witch?" one of the women asked, standing very close to Dougless.

Suddenly, Dougless was afraid. It was one thing to laugh at a man in the twentieth century for calling someone a witch, but in the sixteenth century people were burned for being witches.

"Of course I'm not a witch," Dougless said, backing away, but there was a woman behind her.

A woman pulled on Dougless's sleeve. "Witch's clothes."

"No, of course they aren't. I live . . . ah, in another village, that's all. Next year you'll all be wearing this." She couldn't go back or forward, for the surrounding women were blocking her. You'd better think fast, Dougless, she thought, or you just might be this evening's barbecue. While keeping an eye on the women, she put her hand into her tote bag, digging for she knew not what. Her hand lit on a book of matches she'd taken from a hotel somewhere.

She pulled out the matches, tore off one, and struck it. With a gasp the women moved back. "In the house," she said, holding the lit match at arm's length. "Go on, get in the house."

The women backed up and stepped inside the doorway just as the match burned down to Dougless's fingertips. She dropped the match and began to run.

Leaving the stinking houses and the rutted road behind, she ran into the woods. When she was out of breath, she sat down on the ground and leaned back against a tree.

It appeared that when she'd passed out in the church, she'd awakened in the sixteenth century. So here she was, alone—Nicholas didn't know her—in a time before soap was invented—or at least before it was used much—and the people seemed to regard her as something evil.

"So how am I to tell Nicholas all he needs to know if I don't even see him?" she whispered.

The first drops of rain were cold on Dougless. She pulled an umbrella from her travel bag and opened it. It was at that moment that she really looked at her beat-up old carry-on. She'd had the thing for years. It had traveled with her wherever she'd gone, and she'd gradually filled it with everything anyone could need while traveling. Inside were cosmetics, medicines, toiletries, a sewing kit, an office kit, magazines, a nightgown, airline nut packages, felt-tip pens, and there was no telling what was in the very bottom.

She pulled the bag under the umbrella with her, feeling as though the bag were her only friend. Think, Dougless, think, she told herself. She had to tell Nicholas what he must know; then she had to get back to her own time. Already she knew that she didn't want to stay in this backward place with its filthy, ignorant people. In just this short time she was already missing hot showers and electric blankets.

She huddled under the umbrella as the rain started coming down harder. The ground under her was getting wet, and she thought of sitting on a magazine, but who knows? She might end up selling the magazines in order to live.

She put her head down on her knees. "Oh, Nicholas, where are you?" she whispered.

Then she remembered the evening of the first day she'd met him and how she'd been in that toolshed crying. He'd come to her then, and later he'd said he'd heard her "calling." If it worked then, maybe it would work now.

With her head down, she concentrated on asking Nicholas to come to her. She visualized his riding up to her; then she thought of all their time together. She smiled, remembering a dinner, chosen by her, that their landlady had cooked for them: corn-on-the-cob, avocados, barbecued spareribs, and a mango for dessert. Nicholas had laughed like a small boy. She remembered the music he'd played, his delight over the books, how critical he had been of modern clothes.

"Come to me, Nicholas," she whispered. "Come to me."

It was dusk and the rain was coming down hard and cold when Nicholas appeared, sitting atop his big black horse.

She grinned up at him. "I knew you'd come."

He did not smile but instead glared down at her in anger. "Lady Margaret would see you," he said.

"Your mother? Your mother wants to see *me?*" She couldn't be sure because of the rain, but he seemed to be momentarily shocked at her words. "All right," Dougless said, rising, then handing him her umbrella and raising her hand for him to help her onto his horse.

To her disbelief, he took the umbrella, examined it with interest, then held it over his own head and rode off, leaving Dougless standing with rain pelting down on her. "Of all the—" she began. Was she supposed to walk while he rode?

She moved back to the relative dryness under the tree, and after a while Nicholas returned, the umbrella held over him.

"You are to come with me," he said.

"Am I supposed to go on foot?" she yelled up at him. "You ride while I slog along in the mud and muck behind you? And you use *my* umbrella? Is that what you had in mind?"

He seemed confused for a moment. "Your speech is most strange."

"Not as strange as your outdated ideas. Nicholas, I am cold and hungry and getting wetter by the minute. Help me on your horse and let's go see your mother."

Nicholas gave a bit of a smile at her insolent attitude, then held down his hand for her. Dougless took it, put her foot on his, and swung onto the back of the horse—not into the saddle with him but onto the hard, unsteady rump of the horse. Dougless put her arms around Nicholas's waist, but he pried her loose and pushed her hands down to the high back of the saddle, then handed her the umbrella.

"Hold this over me," he said, and kicked the horse forward.

Dougless wanted to make a retort, but all her attention was on holding on to the horse. She had to use two hands to hold on, so the umbrella hung uselessly to the side as they sped along. Through the rain she saw more hovels, more people working in the rain, apparently oblivious of it. "Maybe it'll wash them," she muttered, hanging on as best she could.

Because she was behind Nicholas and he was too tall to see over, she didn't see the house until they were in front of it. There was a tall stone wall before them, and behind it stood a three-story stone house.

A man wearing clothes somewhat like Nicholas's—no burlap dress but no diamonds either—came running to take the horse's reins. Nicholas dismounted, then stood impatiently by, slapping his gloves against his palm, while Dougless struggled down by herself, lugging her heavy bag and the umbrella.

When she was down, the servant opened the gate and Nicholas went through it, seeming to expect Dougless to follow him. She hurried after him, down a brick path, up a flight of stairs, across a brick terrace, and into the house.

A solemn-faced servant stood inside, waiting to take Nicholas's cloak and wet hat. When Dougless closed the umbrella, Nicholas took it from her and looked inside, obviously trying to figure out how it worked. After the way he'd been treating her, she wasn't about to tell him. She snatched the umbrella from his hands and gave it to the wide-eyed servant. "This is *mine*," she said to the servant. "Remember that, and don't let anyone else have it."

Looking at her, Nicholas snorted. Dougless hitched her bag onto her shoulder and glared back at him. She was beginning to believe that he was not the man she'd fallen in love with. Her Nicholas wouldn't have made a woman ride on the back of a horse.

Turning away, he started up the stairs, and Dougless, dripping and cold, followed him. She had only a brief glimpse of the house, but it didn't look like the Elizabethan houses she'd seen on guided tours. For one thing, the wood wasn't darkened from being four hundred years old. The walls were paneled in golden oak, and everywhere there was color. The plaster above the panels was painted with scenes of people in a meadow. There were bright, pretty new tapestries and painted cloths hanging on the walls. There were silver plates gleaming from tabletops. And under her feet, oddly enough, there seemed to be straw. Upstairs there were carved pieces of furniture in the hall, looking as new as though they'd been made last week. On one table was a tall pitcher that had beautiful, deep fluting on it. It was of a yellow metal that could only be gold.

Before Dougless could ask about the pitcher, Nicholas opened a door and strode inside.

"I have brought the witch," she heard Nicholas say.

"Now, just a minute," Dougless said, then, hurrying into the room behind him, she stopped. She had entered a beautiful room. It was large, with tall ceilings, the walls paneled with more of the beautiful oak, the plaster above painted with colorful birds, butterflies, and animals. The furniture, the window seat, and the enormous bed were draped with hangings of brilliant silk, and dotted with cushions, all of it embroidered in gold and silver and brightly colored thread. Everything in the room, from cups and pitchers, to a mirror and comb, seemed to be a precious object, made of gold or silver, encrusted with jewels. The whole room glittered beautifully.

"My goodness," Dougless said in awe.

"Bring her to me," said an imperious voice.

Dougless pulled her eyes away from the room to look at the bed. Behind its exquisitely carved posts, behind scarlet silk hangings that twinkled with flowers embroidered in gold thread, lay a stern-looking woman wearing a white nightgown with black embroidery on the cuffs and ruffled neck. About her eyes Dougless could see a resemblance to Nicholas.

"Come here," she commanded, and Dougless moved closer.

The woman's voice, for all its command, sounded tired and stuffy, as though she had a cold.

It was when Dougless was closer to the foot of the bed that she saw that the woman had her left arm stretched across a pillow, and a man, wearing a long, voluminous robe of black velvet, was bending over her and tending to . . .

"Are those leeches?" Dougless gasped. Slimy little black worms seemed to be stuck on the woman's arm.

Dougless didn't see Lady Margaret exchange looks with her son.

"I have been told you are a witch, that you make fire from your fingertips."

Dougless couldn't take her eyes off the leeches. "Doesn't that hurt?"

"Aye, it hurts," the woman said in dismissal. "I would see this magic of fire."

The distaste Dougless felt at seeing the leeches on the woman's arm overrode her fear of being called a witch. She walked to the side of the bed and put her tote bag on top of a table, pushing aside a pretty silver box that had emeralds across the top. "You shouldn't let that man do that to you. It sounds to me like you just have a bad cold. Headache? Sneezing? Tired?"

Wide-eyed, the woman stared at her and nodded.

"That's what I thought." She rummaged in her bag. "If you'll make that man take those nasty things away, I'll fix your cold. Ah, here they are. Cold tablets." She held up the package.

"Mother," Nicholas said, stepping forward, "you cannot—"

"Be still, Nicholas," Lady Margaret said. "And remove those from my arm," she ordered the physician.

The man pulled the leeches from Lady Margaret's arm, dropped them into a little leather-bound box, then stepped away from the bed.

"You'll need a glass of water."

"Wine!" Lady Margaret commanded, and Nicholas handed her a tall silver goblet studded with rough-cut jewels.

Dougless was aware of the unnatural hush in the room, and suddenly she realized how brave Lady Margaret was. Or how dumb, she couldn't help thinking, since she was taking medicine from a stranger. Dougless handed her a cold tablet. "Swallow it and in about twenty minutes it should work."

"Mother," Nicholas began, but Lady Margaret waved him away as she swallowed the capsule.

"If she is harmed, you will pay," Nicholas said into Dougless's ear, and Dougless swallowed. What if the Elizabethan body wasn't ready for cold tablets? What if Lady Margaret was allergic?

Dougless stood where she was, still dripping water and beginning to shiver from cold. Her hair was plastered to her head, but no one had offered her a towel. No one in the room seemed to breathe as they looked at Lady Margaret lying against the embroidered pillows. Shifting nervously, Dougless became aware of another person in the room. Near the bed curtains was another woman. Dougless could just see the shape of her in a dress with a tight bodice above a full skirt.

When Dougless coughed, Nicholas, at the foot of the bed, gave her a sharp look.

It was the longest twenty minutes of Dougless's life as she stood there, cold and nervous, and waited for the pill to take effect. When it did work, it worked quickly. Lady Margaret's sinuses cleared and she lost that awful stuffy feeling of having a cold.

Lady Margaret sat up straighter, her eyes wide. "I am cured," she said.

"Not really," Dougless answered. "The pills just mask the symptoms. You should stay in bed and drink lots of orange juice . . . or whatever."

The woman behind Dougless came bustling from the shadows, leaned over Lady Margaret, and tucked the covers around her.

"I am well, I tell you," Lady Margaret said. "You! Go!" she said to the physician, and he backed out of the room. "Nicholas, take her, feed her, dry her, clothe her, and bring her to me on the morrow. Early."

"I?" Nicholas said haughtily. "I?"

"You have found her, you are responsible for her. Now go."

When Nicholas looked at Dougless, he curled his upper lip. "Come," he said, and there was anger as well as distaste in his voice.

She followed him out of the room, and once they were in the hall, she said, "Nicholas, we must talk."

He turned on her, still wearing that expression of distaste. "Nay, madam, we do not talk." He arched one eyebrow. "And I am *Sir* Nicholas, Knight of the Realm." Turning on his heel, he walked away.

"*Sir* Nicholas?" she asked. "Not *Lord* Nicholas?"

"I am but a knight. My brother is lord."

Dougless stopped walking. "Brother? You mean Kit? Kit is *alive?*"

When Nicholas turned toward her, his face was distorted with rage. "I do not know who you are or how you come to know of my family, but I warn you, witch, you harm one person—should a hair on my mother's head change color—and you will forfeit your life in payment. And do not think to use your witchcraft on my brother."

He turned again and started walking. Dougless followed, but she didn't say anything. Great, just great, she thought. She'd come all the way back across four hundred years to save Nicholas's head, and all he could do was threaten to kill her. How was she going to make him listen?

They went upstairs to the top floor, and Nicholas threw open a door. "You sleep here."

She stepped inside. This was no pretty room filled with treasures. It was a cell with one tiny window high up on the wall, and little more than a lumpy mattress in a corner, with a filthy wool blanket on top. "I can't stay here," Dougless said, horrified. But when she turned, she saw that Nicholas had left the room and shut the door behind him. She heard a key turn in a lock.

She yelled and pounded on the heavy door, but he didn't open it. "You bastard!" she shouted, then slid down the door to the floor. "You rotten bastard," she whispered, alone in the dark room.

TWENTY-TWO

*N*o one came to release Dougless that night or the next morning. She had no water, no food, and very little light. There was an old wooden bucket in a corner, and she assumed this was to relieve herself in. She tried lying on the mattress, but within minutes she felt little things crawling on her skin. Clawing herself, she jumped out of the bed and pressed herself against the cold stone wall.

She could tell when morning came only because the room changed to a lighter shade of gloom. During the long night she'd scratched at whatever was on her skin so much that places were bleeding. Expectantly, she waited for someone to release her. Lady Margaret had said she wanted to see Dougless early. But no one came.

By holding her arm up to a narrow ray of light coming in through the window, she could see her wristwatch, and if it was set correctly for Elizabethan time, at noon still no one had come to release her.

She tried to keep her mind active and not give in to despair, so she repeatedly went over everything Lee had told her about the events leading up to Nicholas's execution. Somehow she had to warn

Nicholas. Somehow she had to prevent Lettice and Robert Sydney from using Nicholas.

But how could she do anything when she was locked away in a dark, flea-ridden room? And not only wouldn't Nicholas listen to her, he seemed to hate her. She tried to remember what she'd said when she'd first seen him yesterday that had so offended him. Was it her references to his beloved Lettice?

It was cold in the room, and Dougless shivered as she scratched at her itching scalp. In the twentieth century she had always had the Montgomery name and money to fall back on. Even though she was years from inheriting, she'd always known the money was there, that she could offer a million dollars for information she desperately needed.

But here in the sixteenth century she had nothing, was nothing. All she had was a travel bag full of modern wonders. And she had her knowledge of what was to come. And somehow she had to persuade these people that they couldn't just toss her into a prison and leave her to rot. The first time Nicholas had come to her, she'd failed to find the information needed to stop his execution, but this time she would *not* fail. This time she was going to succeed no matter what she had to do.

As she thought of these things, energy began to replace her lethargy. Her father loved to tell his daughters stories of their ancestors, of the Montgomerys in Scotland, in England, and in early America. There was one story after another of heroic deeds and near escapes.

"If they can do it, so can I," Dougless said aloud. "Nicholas," she said firmly, "come release me from this hideous place." Closing her eyes, she concentrated, imagining Nicholas coming to her.

It didn't seem to take long for him to "hear" her. When he flung open the door, his face was dark with anger.

"Nicholas, I want to talk to you," she said.

He turned away from her. "My mother asks for you."

She stumbled after him, her legs weak from lack of use, her eyes not adjusted to the light in the hall. "You came because I called you," she said. "There is a bond between us, and if you'd let me explain—"

Halting, he glared at her. "I wish to hear naught that you say."

"Will you tell me what you're so angry at me about? What have I done?"

He looked her up and down in an insolent way. "You accuse me of treason. You frighten the villagers. You besmirch the name of the woman I am to marry. You bewitch my mother. You . . ." His voice lowered. "You come into my head."

Reaching out, she put her hand on his arm. "Nicholas, I know I must seem strange to you, but if you'd just listen to me and let me explain—"

"Nay," he said, moving away from her touch. "I have petitioned my brother to cast you out. The villagers will see to you."

"See to me?" she whispered, then shuddered as she remembered those filthy women in that little clump of houses. No doubt those rotten-toothed hags would stone her if given the chance. "You would do that to me? After the way I helped you when you came to me?" Her voice was rising. "After all I did for you when you came forward, you'd throw me out? After the way I've come back across four hundred years to save you, you'd just throw me into the streets?"

He glared at her. "My brother decides." Turning, he started down the stairs.

Dougless stayed close behind him and tried to control her anger enough to think. First, she had to figure out a way to keep from being tossed out of the relative safety of the house and into the muck of the streets. And Lady Margaret seemed to be the answer to that problem.

Lady Margaret was again in bed, and Dougless could see that the twelve-hour cold capsule had worn off.

"You will give me another of the magic tablets," she said, leaning back against the pillows.

In spite of being hungry, tired, filthy, and frightened, Dougless knew that now was the moment when she had to use her wits. "Lady Margaret, I am not a witch. I am merely a poor humble princess set upon by thieves, and I must appeal to you for help until my uncle the king can come to me."

"Princess?" Lady Margaret said.

"King?" Nicholas half-shouted. "Mother, I—"

Lady Margaret put up her hand to silence him. "Who is your uncle?"

Dougless took a deep breath. "He is the king of Lanconia."

"I have heard of this place," Lady Margaret said thoughtfully.

"She is no princess," Nicholas said. "Look you at her."

"This happens to be the style of dress in my country," she snapped at him. "Are you going to throw me in the street and risk a king's wrath?" She looked back at Lady Margaret. "My uncle would be very generous to anyone who protected me."

Dougless could see that Lady Margaret was considering this. "I can be very useful," Dougless said quickly. "I have lots of cold tablets, and I have all sorts of interesting things in my bag. And I . . ." What could she do? "I can tell stories. I know lots of stories."

"Mother, you cannot consider keeping her here," Nicholas said. "She is no better than a flirt-gill."

Dougless guessed that that was a lady of ill repute. She turned angry eyes on him. "Look who's talking. You and Arabella Sydney can't keep your hands off one another."

Nicholas's face turned purple, and he took a step toward her.

Lady Margaret coughed to cover laughter. "Nicholas, fetch Honoria to me. Go! Now!"

With one more look of anger at Dougless, he obediently left the room.

Lady Margaret looked at Dougless. "You amuse me. You may remain in my care until a messenger can be sent to Lanconia to ask after your uncle."

Dougless swallowed. "How long will that take?"

"A month or more." Lady Margaret's eyes were shrewd. "Do you recant your story?"

"No, of course not. My uncle *is* king of Lanconia." Or will be, Dougless amended to herself.

"Now the tablet," Lady Margaret said, leaning back on the pillows. "Then you may go."

Dougless got a cold tablet from her bag but hesitated. "Where am I supposed to sleep?"

"My son will tend to you."

"Your son locked me in a hideous little room, and there were bugs in the bed!"

Judging from the look on Lady Margaret's face, she didn't seem to see anything wrong with what her son had done.

"I want a proper room and some clothes that won't make people stare at me, and I want to be treated with the respect due to . . . to my station in life. And I want a bath."

Lady Margaret looked at her with cold, dark eyes, and Dougless saw where Nicholas got his imperious manner. "Beware you do not amuse me too much."

Dougless tried to keep her knees from knocking. Once, as a child, she'd seen a wax museum that showed a medieval torture chamber. Now she remembered the instruments of torture too well. The rack. The Iron Maiden. "I mean no disrespect, my lady," she said softly. "I will earn my keep. I will do my best to continue to amuse you." Like Scheherazade, she thought. If I don't amuse this woman, tomorrow it's off with my head.

As Lady Margaret studied her, Dougless knew her fate, her very life, was being decided in this single moment. "You shall attend me. Honoria will—"

"That means I can stay? Oh, Lady Margaret, you won't regret this, I promise. I'll show you how to play poker. I'll tell you stories. I'll tell you all of Shakespeare's stories. No, I better not do that, it might upset things. I'll tell you about . . . ah, *The Wizard of Oz* and *My Fair Lady*. Maybe I can remember some of the words and music." Dougless, who had always refused to sing out loud, began to sing, "I Could Have Danced All Night." Funny what the threat of being burned alive could make one do.

"Honoria!" Lady Margaret said sharply. "Take her, clothe her."

"And food and a bath," Dougless added.

"The tablet."

"Oh, sure." Dougless handed the cold tablet to Lady Margaret.

"Let me rest now. Honoria will see to you. She will stay with you, Honoria."

Dougless hadn't heard the other woman enter. She looked to be the same woman who had been in the room last night, but Dougless couldn't see her face as she kept it turned away. Dougless followed Honoria from the room.

She felt better now knowing that she had some time before Lady

Margaret found out she wasn't a princess. Was lying to a lady punished by death or merely torture? Or torture then death? But perhaps if Dougless could entertain Lady Margaret well enough, she wouldn't care whether she was a princess or not. And, too, perhaps a month was long enough to do what she must.

Clasping her travel bag tightly to her, Dougless followed Honoria to her room, which was next to Lady Margaret's. It was about half the size of Lady Margaret's room, but, still, it was large and very pretty. There was a white marble fireplace on one wall, a big four poster bed, some stools, two carved chairs, and a chest at the foot of the bed. Sun came in through a window that had small diamond-shaped panes of glass.

Looking about the pretty room, Dougless was beginning to relax somewhat. She had managed to keep herself from being thrown into the streets.

"Is there a bathroom around here?" she asked the back of Honoria.

Turning, the pretty woman gave Dougless a blank look.

"A privy?" Dougless explained.

Nodding in understanding, she pointed to a small door in the paneling. When Dougless opened the door, she saw a stone seat with a hole cut in it; the little room was the equivalent of an outhouse indoors. And it stunk to high heaven. Beside the seat was a stack of paper, thick, hard paper that had writing all over it. She held one piece of paper up. "So that's what happened to all the medieval documents," she murmured. Quickly, she used the privy and left it.

When she went back into the room, she watched as Honoria opened a chest, pulled clothes out, laid them on the bed, then left the room. When she was alone, Dougless walked about, exploring. This room had no silver or gold ornaments as Lady Margaret's had, but everywhere were embroidered fabrics. Dougless had seen a few examples of Elizabethan embroidery in museums, but they had been old and faded. Here the cushions were brilliant, undimmed by time or use, and the colors were wondrous!

She walked around the room touching everything, marveling at the brightness of all of it. New antiques, she thought as she scratched furiously at bites on her back.

After a while the door opened, and two men came in bearing a big, deep wooden tub. The men wore red, tight-fitting wool jackets, puffy shorts like those Nicholas wore, and black knitted hose. Both men had strong, muscular legs.

There are things to be said for the Elizabethan age, Dougless thought as she admired the men's legs.

Behind the men came four women bearing buckets of steaming hot water. They wore simple, long wool skirts, tight bodices, and little caps on their heads. Two of the women had smallpox scars on their faces.

When the tub was half full of steaming water, Dougless began to undress, and Honoria held out her hands to help, but then stepped back, her eyes wide, when she saw Dougless needed no help in undressing. In other circumstances, Dougless would have been modest, but not when she was as filthy as she was. When she was down to her bra and panties, and Honoria was staring at her in speechlessness, Dougless held out her hand. "Hi, I'm Dougless Montgomery."

Honoria didn't seem to know what to do, so Dougless picked up her hand and clasped it. "So, we're to be roommates."

Honoria gave Dougless a puzzled look. "Lady Margaret has requested that you remain with me, yes." She had a soft, pleasant voice, and Dougless could see that she was quite young, maybe only twenty-one or two.

Dougless stripped off her undergarments and stepped into the tub while Honoria picked up the modern clothes, examining each carefully, unabashedly curious.

Dougless took the soap the servants had left beside the tub, but it felt like a harsh version of Lava and it lathered about as well as a stone. "Would you hand me my bag, please?" she asked Honoria. Looking quite hard at the nylon of the bag, Honoria set it on the floor by Dougless, then watched as she unzipped it. Dougless withdrew a cake of soap—she was always saving the pretty, scented bars from hotels—and began to wash herself.

Honoria was making no attempt to hide her curiosity as she watched Dougless wash.

"Would you tell me about this place?" Dougless asked. "Who lives here? Tell me about Kit and Nicholas, and is he engaged to Lettice, and is John Wilfred here, and what about Arabella Sydney?"

Honoria sat on a chair and tried to answer questions as she watched in awe as Dougless used the marvelous soap, then shampooed her hair.

As far as Dougless could tell from Honoria's words, she'd been transported back in time early enough that only Nicholas's engagement had taken place. Nicholas had not yet made a fool of himself on the table with Arabella, and John Wilfred was insignificant enough that Honoria didn't know who he was. Honoria would give Dougless any facts she wanted, but would not give an opinion. And she absolutely refused to gossip.

After Dougless had bathed and washed her hair, Honoria handed her a coarse, rough towel of linen, and when she was damp-dry, and her hair combed, Honoria began to help her dress.

First went on a long nightgown-like garment, very plain, made of finely woven linen. "What about underpants?" Dougless asked.

Honoria looked blank.

"Knickers. You know." Dougless picked up her own pink lacy briefs from the chest top where Honoria had put them, but Honoria still looked blank.

"There is nothing below," Honoria said.

"My goodness," Dougless said, wide-eyed. Who would have thought that underpants were a recent invention? "When in Rome . . ." she murmured, and tossed her briefs aside.

Dougless wasn't prepared for the next layer of clothing. Honoria held up a corset. Dougless's experience of corsets was seeing *Gone With the Wind* and Mammy pulling Scarlett's laces, but this corset was . . .

"Steel?" Dougless whispered, holding the thing up to look at it.

The corset was made of thin, flexible strips of steel, covered with fine silk, with steel hooks down one side, and since the corset wasn't new, rust was showing through the silk. When Honoria buckled her into it, Dougless thought she might faint. Her rib cage could not expand, her waist was about three inches smaller than it was naturally, and her breasts were pressed flat.

Dougless steadied herself against the bedpost. "And to think that I used to complain that panty hose were uncomfortable," she murmured.

Over the corset went a voluminous, long-sleeved linen shirt, the ruffled collar and sleeves embroidered prettily with black silk thread.

Around her waist was tied a half slip of linen that had wire sewn inside it so that it stood out in a perfect bell shape. "A farthingale," Honoria said when asked, giving Dougless an odd look for not knowing this simple fact.

"This is getting heavy. Is there more?" Dougless asked.

Honoria next put a half slip of lightweight wool over the wired farthingale.

Over this petticoat went another one, this one of emerald green taffeta. Dougless began to cheer up. The taffeta rustled when she moved and the fabric was beautiful.

Honoria picked up a dress of rust-colored brocade with a huge abstract design of black flowers. The dress was not easy to get into. Over Dougless's shoulders was a crisscross network of silk cords, a pearl at every joint. The front of the bodice was fastened with hooks and eyes that looked strong enough to hold army tanks together. An embroidered band concealed the closure.

There were no sleeves on the dress, but Honoria attached them separately, pulling them up over the long sleeves of the linen shirt underneath. At the shoulder the sleeves were big and puffy; then they tapered to the small wrists. The sleeves weren't solid fabric but strips of hemmed emerald taffeta, fastened every few inches by a gold square set with a pearl.

Dougless touched the pearls while Honoria hurriedly and efficiently went around Dougless with a long hatpin type of instrument pulling bits of the white linen out the cuts in the sleeves.

By now it had taken Honoria an hour and a half to put these garments on Dougless and she wasn't finished yet.

Next came the jewels. A belt of gold links with rough-cut square emeralds went around Dougless's now-tiny waist. An enameled brooch with pearls around it was pinned in the middle of the bodice, and two gold link chains went off to either side, fastening under her arms. Honoria picked up a collar that was a limp ruffle of linen, put it around Dougless's neck and tied it in back. (Later, Dougless found out that in 1564, Nicholas's ruff had been stiff with yellow starch, but, now, a mere four years earlier, no one had heard of starch.) To conceal where the ruff joined the dress, Honoria slipped a third belt of square gold links about her neck.

"You may sit," Honoria said softly.

Dougless tried to walk, but she was wearing somewhere around forty to fifty pounds of clothing and the steel corset was preventing her from breathing.

Stiffly, her head up off the scratchy ruff, Dougless made her way to a stool and collapsed. She did not, however, slump. One does not slump when wearing a steel corset.

Dougless sat rigidly while Honoria combed Dougless's thick auburn hair, then pulled it back from her face and braided it. Then, using bone pins, she fastened the braids up. Over the braids, on the back of Dougless's head, she fastened a little cap that was like a hair net, but again, pearls were at each joint.

Honoria helped Dougless stand up. "Yes," she said, smiling, "you are most beautiful."

"As pretty as Lettice?" Dougless asked without thinking.

"Lady Lettice is most beautiful also," Honoria said, her eyes cast downward.

Dougless smiled. Tactful, very tactful.

Honoria had Dougless sit on the edge of the bed, then put out her leg, and Honoria slipped fine, hand-knit wool stockings up to Dougless's knees; then she tied them with pretty ribbon garters embroidered with bumblebees. She slipped cork-soled, soft leather shoes on Dougless's feet, then helped Dougless to again stand up.

Slowly, Dougless walked toward the window, then back. The clothes were ridiculous, of course. They were heavy, unwieldy, terrible for your lungs, and yet . . . She put her hands to her waist. She could practically encircle it with her hands. She was wearing pearls, gold, emeralds, satin, and brocade, and in spite of the fact that she could barely breathe and her shoulders were already aching from the weight, she'd never felt so beautiful in her life.

When she twirled about, the skirts belled out from her prettily. She looked up at Honoria. "Whose dress is this?"

"Mine own," Honoria said softly. "We are near the same size."

Dougless went to her and put her hands on her shoulders. "Thank you very much for lending it to me. It was very generous of you." She kissed Honoria on the cheek.

Confused and blushing, Honoria turned away. "Lady Margaret wishes you to play for her tonight."

"Play?" Dougless was looking at the sleeves of her gown. Real gold, not fake. How she wished she had a full-length mirror! "Play what?" Her head came up. "You mean like play an instrument? I can't play anything."

Honoria was obviously shocked. "They do not teach music in your country?"

"They teach it, but I didn't take any."

"What does a woman learn in your country if not sewing and music?"

"Algebra, literature, history, things like that. Can you play an instrument? Sing?"

"Most certainly."

"Then how about if I teach you some songs and *you* play and sing them?"

"But Lady Margaret—"

"Won't mind. I'll be the bandleader."

From the way Honoria smiled, Dougless guessed that she'd like introducing new songs to the household. "We shall go to the orchard," she said.

When Honoria left the room, Dougless took a few minutes to apply cosmetics very lightly—she didn't want to look like a painted hussy, but it would not hurt her cause to look as appealing as she could.

Moments later, Honoria returned with a lute, and a man handed Dougless a basket that she saw contained bread and cheese and wine; then they were on their way outside.

Now that Dougless wasn't afraid that any minute she was going to be thrown into a dungeon, she looked about her. There were people *everywhere.* There were children running up and down stairs carrying things; men and women scurried hither and yon. Some people wore coarse linen or wool, some dressed in silks, some had jewels, some not; some people wore fur, some men wore shorts like Nicholas, and some men wore long gowns. Nearly all the people seemed young, and what surprised Dougless the most was that the people seemed to be as tall as twentieth-century people. She'd always heard that people of the Elizabethan age were much smaller than modern people. But she found that, at five feet three inches, she was short in the twentieth century and short in the Elizabethan age as well. The people did seem to be a lot slimmer, though. From all the moving about they did, plus the poundage of their clothes, they probably couldn't put on weight.

"Where is Nicholas's room?" Dougless asked, and moments later, Honoria pointed to a closed door.

Dougless had to watch her step as she descended the staircase in her long skirts, but the brocade in her hand made her feel elegant.

As they made their way toward the back of the house, Dougless had glimpses of lovely rooms with gorgeously dressed women bent over embroidery frames. Outside, she and Honoria stopped on a brick terrace that had a low wall around it and a stone balustrade on top, and she had her first look at an Elizabethan garden. Before her, down some steps, was a maze of low, deep green hedges. To her right was another walled garden of vegetables and herbs set in perfectly arranged squares. A pretty little octagonal building stood in the middle. To her left she could see another garden of fruit trees with an odd sort of hill in the middle. On top of the hill was a wooden rail.

"What is that?" she asked.

"A mound," Honoria replied. "Come, we will go to the orchard."

They walked briskly down brick stairs, then across a raised walk beside a rose-covered wall, where Honoria opened an oak door and they entered the orchard. Dougless found that although the gown she wore very much constricted her upper body, from the waist down she was free. The farthingale held the weight of the skirts off her legs, and not wearing any underpants gave her the oddest feeling of being naked.

The orchard was lovely, and it struck Dougless how perfectly in order it was. Everything was planted symmetrically, and all of it was perfectly clean. She could see at least four men and two children using wooden rakes to clean and to generally make the garden beautiful. Now she could see why Nicholas had been so upset by the garden at Bellwood. But to keep a garden like this took the services of many, many people.

Honoria walked along the gravel path on the edge of the orchard to a grape arbor. As far as Dougless could see, there wasn't a dead leaf or twig on the vines, and the unripe grapes hung down abundantly.

"This is very pretty," Dougless whispered. "In fact, I've never seen a garden as pretty as this one."

Smiling, Honoria sat on a bench in front of a pear tree that was perfectly espaliered against the wall and pulled her lute onto her lap. "You will teach me your songs now?"

Sitting beside her, Dougless pulled aside the cloth inside the basket she carried. Inside was a big piece of bread, white bread, but not like modern white bread. It was heavier, and very fresh, but there were odd holes in the crust. It was delicious. The cheese was tangy and fresh. Inside a hard leather bottle was a sour-tasting wine. There was also a little silver goblet.

"Does no one drink water?"

"The water is bad," Honoria said, tuning her fat-bellied lute.

"Bad? You mean undrinkable?" She thought of the little houses she'd seen yesterday. If those people had access to the water, it was sure to be dirty. How odd, she'd always thought that water pollution was a twentieth-century problem.

Dougless spent a lovely two hours with Honoria in the orchard, eating the cheese and bread, sipping the cool wine from a silver goblet, watching the jewels on her own dress and on Honoria's twinkling in the sunlight, and watching the gardeners go about their work. She didn't know many songs, but she'd always loved Broadway musicals and had seen most of them on video, so when she began to think about it, she knew more than she thought. Besides "I Could Have Danced All Night," she knew "Get Me to the Church on Time" from *My Fair Lady.* She made Honoria laugh at the title song from *Hair.* And she knew "They Call the Wind Maria" from *Paint Your Wagon.* She also knew the theme song from *Gilligan's Island,* but she didn't sing that.

After the fifth song, Honoria put up her hand to halt. "I must write these," she said, then went back to the house to get paper and pen.

Dougless was content to sit where she was, like a lazy cat in the sun. Unlike her usual life, she felt no urgency to be somewhere else or do something else.

On the far side of the orchard a little door opened and she saw Nicholas enter. Immediately, Dougless was alert and her heart began to race. Would he like her dress? Would he like her better now that she looked like the other women of his century?

She started to get up, but then she saw a pretty young woman she'd never seen before enter behind him. Nicholas was holding her hand as the two of them went running down the path toward the grape arbor in the opposite corner of the garden. It wasn't difficult to see that they were lovers slipping away to somewhere private.

Dougless stood up, her fists clenched at her side. Damn him, she thought. This is just the sort of thing that had gained him such an awful reputation in the twentieth century. No wonder the history books had nothing good to say about him.

Dougless's first impulse was to run after them and tear the woman's hair out. Nicholas might not remember her, but that didn't change the fact that Dougless was the woman he loved. But, Dougless told herself, that was neither here nor there. She owed it to the future memory of Nicholas to put an end to this cavorting.

Feeling saintly, telling herself she was doing this for Nicholas's own good, she swiftly walked toward the arbor. She was aware that every gardener in the orchard had stopped work and was watching her.

In the secret shade of the arbor, Nicholas already had the woman's skirt up her bare thigh, his hand disappearing underneath. His jacket and shirt were open, the woman's hand was inside, and they were kissing each other with a great deal of enthusiasm.

"Well!" Dougless said loudly, somehow controlling her urge to spring at the two of them. "Nicholas, I don't believe this is the behavior of a gentleman."

The woman pulled away first and looked at Dougless in surprise. She started to push Nicholas away, but he didn't seem able to stop kissing her.

"Nicholas!" Dougless said sharply in her schoolteacher voice.

When Nicholas turned to look at her, she saw that his eyelids were lowered, and he had that sleepy look she'd seen only when he'd made love to her.

Dougless drew in her breath.

When he saw her, Nicholas's expression changed to anger, and he dropped the woman's skirt.

"I think you'd better leave," Dougless, her body shaking with anger, said to the woman.

The woman, looking from Nicholas to Dougless as they glared at each other, hurried out of the arbor.

Nicholas looked Dougless up and down, and the anger on his face almost made her retreat, but she held her ground.

"Nicholas, we have to talk. I have to explain to you who I am and why I'm here."

When he stepped toward her, this time she did step back. "You have charmed my mother," he said in a low voice, "but you do not charm me. If you come between me and my actions again, I will take a batlet to you."

He shoved past her so hard that Dougless nearly fell against the wall, and she watched with a heavy heart as he strode angrily down the path and out through the door in the wall. How was she supposed to accomplish anything if he wouldn't listen to her? He wouldn't even spend ten minutes in her company. What was she supposed to do, lasso him? Right, she thought, tie him up and tell him she was from the future and she had come back through time to save his neck—literally. "And I'm sure he'll believe me," she whispered.

Honoria returned with a wooden lap desk, big feathers that she expertly trimmed into pens, ink, and three sheets of paper. She plucked out the notes of the songs, and asked Dougless to write the music. Her opinion of Dougless's education was further lowered when she found out that Dougless could neither read nor write music.

"What is a batlet?" Dougless asked.

"It is used to beat the dust from the clothes," Honoria answered, writing the notes down.

"Does Nicholas . . . ah, fool around with all the women?"

Honoria stopped playing and looked at Dougless. "You should not lose your heart to Sir Nicholas. A woman should give her heart only to God. People die, but God does not."

Dougless sighed. "True, but while we're alive, people can make living worthwhile or not." Dougless started to say more, but she glanced up, and standing on the terrace of the house, she saw someone's head, and it looked like . . .

"Who is that girl?" Dougless asked, pointing.

"She is to marry Lord Christopher when she is of age. If she lives. She is a sickly child and not often out."

The girl, from this distance, looked just like Gloria, just as fat, just as petulant. Dougless remembered Lee saying that Nicholas's older brother was to marry a French heiress and that was why he'd refused Lettice's offer of marriage.

"So, Nicholas is to marry Lettice, and Christopher is engaged to a child," Dougless said. "Tell me, if that girl were to die, would Kit consider marrying Lettice?"

Honoria looked taken aback at Dougless's casual use of Christian names. "Lord Christopher is heir to an earldom, and he is related to the queen. Lady Lettice is not of his rank."

"But Nicholas is."

"Sir Nicholas is a younger son. He does not inherit the estates or the title. For him Lady Lettice is a good match. She also is related to the queen, but distantly. Her dowry, though, is not large."

"But if Lettice married Nicholas, then, say, Christopher died, Nicholas would be the earl, right?"

"Aye," Honoria said, and stopped writing notes. Looking up at the terrace, she saw the fat, spotty, sickly French heiress go back into the house. "Sir Nicholas would become the earl," she said thoughtfully.

TWENTY-THREE

*B*y *the time Dougless climbed into bed* beside Honoria that night, she was exhausted. No wonder she'd seen so few fat people and the women had such tiny waists. Between the steel corset and the constant activity, fat didn't have a chance to settle on a person's body.

She and Honoria had left the garden to attend a service in the pretty little chapel on the ground floor of the house. They'd listened to a richly dressed minister and they'd spent a great deal of time on their knees. Dougless couldn't pay attention to what the minister was saying for looking at the stunning clothes of the men and women around her: silk, satin, brocade, fur, jewels.

It was in the chapel that she had her first glimpse of Christopher. He looked like Nicholas, but not so young or handsome. But there was a quiet strength coming from him that made Dougless stare at him. When he glanced across at her, there was so much interest in his eyes that Dougless looked away, blushing. She didn't see Nicholas watching the two of them and frowning.

After chapel was supper, which Dougless took in the Presence

Chamber with Lady Margaret, Honoria, and four other women. There was vegetable beef soup, a nasty bitter beer, and fried rabbit. A man, who Honoria said was the butler, had to chip cinders from the crust of a loaf of bread before he served it to them, and thereby explained the holes in the crust of Dougless's earlier loaf.

The other women, Dougless learned, were Lady Margaret's gentle-women and chamberers. As far as Dougless could tell, everyone in the household had a specific rank, and servants had servants who had servants. And, to her surprise, they also had specific duty hours. Her knowledge of servants was based on what she'd read of Victorian house-holds, where the servants worked from very early to very late, but she learned from questioning Honoria, there were so many servants in the Stafford household that no one worked longer than about six hours at a time.

At supper, Dougless was introduced, and the ladies eagerly asked about her country of Lanconia and her uncle the king. Dougless, squirming with the lie, muttered replies, then asked the ladies about their clothes. She received some fascinating information on the Spanish style of dress, the French, the English, and the Italian fashions. Dougless became very involved in this, and soon found herself planning a gown in the Italian style that had something called a bum role under the skirt instead of a farthingale.

After supper, servants cleared the tables, then moved them against the wall, and Lady Margaret asked to hear Dougless's songs. What followed was an energetic and laugh-filled evening. With no TV and professional performances ever seen, no one was shy about singing or dancing. Dougless knew she was terrible compared to the people she'd heard on the radio and on records, but before the evening was over she found herself singing solos.

Christopher came to join them, and Honoria taught him "They Call the Wind Maria," which he played on the lute. Everyone seemed to play an instrument, and before long Lady Margaret and all five of her ladies were playing the melodies on oddly-shaped, strange-sounding instruments. There was a guitar of sorts but shaped like a violin, a three-stringed violin, a tiny piano, an enormous lute, several kinds of flutes, and a couple of horns.

Dougless found herself drawn to Kit. He was so much like Nicholas, the Nicholas she'd known in the twentieth century—certainly not this sixteenth-century Nicholas who went from one woman to another. She sang "Get Me to the Church on Time," and Kit quickly picked up the melody. In no time they were all singing the funny song.

At one point she saw Nicholas standing in the doorway glowering. He refused to enter even when Lady Margaret motioned to him.

It was only about nine o'clock when Lady Margaret said it was time to retire. Kit kissed Dougless's hand, and she smiled at him; then she followed Honoria off to bed.

Honoria's maid came to help the two women undress. Dougless took several lovely, deep breaths after the steel corset was removed; then, wearing the long linen undergarment she'd worn under her dress all day and a little cap to protect her hair, she climbed into bed beside Honoria. The sheets were linen and scratchy and not too clean, but the mattress was of goose down and as soft as a whisper. She was asleep before she'd pulled the coverlet over her.

She didn't know how long she'd been asleep when she awoke. She felt as though someone was calling her, but when she lifted her head and listened, she heard no one, so she lay back down. But the feeling that someone wanted her would not go away. Although the room was silent, she couldn't get rid of the feeling that she was needed by someone.

"Nicholas!" she said, coming bolt upright.

After a glance at the sleeping back of Honoria, Dougless crept out of bed. She put on a heavy brocade robe that was at the foot of the bed; then she slipped her feet into the soft, wide shoes. Elizabethan corsets might be murder but the shoes were heaven.

Silently, she left the room, then stood outside the closed door and listened. There was no sound, and what with the straw on the floor, she'd have been able to hear any footsteps. She started walking to the right, for she felt the call strongest there. She went to one closed door, put her hand on it, but felt nothing. The same at the second door. It was at the third door that she could feel the call the strongest.

When she opened the door, she wasn't surprised to see Nicholas sitting on a chair wearing his tight hose, the baggy shorts, and a big linen shirt open to the waist. A fire burned in the fireplace, and he held a silver tankard. He looked as though he'd been drinking for a while.

"What do you want of me?" she asked. She was more than a little afraid of this Nicholas, as he didn't seem remotely like the man who had come to her own century.

He didn't look at her, just stared at the fire.

"Nicholas, I'm willing to talk, but if you're just going to give me the silent treatment, then I'd like to go back to bed."

"Who are you?" he asked softly. "How do I know of you?"

She sat on the chair next to him, facing the fire. "We are bonded somehow. I can't explain it. I cried for help and you came to me. I needed you and you heard my call. You gave me . . ." Love, she almost said. Somehow that seemed long ago and this man was a stranger to her. "It seems to be my turn now. I've come to warn you."

He looked at her. "Warn me? Ah, yes, I must not commit treason."

"You don't have to sound so cynical. If I can come all this way back here, the least you can do is listen. That is, if you can keep your hands from under some woman's skirt long enough."

She could see his face turning red with rage. "Callet!" he said under his breath. "You who use your witchcraft to befuddle my mother, who exhibit yourself to my brother, dare to speak ill of me?"

"I am *not* a witch. I've told you that a thousand times. All I've done is what I've had to do to get myself inside your house so I can warn you." Standing up, she tried to calm herself. "Nicholas, we have to stop arguing. I've been sent back to warn you, but unless you listen to me, everything's going to happen the same way it did before. Kit will—"

He stood up, cutting her off, then leaned over her threateningly. "When you came to me this night, did you come from my brother's bed?"

Dougless didn't think about what she did. She just slapped him across the face.

He grabbed her against him, his body forcing hers backward as he put his mouth on hers, hard, angry.

Dougless wasn't going to allow a man to use force to kiss her. She pushed at him with all her strength, but he didn't release her. One of his hands was on the back of her head, forcing her head sideways, while the other hand slipped to the small of her back and pushed her body intimately to his.

When his lips touched hers, Dougless stopped fighting him. This was Nicholas, the Nicholas she'd come to love, the man that even time couldn't separate her from. Her arms went about his neck, and she opened her mouth under his. As she kissed him in return, her body began to melt into his. Her legs were weak, trembling.

His lips moved to her neck.

"Colin," she whispered, "my beloved Colin."

He pulled his face away from her, looking puzzled. She touched the hair at his temples, ran her fingertips down his cheeks.

"I thought I had lost you," she whispered. "I thought I'd never see you again."

"You may see all of me that you wish," he said, smiling; then he put his hand under her knees and carried her to his bed. He stretched out beside her and Dougless closed her eyes as his hand went under her robe, then untied the neck of her gown. He kissed her ear, nibbling at her lobe, then ran his tongue down the sensitive cord of her neck while his hand slipped inside her gown to touch her breast.

As his thumb rubbed the peak of her breast, as his breath was on her ear, he whispered, "Who has sent you to me?"

"*Mmm,*" Dougless murmured. "God, I suppose."

"What is the name of the god you worship?"

Dougless could barely hear him as he slipped one leg over hers. "God. Jehovah. Allah. Whoever."

"What man worships this god?"

Dougless was beginning to hear him. She opened her eyes. "Man? God? What are you talking about?"

Nicholas squeezed her breast. "What man has sent you to my house?"

She was beginning to understand his motive in making love to her. She pushed away from him, and sitting up, she tied her gown and robe. "I see," she said, trying to control her anger. "This is how you always get what you want from women, isn't it? At Thornwyck all you had to do was kiss my arm and I'd agree to do whatever you wanted. So now you've decided that I'm up to no good, so you're going to seduce a confession out of me."

She got off the bed and stood glaring at him. But Nicholas lounged on the bed, not at all upset by the revelation of his devious actions. "Let me tell you something, Nicholas Stafford, you're not the man I thought you were. The Nicholas I knew was a man who cared about honor and justice. All *you* care about is the number of women you can bed."

She stood up straighter. "All right, I'm going to tell you who sent me and why I'm here." She took a deep breath. "I'm from the future, the twentieth century actually, and you came to me there. We spent several lovely days together."

His mouth dropped open and he started to speak, but Dougless put up her hand. "Hear me out. When you came to me the time here was September of 1564, four years from now and you were sitting in a prison awaiting your execution for treason."

Nicholas's eyes began to twinkle in amusement as he rolled off the bed and picked up his tankard. "I see why my mother has taken you to amuse her. Tell me more. What treason had I committed?"

Dougless clenched her fists at her side. It was difficult to be caring toward a man who was smirking in derision. "You hadn't. You were innocent."

"Ah, yes," he said patronizingly. "I would be."

"You were gathering an army to protect your lands in Wales, but in your haste, you didn't petition the queen for permission to raise the army. Someone told her you were planning to use the army to take her throne."

Nicholas sat down and looked at her, his eyes filled with amazement. "Pray tell me, who lied to the queen about these lands I do not own and this army I do not possess?"

She was so angry at his attitude that she wanted to leave the room. Why bother to try to save him? Let the history books record that he was a wastrel. He *was* a wastrel. "They were your lands and your army because Kit was dead, and Robert Sydney and your beloved Lettice had lied to the queen."

Nicholas's face changed to cold rage. He advanced on her. "Do you enter this household to threaten my brother's life? Do you think to cast your spells on me so that I feel all that you do in the hopes that I will take you to wife and make you a countess? Do you stop at nothing?

You besmirch the name of my betrothed as well as my cater-cousin to gain your desires?"

She backed away from him, afraid of him now. "I can't marry you because my life doesn't belong in this century. I certainly can't go to bed with you because if I did I'd probably disappear, and if I disappeared now, I'm sure nothing would be changed. And besides that, I don't *want* to marry you. Okay, so I came back to give you a message and that's it. So now maybe I'll get lucky and disappear. I *hope* I do. Truthfully, I hope I never have to see you again."

She grabbed the door handle, but he slammed the door shut and wouldn't let her leave.

"I will watch you. If my brother has one pain, I will know it is caused by you and you will pay."

"I left my voodoo doll on the plane. Now, will you let me out or do I scream?"

"Heed me, woman."

"I understand you perfectly, but since I'm not a witch, I don't have any fears, do I? Now open the door and let me out of here."

He stepped back, and Dougless, with her head high, left the room. She was all the way down the corridor to the room she shared with Honoria before she started crying. She thought she'd lost Nicholas when he'd returned to the sixteenth century, but that hadn't been as complete as this. Now he wasn't even the same man she'd known and loved such a short time ago.

She didn't return to Honoria's bedroom, but went to the Presence Chamber to curl up on a window seat. The tiny diamond-shaped panes of glass were too thick and rippled to see out of, but Dougless didn't care about seeing out. How many times was she going to lose the man she loved? Was the Nicholas who came to her in the twentieth century the man who'd just kissed her? Other than looks, the two seemed to have nothing in common.

Once again, Dougless, she told herself, you've fallen for the wrong man. If he wasn't a man with one foot in jail, then he was a man who chased after every woman around. One minute Nicholas was cursing Dougless for being a witch, and the next he was kissing her.

When Nicholas had gone back before, he'd been executed, because they'd not had enough information. Afterward, she'd felt that they might have found the information they needed if she hadn't spent so much time being jealous of Arabella. If Douglass had spent more time researching and asking questions, she might have saved Nicholas's life.

So now she'd been given a second chance, yet she was repeating the same mistakes. She was letting emotion blind her to what must be done. This extraordinary, unbelievable thing of switching two people back and forth through time had been done to her and Nicholas so that lives and fortunes could be saved. But all Douglass could think of was whether Nicholas still loved her or not. She threw jealous fits like a junior-high-school-girl because a grown man was fooling around with some woman in a grape arbor.

Douglass stood up. She had a job to do and she had to do it without allowing petty emotion to get in her way.

She went back into Honoria's bedroom and slipped into bed beside her. Today she would start finding out what she could do to prevent the treachery of Lettice Culpin.

Douglass had merely closed her eyes when the bedroom door was flung open and Honoria's maid entered. She pulled back the hangings to the four-poster bed, opened the shutters to the windows, took Honoria's and Douglass's gowns and the layers of underwear from the chest at the foot of the bed, and shook them. Minutes later Douglass was caught up in the bustle of the day, of dressing again in Honoria's second-best gown and eating a breakfast of beef and beer and bread. Honoria started to clean her teeth with a linen cloth and some soap, but Douglass didn't want to try the flavor, so she gave Honoria one of the several hotel giveaway toothbrushes she had in her bag. After a demonstration of its use and some exclamations over the toothpaste, she and Honoria companionably brushed their teeth, spitting into a lovely hammered copper basin.

After breakfast in their chamber, Douglass followed Honoria into a bustle of activity as she attended Lady Margaret in directing the large household. There was a morning church service to attend, then the servants to see to. Douglass stood by and watched in awe as Lady Margaret went over every problem, talked and listened to every complaint.

Dougless asked Honoria a thousand questions as Lady Margaret competently and efficiently dealt with what seemed to be hundreds of servants: marshals of the hall, yeomen of the chamber, yeomen waiters. Honoria explained that these were only the household heads and that each of these men had many servants under him. She said that Lady Margaret was unusual in that she dealt personally with the household servants.

"There are more servants than these?" Dougless asked.

"Many more, but Sir Nicholas deals with them."

There is no mention in your history books that I was chamberlain to my brother? Dougless remembered Nicholas asking.

After an exhausting morning, at about eleven A.M., the servants were dismissed and Dougless followed Lady Margaret, Honoria, and the other ladies downstairs to what Honoria said was the winter parlor. Here a long table was beautifully laid with a snowy white linen cloth, and each place setting consisted of a large plate, a spoon, and a big napkin. In the center of the table, the plates were . . . Dougless could hardly believe her eyes: the plates were gold. The plates further down the table were silver, then came pewter plates, until a couple on the end were made of wood. There were chairs behind the gold plates and stools for the other diners. There was no disguising who was considered of higher rank than someone else. Obviously, equality was not something these people pursued.

Dougless was happy to see that Honoria led her to a silver plate, and Dougless was further pleased to find herself sitting across from Kit.

"What amusement do you plan for us this eve'n?" he asked.

Dougless looked into his deep blue eyes and thought, How about spin the bottle? "Ah . . ." She had been so involved with the problem of Nicholas she had given her job little thought. "Waltzing," she said. "It's the national dance of my country."

When he smiled at her, Dougless smiled back warmly.

Her concentration was broken when a servant brought a ewer and basin and towel for each guest to wash his hands. Dougless saw that, three seats down from Kit was Nicholas, and he was in serious conversation with a tall, dark-haired woman who wasn't beautiful exactly but very handsome. For a moment, Dougless stared at the woman, thinking that she'd seen her before, but she couldn't place her.

Turning away, she looked at the other people and thought how odd it was to see women without makeup, but the women obviously took care of their skin. They didn't just get up, wash their faces, and go.

On the other side of Nicholas was the French heiress who was to marry Kit. The girl sat quietly, her lower lip stuck out, a frown on her plain face. No one spoke to her, but she didn't seem to mind. Behind her hovered a fierce-looking older woman who, when the girl knocked her napkin askew, straightened it.

Dougless caught the girl's eye and smiled, but the girl glowered back, and the hovering woman looked as though Dougless had threatened her charge. Dougless turned away.

When the food arrived, Dougless saw that it was presented with great ceremony. And cooking like this deserved ceremony. The first course of meat was brought in on enormous silver trays: roast beef, veal, mutton, salted beef. Wine, which was kept cool in copper tubs of cold water, was poured into jewel-colored, translucent goblets of Venetian glass.

The next course was fowl: turkey, boiled capon, chicken stewed with leeks, partridge, pheasant, quail, woodcock. Next came fish: sole, turbot, whiting, lobster, crayfish, eels.

Everything seemed to be cooked in a sauce, all of it highly spiced and delicious.

Vegetables came next: turnips, green peas, cucumbers, carrots, spinach. Dougless did not find the vegetables as good as the other courses because they had been cooked to a pulp. When she asked, she was told that vegetables must be cooked thoroughly to remove the poisons from them.

With every course a different wine was served, and servants rinsed the glasses before filling them with the next wine.

Salads came after the vegetables. Not salads as she knew them but cooked lettuce and even cooked violet buds.

When Dougless was so full she felt like lying down and sleeping the afternoon away, dessert was brought in. There were almond tarts and pies of nearly every fruit imaginable, and there were cheeses that ranged from creamy to hard. The fat, sun-warmed strawberries were more flavorful than any Dougless had ever tasted in the modern world.

For once Dougless was thankful for her steel corset, which kept her from gorging herself.

After the meal the ewer of water was brought around again because the food had been eaten with spoons and fingers.

At last, after three hours, the group broke up and Dougless waddled up the stairs to Honoria's room and flopped on the bed. "I am dying," she said woefully. "I'll never be able to walk again. And to think I expected Nicholas to be happy with a club sandwich for lunch."

Honoria laughed at her. "Now we must attend Lady Margaret."

Dougless soon found out that the Elizabethan people worked as hard as they ate. With her hand on her full belly, Dougless followed Honoria downstairs, through a beautiful knot garden, and out to the stables. Dougless was helped onto a horse with a sidesaddle, which she had a great deal of trouble holding on to; then Lady Margaret, her five women and four male guards wearing swords and daggers, set off at a mad pace. Dougless had a hard time keeping up because she was so unbalanced, with one leg hooked over a tall wooden pommel and the other in a short stirrup. Dougless knew her Colorado cousins wouldn't be very proud of her because she used both hands to hold on to the reins.

"They have no horses in Lanconia?" one of the men asked her.

"Horses, yes; sidesaddles, no," she answered as she held on fearfully.

After about an hour she began to feel less like she was going to fall off at any second, so she could look around her. Going from the beautiful Stafford house to the English countryside was like going from a fairy castle to a slum, or maybe from Beverley Hills to Calcutta.

Cleanliness was not part of the villagers' lives. Animals and people lived in the same buildings and on the same sanitary level. Kitchen and privy slops were thrown outside the doors of the dark little houses. The people were as dirty as only years' worth of dirt and sweat could make them. Their clothes were coarse and stiff with grease and use.

And diseases! Dougless stared at the people they passed. They were marked with smallpox; they had neck goiter, ringworm, running sores on their faces. Many times she saw crippled and maimed people. And no one over the age of ten seemed to have all his teeth—and the ones they did have were usually black.

Dougless's huge lunch threatened to come up. What made her feel worse than the sights and smells was the fact that most of the illnesses could be cured with modern medicine. As she rode, holding on to the saddle, she could see that there were very few people past the age of thirty, and it occurred to Dougless that had she been born in the sixteenth century, she wouldn't have lived past ten years old. At ten her appendix had ruptured and she'd required emergency surgery. There was no surgery in the sixteenth century. But then she probably wouldn't even have survived birth because Dougless had been a breech birth and her mother had hemorrhaged. As she thought about this, she looked at these people with new eyes. These people were the survivors, the healthiest of the healthy.

As Lady Margaret's group rode by, the villagers came out of their huts or stopped working in the fields to stare at the procession of beautifully dressed people on their sleek horses. Lady Margaret and her attendants waved to the villagers, and the villagers grinned back. We're rock stars, movie stars, and royalty all rolled into one, Dougless thought, and she waved at the people too.

They rode for what seemed to be hours to Dougless's sore backside and cramped legs before they halted in a pretty little meadow that overlooked a field full of grazing sheep. One of the grooms helped Dougless from her horse, and she limped to where Honoria sat on a cloth on the damp ground.

"You have enjoyed the ride?" Honoria asked.

"About as much as measles and whooping cough," Dougless murmured. "I take it Lady Margaret is over her flu?"

"She is a most energetic woman."

"I can see that."

They sat in companionable silence for a while, Dougless looking at the pretty view and trying not to think of her encounter with Nicholas the night before. She asked Honoria what a callet was and found out it was a lewd woman. Dougless bit her tongue on renewed anger.

"And a cater-cousin?" she asked Honoria.

"A friend of the heart."

Dougless sighed. So Nicholas and Robert Sydney were "friends of the heart." No wonder Nicholas would believe nothing bad about the man. Some friendship, she thought. Nicholas rolls about on the table with Robert's wife, and Robert plots to have his friend executed.

"Robert Sydney is a pillicock," Dougless muttered.

Honoria looked shocked. "You know him? You care for him?"

"I don't know him, and I certainly don't care for him."

Honoria looked so puzzled that Dougless asked what a pillicock was. "It is a term of endearment; it means a pretty rogue."

"Endearment? But—" She broke off. When Nicholas had asked her to return to the sixteenth century to cook for him and she'd been so angry, she'd called him rotten names and Nicholas had supplied "pillicock" to the list. He must have loved hearing an angry woman call him a term of endearment.

She smiled in memory. He could indeed be a pillicock.

One of the women, who was a maid to a maid to Lady Margaret, passed about little cookies made of crushed almonds.

Munching, Dougless asked, "Who was the handsome dark-haired woman sitting next to Nicholas at dinner today?"

"Lady Arabella Sydney."

Dougless choked and coughed, sputtering crumbs. "Lady Arabella? Has she been here long? When did she come? When will she leave?" The postcard, Dougless thought. That's where she'd seen the woman: in the portrait on the postcard she'd bought at Bellwood.

Honoria smiled. "She arrived yester eve and leaves early on the morrow. She journeys with her husband to France. They will not return for years, so she came to bid my Lady Margaret farewell."

Dougless's mind raced. If Nicholas hadn't had Arabella on the table yet and tomorrow Arabella left, then *this* had to be the day. She had to stop it!

Suddenly, she doubled over, her hands on her stomach, and began to groan.

"What ails you?" Honoria asked, concerned.

"Something I ate. I must return to the house."

"But—" Honoria began.

"I *must*." Dougless gave a few more groans.

Quickly, Honoria went to Lady Margaret and returned in a few minutes. "We have permission. I will accompany you with one groom."

"Great. Let's just go fast."

Honoria looked confused as Dougless hurried toward the horses. As a groom helped her onto the saddle, Dougless didn't look at all ill.

Dougless would have thrown her leg over the idiot sidesaddle, but there was no stirrup on one side, so she tightened her leg around the big protrusion in the front, took a little riding crop, and applied it to the horse's flanks. Leaning forward, she hung on as the horse thundered down the rutted, dirty road.

Behind her came the groom and Honoria, doing their best to keep up with her.

Twice Dougless had to make the horse jump, once over a wagon tongue, once over a small wooden wheelbarrel. She reined in sharply as a child ran across the road and managed to miss him. She ran through a flock of geese that set up a terrible clatter.

When she reached the house, she leaped from the saddle, tripped on the heavy skirts, and fell face forward. But she didn't waste a moment as she got up and began running, flinging open the gate, then running down the brick walk and up the stairs, across the terrace and in through the front door.

Once she was inside the house, she stopped and stared up at the staircase. Where? Where was Nicholas? Arabella? The table?

To her left came voices, and when she heard Kit, she ran to him. "Do you know where there's a table, about six feet long, three feet wide? The legs are turned in a spiral."

Kit smiled at the urgency in her voice—and at the wild look of her. Her face was running with perspiration, her cap was half off, and her auburn hair was falling about her shoulders. "We have many such tables."

"This one is special." She was trying to remain calm, but she couldn't quite do it. And she was trying to breathe, but the corset was constricting her lungs. "It's in a room Nicholas uses, and there's a closet in the room, a place big enough that two people can hide in it."

"Closet?" Kit said, puzzled, and Dougless realized that a closet in Elizabethan England wasn't a place to hang clothes.

An older man behind Kit whispered something to him, and Kit smiled. "The chamber next to Nicholas's bedchamber has such a table. He often—"

Dougless didn't hear the rest. Tossing her skirt and petticoats over her arm, she ran up the stairs. Nicholas's bedroom was two rooms down on the right and next to it was a door. She tried the handle, but it was locked. She ran into his bedroom, and through it, but the connecting door was also locked.

She banged on the door with her open palms. "Nicholas! If you're in there, let me in. Nicholas! Do you hear me?"

She could swear she heard sounds inside the room. "Nicholas!" she screamed as she pounded and kicked the door. "Nicholas!"

When he opened the door, he had a lethal-looking dagger in his hand. "Is my mother well?" he asked.

Dougless pushed past him. There, against the wall was the table she'd seen in the Harewoods' library. It was four hundred years younger, but it was the same table. And sitting on a chair, trying to look innocent, was Lady Arabella.

"I will have your—" Nicholas began.

But Dougless cut him off when she flung open a little door to the left of the window. There, huddled against the shelves, were two servants. *"This* is why I wanted you to open the door," she said to Nicholas. "These two spies would have seen everything you two were about to do."

Nicholas and Arabella were gaping at her, speechless.

Dougless looked at the two servants. "If one word of this gets out, we'll know who told. Do you understand me?"

In spite of Dougless's odd speech pattern, they did indeed understand her. "Now get out of here," she said.

As quickly as mice, they scurried from the room.

"You—" Nicholas began.

Ignoring him, Dougless turned to Arabella. "I've saved your life, because your husband would have heard of this and eventually he would have—" Dougless took a deep breath. "I think you'd better go."

Arabella, not used to being spoken to like this, started to protest, but then she thought of her husband's temper. She hurried from the room.

When Dougless turned to Nicholas, she saw the rage on his face—which was nothing new, since he'd hardly looked at her any other way since she'd arrived. She gave him a hard glare, then started to leave.

She didn't make it out the door because Nicholas slammed it in her face.

"Do you spy on me?" he asked. "Do you enjoy watching what I do with other women?"

Count to ten, Dougless thought, or better yet, twenty. She drew a deep breath. "I do not get my kicks from watching you make a fool of yourself with women," she said calmly. "I've told you why I'm here. I knew you were about . . . about to have Arabella on the table because you'd already done so. The servants told everybody, John Wilfred wrote the story, Arabella had your kid, and Robert Sydney did her in. Now, may I go?"

She watched the emotions running across Nicholas's face, the anger, the confusion, and Dougless felt sympathy for him. "I know that what I'm saying is impossible to believe. When you came to me, I didn't believe you either, but, Nicholas, I'm from the future and I've been sent back in time to try to prevent the ruin of your entire family. Lettice—"

His look cut her off. "Do you accuse an innocent woman? Or are you jealous of all women I touch?"

Dougless's vow to control her emotions flew out the window. "You vain peacock! I couldn't care less how many women you bed. It's nothing to me. You aren't the man I once knew. In fact you're half the man your brother is. I was sent back in time to right a wrong, and I'm going to do the best I can, no matter how hard you try to thwart me. Maybe if I can prevent Kit's death, *that* will save the Stafford estates, then nobody will have to try to change you from being a randy satyr. Now, let me out of here."

Nicholas didn't move from in front of the door. "You speak of my brother's death. Do you mean to cast—"

Dougless threw up her hands and turned away. "I am *not* a witch. Can't you understand that? I'm a regular, ordinary person who's been caught in very strange circumstances." She turned back to him. "I don't know all of what happened when Kit died. You said you were at sword practice and you cut your arm, so you couldn't go riding with him. He saw some girl in a lake and went after her. He drowned. That's all I know." Except that Lettice might have been responsible, Dougless thought, but she didn't add that.

He was staring at her, his eyes hostile.

Her voice softened. "When you came to me, I didn't believe you either," she repeated. "You told me several things that weren't in the history books, but I still didn't believe you. Finally, you took me to Bellwood and showed me a secret door that held a little ivory box. No one, in all the years of the many different owners of the castle had found the door. You said Kit showed you the door the week before he died." She didn't like to think of Kit dying.

Nicholas gaped at her. She *was* a witch, for, just recently, Kit mentioned a hidden door at Bellwood, a door he had not yet shown his younger brother. What had she done to Kit to persuade him to tell her of this door that by right should be known only to family members?

In truth, what was she doing to his family and his household? Yesterday he'd heard a stableman singing some absurdity of a song called "Zip-A-Dee-Doo-Dah." Three of his mother's women now applied paint to their eyelids that they said came from "Lady" Dougless. His mother—his sane, level-headed, wise mother—took medicine from her hand with the trust of a child. And Kit watched the red-haired wench with the intensity of a bird of prey.

In the few days she had been in the Stafford house, she had upset everything. Her songs, her outrageous dances, the stories she told (lately the castle folk had been talking about some people named Scarlett and Rhett), even how she painted her face was affecting everyone. She was a sorceress, and she was gradually putting everyone under her spell.

Nicholas was the only person who made any attempt to resist her. When he tried to talk to Kit of the power the woman was gaining, Kit had laughed. "Of what consequence are a few stories and songs?" Kit had said.

Nicholas didn't know what the woman wanted, but he did not mean to so easily fall under her spell as the others had. He meant to resist her no matter how difficult that might be.

Now, glaring at her, he knew that resisting her would never be easy. Her auburn hair was about her shoulders, and she held the little pearl cap in her hands. Never had he seen a woman as beautiful as she. Lettice, perhaps, was more perfect-featured, but this woman, this

Dougless, who enraged him, had something more, something he could not name.

From the first moment he'd seen her, it had been as though she had some secret hold over him. He liked being in control with women, like kissing them and feeling them melt against him. He liked the challenge of winning a difficult woman, and he liked the sense of power it gave him when he walked away from her.

But from the first this woman had been different. He watched her far more than she did him. He was aware of every time she looked at Kit, of every glance she gave some handsome servant, of every time she smiled or laughed. Last night in his room his awareness of her had been to the point of pain, and this awareness had made him so angry he could barely speak or think coherently. Her effect on him enraged him. After she left, he had not slept because he knew she wept. The tears of women had never bothered him before. Women always cried. They wept when you left them, when you would not do what they wanted, when you told them you did not love them. He liked women like Arabella and Lettice who never cried for any reason.

But last night this woman had spent the night weeping, and even though he could neither hear nor see her, he had felt her tears. Three times he had almost gone to her but he'd managed to restrain himself. He had no intention of letting her know she had power over him.

As for her story of past and future, he did not so much as consider it. But something about her was strange. He did not for a moment believe she was a Lanconian princess—nor did he think his mother believed her, but Lady Margaret liked the odd songs and the woman's strange manner of speaking. His mother liked the way this woman acted as though everything were new to her, from the food to the clothes to the servants.

" . . . you'll tell me, won't you?"

Nicholas stared at her; he had no idea what she'd been saying. But suddenly a wave of such desire for her flooded his veins that he stepped back against the door. "You will not bewitch me as you have my family," he said as though he meant to convince himself.

Dougless saw the lust in his eyes, saw the way his lids lowered. In spite of herself, her heart began to pound. You touch him and you return, she told herself, but you can't leave until Kit is safe and Lettice's treachery is exposed.

"Nicholas, I don't mean to bewitch you, and I haven't done anything with your family that I haven't needed to do to survive." She put out her hand to touch him. "If you would only listen to me . . ."

"Listen to your talk of past and future?" he said with a sneer. He leaned his face close to hers. "Beware of what you do, woman, for I watch you. When word comes that you have no uncle who is king, I myself will toss you from my home. Now get you from me, and do not spy on me again." Turning, he stormed from the room, leaving Dougless alone and feeling helpless.

She looked through his bedroom toward his retreating back. "Please, God," she prayed, "show me how I am to help Nicholas. Let me do what I failed to do the first time. Please show me the way."

Feeling older than she had when she entered, she left the room.

TWENTY-FOUR

*I*n the morning, Dougless saw Arabella just as she was stepping on a block to mount her beautiful black horse. Near her was a man who Dougless assumed was her husband, Robert Sydney. Dougless wanted to see him, wanted to see the face of the man whom Nicholas considered his friend, yet had sent his "friend" to be executed.

Sydney turned, and Dougless drew in her breath. Robert Sydney looked very, very much like Dr. Robert Whitley, the man she had once hoped to marry.

Dougless turned away, her hands shaking. Coincidence, she told herself. Nothing more than coincidence. But later that day she remembered how, in the twentieth century, Nicholas, when he'd first seen Robert, had looked as though he'd seen a ghost. And Robert had looked at Nicholas with hatred in his eyes.

Coincidence, she told herself again. It could be nothing more.

During the next two days Dougless rarely saw Nicholas. When she did see him, he was glowering at her from a doorway or frowning at her across a table. Dougless was kept very busy by the household because they had come to regard her as TV, movies, carnival, and concert all in one. They wanted games, songs, stories; their demand to be entertained was insatiable. Dougless could not walk in the garden or in the house without someone stopping her and asking for one more bit of entertainment. She was kept busy for long hours trying to remember everything she'd ever read or heard. With Honoria's help, she devised a crude version of Monopoly. They played Pictionary with slate tablets. When she ran out of fiction stories she'd read, she started telling them history stories about America—Lady Margaret especially loved these. Nathan Hale became a favorite hero of the household, and Lady Margaret kept Dougless up half of one night asking questions about Abraham Lincoln.

Dougless tried her best to stay in the entertainment field and not talk about religion or politics. After all, just a few years before Queen Mary had been burning people for being of the wrong religion. Twice Kit asked her questions about farming in her country, and, despite knowing little, she was able to make a few suggestions about compost and how it could be used with the crops.

Dougless knew that Lady Margaret's ladies were appalled at Dougless's poor education, at her speaking only one language and at her not being able to play a musical instrument. And they could not read her handwriting. But for the most part they forgave her.

While Dougless was teaching, she was also learning. These women did not have the pressure on them that twentieth-century American women did to be everything to everyone. The sixteenth-century woman was not supposed to be a corporate executive, an adoring mother, a gourmet cook and hostess, as well as a creative lover with the body of an athlete. If the woman was rich, she was to sew, look after her household and enjoy herself. Of course she didn't expect to live past about forty, but at least during her few years on earth, she wasn't under society's constant pressure to do more and be more.

As the days in sixteenth-century England accumulated, Dougless remembered her time of living with Robert. The alarm went off at six A.M., and she hit the floor running. She had to run to get a day's work done in a day. There were meals to prepare, groceries to buy, the house to be straightened (Robert had a cleaning woman once a week), and the kitchen to be cleaned again and again and again. And in her "spare time" she had a full time job. Sometimes she'd wished she could stay in bed for three days and read murder mysteries, but there was always too much to do to consider being lazy.

Besides, there was the guilt. If she was resting, she felt she "should" be at the gym trying to keep her thighs from spreading, or she "should" be planning some scrumptious dinner party for Robert's colleagues. She felt guilty when, exhausted, she served a pizza from the freezer for dinner.

But now, here in the sixteenth century, the modern-day pressures seemed far away. People didn't live alone and isolated. This wasn't one house with one woman to do twenty jobs; this was one house with a hundred and forty-some people to do maybe seventy jobs. One tired, lonely woman didn't have to cook, clean, wash, and so on, plus hold an outside job. Here one person had one job.

Modern women had their own self-made guilt to make them miserable, but the sixteenth-century people had diseases, their fear of the unknown, their ignorance of medicine, and constant and ever-present death to haunt them. People in the sixteenth century died frequently, and death was always nearby for the Elizabethans. There had been four deaths in the household since Dougless had arrived, and all of them could have been avoided with decent emergency room care. One man died when a wagon fell on him. Internal bleeding. When Dougless saw the man, she would have given anything to have been a doctor and able to stop the bleeding. People died from pneumonia, flu, or a blister that became infected. Dougless passed out aspirin, dabbed wounds with Neosporin ointment, gave out spoonfuls of Pepto-Bismol. She might help people temporarily, but she could do nothing about decaying teeth, about torn ligaments that left people crippled for life, or about appendixes that burst and killed children.

Nor could she do anything about the poverty. Once she tried to talk to Honoria about the vast difference between the way the Stafford family lived and the way the villagers lived. It was then that Dougless learned about sumptuary laws. In America everyone pretended to be equal, saying that a man who was worth millions was no better than some guy who sweated for a living. But no one believed that. Rich criminals got off with light sentences; poor men got maximum sentences.

In the sixteenth century Dougless had found that the idea of equality was a concept that was met with laughter. People were not equal, and by law they were not even allowed to dress equally. In disbelief, Dougless had asked Honoria to explain these sumptuary laws. Earls could wear sable, but barons could wear only the arctic fox. If a man had an income of a hundred pounds a year or less, he could wear velvet in his doublet but not in his gown. If he made twenty pounds a year, he could wear only satin or damask doublets and silk gowns. A man making ten pounds or less a year could not wear cloth costing more than two shillings a yard. Servants could not wear a gown that reached below their calves, and apprentices constantly wore blue (which is why the upper classes rarely wore the color).

On and on the rules went. They covered income, furs, colors, cloth, cut. Dougless was allowed to wear whatever a countess did because she was one of Lady Margaret's ladies. Laughing at it all, Honoria said that everyone wore what he could afford, but if a person was found out, he had to pay a fine to the city coffers; then he returned to wearing whatever he wanted to.

In the twentieth century Dougless had never cared much about clothes. She liked them to be comfortable and long-wearing, but other than that she paid little attention to them. But these beautiful Elizabethan gowns were another matter! In the few days she'd been in the sixteenth century, she'd found the people to be obsessed with clothes. Lady Margaret's ladies spent hours planning gowns.

One day a merchant arrived from Italy, and he and his two cartloads of fabrics had been welcomed into the Presence Chamber as though he'd discovered a cure for flea bites. Dougless had found herself joining in the frenzy of pulling out bolts of narrow fabrics and holding them up to herself and the other women.

Both Nicholas and Kit had joined them. Like most men, they loved being surrounded by laughing, excited, pretty women. To Dougless's embarrassment, but also her delight, Kit had chosen fabric for two gowns for her, saying that it was time she wore her own clothes.

That night in bed, Dougless had lain awake for a while and

thought how different, yet how much alike these Elizabethans were from people of her own time. From reading novels set in Elizabethan times, Dougless had thought the people did nothing but discuss politics. Even with TV, radio, and weekly news magazines, the American people weren't half as well informed as the players in medieval novels seemed to be. But Dougless found these people, like ordinary Americans, much more concerned with clothes and gossip, and the smooth running of the enormous and complicated household, than in what the queen was doing.

In the end, Dougless decided to do what she could to help, but she didn't believe her job was to change sixteenth century life. She had been sent back through time to save Nicholas, and that was what she planned to concentrate on. She was an observer, not a missionary.

However, there was one aspect of medieval life Dougless could not tolerate, and that was the lack of bathing. The people washed their faces and hands and feet, but a full bath was a rare occurrence. Honoria kept warning Dougless against her "frequent" bathing (three baths a week), and Dougless hated that the servants had to haul the tub into the bedroom, then lug in buckets of hot water. The ordeal of preparing a bath was so enormous that after Dougless bathed, two more people would use the water. Once Dougless was the third bather and she saw lice floating on top of the water.

Bathing was close to becoming an obsession with her until Honoria showed her a fountain in the knot garden. The "knots" were hedges that had been planted into intricate designs, with bright flowers in the loops. In the center of the four knots was a tall stone fountain set in a little pool. When Honoria motioned to a child weeding the garden, he ran out of sight behind a wall; then, to Dougless's delight, water came from the top of the fountain and flowed down into the pool. The child had been sent to turn a wheel.

"How lovely," Dougless had said. "Just like a waterfall, or a . . ." Her eyes began to gleam. "Or like a shower." It was at that moment that a plan began to form in her mind. Privately, she talked to the child who had turned the wheel and arranged to pay him a penny if he'd meet her at four A.M. the next morning.

So, at four A.M. the next morning, Dougless tiptoed out of

Honoria's room, down the stairs, and out to the knot garden. She carried her shampoo and rinse, a towel, and a washcloth. The child, sleepy-eyed but smiling, took the penny (which Honoria had given Dougless) and went to turn the wheel. Dougless hesitated for a moment about whether to remove all her clothes or not, but it was still quite dark and it would be a while before the rest of the household woke. So, she slipped off her borrowed robe and the long linen shirt and stepped, naked, under the fountain.

Never has anyone in history enjoyed a shower more! Dougless felt as though years of dirt and oil and sweat were washing off of her. She'd never been able to feel clean using a bathtub, and after weeks of not showering, she felt grimy. She shampooed her hair three times, then conditioned it, shaved her legs and underarms, then rinsed. Heaven. Sheer, perfect heaven.

At long last she stepped out of the fountain, gave a whistle to the boy to stop turning the wheel, then dried and put on her robe.

She was smiling broadly as she started back down the path toward the house. Perhaps she was grinning too broadly to be able to see properly, or maybe it was still too dark yet to see well, because she ran into someone.

"Gloria!" she said before she realized it was the French heiress. "I mean," she said, stumbling, "I guess you're not Gloria, are you? Where's the lioness?" Dougless gasped at what she'd said. She'd rarely seen this girl, but when she had, she'd always been accompanied by her tall, overbearing guardian of a nurse. "I didn't mean—" Dougless began, apologizing.

The heiress didn't reply but sailed past Dougless with her nose in the air. "I am of an age to care for myself. I need no nurse."

Dougless smiled at the girl's plump back. She sounded just like Dougless's fifth graders. They, too, thought they were old enough to take care of themselves. "Sneaked out, did you?" Dougless said, smiling.

The girl turned quickly and glared at Dougless, then her face softened. "She does snore," she said with a bit of a smile; then she looked back at the fountain. "What do you here?"

When Dougless looked at the fountain, to her horror, she saw that the little pool was full of soap bubbles. To Dougless, the bubbles were pollution, but the heiress seemed to think they were wonderful. The girl lifted a handful of suds.

"I took a bath," Dougless said. "Want one?"

The girl gave a delicate shudder. "Nay, my health is most delicate."

"Bathing won't hurt—" Dougless began but stopped. No missionary work, remember? she reminded herself. Moving to stand by the girl, Dougless looked at her closely in the early light. "Who told you you were delicate?"

"Lady Hallet." She looked at Dougless. "My lioness." There were tiny dimples in her cheeks.

Dougless considered what she was about to say, and she knew she was taking a chance, but the child looked as though she needed a friend. "Lady Hallet says you're delicate so she gets to tell you what to eat, and where you can and cannot go, and who may be your friend and who not. In fact, she gets to keep you under her thumb so much that you have to sneak out before daylight just to see the gardens. Is that about right?"

For a moment, the girl's mouth dropped open, but then she stiffened and gave Dougless a haughty look. "Lady Hallet guards me from the lower classes." She looked Dougless up and down.

"Such as me?" Dougless asked, suppressing a smile.

"You are not a princess. Lady Hallet says a princess would not make a spectacle of herself as you do. She says you are not educated. You do not even speak French."

"That's what Lady Hallet says. But what do *you* think of me?"

"That you are not a princess or you would not—"

"No." Dougless cut her off. "Not what Lady Hallet says, what do *you* think?"

The girl gaped at Dougless, obviously not knowing what to say.

Dougless smiled at her. "Do you like Kit?"

The girl looked down at her hands, and Dougless thought her face turned red. "As bad as that?"

"He does not notice me," the girl whispered, tears in her voice. When her head came up and she glared in hate at Dougless, at that moment she looked so much like Gloria that it was eerie. "He looks at you."

"Me?" Dougless gasped. "Kit isn't interested in me."

"All the men like you. Lady Hallet says you are close to being a . . .
a . . ."

Dougless grimaced. "Don't tell me. I've already been called that.
Look . . . What's your name?"

"Lady Allegra Lucinda Nicolletta de Couret," she said proudly.

"But what do your friends call you?"

The girl looked puzzled for a moment, then smiled. "My first nurse
called me Lucy."

"Lucy," Dougless said, smiling, but then she looked at the lightening sky. "I guess we better get back. People will be searching for . . .
us."

Lucy looked startled, then gathered her heavy, expensive skirt and
started to run. She was obviously terrified of being found missing.

"Tomorrow morning," Dougless called after her. "Same time." She
wasn't sure Lucy heard or not.

Dougless went back to the house, ignoring the servants' looks at
her wet hair and her robe. When she opened the door to Honoria's bedroom, she sighed. Now began the long, painful process of dressing, and
she wished just now for the ease and comfort of jeans and a sweatshirt.

After breakfast she sneaked away from the other women to look for
Nicholas. The women were demanding new songs, and already
Dougless's small store was depleted. She was down to humming tunes
and persuading the women to make up their own words. But today she
had to talk to Nicholas. Nothing was going to be changed about his
execution if she didn't talk to him.

She found him in a room that could only be an office, sitting at a
table surrounded by papers. He appeared to be adding a column of figures.

He looked up at her, raised one eyebrow, then looked back down at
his paper.

"Nicholas, you can't ignore me. We must talk. Sometime you're
going to *have* to listen to me."

"I am occupied. Do not plague me with your nonsensical chatter."

"Chatter! Nonsense!" she said in anger. "What I need to say means
more than that."

He gave her another look to be quiet, then returned to his column of numbers.

Dougless glanced at the paper, but the numbers made no sense to her. Some were Roman numerals, some written with a *j* instead of an *i,* and some numbers were Arabic. No wonder he had a difficult time adding them, she thought. Opening the little embroidered pouch that hung at her waist, she took out her solar calculator. She carried it with her because Honoria and the other ladies were always counting stitches in their embroidery, so Dougless often added and subtracted for them so their patterns would be accurate. But she had more important things to do than help him add, she thought as she set the calculator down beside Nicholas's hand.

"You and Kit were gone for a few days. Did you go to Bellwood? Did he show you the secret door?" she asked.

"*Lord* Kit," he said emphatically, "is not your concern. Nor am I. Nor, for that matter, is my mother's household. Madam, you are not wanted here."

She was standing over him, looking down at him and trying to think of what to say to make him listen to her. Then, as she watched, in his anger Nicholas snatched up the calculator and began punching the buttons. He punched in the numbers, hit the plus key between them, then the equal at the end. Still speaking, obviously not even noticing what he'd done, he wrote down the total on his piece of paper.

"And furthermore——" he said as he started to add the second column.

"Nicholas," she whispered, "you remember." She drew in her breath; then louder, she said, "You remember."

"I remember naught," he said angrily, but even as he spoke, he stared down at the calculator in his hands. He realized he'd been using it, but now the knowledge of what it was and how it was used fled him. He dropped the thing as though it were evil.

Seeing him use the calculator was a revelation to Dougless. Somehow, what he'd experienced in the twentieth century was buried in his memory. It was four years before it happened, but now also happened to be four hundred years before Dougless's birth. So many strange experiences were happening to her that she couldn't question his knowledge of a calculator. But if he remembered that little machine, then he remembered *her.*

She went to her knees beside him and put her hands on his arm. "Nicholas, you do remember."

Nicholas wanted to pull away from her, but he couldn't. What was it about the woman? he asked himself. She was pretty, yes, but he'd seen women more beautiful. He'd certainly been around women more pleasing than she was. But this woman . . . this woman never left his mind.

"Please," she whispered, "don't close your mind to me. Don't fight me. You might remember more if you'd allow yourself."

"I remember naught," he said firmly, looking down into her eyes. He'd like to take her hair out of the little cap, out of its braid.

"You *do* remember. How else would you know how to use the calculator?"

"I did not—" he began, then glanced at the thing sitting on top of the papers. But he knew that, somehow, he had known how to use it; he'd known how to add the numbers with it. He jerked his arm from under her hands. "Leave me."

"Nicholas, please listen to me," she pleaded. "You must tell me if Kit has shown you the door at Bellwood or not. That information will give us an idea of how long we have until he's . . . he's drowned." Until Lettice orders him killed, she thought. "It may be weeks yet or even months, but if he's shown you the door, his . . . accident is a matter of days from now. Please, Nicholas, don't fight me on this."

He was not going to allow her to control him. He was not going to be like the rest of the household and follow her about begging for her favors. Any day now he expected her to ask for a purse of gold in exchange for another song. And his mother was so enamored of her that she'd no doubt give the gold. As it was, Lady Margaret showered this woman with dresses and fans, and dug into the Stafford jewel chests to lend her all sorts of riches.

"I know of no door," Nicholas said, lying. It had been but days since Kit had shown him the door at Bellwood. That this witch-woman knew of it was further proof that she was not what she seemed.

Dougless sat back on her heels, her green satin skirt billowing about her, and sighed in relief. "Good," she whispered. "Good." She didn't want to think that Kit was close to death. If Kit didn't die, then perhaps Lettice wouldn't have a chance to get her hooks into Nicholas, and the great injustice would be prevented. And, besides, perhaps after Kit was saved, she would be sent back to the twentieth century.

"You care for my brother?" Nicholas asked, looking down at her.

She smiled. "He seems like a nice guy, but he'll never be . . ." She trailed off. The love of my life, she'd almost said. Looking into Nicholas's blue eyes, she remembered the night they'd made love. She remembered his laughter and his interest in the modern world. Without thinking, she reached her hand out toward him. He didn't seem to think either as he took her hand and raised her fingertips to his lips.

"Colin," she whispered.

"Sir," came a voice from the doorway. "My pardon."

Nicholas dropped her hand, and Dougless, knowing the moment was lost, rose and smoothed her skirts. "You'll tell me about the door, won't you? We'll have to keep watch over Kit," she said softly.

Nicholas didn't look at her. All the woman spoke of was his brother. She haunted his mind, yet she seemed to feel no such pull toward him. Her thoughts were of Kit alone. "Go," he murmured, then louder, "Go and sing your songs to the others. It will take more than a song to enchant me. And take that." He looked at the calculator as though it were something from the devil.

"You can keep it and use it if you want."

He turned hard eyes toward her. "I know not how."

With a sigh, Dougless took the calculator, then left the room. So far, every attempt she'd made to talk to Nicholas had failed. But at least now she was beginning to understand that he thought he was protecting his family from her. She couldn't help smiling at that thought. The Nicholas she'd loved so much had also put his family first. In the twentieth century, he'd wanted to return to a possible execution in order to save his family's honor.

This man *was* the Nicholas she'd come to love, she thought, smiling. On the surface, what with the women on the table and in the arbor, he had seemed like the rake the history books had portrayed him to be.

And of course she'd hated his anger and animosity toward her. And it didn't help any that the rest of his family couldn't be nicer to her, with only Nicholas being hostile. But, under it all, she knew that he was the man she'd come to love, the man who put others before himself.

This thought made her forgive him for his hostility. What if she'd had an ulterior motive for wanting to be near his family? It wasn't good to be as trusting as the family was. Nicholas was the one who was right. He should mistrust her. Since he consciously remembered nothing of her from before, he had no reason to trust her. And what with the bond between them and the way he "heard" her calling him at times, he had every reason to believe her to be a witch.

But he did remember, she thought. He said he remembered nothing, but he'd remembered the calculator enough to use it correctly. She wondered if there were other things he remembered and she began to think of the contents of her tote bag. What else could she show him that might further jog his memory?

In the Presence Chamber everyone was in a flurry. It seemed that the caterer's goods had arrived. Dougless learned that this was a man who traveled all over England to buy special foods for the Stafford family, then sent them back once a month. This month he'd sent back pineapples and cocoa powder that had been imported from Mexico to Spain, then into England. There was also sugar from Brazil.

Standing back and watching as the women exclaimed over these delicacies, Dougless couldn't help but think how the twentieth century took food for granted. Americans could have any food at any time of the year.

As Dougless looked at the chocolate powder, carefully wrapped in cloth, she thought of the American picnic she'd cooked for Nicholas: fried chicken, potato salad, deviled eggs, and chocolate brownies.

Suddenly an idea hit her. She'd heard that smells and flavors were some of the strongest memory generators. She knew that certain foods reminded her of her grandmother, Amanda, for there was always an astonishing variety of food in her grandmother's house. And the smell of jasmine always reminded Dougless of her mother. If Nicholas was served the same meal he'd eaten in the twentieth century, would it help him remember more of the time he'd spent with her?

Dougless went to Lady Margaret and asked permission to be allowed to prepare the evening meal. Lady Margaret was pleased with the idea, but horrified that Dougless wanted to work in the kitchen herself. She proposed that Dougless tell the Groom of the Pantry what she wanted and that she talk to the Groom of the Kitchen (the one "for the mouth") and not go to the kitchen herself.

Dougless did her best to insist; besides, Lady Margaret had piqued her curiosity about the kitchen. And what in the world was a Groom of the Kitchen "for the mouth"?

After the long, sumptuous dinner, Dougless went downstairs to the kitchen and was awed at what she saw: room after room with enormous fireplaces, huge tables, and many, many people scurrying about. But she soon discovered that each person had a job. There were two slaughtermen, two bakers, two brewers, a maltmaker, a couple of hop men, laundresses, children to do odd jobs, and even a man called a roughcaster whose job it was to patch the plaster when it fell down. There were also clerks to record every penny of expense. And all of these people had helpers.

Huge carcasses of beef and pork were delivered into the kitchen in wagons, then passed through to the slaughtering room. Storage rooms, bigger than houses, were filled with barrels. Sausages as big as an arm and several feet long hung from the tall ceilings. In two rooms, set back in the wall high above the double fireplaces, were tiers of beds with straw mattresses where many of the kitchen workers slept.

The head groom took her through the rooms, and after Dougless was able to close her mouth in awe at the size of the place and at the vast quantity of food prepared in the kitchen room, she began to tell the man what she wanted to do.

Swallowing, she saw crates of chickens brought in; then a large woman began wringing necks. Cauldrons of water were put on to boil to scald the chickens so their feathers could be plucked, and she was told that the softest of these chicken feathers were saved to be used for pillows for the servants.

She was surprised that potatoes were found in a sixteenth-century household but not eaten often. But under Dougless's directions, women were soon set to peeling potatoes, and others to boiling eggs that were much smaller than twentieth-century eggs.

To get the flour for the batter for the chicken and for the brownies, Dougless was taken to the bolting room. Here flour was repeatedly sifted through fabric sieves, each one of increasing fineness. Dougless began to understand why pure white bread, called manchet, was so prized. The lower the status of the person in the household, the coarser his bread. Bread that had been bolted only once still had lots of bran—and sand and dirt—in it. Only the family and their immediate retainers got bread that had been bolted until it was perfectly clean.

Dougless knew there would be enough chicken, eggs, and potatoes for the whole household, but the brownies with the precious, expensive chocolate would be for the family only. One of the cooks helped her decide how much chicken got coated with rough flour and how much got flour from the next bolting, how much from the next, and so on. Dougless wasn't about to give a lecture on equality, especially since she knew the finest flour had no bran in it and many of the vitamins were missing, and therefore was not as nutritious as the flour that had been bolted fewer times. Dougless just concentrated on preparing a meal that could feed an army.

The meal, which had been so easy when prepared in a modern English kitchen and done on a small scale, was not easy in the sixteenth century. Everything had to be made in vats and from scratch. There was no mustard or mayonnaise from the grocery for the eggs and pota-toes. All the pepper, kept under lock and key, was whole and someone had to pick out the stones; then the peppercorns had to be crushed in a mortar the size of a bathtub. The nuts for the brownies didn't come in a plastic bag but had to be shelled.

As Dougless supervised, she watched and learned. Her only moment of panic came when she saw that the cake pans were lined with paper that had been written on. She watched in horror when she saw chocolate batter being poured over a deed that she was sure had been signed by Henry the Seventh.

By the time the meal was nearly ready to be served, Dougless knew that the meal had to be a picnic. As though she'd always ruled an army, she sent men into the orchard to spread cloths on the ground, then had pillows brought down from upstairs.

Supper was late that evening, not served until six P.M., but from the looks on people's faces as they began to taste everything, they thought the wait was worth it. They ate their potato salad with spoons and devoured platefuls of deviled eggs. They loved the high seasoning of the chicken.

Dougless sat across from Nicholas and watched him so closely she hardly ate. But as far as she could see, nothing sparked a memory.

At the end of the meal, the servants triumphantly carried out silver platters heaped high with nut-filled chewy brownies. At the first bite there were tears of gratitude in the eyes of some of the diners.

But Dougless looked only at Nicholas. He bit; he chewed. Then slowly, he looked at Dougless, and her heart leaped to her throat. He does remember, she thought. He remembers something.

Nicholas put down the brownie; then, not knowing why he did it, he removed the ring from his left hand and handed it to her.

Dougless put out a shaking hand and took the ring. It was an emerald ring, the same ring he'd given her on that day at Arabella's house when she'd first made brownies for him. She could see by his expression that he was puzzled by his action.

"You gave me this ring before," she said softly. "When I cooked this meal for you the first time, you gave me this same ring."

Nicholas could only stare at her. He started to ask her to explain, but Kit's laughter broke the spell of the moment.

"I do not blame you." Kit laughed. "These cakes are worth gold. Here," he said as he pulled off a simple gold ring and gave it to Dougless.

Smiling and frowning at the same time, she took the ring Kit offered. The ring was worth nothing compared to Nicholas's emerald, but had the values been reversed, Nicholas's ring would have been worth much more to Dougless. "Thank you," she murmured, then looked back at Nicholas. But he was looking away now and she knew that what he had remembered was gone.

TWENTY-FIVE

*Y*ou *are too silent, brother,"* Kit said, smiling at Nicholas. "You should come and make merry. Dougless is to teach us a card game called poker this night."

Nicholas looked away from his brother. Something had happened tonight, he thought, something he couldn't understand. At supper he had bitten into one of the chocolate cakes the woman had prepared and he'd known, quite suddenly, without words, that she was not his enemy.

Even as he handed her his ring, he told himself he was being a fool. Often, when it came to this woman, he was sure he was the one sane person in his household. He was the only person who did not believe her to be a gift from God. And if her good works did turn out to be treachery, he would be the only one who was able to see her as she truly was.

But this evening, as he'd eaten that wonderful cake, images had flashed across his mind. He saw her with her hair loose, her legs bare, and sitting on an odd two-wheeled metal frame of sorts. He saw her with water pouring down over her beautiful, nude body. And he saw her clutching his emerald ring to her breast and looking at him with love. Without a thought, he had slipped the ring from his finger and given it to her, because, somehow, the ring seemed to belong to her.

"Nicholas?" Kit was saying. "Are you well?"

"Yes," Nicholas said absently. "I am well."

"Do you join us in this new game?"

"Nay," Nicholas murmured. He didn't want to be near the woman, didn't want her to cause him to see images of something he knew had not happened. It was better for him to stay away from her. If he spent time with her, perhaps he would begin to listen to her, even begin to believe her absurd stories of past and future.

"Nay, I do not go," he said to Kit. "I work this night."

"Work?" Kit asked, his voice teasing. "No women? When I think on it, have you had a woman to your bed since Lady Dougless arrived?"

"She is no—" Nicholas began. He suddenly had another image of her smiling down at him, of her hair soft and full about her shoulders.

Kit laughed knowingly. "It goes that way, does it? I cannot blame you; the woman is beautiful. Do you mean to make her your mistress after your marriage?"

"Nay!" Nicholas said forcibly. "The woman is naught to me. Take her away with you. I wish never to see her again, never to hear her voice. I wish she had never come into my life."

Kit stepped back, still smiling. "So the thunderbolt has hit," he said, obviously enjoying Nicholas's agony.

Nicholas came out of his chair, ready to do battle over his brother's smirking, knowing tone. But Kit backed toward the door, and when Nicholas came close, Kit left the room, laughing loudly as he shut the door in his brother's face.

Nicholas sat down at the table again and tried to give his attention to the accounts before him, but all he could think of was the red-haired woman. He knew that she was laughing now, amused at what she was doing. He knew that, somehow, he'd feel it if she wasn't happy.

He walked toward the window, turned its latch, opened it, then looked down into the garden. Unwanted, an image came to him. In his mind's eye, he saw another garden. It was night, and it was raining, and the woman was calling to him. He saw lights, strange, purple-blue lights on poles, and he saw himself in the rain, clean-shaven and wearing strange clothes.

Pulling away from the window, Nicholas slammed it shut, then rubbed his hands over his eyes as though to clear the vision. He would not let this woman ensorcell him. He must not let her control his mind!

Leaving the office, he went to his bedchamber, poured himself a tall goblet of sack, then downed it. Only after he'd downed a second and third helping as quickly as possible, did he feel the warmth of the wine coursing through his veins. He would drown his images of her. He would drink until he couldn't hear her, see her, smell her . . . or remember her.

For a while the wine worked and he was able to still the images in his head. Content, feeling calm, Nicholas stretched out on his bed and was asleep instantly.

But then the images came again, this time in the form of dreams.

"You must tell me if Kit has shown you the door," he heard the woman saying. "Tell me if you cut your arm." "Kit died and you caused it." "What if you are wrong?" The woman's voice grew louder, urgent. "What if you are wrong and Kit dies because you won't listen?"

Nicholas awoke sweating, and the rest of the night he lay with his eyes open, afraid to go back to sleep. Something had to be done about the woman if she wouldn't let him sleep. Something had to be done.

TWENTY-SIX

*A*t four A.M. *Dougless crept out of the house* to go to the fountain to take a shower. Yesterday a couple of the ladies had been talking about the suds in the fountain and Lady Margaret had looked at Dougless knowingly. Flushing, Dougless looked away, wondering if there was anything that went on in the Stafford household that Lady Margaret didn't know about.

Now Dougless smiled in memory. If it weren't all right for her to use the fountain for a shower, no doubt Lady Margaret would have told her so.

Even in the faint light, Dougless could see Lucy waiting for her. Poor lonely kid, she thought. Since yesterday, Dougless had asked questions and found out that Lucy and her guardian had been brought to England to the Stafford household when Lucy was just three years old. It was believed that she'd make a better wife for Kit if she knew English ways and got to know her husband's family before marriage.

But from the moment Lucy had arrived, Lady Hallet had denied anyone access to the child, who had been very ill from the voyage across the Channel and the rough road journey across England. By the time Lucy was well, no one seemed to remember she was living with them.

Something Dougless had noticed about the sixteenth century was that the adults didn't idolize children the way twentieth-century Americans did. It had surprised Dougless to find out that most of Lady Margaret's ladies were married, and two of them had young children at their homes, which were often a hundred miles away. The women didn't seem to be in any throes of agony over whether or not they were spending "quality time" with their children. Dougless once, over embroidery—which they did very well and at which Dougless was hopelessly clumsy—mentioned that in her country women spent whole days with their children, entertaining them, teaching them, and trying never to be bored by them. The women had been horrified by this idea. They believed you should ignore children until they were of marriageable age. After all, they said, children died easily and their souls weren't formed until they were of age.

Dougless had returned to her embroidery. Heretofore, she'd thought parents had always, throughout time, adored their children. She'd thought that mothers were always agonizing over whether or not they gave enough to their children. But there seemed to be more differences between the twentieth century and the sixteenth than just clothes and politics.

Now, looking at Lucy, she could feel the girl's loneliness. She was a stranger in a house where she'd lived since she was a toddler, yet she knew fewer people than Dougless did.

"Hello," Dougless said.

Lucy smiled broadly, then caught herself and resumed her stiff pose. "Good morn," she said formally. "Do you mean to do this again?" she asked as Dougless started to remove her robe, then turned away as Dougless stepped, nude, into the fountain.

"Every day," Dougless said as she gave a whistle for the boy to turn the wheel. She gasped at the icy water, but a clean body was worth some discomfort.

Lucy remained turned away while Dougless bathed and washed her hair, but when the girl didn't leave, Dougless sensed that there was something she wanted. But perhaps it was only that she wanted a friend.

Dougless got out of the fountain-shower, dried, then turned to Lucy. "This morning we're going to play charades. Maybe you'd like to join us."

"Will Lord Christopher attend?" she asked quickly.

"Ah," Dougless said, understanding. "I don't think so."

Lucy slumped down on a bench as though she were a beach ball that had suddenly been deflated. "Nay, I will not attend."

As Dougless toweled her wet hair, she looked at Lucy thoughtfully. How did a dumpy-figured, not-very-pretty adolescent capture the attention of a gorgeous hunk like Kit?

"He talks of you," Lucy said sullenly.

Dougless sat beside her on the bench. "Kit talks about *me?* When do you see him?"

"He visits me most days."

Kit would, Dougless thought. He seemed awfully thoughtful and kind—and he probably considered visiting his future wife his duty. "Kit talks to you of me, but what do you talk to him about?"

Lucy wrung her hands in her lap. "I say naught."

"Nothing? You don't say anything to him? He comes to visit you every day and you just sit there like a bump on a log?"

"Lady Hallet says it would be unseemly for me to—"

Dougless couldn't control her anger. "Lady Hallet! That ogre? That woman is so ugly that the sight of the back of her head would crack a mirror."

Lucy giggled. "A hawk once went to her instead of to its master. I thought the hawk mistook her for its mate."

Dougless laughed. "With that beak of hers I can understand the mistake."

Lucy laughed aloud, then covered her mouth. "I wish I were like you," she said wistfully. "If I could make my Kit laugh . . ."

She didn't have to say more to make Dougless understand. "My Kit," as in *"my* Nicholas."

"Maybe we could find a way to make Kit laugh. I was thinking about doing a vaudeville routine with Honoria, but maybe you and I could do it together."

"'Vaudeville'? 'Routine'? I do not believe Lady Hallet will—"

"Lucy"—Dougless took the girl's hands in hers—"something that I've found that hasn't changed over time is that if you want the man, you have to fight for him. Now, what you want is for Kit to notice you, and what you *need* is a little self-confidence. You also need to trust your own judgment and not someone else's. So maybe we can accomplish a few of these things by putting on a show. Kit will see that you're no longer a little girl—and so will Lady Hallet, for that matter—and we'll both have a good time. So how about it?"

"I . . . I don't know. I . . ."

"What did one duke say to the other duke?"

Lucy looked blank.

"'That was no lady, that was my wife.'"

Lucy's mouth opened in shock; then she giggled.

"Where does a three-hundred-pound canary sit?" Dougless paused. "Anywhere he wants to."

Lucy laughed harder.

"You'll do," Dougless said. "You'll do very well. Now, let's plan. When can we rehearse? No excuses. You're the heiress, remember, and Lady Hallet works for you."

By the time Dougless got back to the house, it was full daylight. She knew that many people had an idea of what she was doing each morning, for there were no secrets in the household, but everyone politely refrained from asking her point-blank.

In the mornings Lady Margaret was too busy to want any new games, so Dougless wandered into the gardens and soon found herself drawing the ABCs in the dirt for three children who worked in the kitchen. Before she realized it, it was time for dinner.

Neither Nicholas nor Kit came to dinner. Dougless vowed that after the meal she would look for Nicholas and again try to talk to him. At least now that she knew that Kit hadn't shown Nicholas the secret door at Bellwood, she knew Kit's "accident" was not imminent.

Smiling, she left the table and allowed Honoria to again try to teach her how to make lace from a bit of linen. Honoria was making a beautiful cuff with the word *Dougless* in it, surrounded by odd little birds and animals.

Bent over her embroidery frame, Dougless felt at peace. She was going to be able to help Lucy, and yesterday Nicholas had remembered something about their time in the twentieth century. She glanced at the big emerald ring on her thumb. Now that his memory had been jogged, surely he'd soon remember more. She was going to be able to accomplish what she had failed to do the first time.

TWENTY-SEVEN

*N*icholas's head hurt, and he didn't feel too steady on his feet. He'd seen no more images after he stopped sleeping last night, but this morning he was still haunted by the dreams. "What if you are wrong?" he kept hearing in the woman's voice. Wrong about what? About her being a witch? The images she'd put into his head were proof that he was right.

Groggily, he went downstairs to sword practice. He lunged with his sword at the man before him, not seeing the startled look on the knight's face. Nicholas wasn't usually aggressive in sword practice, but today, what with his head pounding and his anger, he felt aggressive. Again and again he lunged. The knight stepped back, his sword at his side.

"Sir?" the man said, astonished.

"Do you mean to give me a good fight or not?" Nicholas challenged, then lunged again. Perhaps if he was tired enough, he wouldn't be able to hear the woman or see her inside his mind.

Nicholas wore out three men before a fourth, fresh man brought him low. Nicholas went right when he should have gone left, and the man's blade neatly sliced his left forearm open almost to the bone. While Nicholas stood there staring at his bleeding arm, an image came to him. But this image was different, he didn't just see it, he was *in* the dream.

He was walking beside the red-haired woman in a strange place, and they stopped before a building with glass windows, but windows such as he'd never dreamed existed, with glass so clear it was as though it were not there. A machine, a big, strange machine with wheels went by, but he didn't seem to be interested in it. Instead, he was intent only on talking to the woman and telling her of the scar on his arm. He was telling her that Kit had drowned on the day he'd hurt his arm at sword practice.

He came out of the dream as abruptly as he went into it, and when he returned to the present, he was lying on the ground, his men hovering anxiously over him, one of them trying to stop the flow of blood.

Nicholas had no time to give over to pain. "Saddle two horses," he said quietly, "one with a woman's saddle."

"Ride?" asked one man. "You mean to ride with a woman? But, my lord, your arm—"

Nicholas turned to him with cold eyes. "For the Montgomery woman, she—"

"She can ride only enough to keep from falling from the horse," said another man, contempt in his voice.

Awkwardly, and with help, Nicholas got to his feet. "Bind my arm so the bleeding stops, then saddle two horses—with men's saddles. Do it now," he said. "Waste no time." His voice was low, but there was command in it.

"Should I fetch the woman?" another man asked.

Nicholas, his arm held out while a man bound a cloth tightly about it, looked up at the windows of the house. "She will come," he said with confidence. "We do but wait."

Hunched over her embroidery frame, Dougless was listening to one of the ladies telling a juicy story about a woman who'd tried to bed another woman's husband. Dougless was listening to the story with all her attention when suddenly a fierce, burning pain stabbed her left fore-arm.

With a cry of pain, Douglass fell back on the stool and landed on the floor. "My arm. Something has hurt my arm." She cradled her arm to her, tears of pain coming instantly.

Leaping to her feet, Honoria ran to kneel by Douglass. "Rub her hands, do not let her faint," Honoria commanded as she quickly untied Douglass's sleeve at the shoulder and slipped it down. Honoria winced at Douglass's moan of pain as she had to pull Douglass's arm away from her breast to remove the sleeve. Once the sleeve was off, Honoria pushed the linen undersleeve up to look at Douglass's arm.

There was nothing wrong with it. The skin was not even reddened.

"I see nothing," Honoria said, suddenly afraid. She'd grown to care for Douglass, but the woman was very odd. Sir Nicholas accused her of being a witch. Was this pain a manifestation of her witchcraft?

The pain in her arm was blinding, but when Douglass looked down, she saw that there was nothing wrong with her forearm. "It feels as though it's been cut," she whispered, "as though someone has cut it deeply with a knife."

She used her right hand to rub her forearm, but she could barely feel her own touch. "I can feel the cut," she whispered, trying not to whimper. The women around her were looking at her strangely, as though Douglass weren't quite sane.

Suddenly, Douglass could hear Nicholas's voice in her head. They were in bed together and she'd touched the scar on his left forearm. He said he'd been injured on the day Kit had drowned.

Douglass was on her feet instantly. "Where do the men practice swords?" she asked, trying not to sound frantic. Please, God, she prayed, do not let me be too late.

At her remark, the other women seemed to be assured of Douglass's lack of sanity, but Honoria answered. Nothing Douglass did could surprise her. "To the back, past the maze, through the northeast gate."

Nodding, Douglass wasted no more time. She grabbed her skirts, thanked heaven for the farthingale that held the skirts away from her legs, then began to run. In the hall she crashed into a man, and when he fell, she leaped over him. A woman in the kitchen was getting something off a high shelf. Crouching, Dougless kept running under her arms. A wagonload of barrels had come untied, and Dougless leaped five barrels, one after another, looking like an oddly dressed Olympic hurdler. She ran past Lady Margaret outside the maze, but when the woman called to her, Dougless didn't answer. When the gate in the wall at the back of the maze stuck, Dougless lifted her foot and smashed it open.

Once outside the gardens, she ran as fast as she could.

Nicholas, his arm swathed in a bloody bandage, was sitting on a horse and watching her progress toward him.

"Kit!" Dougless screamed, still running. "We have to save Kit."

Dougless didn't say any more because a man swooped her into his arms and dumped her onto a horse, and, oh, thank all that was holy, it was a man's saddle. She jammed her feet into the stirrups, grabbed the reins, and looked at Nicholas.

"We ride!" he shouted as he kicked his horse forward.

The wind in her eyes stung and her arm still hurt, but most of Dougless's concentration was on following Nicholas. Behind them thundered three men trying to keep up with them.

They ran across plowed fields, through gardens of cabbages and turnips. They ran through the dirty, barren yards of peasants, and for once Dougless gave no thought to equality as their horses' hooves destroyed crops and even once, a shed. They ran into the woods, tree branches low overhead. Dougless put her head down on the horse's neck and kept going. Leaving the trail, Nicholas headed into the forest. Even though there was no path, the forest floor was clear of deadfall, for even twigs were needed for firewood, so, except for the overhanging branches, their way was unhampered.

Dougless never thought to question how Nicholas knew where Kit was, but she was sure he did know. Just as he'd known she would come when he hurt his arm, he knew where his brother was.

They broke through the trees into a clearing, and ahead, surrounded by more trees, sparkled a pretty, spring-fed pond. Nicholas was off his horse while it was still running, and Dougless followed him, tearing her heavy, long skirt when it caught on the saddle.

When she reached the pond and looked down, what she saw chilled her. Three men were carrying Kit's nude, lifeless body out of the water. Kit's body was facedown, his long dark hair falling forward, his neck limp and lifeless.

Nicholas was staring at his brother. "No," he said, then, "NO!"

Shoving past Nicholas, Dougless went to the men holding Kit. "Put him down here," she ordered. "On his back."

Kit's men hesitated.

"Obey her!" Nicholas bellowed from close behind her.

"Pray," she said to the man nearest her as she straddled Kit. "I need all the help I can get. Pray for a miracle."

Instantly, the men went to their knees, their hands clasped, their heads bowed.

Nicholas knelt before Kit's inert body and placed his hands on Kit's wet head. When he looked at Dougless, his eyes showed that he trusted her in whatever she did to his beloved brother's inert body.

Dougless pushed Kit's head back to make a straight line of his air ducts, then began to give him mouth-to-mouth resuscitation. Nicholas's eyes widened as he watched, but he did not try to stop her. "Kit, please," she whispered. "Please live," then she again forced air into his lungs.

When she was ready to give up hope, Kit coughed, then was silent.

Nicholas's head came up as he looked at Dougless. "Come on, come on," she said. "Breathe, damn you!" With Nicholas's help, she pushed Kit onto his side.

Kit gave another cough, then another, then he vomited water as his lungs cleared.

Rolling off of him, Dougless put her face in her hands and burst into tears.

Nicholas held his brother's shoulders while Kit got rid of the water. A knight draped his cape about Kit's bare lower half, while the other men stared down at Dougless. Her hair was down, her dress torn, she'd lost a shoe, and Nicholas's blood was on one sleeve and the other sleeve was missing.

At last Kit quit coughing and leaned back against his brother. Tiredly, Kit looked at Nicholas's arm that was wrapped tightly about his chest. His brother's blood trickled down Kit's bare, wet chest. Kit looked up at his men, and saw all six of them staring down at the Montgomery woman who was crying softly into her hands.

"This is a fine way to treat a man back from the dead," Kit managed to croak out. "My brother bleeds on me, and a pretty woman sheds tears. Is no one glad that I yet live?"

If anything, Nicholas's grip on Kit tightened. Dougless looked up, wiped her eyes with the back of her hand, and sniffed. A knight handed her a handkerchief. "Thank you," she murmured, then blew her nose.

"The maid has saved you," one of the knights said, awe in his voice. "It is a miracle."

"Witchcraft," muttered another man.

Nicholas looked up at the man, his eyes black with threat. "You call her witch again and you will not live to repeat the words."

The men knew that Nicholas meant what he said.

When Dougless looked at Nicholas, she knew that his hatred of her was over, and that now he'd listen to her. She blew her nose again, then tried to stand. When she stumbled, one of the men helped her up, but they were all looking at her as though she were part saint, part demon.

"Oh, heavens," she said, "stop looking at me like that. This is a common practice in my country. We have lots of water and people are always drowning. Really, what I did was no miracle."

To her relief, she could see the men believed her, but probably only because they wanted to.

"Now, I want all of you to stop standing around and get busy. Poor Kit must be freezing, and, Nicholas, your arm is a mess. You two help Kit, and you two see if there are any clean bandages for Nicholas's arm, and you two go see if the horses survived the trip. Now go! Scurry!"

One advantage women throughout time have had is that the little boy in men always remembers a time when women were all-powerful. The men bumped into each other as they ran to do her bidding.

"You have a shrew on your hands, brother," Kit said happily. Nicholas still held his brother tightly, as though he were afraid Kit would die if he released him. "Perhaps you would fetch my clothes for me," Kit said softly to Nicholas, then shook his head as Dougless started for Kit's clothes piled on the bank of the pond.

Slowly, Nicholas released his hold on his brother and started to rise, but he swayed on his feet. The loss of blood, combined with his ride and his fear, had weakened him. Standing to one side, Dougless watched as Nicholas slowly made his way to the bank, picked up Kit's clothes, then took them back to his brother.

Kit accepted the clothes with the solemnity of a king receiving the crown at his coronation, then he grinned. "Sit down, little brother," he said.

When Nicholas took a step, he swayed, so Dougless caught him in her arms and led him to sit down; then she sat beside him. Turning, Nicholas put his head on her lap.

Kit laughed. "Now that is more the brother I know." He looked up as his men came back into the clearing.

Dougless looked down at Nicholas and stroked his sweat-dampened black curls. This was, at long last, her Nicholas. Here again was the man she'd loved and lost.

"Do you grow onion-eyed again?"

His words, so heart-stoppingly familiar, did indeed bring tears to her eyes. "The wind," she murmured. "Nothing more." She smiled at him. "Give me your arm. I want to see what you've done to it."

Obediently, he held up his arm, and her stomach lurched. The bandage was saturated with blood and his hand was encrusted, as well as his sleeve above the wrappings.

"How bad is it?" she whispered.

"I do not believe I will lose the arm. The leeches—"

"Leeches!" Dougless said. "You can't afford more blood loss." Glancing up, she saw that Kit was now dressed, but he was so weak that he was being supported as the men led him to his horse.

"Nicholas, get up. We're going back to take care of that arm," Dougless said.

"Nay," he said. "I would the two of us stayed here."

He had that look in his eye, that soft, sexy, hooded look that promised he would make Dougless glad she stayed.

"No," she said, even as she bent down to kiss him.

"A woman's 'no' pleases me much," Nicholas said softly, his uninjured arm moving up to her hair.

Their lips didn't meet.

"Oh, no, you don't," Dougless said sternly. "Up! I mean it, Nicholas, get up. You aren't going to sweet-talk me into doing whatever you want while your arm turns to gangrene. We're going back to the house and clean up the wound; then we'll get Honoria to sew it back together."

"Honoria?"

"She can sew better than anyone else."

He frowned. "The arm does pain me some." Slowly, reluctantly, he lifted his head from her lap, but, as he moved past her lips, he planted a quick, sweet kiss on them.

They rode slowly back to the Stafford house, and as they approached, Dougless tried to straighten her spine and her clothing. But her dress, torn and bloody, was beyond repair. In the wild ride, she'd lost her little pearl-studded cap. As they drew nearer to the house, Dougless remembered running past Lady Margaret and not speaking, and, too, practically before the lady's face, she'd kicked the gate open. And now here she was, looking like something off the streets, riding astride, her skirts up to her calves.

"I don't think I can face your mother," Dougless said to Nicholas.

He gave her a puzzled look, but turned away when he heard a shout. One of the guards had ridden ahead, so the news of Kit's near-death had reached the household. Lady Margaret and all her ladies were waiting to greet them. At the sight, Dougless swallowed in fear. Would she again be accused of witchcraft?

As soon as Kit dismounted, Lady Margaret clasped her eldest son to her; then she turned to Dougless.

"I beg your pardon, my lady," Dougless said, "for my appearance. I—"

Taking Dougless's face in her hands, Lady Margaret kissed her on both cheeks. "You are beautiful to me," she said, her voice full of her gratitude.

Dougless felt her face grow pink with embarrassment, but also with pleasure.

Turning to Nicholas, Lady Margaret glanced at his bloody arm, then yelled, "Leech!"

At that, Dougless put herself between mother and son. "Please, my lady, may I see to his arm? Please," she whispered. "Honoria will help me."

Lady Margaret seemed to be torn. "Do you have a tablet for wounds?"

"No, just soap and water and disinfectant. Please, let me care for him."

After a look over Dougless's shoulder to Nicholas, Lady Margaret nodded.

Once upstairs in Nicholas's bedchamber, Dougless gave Honoria a list of things she'd need. "The strongest, harshest soap you have, something with lye in it; then I want a kettle for boiling water, and I'll need needles—silver needles—white silk thread, beeswax, my tote bag, and the cleanest, whitest linen in this house." Three maids scurried to do her bidding.

When she was alone with Nicholas, she had him soak his bandaged arm in a long copper pan of boiled water she had taken from the kettle over the fireplace. He was bare from the waist up, and as efficient as Dougless tried to be, she could feel his hot eyes on her.

"Tell me of what we once were each to the other."

Dougless put more water on to boil. "You came to me in my time." Now that he was ready to listen, she found herself reluctant to talk. The Nicholas who accused her of witchcraft had no power over her, but this Nicholas, who looked at her with sparkling eyes, made her toes curl.

When she went back to him, she saw that the dried blood had softened away from the bandages. Propping his arm on the pan, she took small sewing scissors and began to snip away the encrusted bandage.

"Were we lovers?" he asked softly.

Dougless's breath drew in sharply. "I cannot do this if you don't hold still."

"I did not move, you did," he said, then watched her for a while. "Were we together long? Did we love much?"

"Oh, Nicholas," she said and found to her shame that tears were again coming to her eyes. "It wasn't like that. You came to me for a *reason*. You had been found guilty of treason, and you came to my time because Lady Margaret's papers had been found. You and I researched to find out who had betrayed you."

Slowly, she began to peel strips of linen off his arm.

"Did we find the truth?"

"No," she said softly. "*We* did not. I found out the truth after you went back, after you . . ." She looked up at him. "After you had been executed."

Nicholas's face was changing, losing its look of sex. He could no longer continue to not listen to the woman. She had known about the servants in the closet when he and Arabella had been fumbling on the table. And she had known about Kit. His heart hammered in his chest when he thought how close he had come to losing Kit. If the woman had not been there, Kit would have died.

And it would have been Nicholas's fault, he thought. His own fault and no one else's, because he'd lied when she'd asked him about the cabinet at Bellwood. She had said that Kit showed Nicholas the cabinet a week before his death, but Nicholas had not listened. He had heard only that she spoke of his handsome brother. His jealousy had nearly cost his brother's life.

Nicholas leaned back against the pillows. "What more do you know?"

She opened her mouth to tell him of Lettice, but she couldn't, not yet. It was too soon and he didn't yet trust her enough. She knew he loved Lettice deeply. He had so much wanted to leave the twentieth century—and Dougless—to get back to his beloved wife. It would take more time before she had his trust enough that she could talk to him about his beloved Lettice. Certainly, now was not the time.

"I will tell you everything later," she said, "but now I must see to your arm."

Dougless continued pulling the bandage from his wound until she at last saw the deep slash. She'd never been good with bloody wounds, but years of teaching elementary school had taught her to look at chipped teeth, blood-dripping wounds, and broken limbs while remaining cheerful for the child's sake. She knew Nicholas's wound needed a doctor, but she also knew that now she was the best that was available.

When Honoria and the maids returned with all Dougless had

ordered, she set them to work. Honoria did not allow the maids to question anything Dougless told them to do. The four women removed their outer sleeves, rolled up the linen sleeves above the elbow; then Dougless had them scour their hands and arms while she boiled needles and silk thread.

The only sedative-type pills she had in her tote bag were what she took to calm her nervous stomach. She wished she had good ol' Valium, but she didn't. She gave Nicholas two pills and hoped they'd make him drowsy.

They did, and within minutes, he was asleep.

When all the equipment was as clean as she could get it, Dougless set Honoria to sewing Nicholas's arm. Honoria blanched, but Dougless insisted because Honoria's stitches were fine and accurate.

Dougless wasn't sure exactly how to do it, but she directed Honoria to sew the gash in Nicholas's arm in two layers. The inside stitches would have to remain in his arm forever, but Dougless's father had a steel plate in his leg from his time in the military, so she guessed Nicholas could live with some silk inside his arm. Dougless carefully held Nicholas's skin together while Honoria sewed it.

When Nicholas's wound was sewn together, Dougless wrapped his arm in clean linen. She told the maids she wanted them to boil linen to be used the next day, and when they touched the linen, their hands were to be very clean. Honoria said she would see to it.

Finally, Dougless dismissed all of them; then she sat down on a chair by the fire and proceeded to wait—and to worry. If Nicholas developed a fever she had no penicillin, no oral antibiotics, nothing but a few aspirin. She told herself she needn't worry because she knew Nicholas's future, but today she had changed history. If Kit didn't die, then perhaps Nicholas would. Would she go back to the twentieth century and find that Kit had lived to a grand old age, but his younger brother had died from an infected cut on his arm? History, or in this case, the future, was different from now on.

Hours later, Dougless was dozing in the chair when the door opened and Honoria entered. In her arms was a beautiful gown of deep purple velvet, the color of an eggplant, with wide, trailing sleeves of soft white ermine, the little black tails sewn on at intervals.

"Lady Margaret sends this to you," Honoria whispered so as not to disturb Nicholas. "It will have to be fit to you, but I thought you might see it now."

Dougless touched the soft velvet. It wasn't like modern rayon velvet or heavy cotton velvet, but this was all silk and glistened as only silk could. "How is Kit?" Dougless whispered.

"Sleeping. He says someone tried to kill him. When he swam out to the girl, someone, or maybe two of them, came from under the water, caught his legs, and pulled him under."

Dougless looked away. In Lady Margaret's account found in the wall, she said she believed that Kit had been murdered, that his drowning had not been an accident.

"If you had not known how to raise him from the dead . . ." Honoria whispered.

"I didn't raise anyone from the dead," Dougless said sharply. "There was no magic or witchcraft involved."

Honoria gave her a hard look. "Your arm no longer pains you? It is well?"

"It's fine now, just a dull ache. It's—" Breaking off, she refused to meet Honoria's eyes. Yes, there was magic involved. Her feeling the pain of Nicholas's cut arm was the least of the magic, but Honoria didn't need to be told that.

"You should rest now," Honoria said. "And change your gown."

Dougless glanced at Nicholas, still asleep. "I must stay with him. If he wakes, I want to be here. I can't risk his having a fever. Do you think Lady Margaret would mind if I stay here?"

Honoria smiled. "Were you now to ask for deeds to half the Stafford estates, I do not believe Lady Margaret would deny you."

Dougless smiled back. "I just want Nicholas to be safe."

"I will bring you a robe," Honoria said, then left the room.

An hour later, Dougless had removed her torn and dirty gown, as well as her steel corset, and now she sat before a warm fire, wearing a pretty ruby red brocade robe. Every few minutes she put her hand to Nicholas's forehead. It was warm, but he didn't seem to be running more than a few degrees of temperature.

TWENTY-EIGHT

*T*he shadows in the room lengthened and still Nicholas slept. A maid brought Dougless food on a tray, but Nicholas did not waken. As night fell, she lit candles and looked down at him, so peaceful on the bed, his dark curls vivid against his pale skin. For hours she'd done nothing but watch him, but when she saw no signs of fever, she began to relax and look about her.

Nicholas's room was adorned richly, as befitted a son of the house. His mantelpiece had several plates and goblets of gold and silver on it, and Dougless smiled when she looked at them. She'd come to understand what Nicholas had meant when he'd said his wealth was in his house. Since there were no banks to hold the wealth of a great family like the Staffords, all they had was put into gold and silver and jewels, which were formed into beautiful objects. Smiling, she touched a pitcher and thought that her family's wealth would be a lot more enjoyable if their stocks and bonds were turned into gold dishes.

Beside the fireplace was a long row of tiny oval portraits, all done in exquisite colors. Most of them were people she didn't know, but one of them had to be Lady Margaret as a young woman. There was a hint of Nicholas's eyes in hers. There was an older man who had the shape of Nicholas's jaw. His father? she wondered. There was a miniature oil of Kit. And on the bottom was Nicholas.

She took the portrait from the wall, held it a moment and caressed it. What had happened to these portraits in the twentieth century? she wondered. Were they hanging on some museum wall with "Unknown Man" on a card beside them?

Still holding the portrait, she walked about the room. There was a cushioned seat beneath the window, and Dougless went to it. She knew the top lifted and she wondered what Nicholas kept inside. Glancing at him to make sure he was asleep, she put the portrait on a shelf, then lifted the seat. It creaked but not too loudly.

Inside the seat were rolls of paper tied with pieces of yarn. She took one, untied the string, then unrolled it out on a table. It was a sketch of a house, and Dougless knew instantly that the house was Thornwyck Castle.

"Do you pry?" Nicholas asked from the bed, making Dougless jump.

She went to him and felt his forehead. "How do you feel?"

"Less well than if there were not a woman invading my private goods."

Dougless thought he sounded just like a little boy whose mother had looked inside his secret box. She picked up the plan. "Have you shown these to anyone besides me?"

"I have not shown them to you," he said as he made a lunge for the corner of the paper, but Dougless moved away. Weakly, he lay back against the pillows.

Dougless put the plan down. "Hungry?" She ladled soup into a silver bowl from a pan on the hearth, which had been set there to keep the soup warm. Sitting beside Nicholas, she began to feed him. At first he protested that he could feed himself but, like all men, he soon adjusted to being pampered.

"You have looked long at the drawings?" he asked between bites.

"I had just opened the one. When do you plan to start building?"

"It is merely foolishness. Kit will—" He broke off, then smiled.

Dougless knew what he was thinking, that he'd come so very close to losing Kit.

"My brother is well?" Nicholas asked.

"Perfectly healthy. Better than you. He didn't lose enough blood to flood a river." When she wiped his lips with a napkin, he caught her fingertips and kissed them.

"If I live, then I owe you my life as well as my brother's. What can I do to repay you?"

Love me, Dougless almost said. Fall in love with me again, just as you did before. Look at me with eyes of love. I'll stay in the sixteenth century forever, if you'll love me. I would give up cars and dentists and proper bathrooms if you'd love me again. "I don't want anything," she said. "I just want both of you to be well and for history to come out all right." She put the empty bowl on a table. "You should sleep more. Your arm needs to heal."

"I have slept all I need. Stay and entertain me."

Dougless grimaced. "I've run out of entertainments. There isn't a game I ever played or a song I ever heard that I haven't dredged out of my memory. I'm just about played out."

Nicholas smiled at her. Sometimes he didn't understand her words, but he nearly always got the meaning.

"Why don't you entertain me?" She picked up his sketch. "Why don't you tell me about this?"

"Nay," he said quickly. "Put those away!" He started to sit up, but Dougless pushed him back to the pillows.

"Nicholas, please don't tear your stitches. You must be still. And stop glowering at me! I know all about your love of architecture. When you came to me in the future, you had already started building Thornwyck Castle." She almost laughed at the expression on his face.

"How did you know I planned this for Thornwyck?"

"I told you. When you came to me, it was four years from now and you'd already done it. Actually you'd only started it. It was never finished because you . . . you . . ."

"Were executed," he said, and for the first time he really thought about her words. "I wish you to tell me all."

"From the beginning?" Dougless asked. "It will take a long time."

"Now that Kit is safe, I have time."

Until Lettice gets hold of you, she thought. "I was in a church in Ashburton, and I was crying," she said, "and—"

"Why did you weep? Why were you in Ashburton? And you cannot stand and tell me this long story. No, do not sit there. Here."

He patted the empty half of the bed beside him.

"Nicholas, I can't get in bed with you." Just the thought of being so near him made her heart beat faster.

Opening his eyes, he smiled at her. "I saw a . . . a dream of you. You were in a white box of sorts, water was pouring on you, and you wore no clothes." He looked her up and down, as though he could see through the voluminous robe. "I do not believe you have always been so shy of me."

"No," she said hoarsely, remembering being in the shower stall with him, the "white box" of his dream. "One night we were not shy of each other, and the next morning you were taken away from me. I'm afraid now that if I touch you, I'll be returned to my own time, and I can't go yet. There is more for me to do."

"More?" he asked. "You know of others who die? My mother? Is Kit not yet safe?"

She smiled at him. *Her* Nicholas. Her lovely Nicholas who thought of others before himself. "You are the one who is in danger."

He smiled in relief. "I can care for myself."

"In a pig's eye you can! If I hadn't been here, you'd probably have lost your arm or died from the wound. One of those idiots you call a physician had only to touch that cut with his filthy hands and presto! you're a goner." Of course that hadn't happened the first time he'd cut his arm, but . . .

Nicholas blinked at her. "You do talk most strangely. Come, sit by me and tell me all." When Dougless didn't move, he sighed. "I swear to you on my honor I will not touch you."

"All right," she said. Truthfully, she felt that she could trust him more than she could trust herself. Moving to the other side of the bed, she climbed up on it, for it was a few feet off the floor, then sank into the feather mattress.

"Why did you cry in the church?" he asked softly.

If Dougless could say nothing else about Nicholas, he was a good listener. He was more than a good listener, since he pulled from her things that she didn't want to tell him. In the end, she told him everything about Robert.

"You lived with him without marriage? Did not your father kill him for abducting you?"

"It's not like that in the twentieth century. Women have free choice, and fathers don't tell daughters what to do. Men and women are more equal in my time."

Nicholas snorted. "It seems that men still rule, for this man had all of you he wanted, but he did not make you his wife. He did not share his goods with you or demand his daughter respect you. And you say you chose this freely?"

"I . . . Well . . . It's not like you make it sound. Most of the time, Robert was very good to me. He and I had some good times together. It was only when Gloria was around that it was awful."

"Were a beautiful woman to give me all and in return I was only to give her, what do you say, a 'good time,' I, too, would be most grateful. Do all women of your time give themselves so cheaply?"

"It's not cheap. You just don't understand. Nearly everyone lives together before they get married. It's to see if we're compatible. And, besides, I thought Robert was going to ask me to marry him, but instead, he bought—" She stopped. Nicholas was making her feel as though she thought very little of herself. "You just don't understand, that's all. Men and women are different in the twentieth century."

"*Hmmm.* I see. Yes. Women no longer want respect from a man, they want a 'good time'."

"Of course they want respect; it's just that . . ." She didn't know how to explain her living with Robert to a sixteenth-century man. In fact, now, living in the Elizabethan world, she could see that living with a man *had* cheapened her. Of course marriage was no guarantee that a man was going to respect her, but why hadn't she stood up to Robert and said, "How dare you treat me like this?" or, "No, I will not pay for half of Gloria's plane fare," or, "No, I have too many things to do to pick up your dry cleaning?" Right now she couldn't remember why she'd let him walk over her that way.

"Do you want to hear this story or not?" she snapped.

Smiling, Nicholas lay back against the pillows. "I wish to hear all of it."

After she was past his many questions about her relationship to Robert, she was able to continue. She told of crying on his tomb and of his suddenly being there and of her not believing who he was. She told of his walking in front of a bus.

She didn't get far after that because Nicholas started asking questions. It seemed he'd had a vision of her on a two-wheeled vehicle and he wanted her to explain what it was. He wanted to know what a bus was. When she said she'd called her sister, he wanted her to explain how a telephone worked.

Dougless couldn't describe all he wanted to know, so she got off the bed and got her tote bag. She pulled out her three magazines and started looking for photographs.

Once she showed him the magazines, there was no hope of continuing with her story. There was an Elizabethan saying, "Better unborn than untaught," and Nicholas seemed to epitomize that belief. He was insatiable in his curiosity, and he asked questions faster than Dougless could answer them.

When she couldn't find pictures to show him, she pulled out a spiral notebook, colored felt-tips, and began to draw. The pens and paper caused more questions.

Dougless was beginning to be exasperated because she couldn't continue her story, but then she realized that now that he believed her, she'd have time in the future to tell him everything. "You know," she said, "when I saw Thornwyck Castle, the tower on the left looked different than you drew it. And where are those curved windows?"

"Curved windows?"

"Like this." Dougless began to sketch, but she wasn't very good at architectural rendering.

Rolling onto his side, Nicholas took the pen and made a beautiful perspective sketch of the windows. "This is like the windows?"

"Yes, exactly. We stayed in one of those rooms, and we could see the garden below. The church is just next door, and the guidebook said there used to be a wooden walkway from the church to the house."

Leaning back, Nicholas began to sketch. "I have told no one of my plans, but you say that this was half built before I . . . before I was . . ."

"Right. Yes. After Kit died and you were the earl, you had complete freedom to do what you wanted. I guess now that Kit's alive, you'll have to get his approval to build this place."

"I am no master builder," Nicholas said, looking at his sketch. "Were Kit to need a new house, he would hire someone."

"*Hire* someone? Why? You can do it. These are beautiful drawings, and I've seen Thornwyck Castle and happen to know it's beautiful."

"I to be a tradesman?" he asked, one eyebrow aloft haughtily.

"Nicholas," she said sternly, "there are many things I like about your century, but your class system and your sumptuary laws aren't part of what I like. In my century everyone works. It's embarrassing to be 'idle rich.' In England even royalty works. Princess Diana goes all over the world raising money for one charity after another. And the Princess Royal, well, I get tired just reading her schedule. Prince Andrew takes pictures; Princess Michael writes books. Prince Charles tries to keep England from looking like a Dallas office complex, and—"

Nicholas chuckled. "It is not so rare now that royalty works. Do you think our lovely new queen sits idle?"

Suddenly Dougless remembered having read that one of the reasons Nicholas was executed was that some people were worried that he might go to court and seduce the young Queen Elizabeth. "Nicholas, you aren't thinking of going to court, are you? You wouldn't want to be one of her courtiers, would you?"

"One of her—" Nicholas asked, aghast. "What do you know of this woman who is queen? Some say Mary of Scotland is the true queen and that the Staffords should join forces with others to put her on the throne."

"Don't do that! Whatever you do, don't put your money on anyone but Elizabeth." As she spoke, Dougless wondered if she was changing history. If the Staffords and all their money had been put at Mary's disposal, would she have taken the throne? If Elizabeth weren't queen, would there have been a time when England was the reigning world power? If England weren't a world power that sent settlers to America, would America be speaking English? "Heavy," she said under her breath, mocking a young cousin of hers.

"Who will Elizabeth marry?" Nicholas asked. "Who will she put on the throne beside her?"

"No one, and don't start on me, because we've already had this argument. Elizabeth marries no one, and she does a super job of running the country and a lot of the world with it. Now, are you going to let me tell you the rest of our story, or are you going to keep telling me that what did happen didn't?"

He grinned at her. "You gave yourself to a man for free and I came to save you. Yes, please continue."

"That's not exactly what happened, but . . ." Trailing off, she looked at him. He *had* saved her. He'd appeared in that church, sunlight flashing off his armor, taken her away from a man who didn't love her, and shown her the true give-and-take of love. With Nicholas she could be herself. She never had to think about having to please him; she just seemed to naturally please him. When she was growing up, she'd tried so hard to be as perfect as her older sisters. But it seemed that every schoolteacher she ever had, had had all of her sisters in her classes before Dougless. And, by comparison, Dougless was always a disappointment. Dougless daydreamed, but her sisters never did. Dougless wasn't much good at sports, but her sisters had excelled. Her sisters had had millions of friends, but Dougless was always a bit shy and had always felt like an outsider.

Her parents had never compared her to her sisters. They never seemed to notice that the tennis trophies, equestrian trophies, baseball trophies, spelling bee medals, and science fair ribbons all belonged to their eldest daughters. Dougless had once won a third prize yellow ribbon at church for the best apple pie, and her father had proudly hung it up beside his other daughters' blue ribbons and purple best-of-show ribbons. The yellow had looked so strange and, to Dougless, so embarrassing, that she took the ribbon down.

All her life it seemed that Dougless had wanted to please people, but, somehow, she'd never been able to. Her father kept saying that whatever she did was okay with him, but Dougless merely had to look at her sisters' accomplishments and she knew she needed to do something great. Robert had been an attempt to impress her family. Maybe Robert, a distinguished surgeon, was supposed to be the biggest trophy of all.

But Nicholas had saved her, she thought. Not in the way he meant. He hadn't saved her because he'd pushed Robert out a door. No, he'd saved her by respecting her, and, because of him, Dougless had begun to see herself through his eyes. When she thought about it, Dougless doubted very much if her sisters could have handled what had happened as well as she had. All of them were so sensible and so levelheaded they would probably have called the police on a man in armor who said he was from the sixteenth century. Not one of them would have been softhearted enough to take pity on a poor crazy man.

"What makes you smile so?" Nicholas asked softly.

"I was thinking about my sisters. They're perfect people. Not a flaw in them, but I just realized that perfect can sometimes be a little lonely. Maybe I do try to please people, but I guess there are worse things. Maybe I should just find the right person to please."

Nicholas was obviously confused by this. He took her hand and began to kiss the palm. "You please me much."

She snatched her hand away. "We can't . . . touch each other," she said, stammering.

He looked at her through his lashes, his voice low. "But we have touched, have we not? I remember seeing you. I seem to know of touching you."

"Yes," Dougless whispered. "We have touched." They were alone on the bed, the room dark except for the golden glow of three candles.

"If we have touched, then it will not matter if we touch again in this life." His hands were reaching for her.

"No," she said, her eyes pleading. "We cannot. I would be returned to my own time."

Nicholas didn't move closer to her, and he couldn't understand why he stopped. But he could feel the urgency in her. Never before had a woman's "no" stopped him, because he soon found the women hadn't really meant no. But now, on the bed with this most desirable woman, he found himself listening to her words.

Leaning back against the pillows, he sighed. "I am too weak to accomplish much," he said heavily.

Dougless laughed. "Sure, and if you believe that, I have some land in Florida to sell you."

Nicholas grinned, understanding her meaning. "Come, then, sit close by me and tell me more of your time and of what we did there." He held up his uninjured arm, and Dougless, against her better judgment, moved near him.

Pulling her very close to the side of him, he wrapped his strong right arm about her. She pushed at him for a moment, then sighed and snuggled against his bare chest. "We bought you some clothes," she said, smiling in memory. "And you attacked the poor clerk because the prices were so high. Afterward we went to tea. You *loved* tea. Then we found you a bed-and-breakfast." She paused. "That was the night you found me in the rain."

Nicholas was listening to her with half an ear. He wasn't yet sure he believed her story of past and future, but he was sure of how she felt in his arms. Her body next to his was something he remembered very well.

She was explaining that he'd seemed able to "hear" her. She said she wasn't quite sure how it worked, but she'd used it the first day she'd come to the sixteenth century. She had "called" to him in the rain, and he had come to her. She chided him for his rudeness on that day and for making her ride on the back of the horse. Later, when she was in the room in the attic, she had again "called" him.

Nicholas didn't need further explanation of this, for he seemed to always feel what she felt. Now, as she lay in his arms, her head on his chest, he could feel her sense of comfort, but at the same time he felt her sexual excitement. He'd never wanted to make love to a woman as much as he wanted to make love to her, but something stopped him.

She was telling of going to Bellwood and how he had shown her the secret door.

"I believed you after that," she said. "Not because you knew of the door, but because you were so hurt that the world remembered your misdeeds instead of all the good you had done. No one in the twentieth century knew for sure that you had designed Thornwyck Castle. There was nothing left behind to prove that you were the designer."

"I am not a tradesman. I will not—"

She looked up at him. "I told you that in our world it's different. Talent is appreciated."

He looked down at her, her face close to his, and put his fingertips under her chin. Ever so slowly he brought his lips to hers and kissed her gently.

Then he pulled back, startled. Her eyes were closed and her body was soft and pliant against his. He could take her, he knew that, but, still, something was stopping him. When he moved his hand from her chin, he found that it was trembling. He felt like a boy with his first woman. Except that the first time Nicholas had bedded a woman, he had been eager and enthusiastic, not trembling as he was now.

"What do you to me?" he whispered.

"I don't know," Dougless said, her voice husky. "I think maybe we were meant to be together. Even though we were born four hundred years apart, we were meant for each other."

He ran his hand down her face, then her neck, shoulder, and arm. "Yet I am not to bed you? I cannot take the clothes from your body and kiss your breasts, kiss your legs, kiss—"

"Nicholas, please," she said, pushing out of his arms. "This is difficult enough as it is. All I know is that when we were together in the twentieth century, after we made love, you disappeared. I was holding you and you slipped right out of my grasp. I have you again now, so I don't want to lose you a second time. We can spend time together, we can talk, and we can be together in every way except physically." She paused. "That is, if you want me to stay with you."

As Nicholas looked at her, he felt the pain she'd felt at their separation, but at the moment, he wanted to make love to her more than he wanted to understand anything.

Dougless saw what he was thinking, so when he lunged at her, she rolled off the bed. "One of us has to keep his wits. I want you to get some rest. Tomorrow we can talk more."

"I do not want to talk to you," he said sullenly.

Laughing, Dougless remembered all the things she'd once done to entice him. She didn't need high heels now! "Tomorrow, my love. I must go now. It's almost dawn, and I must meet Lucy and—"

"Who is Lucy?"

"Lady Lucinda something or other. The girl Kit's to marry."

Nicholas snorted. "A fat lump that."

Dougless's anger flared. "Not beautiful like the woman *you're* to marry, is she?"

Nicholas smiled. "Jealousy becomes you."

"I'm not jealous; I'm—" She turned away. Jealousy didn't begin to describe what she felt for Lettice, but she said nothing. Nicholas had already made it clear that he loved the woman he was to marry, so she was sure he wouldn't listen to anything Dougless said against her. "I have to go," she said at last. "And I want you to sleep."

"I would sleep well if you would but stay with me."

"Liar," she said, smiling. She didn't dare go too near him again. She was tired from the excitement of the day and from a night without sleep. Lifting her tote bag, she stepped to the door, gave one last look at his bare chest, his skin dark against the white of the pillows; then hurriedly, before she changed her mind, she left the room.

Lucy was waiting for her by the fountain, and after Dougless had showered, they rehearsed their vaudeville act. Dougless was going to play the straight man, the dummy who asked the questions, so Lucy would get all the laughs.

At daybreak, Dougless made her way back to the house, and Honoria was waiting for her, holding up the purple velvet dress.

"I thought I might take a nap," Dougless said, yawning.

"Lady Margaret and Lord Christopher await you. You are to be rewarded."

"I don't want any reward. I just want to help." Even as she said it, she knew her words were a lie. She wanted to live with Nicholas for the rest of her life. Sixteenth century, twentieth century, she didn't care which if she could just stay with him.

"You must come. You may ask for whatever you wish. A house. An income. A husband. A—"

"Think they'd let me have Nicholas?"

"He is pledged," Honoria said softly.

"I know that only too well. Shall we start getting me harnessed?"

After Dougless was dressed, Honoria led her to the Presence Chamber, where Lady Margaret and her oldest son were playing a game of chess.

"Ah," Kit said when Dougless entered; then he lifted her hand and kissed it. "The angel of life who gave me back mine."

Smiling, Dougless blushed.

"Come, sit," Lady Margaret said, pointing to a chair. A chair, not a stool, so Dougless knew she was being greatly honored.

Kit stood behind his mother's chair. "I wish to thank you for my life, and I wish to give you a gift, but I know not what you would wish. Name what you would have of me. And think high," he said, eyes twinkling, "my life is worth much to me."

"There is nothing I want," Dougless said. "You have given me kindness. You have fed and clothed me most sumptuously. There is nothing more I could want." Except Nicholas, she thought. Could you gift wrap him and send him to my apartment in Maine?

"Come," Kit said, laughing. "There is something you must want. A chest of jewels perhaps. I have a house in Wales that—"

"A house," Dougless said. "Yes, a house. I'd like you to build a house in Thornwyck, and Nicholas is to draw the plans for it."

"My son?" Lady Margaret asked, aghast.

"Yes, Nicholas. He's made some sketches for a house, and it will be beautiful. But he must have Kit's . . . I mean, Lord Christopher's backing."

"And you would live in this house?" Kit asked.

"Oh, no. I mean, I don't want to own it. I just want Nicholas to be allowed to design it."

Both Kit and Lady Margaret stared at her. Dougless looked at the women around them, sitting at their embroidery frames. They were gaping.

Kit recovered first. "You may have your wish. My brother will get his house."

"Thank you. Thank you so very much."

No one in the room spoke again, so Dougless stood up. "I believe I owe you a game of charades," she said to Lady Margaret.

Lady Margaret smiled. "You no longer need to earn your keep. My son's life has paid for you. Go and do what you wish."

Dougless at first started to protest that she didn't know what to do with herself, but then she figured she'd think of something. "Thank you, my lady," she said, and bobbed a curtsy before leaving the room. Freedom, she thought, as she went back to Honoria's bedroom. No more having to entertain people. Good thing, since her store of songs was down to the McDonald's jingle.

Honoria's maid helped Dougless remove her new dress and corset (her old corset that was beginning to rust through its silk covering), and she went to bed smiling. She had prevented Nicholas from impregnating Arabella, and she'd saved Kit. All that was left was to get rid of Lettice. If she could do that, she would change history. She fell asleep smiling.

TWENTY-NINE

What *followed was, for Douglass,* the happiest week of her life. Everyone in the Stafford household was pleased with her, and it seemed that she could do no wrong. She figured it would wear off in a few days, so she planned to enjoy it while it lasted.

She spent every minute she could with Nicholas. He wanted to know all about her twentieth century world, and he never tired of asking questions. He had difficulty believing her talk of automobiles, and airplanes he didn't believe at all. He went through everything in her tote bag. In the bottom were a couple of foil-wrapped tea bags, and Douglass made him a cup of tea with milk. As he'd done the first time, he kissed her soundly in pleasure at the taste.

In return for telling him of the twentieth century, he told her of his life. He showed her dances, took her hawking one day, then laughed at her when she refused to allow the lovely bird on her arm to fly away so it could kill its prey. He showed her buzzards in pens that were fed nothing but white bread for days to clean the carrion from their craws before they were butchered and eaten.

They argued about educating the "lower classes." And that led to a squabble about equality. When Nicholas said her America sounded violent and lonely, Dougless wished she hadn't told him so much.

He asked her hundreds of questions about the immediate future of England and especially about Queen Elizabeth. Dougless so wished she remembered more of what her father had told her so she could tell Nicholas.

He seemed fascinated with the idea of sea travel and with exploring her new country.

"But you'll be here married to Lettice. You won't be able to go anywhere if you're executed."

As she'd already found out, Nicholas would *not* listen to her when she spoke of his execution. He had a young man's belief that he was invincible and that nothing could hurt him. "I will not raise an army to protect my lands in Wales because they are not my lands. They are Kit's, and if he is alive, then the future I once had will not be."

She had no argument for him. When she asked him who he thought had tried to kill Kit, Nicholas merely shrugged and said it was no doubt some ruffian. Dougless still couldn't get used to the idea of a land where there was no federal government and no police force. The nobility, besides having all the money, had all the power. They judged disputes, hanged people when they wanted to, and answered only to the queen. If the peasants had a good family to rule them, they were lucky, but many were not so fortunate.

One day Dougless asked Nicholas to take her to see a town. He raised an eyebrow at her and told her she would not like it, but he agreed to take her.

He was right. The peace and relative cleanliness of the Stafford household had not prepared her for the filth of a medieval town. Eight of Nicholas's men accompanied them to protect them from highwaymen. As they rode along the rutted road, Dougless looked at every shadow behind every tree. Being attacked by a dashing highwayman in a romantic novel was one thing, but she knew that, in reality, highwaymen were dangerous.

The town was dirty beyond anything Dougless had ever imagined. People emptied kitchen slops and chamber pots into the streets. She saw adults who she was sure had never had a bath in their lives. At the corner of a bridge over a little river were tall pikes with rotting human heads on them.

She tried to look at all of it and see only the good. She tried to memorize what houses looked like and what the streets were like. If she did return to her time, she wanted to tell her father everything she'd seen. But try as she might, she was so overwhelmed by the bad that it was all she could see. The houses were so close together that women passed things from the windows to each other. People shouted, animals screamed, and someone was beating on metal with a hammer. Filthy, diseased children ran up to them, clutching their legs and begging. Nicholas's men kicked them away, and Dougless, instead of feeling sympathy, felt herself recoiling from their touch.

When Nicholas turned and saw her pale face, he ordered his men to start for home. Once they were again in the open air, Dougless could breathe.

When Nicholas called a halt, tablecloths were spread under some trees and food was brought out. Nicholas handed her a goblet full of strong wine. With trembling hands, Dougless took the wine and drank deeply.

"Our world is not like yours," Nicholas said. In the past days he had questioned her on every aspect of modern society, and his questions had included bathing and sewage drains.

"No," she said, trying not to remember what that town had looked and smelled like. America had many homeless, but they did not live like these people did. Of course she had seen some well-dressed people in the town, but the sight of them could not take away from the stench. "No, a modern town is not like that."

He stretched out beside her while she drank her wine. "Do you still wish to remain in my time?"

She was looking at him, but between them were the images of what she had just seen. If she stayed with Nicholas, that town would be part of her life. Whenever she left the safety of the Stafford house, she would see rotting heads on pikes and streets filled with the contents of chamber pots.

"Yes," she said, looking into his eyes. "I would stay if I could."

He lifted her hand and kissed it.

"But I'd make the midwives wash their hands."

"Midwives? Ah, then you plan to have my children?"

The thought of bearing a child without a proper doctor and hospital terrified her, but she didn't tell him that. "A dozen at least," she said.

Her sleeve was too tight to push up, but she could feel his hot lips through her clothing. "When shall we begin making them? I should like more children."

Her eyes were closed, her head back. "More?" Suddenly, something that Nicholas said came back to her. A son. He'd said he had no children but he'd once had a son. What exactly had he said?

She pulled her arm from him. "Nicholas, do you have a son?"

"Aye, an infant. But you need not worry, his mother died long ago."

She was concentrating hard. A son. What had Nicholas said? *I had a son, but he died in a fall the week after my brother drowned.* "We have to return," she said.

"But we will eat first."

"No." She stood up. "We have to see about your son. You said he died a week after Kit drowned. Tomorrow will be a week. We must go to him now."

Nicholas didn't hesitate. He left a man to pack the food and dishes, while he and the other men and Dougless tore back to the Stafford house. They jumped off their horses at the front gate. Lifting her skirts, Dougless ran after Nicholas.

He led her to a wing of the house she'd never been in before, then threw open a door. What Dougless saw horrified her more than anything she'd yet seen in the sixteenth century. A little boy, barely over a year old, was wrapped from his neck to his feet in tight bindings of linen—and he was hanging from a peg on the wall. His arms and legs were pinned to him exactly like a mummy. The bottom half of the bindings were filthy where he'd relieved himself but not been changed. Below him on the floor was a wooden bucket to catch excess "drippings."

Dougless could not move as she stared in horror at the child, whose eyes were half open, half closed.

"The child is fine," Nicholas said. "No harm has come to him."

"No harm?" Dougless said under her breath. If a child in the twentieth century were treated like this, it would be taken from its parents, but Nicholas was saying the child was fine. "Take him down," she said.

"Down? But he is safe. There is no reason to—"

Dougless glared at him. "Down!"

With a look of resignation, Nicholas took the boy by the shoulders and, holding him at arms' length so he'd drip onto the floor and not on his father, he turned to Dougless. "And what am I to do with him?"

"We are going to bathe him and dress him properly. Can he walk? Talk?"

Nicholas looked astonished. "How am I to know this?"

Dougless blinked. There was more than mere time between their two worlds. It took Dougless a while, but she got a big wooden bucket brought to the room and filled with hot water. Nicholas complained and cursed, but he unwrapped his smelly, dirty son and plunked him into the warm water. The poor child was covered with diaper rash from the waist down. Dougless used some of her precious soft soap to gently wash him.

At one point the boy's nurse came in and was very upset, saying Dougless was going to kill the child. At first Nicholas wouldn't get involved—probably because he agreed with the nurse, Dougless thought—but when Dougless glared at him, he made the woman leave.

The warm water made the boy perk up, and Dougless guessed that the bindings had been so tight the boy had been in a bit of a stupor. She said as much to Nicholas.

"It keeps them quiet. Loosen the swaddlings and they weep most loudly."

"Let's wrap *you* in bindings like that, hang *you* on a peg, and see if *you* don't cry bloody murder."

"A child has no sense." Obviously, he was puzzled by her actions and her thoughts.

"He has the brain now that he'll go to Yale with."

"Yale?"

"Never mind. Have safety pins been invented yet?"

Dougless had to improvise diapers. Nicholas protested when she used one diamond and one emerald brooch to fasten the corners of the boy's linen diaper. She wished she had some zinc ointment for his rash.

When at last the child was clean, dry, and powdered (thanks to another hotel giveaway sample from her tote bag), she handed the boy to his father. Nicholas looked horrified and bewildered at the same time, but he took the boy, and after a moment he even smiled at him. The child smiled back.

"What's his name?" Dougless asked.

"James."

She took the boy from Nicholas. He was already a very good looking child, with his father's dark hair and blue eyes, and he had a tiny cleft in his chin. "Let's see if you can walk." She put the boy on the floor, and after a few stumbles, he walked to Dougless's outstretched arms.

Nicholas stayed with her, watching as she spent an hour playing with the boy. And when Dougless put him down for the night, she found out more about Elizabethan child care. James's crib had a hole in the middle, and the child was strapped in at night, his bottom over the hole, and once again a bucket was put under him.

Nicholas did little more than roll his eyes when she demanded that the child be given a proper mattress. The nurse complained, and Dougless could see her point. If the child had no rubber pants, by morning the mattress would be filthy, and how does one clean goose feathers? She solved the problem by putting a piece of waxed cloth, such as rain gear was made out of, over the mattress. The nurse did as Dougless bid, but she was grumbling when Dougless and Nicholas left.

Nicholas was chuckling as they left the room. "Come and have supper with me," he said. "We will celebrate the cleansing of my son." Taking Dougless's hand, he tucked it under his arm.

THIRTY

Nicholas leaned back on the bench and watched Dougless playing with his son. The sun was bright, the air heavy with the scent of roses, and as far as Nicholas could tell, all was perfect in the world. It had been three days since she'd taken the boy off the peg and out of swaddling, and during those three days the child had spent a great deal of time with them. But then so had many people spent time with them. Nicholas was amazed to discover how much Dougless had involved herself in in the short time she'd been with the Stafford family. Early mornings she "rehearsed," as she called it, with the fat heiress, and yesterday she and the heiress had put on a ridiculous play while wearing even more ridiculous peasant clothes. They had sung a song about "Travelin' along, singin' a song . . . ," then told jokes that bordered on blasphemy.

Throughout the play, Nicholas had refused to laugh, because he knew she had done this work for Kit. She had even told Nicholas so. The rest of his family had laughed uproariously at the play, but Nicholas refused to do so.

Later, when he got her alone, she had laughed at him and accused him of being jealous. Jealous? Nicholas Stafford jealous? He could have any woman he wanted, so why should he be jealous? She had smiled so knowingly that, to stop her, he had grabbed her to him and kissed her until she couldn't remember her own name, much less think of another man.

Now, leaning back against the garden wall and watching her toss a ball to his son, he felt at peace. Was this love? he wondered. Was this the love that the troubadours sang of? How could he be in love with a woman he hadn't taken to bed? Once he'd thought he was in love with a half-gypsy girl who had done splendid things to his body. But with this Dougless all they did was talk—and laugh.

She had nagged him so much about the sketches she'd found while snooping in his belongings that he had started making new drawings. Kit had told Nicholas that he could begin building Thornwyck Castle in the spring.

During their days spent together, he and Dougless talked and sang together, rode, and walked. And he found himself telling her things about himself that he had never told another soul.

Two days ago a portrait painter had come to the Stafford household and Nicholas had commissioned him to paint a miniature oil of Dougless. It should be finished soon.

Looking at her now, he was beginning to wonder if he could live without her. But, regularly, she mentioned leaving. She talked about what he must do when she was gone. She talked of cleanliness until he could bear no more, but she kept saying cleanliness was of utmost importance.

When she was gone. He couldn't bear to think of not being with her. Many times during the day he'd found himself thinking, I must tell Dougless that. She said that in her time men and women were partners and they shared thoughts and ideas. He knew his mother's last husband had often asked Lady Margaret's opinion, but he couldn't remember his stepfather saying, "How was your day?" as Dougless asked.

And there was the child. The child was a bother, of course, but there were times when he enjoyed the boy's smiles. The boy looked up at Nicholas as though his father were a god. Yesterday Nicholas had taken the boy into the saddle before him, and the child's squeals of laughter had made Nicholas smile.

Suddenly Dougless laughed at something the boy did and brought Nicholas back to the present. The sunlight was shining on her hair, but then the sunlight seemed to come out only when she was near. He wanted to touch her, hold her, make love to her, but the threat of her disappearance kept him from pulling her into his bed. Oh, he kissed her when he could and touched every part of her body he could reach. They snuggled together in the evenings, alone in some deserted nook, and watched the firelight or the stars out an open window. He touched her and held her, but they went no further. The possibility of her leaving was too great for him to risk.

A boy came to tell Nicholas that Lady Margaret wanted to see him, so, reluctantly, he left the garden and went into the house.

His mother awaited him in her private closet off her bedchamber.

"Have you told her?" Lady Margaret asked, her face stern.

Nicholas didn't have to be told what she meant. "Nay, I have not."

"Nicholas, this has gone too far. I have been lenient with the woman because she saved Kit's life, but your behavior . . ." She trailed off because there was no need to say more.

Nicholas went to the window, opened it, and looked down into the garden. He could just see Dougless below. "I would spend my life with the Montgomery woman," he said softly.

Lady Margaret slammed the window shut and glared at her son. She had eyes that could pierce a man. "You cannot. The dowry for Lettice Culpin has been accepted and part of it spent to buy sheep. The woman brings land with her and a good name. Your children will be related to the throne. You cannot throw that away for this woman who is nothing."

"She is all to me."

Lady Margaret glared at him. "She is nothing. Two days ago the rider returned from Lanconia. There is no Montgomery king. This Dougless Montgomery is no more than a fast-tongued—"

"Say no more," Nicholas said, cutting her off. "I have never believed her to be of royal blood, but she has come to mean more to me than bloodlines and property."

Lady Margaret groaned. "Do you think you are the first to love? When I was a girl, I loved my cousin, so I refused to marry your father.

My mother beat me until I was willing." She narrowed her eyes at Nicholas. "And she was right. Your father gave me two sons who lived to manhood, while my cousin gambled his fortune away."

"Dougless is not likely to gamble my fortune away."

"Nor will she increase your fortune!" Lady Margaret calmed herself. "What ails you? Kit is to marry a fat child, while you are to marry one of the great beauties of England. Lettice is much more beautiful than the Montgomery woman."

"What do I care for money and beauty? Lettice has a heart of stone. She marries me, a younger son, only for my connection to the throne. Let her find another who will overlook her lack of warmth and will see only the perfection of her face."

"You mean to unkiss this bargain? You will break your betrothal?" Lady Margaret was aghast.

"How can I marry one woman when another owns my heart?"

Lady Margaret gave a derisive snort of laughter. "I did not raise you to be a fool. Keep the Montgomery woman after your marriage. Make her a maid to your wife. I cannot believe Lettice will mind that you do not go to her every night. Get Lettice with child, then go to your Montgomery woman. It was an arrangement my second husband had, and I did not mind. Although he gave his woman three children and me only one and that one died," she added bitterly.

Nicholas turned away from his mother. "I do not believe Dougless would agree to such an arrangement. In her country I do not believe such things are done."

"Her country? Where is this country of hers? It is not Lanconia. Where does she get these games and amusements? Where do these strange implements she carries come from? She adds on a machine. She has pills that are magic. Is she from the devil? Do you wish to cohabit with one of the devil's own?"

"She is no witch. She's from—" He stopped and looked at his mother. He could not tell her the truth about Dougless. Dougless had made a remark about the household loving her now because she had saved Kit, but that it would soon cease.

Lady Margaret glared at her son. "Do you sell yourself to her? Do you believe whatever story she tells you? The woman is a liar and . . ."

She hesitated. "She interferes too much. She has you drawing houses like a tradesman. She has the girl Kit is to marry dressing like a peasant. She takes children from the nursery. She teaches the servant children to read and write—as though that were needed. She—"

"But you have encouraged all of this," Nicholas said in astonishment. "I was the one who preached caution when she came. You took the tablet she offered."

"Aye, I did. I was much amused by her at first. And I would be amused now were not my youngest son thinking himself in love with her." Lady Margaret softened and put her hand on Nicholas's arm. "Love God, love your children when they are grown if you must, but do not give your love to a lying woman. What does she want from you? What does she want from all of us? Listen to me, Nicholas, beware of her. She changes too much in our family. She wants something."

"No," Nicholas said softly. "She wants naught but to help. She has been sent—"

"Sent? She has been sent here by whom? Who sent her? What can she gain?" Lady Margaret's eyes widened. "Kit said men tried to pull him under when he nearly drowned. Did the Montgomery woman arrange to have him drowned, then pretend to save him? Such a trick would gain her much in our family. Or mayhap she meant for him to die. Twere Kit dead, you would be earl and she has you in her palm."

"No, no, no," Nicholas said. "Her character is not like that. She did not know about Kit because I had lied to her about the door at Bellwood."

Lady Margaret's handsome face showed her confusion at his words. "What do you know of her?"

"Naught. I know naught bad of her. You must believe me, the woman wants only good for us. She has no evil intent."

"Then why does she want to prevent your marriage?"

"She does not," Nicholas said, but turned away. When he had first met Dougless, she had said several derogatory things about Lettice, but lately she had said nothing. Nicholas realized his mother's words were making him doubt Dougless.

Lady Margaret moved to stand before her son. "Does the Montgomery woman love you?" she asked softly.

"Aye, she does," he answered.

"Then she will want what is best for you. And Lettice Culpin is best. The Montgomery woman must see that she can bring no dowry to the marriage. She has lied about having an uncle who is king, so I doubt if she has any relative who matters. What is she? The daughter of a tradesman?"

"Her father teaches."

"Ah," Lady Margaret said. "The truth at last. What can she offer the Stafford family? She has nothing." She put her hand on Nicholas's arm. "I do not ask you to give her up. She will stay in this house with you, or go with you and your wife. Breed with the woman. Love her. Make free with her." Her face became stern again. "But you cannot make her your wife. Do you understand me? Staffords do not marry the penniless daughters of teachers."

"I understand full well, madam," Nicholas said, eyes dark with anger. "I, more than anyone, feel the weight of my family's name on my shoulders. I will do my duty and marry the beauteous, coldhearted Lettice."

"Good," Lady Margaret said, then lowered her voice. "I should hate for something to happen to the Montgomery woman. I have grown fond of her."

Nicholas stared at his mother for a moment, then turned and left the room. He stalked angrily to his bedchamber, and there, alone, he leaned against the door and closed his eyes. His mother's words had been clear enough: do your duty and marry Lettice Culpin or "something" will happen to Dougless. Even as he thought the words, he knew how Dougless would react to his marrying another woman. Dougless would not remain in his household to wait on his wife.

To lose Dougless and gain Lettice, he thought. To trade Dougless's eyes of love for Lettice's cold, calculating eyes. The first time he had met Lettice, he had been taken with her beauty. Dark eyes, dark hair, full red lips. But Nicholas had been around enough beautiful women that he was soon able to see beneath her beauty. She walked about the Stafford household, her eyes on gold vessels, tallying them, her mind like a scale, weighing how much gold the Staffords owned, how much silver.

Nicholas had tried to seduce the woman, but had failed. He had failed, not because Lettice was unwilling, but because she was uninterested. Kissing Lettice was like kissing warm marble.

Duty, he thought. His duty was to marry the woman who had more money, the woman with the bluest blood. "Dougless," he whispered, then closed his eyes.

Tonight he must tell her, he thought. Tonight he had to tell Dougless of his impending marriage. He could put it off no longer.

THIRTY-ONE

*Y*ou can't marry her," Dougless said quite calmly.

"My love," Nicholas said, walking toward her, his hands out-stretched.

He had asked her to go riding with him, then had taken her to a neighboring estate where there was a mature maze in the garden. The hedges were twelve feet tall, and the way in and out was complicated. He knew she didn't know her way out of the maze and therefore she was less likely to run from him when he told her what he had to.

"I must marry her," Nicholas said. "It is my duty to my family."

Dougless told herself to remain calm. She told herself that she had a job to do, and that she must explain to Nicholas why he couldn't marry Lettice. But when faced with having the man she loved tell her he was going to marry another, logic fled.

"Duty?" she said through her teeth. "No doubt it's a great hardship for you to marry a beautiful babe like Lettice. I'll just bet you're dreading it. And I guess you want me too. Is that it? A wife *and* a lover? Only I can't be your lover, can I?" She glared at him. "Or maybe I can be. If I went to bed with you, would that keep you from marrying that evil woman?"

Nicholas was moving toward her, trying to take her in his arms, but he halted. "Evil? Lettice is greedy perhaps, but evil?"

Dougless's fists were clenched at her side. "What do you know of evil? You men are all alike no matter when you were born. All you can see is the outside of a person. If a woman is beautiful, she can have any man she wants, no matter how rotten she is inside. And if a woman is ugly, nothing else matters."

Nicholas dropped his hands; his eyes were angry. "Aye, that is all that interests me. I care naught for duty or family or for the woman I love. Tearing the clothes from Lettice's divine body is all that interests me."

Dougless gasped, feeling as though he'd slapped her. She wanted to leave the maze, but she knew she didn't know the way out. She turned back to him. Anger was holding her upright, but, quite suddenly, the anger left her. She collapsed on a bench, her face in her hands. "Oh, God," she whispered.

Nicholas sat beside her and pulled her into his arms, holding her while she cried against his chest. "The marriage is something I must do. It has been arranged. I do not wish it, not now, not since I have you, but it is what I must do. Were something to befall Kit, I would be earl and it is my duty to produce an heir."

"Lettice can't bave chilled," Dougless said against his chest.

He pulled a handkerchief from inside his slops. "What?"

Dougless blew her nose. "Lettice can't have children."

"How do you know of this?"

"Lettice was the one who caused your execution. Oh, Nicholas, please don't marry her. You *can't* marry her. She will kill you." Dougless was calming somewhat, and beginning to remember what she must tell him. "I was going to tell you, but I thought we would have more time together. I wanted you to trust me more before I told you. I know how much you love Lettice, and—"

"Love her? I love Lettice Culpin? Who has told you this?"

"You did. You told me she's one of the major reasons you wanted to return to the sixteenth century, because you loved her so very much."

Pulling away from her, he stood up. "I came to love her?"

Dougless sniffed and blew her nose again. "When you came to me, you'd been married to her for four years."

"It would take more than four years to make me love that woman," Nicholas muttered.

"What?"

"Tell me more of this love I bore for my wife."

There was a knot in Dougless's throat, so she had difficulty speaking, but she did her best to explain all that he'd said to her. He questioned her thoroughly, asking about their last days together. Dougless held on to one of his big hands with both of hers while she answered his questions.

At last he put his fingertips under her chin and lifted her face. "When I was with you before, I knew I must return. Perhaps I did not want to cause you pain when I left. Perhaps I meant to prevent your loving a man who would not stay."

Dougless's eyes widened, tears sparkling. "You said that," she whispered. "On our last night together, you said you wouldn't touch me because I'd grieve too much for you."

Smiling at her, he smoothed a damp tendril of hair away from her face. "I could not love Lettice were I to live with her a thousand years."

"Oh, Nicholas," she said, then threw her arms around his neck and began kissing him. "I knew you'd do the right thing. I knew you wouldn't marry her. Now everything will come out right. You won't be executed because Lettice won't have any reason to try to kill you or Kit. And she won't get hooked up with Robert Sydney because Arabella hasn't had your baby. Oh, Nicholas, I knew you wouldn't marry her."

Nicholas pulled her arms from around him and held her hands, his eyes locked with hers. "I am pledged to marry Lettice, and I shall leave for the marriage in three days' time." When Dougless struggled for release, he held her hands firmly. "My way is not yours. My time is not the same as yours, and I have not the freedom you have. I cannot marry to suit myself only."

He leaned closer to her and put his lips to her cheek. "You must understand me. My marriage was arranged years ago, and it is a good alliance. My wife will bring property and relatives into the Stafford family."

"Will this property and these relatives help you when the axman removes your head?" she asked angrily. "Will you go to your death thinking how good this marriage was?"

"You must tell me all. What you tell me will help me prevent an accusation of treason."

She jerked out of his grasp, then walked to the far side of the grassed area at the heart of the maze. "You'll be able to prevent your execution as well as you could have prevented Kit's drowning. If I hadn't been here, your brother would be dead and your lovely Lettice would be marrying an earl."

A smile twitched at the corners of Nicholas's mouth. "Were I the earl, I would not marry Lettice. No doubt my mother would marry me to your fat Lucy."

"You *did* marry Lettice after you became the earl. Maybe you owed her something and had to marry her."

"Ah, yes, the sheep," Nicholas said, smiling.

"You can laugh at me if you want, but I can assure you that when you came to me, you weren't laughing. Facing an executioner's ax doesn't make a person feel jovial."

Nicholas sobered. "Nay, it would not. You would tell me of Lettice? Tell me all that you know?"

Dougless sat down on the bench, at the far end from him, away from his touch. As she stared ahead at the green wall of trimmed hedge, she didn't look at him.

She started slowly, at the very beginning, telling him of reading Lady Margaret's papers that were found in a hole in a wall. She told how Nicholas had finagled an invitation into the Harewood's home, where they'd met Lee and Arabella.

"We read the papers and asked questions all weekend, but we found out little. In the end you drew your sword on Lee and he told you that the traitor's name was Robert Sydney. You and I both thought you'd return to this century after that, but you didn't. You stayed." She closed her eyes for a moment. "After that, we had a wonderful time together, but then we . . ." The pain of that morning in the church when Nicholas had disappeared was still fresh. "We made love and the next day you went back. Later I found out you'd been executed."

She drew a deep breath and told him more. She told of afterward meeting Lee, and Lee's telling her of finding Lady Margaret's account of the truth of what had happened, the truth that became known only after Nicholas's death.

She told how Lettice had planned to marry a Stafford, produce an heir, and put the child on the throne of England. She repeated Lady Margaret's belief that Lettice had had Kit killed so she'd be marrying an earl instead of a younger son.

"After you married her, she tried to persuade you to raise yourself at court. She wanted to gain as many people to back her as possible, but you refused."

"I do not like court," Nicholas said. "Too many people conspire against one another."

She turned to look at him. "You refused to stay at court with your wife, so she tried to kill you. When I met you, you had a long, deep scar on your calf where you had fallen from a horse about a year after your marriage. Your mother wrote that you had many 'accidents' after your marriage."

When Nicholas didn't speak, Dougless continued. She told him that Lettice had begun to look for someone to help rid her of Nicholas and she'd found Robert Sydney. "He hated you for being his wife's lover and impregnating her. Lady Margaret thinks he killed both Arabella and the baby."

"But this time I did not impregnate Arabella," Nicholas said softly.

"True," Dougless said, smiling, then continued. "When you started to raise an army to fight in Wales, it was easy for Lettice to get Robert to tell the queen it was treason. Queen Elizabeth was jittery about Mary of Scotland anyway, and maybe she'd heard rumors that the Staffords were considering joining with Mary."

Dougless looked at him, at his beautiful face, at his blue eyes. She reached out her hand and put her palm on his soft, dark beard. "They cut off your head," she whispered, blinking back tears.

Nicholas kissed her palm.

Dougless dropped her hand and looked away. "After your . . . death, Robert Sydney blackmailed Lettice into marrying him. He wanted to put his own child on the throne, only the beauteous Lettice, the woman a man had died for, was barren. She could have no children."

Dougless grimaced. "Lee said it was all ironic. Lettice destroyed the Stafford family for a child she would never have."

There was silence between them for a while.

"And what of my mother?"

She looked back at him. "The queen confiscated all that the

Staffords owned, and Robert Sydney married her to Dickie Harewood."

"Harewood?!" Nicholas said with disgust.

"It was either that or starve to death. The queen gave Sydney a couple of your estates, then someone pushed your mother down a flight of stairs and broke her neck."

She paused at Nicholas's intake of breath. "After that there were no more Staffords. Lettice had managed to wipe out all of you."

When she turned back to look at him, his face was pale.

Nicholas got up and walked toward the hedge. He stood in silence for a while, thinking over her words, then turned back to her. "What you say could have happened once but could not now."

She understood what he was saying, that now it would be all right to marry Lettice. Anger began to swell her veins. "You wouldn't be such a fool to marry her after what I've told you, would you?"

"But your story could not happen now. Arabella does not carry my child, so Robin has no reason to hate me. Kit is alive, so I have no reason to raise an army, and if Kit must raise the army, you will be assured that I will petition the queen's permission."

Dougless came to her feet. "Nicholas, don't you understand that you don't know the future? When you were in my time, the books said you had died three days before your execution. After you returned, the books told of your execution. History is so very easy to change. If you marry Lettice, when I return will I read that Kit was killed another way? That maybe Lettice came up with another way to have you executed? Maybe she'll find someone else to help her. I'm sure there are other men with pretty wives who hate you."

Nicholas smiled at the last. "A man or two."

"You're laughing at me! I am talking life and death, and you stand there *laughing* at me."

He pulled Dougless's rigid body into his arms. "My love, it is good that you care so much, and it is good that you have warned me. I will be cautious from now on."

She pushed away from him. Her voice and body showed her anger. "You are thinking like a *man,*" she accused. "You think that no woman could ever really do *you* harm, don't you? I tell you all of this, and you chuckle at me. Why not wink at me and pat me on the head as well?

Why not tell me to go back to my sewing and leave men things, like life and death, to males who are capable of understanding?"

"Dougless, please," he said, reaching out his hands.

"Don't you touch me. Save your touches for your lovely Lettice. Tell me, is she so beautiful that she's worth all the tragedy that she'll cause? Your death, Kit's death, your mother's death, the end of the noble Stafford family?"

Nicholas let his arms fall to his side. "Do you not see that I have no choice? Am I to tell my family and the Culpins I must break the betrothal because a woman from the future says my bride might kill all of the Staffords? I would be considered a fool and you . . . you would not be treated well."

"You risk everything because of what people might say?"

Nicholas searched for a way to explain what must be so that she could understand. "In your time do you not contract bargains? Legal bargains on paper?"

"Of course. We have contracts for everything. We even have marriage contracts but marriages should be made for love, not—"

"My class does not marry for love. We cannot. Look you about. See the wealth of this house? This is but one house my family owns. These riches have come to us because my ancestors married for estate, not for love. My grandfather married a shrew of a woman, but she brought three houses with her and much plate."

"Nicholas, I understand the theory, but marriage is so . . . so intimate. It's not like signing a contract to do some work for someone. Marriage has to do with love and children, and a home and safety, and having a friend."

"So you live in poverty with the one you love. Does this love feed you, clothe you, keep you warm in winter? There is more to marriage than what you say. You are poor, so you cannot understand."

Her eyes blazed. "For your information I am *not* poor. Not by a long shot. My family is very rich. Lots of money. But just because my family has money doesn't mean I don't want love, or that I'd sell myself to the highest bidder."

"How did your family obtain its wealth?" he asked softly.

"I don't know. We've had it forever. My father said that our ancestors married—" She broke off and looked at him with wide eyes.

"Your ancestors married who?"

"Nothing. It was a joke. He didn't mean anything."

"Who?" Nicholas asked.

"Rich women," she said angrily. "He said our ancestors were quite good at marrying rich women."

Nicholas said nothing, just stood there looking at her.

Her anger left her and she went to him, putting her arms about his waist, holding him tightly. "Marry for money," she said. "Marry the richest woman in the world, but please don't marry Lettice. She is bad. She'll hurt you, Nicholas, hurt all of you."

Nicholas pushed her out to arm's length to look into her eyes. "Lettice Culpin is the highest I can hope for. I am a younger son, a mere knight. I have naught but what Kit allows me. I am fortunate he is so generous as to allow me to live at his expense. The lands Lettice brings to this family will benefit us all. How can I not do this for a brother who has given me so much?"

"Lettice isn't the best you can hope for. Lots of women like you. You can get someone else. If you have to marry someone for money, we'll find her. Somebody rich but not ambitious like Lettice."

Nicholas smiled down at her. "Having a woman in bed is not the same as a marriage alliance. You must trust me on this. Lettice is a good match for me. No, do not frown. I will be safe. Do you not see? The danger of her is in not knowing. Now that I know, I can save my family and myself."

"If she finds out that you aren't interested in overthrowing the queen or even in going to court, perhaps *she* will break the engagement."

"For all that she is related to the Throne and has money, her family is not so old as mine. If what you say about her plans is true, she will not release me. What woman does not believe that she can bend a man to her will?"

"Then she's going to kill you," Dougless said. "Are you going to check every saddle cinch to see if it's been cut? What about poison in your food? What about a wire stretched across the stairs? What if she hires thugs to beat you up? What about drowning? Burning?"

He chuckled in a patronizing way. "I am pleased you care. You shall help me keep watch."

"Me?" She pulled away from him. "Me?"

"Aye. You shall stay in my household." He gave her a look through his lashes. "You shall attend to my wife."

It took Dougless a moment to react. "Attend to your wife?" she said evenly. "You mean like help her dress, check that her bathwater isn't too hot? That sort of thing?"

Her calm tone didn't fool him. "Dougless, my love, my one and only love, it will not be so bad. We will spend much time together."

"Do we spend the time together with or without a permission slip from your wife?"

"Dougless," he pleaded.

"You can ask this of me after the way you talked about my living with Robert? At least with Robert I was his *only* woman. But you . . . you're asking me to wait on that . . . that killer! What am I supposed to do at night while you're trying to produce an heir with her?"

Nicholas stiffened. "You cannot ask me to be celibate. You say you cannot share my bed for fear of returning."

"Oh, I see, *I* can be celibate; that's perfectly okay. But you, Mr. Macho Stud, you have to have a different woman every night. What do you do on the nights when Lettice tells you no? Chase the maids into the arbor?"

"You may not speak to me like this," he said, his eyes darkening with anger.

"Oh, I can't, can't I? If someone travels four hundred years just to warn another person, and that person won't listen for no reason except his own vanity, then the party of the first part can say any damn thing she pleases. Go ahead, marry Lettice, see if I care. Kill Kit. Kill your mother. Lose your estates you think are so bloody valuable. *Lose your head!*"

She shouted the last part, then pushed past him and ran through the maze, tears blinding her.

She was lost within three minutes and she just stood where she was crying. Maybe a person *couldn't* change history. Maybe it was predestined that Kit was going to die and Nicholas was going to be executed. Maybe it was never meant that the Stafford family should continue to live. Maybe no one could change what was going to happen.

Nicholas came to her, but he didn't speak, and Dougless was glad. She knew that mere words would not change what each felt must be done. Silently, she followed him out of the maze.

THIRTY-TWO

*F*or Dougless the next three days were hell. Everyone in the Stafford household was very excited about Nicholas's forthcoming marriage, and it was all anyone could talk of. The food, the clothes, who would be there, who from the Stafford household would get to go, and who would stay at home with Lady Margaret, were all topics of conversation. Huge carts were packed with the goods Nicholas and Kit would take with them to the Culpin estate, where the wedding would be held. With a feeling of doom, Dougless watched the preparations for the long visit. Nicholas and Kit were taking not only their clothes with them, but furniture and servants as well.

To Dougless it seemed that every item that was loaded onto the carts was a weight on her heart. She tried to talk to Nicholas. Tried and tried and tried. But he wouldn't listen. Duty meant more to him than anything else in the world. He would not forsake his duty to his family for any reason on earth, not for love, not even to avoid the possibility of his own death.

On the night before the day Nicholas was to leave, Dougless felt the worst she ever had. Only the day Nicholas had returned to the six-teenth century and left her in the church was comparable.

At night, after the maid had helped her undress, she removed her thin, silky slip from her tote bag and put it on. With her borrowed robe about her, she went to Nicholas's bedchamber.

Outside his room she put her hand to the door. She knew he was awake; she could feel it. Without knocking, she opened the door. He was sitting up in bed, the rough sheet covering his legs, leaving his chest and hard, flat stomach bare and exposed. He was drinking from a silver tankard, and he didn't look up when she entered.

"We must talk," she whispered. The room was silent except for the crackle of a fire and the sputter of candles.

"Nay, we have no more to say," he answered. "We both must do what we must."

"Nicholas," she whispered, but he still didn't look at her. She slipped the concealing robe from her. The nightgown she wore wasn't outrageous by twentieth-century standards, but it was when compared to Elizabethan modes of dress. Its thin straps, low neck, and clinging fabric left nothing to the imagination.

She crawled across the bed to him, like a tigress on the stalk. "Nicholas," she whispered. "Do not marry her."

When she was near him, he looked at her—and the wine sloshed from his tankard. "What do you?" he asked hoarsely, his eyes at first shocked, then hot.

"Perhaps you'll stay with me this night," she said, drawing nearer to him.

Nicholas looked down the front of her nightgown, and when he put out a hand to touch her shoulder, his hand trembled.

"One night," she whispered, moving her face close to his.

Nicholas reacted instantly. His arms were around her, his lips on hers; he was drinking of her, taking of her, as he'd wanted to do for so long. The fabric of her nightgown tore away as his hands and his lips were on her breasts, his face buried in them.

"This one night for your promise," Dougless was saying, her head back. She was trying to remember what she had to do before Nicholas's lips and hands drove all thoughts from her mind. "Swear to me," she said.

"All that I have is yours. Do you not know that?" he said, his lips moving lower on her body, down her stomach. His hands were on her hips, his fingers digging into her flesh.

"Then do not go tomorrow," she said. "This one night for tomorrow."

Nicholas's strong hands were lifting her hips up, and the remains of the gown were sliding farther down. "You may have all my tomorrows."

"Nicholas, please." Dougless was trying to remember what she meant to say, but Nicholas's touch was making her unable to think. "Please, my love. I do not believe I will be here after tonight, so you must swear to me."

After a moment Nicholas raised his head and looked up at her, up past her lovely body to her face. His mind was reeling with the sensations of touching this woman who had come to mean so much to him, but he was beginning to hear her. "What would you have me swear to you?" he asked in a low voice.

Dougless lifted her head. "I will spend tonight with you if you'll swear not to marry Lettice after I'm gone," she said evenly.

For a long moment Nicholas looked at her, his bare body poised over her half-nude body, and Dougless held her breath. She had not come to this decision easily, but she knew that, even if it meant losing Nicholas forever, she had to stop this marriage.

He rolled off of her and the bed in one smooth motion, pulled on a loose robe, then went to stand before the fire, his back to her. When he spoke, his voice was low and husky. "Do you think so little of me to believe I would risk the loss of you for one night's pleasure? Do you think so little of yourself to sell yourself to me for a promise?"

His words were making Dougless feel very small. She pulled her torn gown up over her shoulders. "I couldn't think of any other way," she said as an excuse. "I'd do *anything* to stop your marriage."

He turned to look at her, his eyes dark with emotion. "You have told me of your country and of your ways. Do you think yours is the only way? This marriage means naught to me, yet it means all to you."

"I can't have you risk your life for—"

His eyes blazed. "You risk *our* life for her!" he said angrily. "You tell me again and again that you cannot come to my bed. Yet you are here now, dressed as a . . . as a . . ."

Dougless pulled the sheet over her bare shoulders, feeling like a strumpet. "I only meant to try to get you to promise you wouldn't marry her," she said, feeling near to tears.

He went to the bed, looming over her. "What love is this you bear for me? You come creeping to my bed, appealing to me like a whore. Only you do not want gold, nay, you want me to dishonor my family, to put aside what means most to me."

Dougless put her hands over her face. "Don't, please. I can't bear this. I never meant—"

He sat on the edge of the bed and pulled her hands away. "Do you have any idea how much I dread the morrow? That I dread the woman who I must make my wife? Were I free, were I in your time, I could freely choose where I love. But here and now, I cannot. Were I to marry you, I could not feed you. Kit would no longer give me a place to live, food to eat, clothes to—"

"Kit's not like that. Surely there would be a way for us to live. You help Kit with the estates, so he'd not throw you out. He'd—"

Nicholas's hands tightened on her wrists. "Can you not hear? Can you not understand? I *must* make this marriage."

"No," she whispered. "No."

"You cannot stop what must be. You can only help me."

"How? How can I help you? Can I stop an axman's blade?"

"Aye," he said. "You can. You can stay by me for always."

"Always? While you live with another woman? Sleep with her? Make love to her?"

He released her hands. "So you do this," he said, looking at her bare shoulders above the sheet. "You would take yourself from me for all eternity rather than see me with another woman?"

"No, that's not it. It's just that Lettice is evil. I've told you what she'll do. Choose another woman."

He gave a smile that had no mirth in it. "You would allow me another wife? Allow me to touch another woman when I cannot touch you? You are willing to stand to one side for the rest of our lives?"

Dougless swallowed. Could she live in the same house with him while he lived with another woman? What would she do, be a maiden aunt to Nicholas's children? How would she feel when, each night, he went off to bed with another woman? And how long would he continue to love her if he couldn't touch her? Were either of them strong enough for a platonic love?

"I don't know," she said softly. "I don't know if I could stand by and see you with another woman. Nicholas, oh Nicholas, I don't know what to do."

He sat on the bed beside her and gathered her into his arms. "I will not risk losing you for a hundred women like Lettice. You are worth all to me. God has sent you to me, and I mean to hold you."

She put her head on his chest, parting the robe so her cheek was on his skin. In spite of herself, tears came to her eyes. "I am frightened. Lettice is—"

"A mere woman. No more, no less. She possesses no great wisdom, no amulets of power. If you are by me, she can do me or my family no harm."

"By you?" Her hand went under his robe, touching his skin. "Can I stay by you and not touch you?"

He moved her roaming fingers from inside his robe. "You are sure you will return if I . . ."

"Sure," she answered firmly. "At least I *think* I'm sure."

He held her fingers up and looked at them as a starving man might look at a feast. "It would be much to lose were we to try, would it not?"

"Yes," she said, sadly. "Much, much too much."

He dropped her hand. "You must go. I am a man, and you tempt me more than I can bear."

Dougless knew she should go, but she hesitated. Once again she put her hand on Nicholas's skin.

"Go!" he commanded.

Quickly, she rolled away from him, then ran from the room. She went back to Honoria's room and slipped into bed, but she didn't sleep.

Tomorrow the man she loved, no, more than loved, the man who meant so much that even time could not separate them, was leaving to marry another woman. What was she to do when Nicholas returned with his beautiful wife? (Dougless had heard so much of Lettice's beauty that she would have hated the woman even if she knew nothing else about her.) Should she curtsy and congratulate her? Something like, "Hope you enjoy him. And I certainly hope he's as good a lover with you as he was with me."

Dougless had a vision of Nicholas and his pretty wife laughing together over some private joke. She saw Nicholas sweeping Lettice into his arms and carrying her off to the room they shared. Would they put their heads together over meals and smile at each other?

Dougless slammed her fist into the pillow, making Honoria stir. Men were such fools. They never saw past a pretty face. When a man asked about a woman, all he wanted to know was, was she pretty? No man ever asked if a woman had morals, whether she was honest, kind, did she like children or not? Dougless imagined a beautiful Lettice torturing a puppy in front of Nicholas, but Nicholas not noticing because dear, luscious Lettice had looked at him through fluttering lashes.

"Men!" Dougless muttered, but even as she said it, she didn't mean it. Nicholas had not allowed himself to be seduced tonight because he was afraid he'd lose Dougless. If that wasn't love, what was?

"Maybe he was saving himself for Lettice," Dougless said into the pillow, and that's when she began to cry.

The sun came up and still Dougless cried. It was as though she couldn't stop. Honoria did everything she could to cheer Dougless up, but nothing worked.

Dougless could see, hear, think of nothing but Nicholas and the beautiful woman he was to marry. When Dougless thought of the hideous non-choices she had, she began to cry harder. She could stay in the sixteenth century and watch Nicholas with his wife, watch them talking together, watch while Lettice was given an honored place in the family as a son's wife. Or she could threaten Nicholas that he had to give up his wife or she, Dougless, would leave the house. And if she left the Stafford household, what would she do? How could she earn her living in the sixteenth century? Drive a taxi? Maybe become an executive secretary? She was rather good with computers. She'd been in the Elizabethan age long enough to see how well a lone woman would fare without a man. She couldn't so much as go two miles from the house without fear of being set upon by thieves.

And even if she could leave him, that would mean he'd be left in the hands of the scheming Lettice.

So what could she do if she couldn't leave and she couldn't stay? She could work harder at seducing Nicholas; then, after one lovely night of passion, she would be returned to the twentieth century. Without Nicholas. Alone. Never to see him again. She imagined herself at home in Maine, sitting by herself and thinking that she would give all she possessed to see Nicholas, to speak to him just one more time. By that time, she'd be so lonely she wouldn't care if he were with a hundred women, if she could just see him one more time.

"Women's lib doesn't cover this situation," she said through her tears. The ideal of equality for women said you weren't supposed to put up with the man in your life having affairs, so she guessed she certainly wasn't supposed to let him *marry* someone else.

It was all or nothing. To have Nicholas she had to share him; she'd have to share him physically, mentally, share him in every way possible. To leave him meant absolute, eternal loneliness for Dougless, and possibly death for Nicholas and his family.

Every thought made her cry harder. Days went by and still she cried. Honoria made sure that Dougless was dressed each day and she tried to see that she ate, but Dougless couldn't eat. She didn't care about eating or sleeping. Her mind was on Nicholas.

At first the other people in the Stafford household were sympathetic to Dougless's tears. They knew why she cried. They had seen the way she and Nicholas looked at each other, the way they touched. Some of them sighed and remembered their first loves. They felt sorry for Dougless when Nicholas went off to be married, and they saw the way Dougless cried in heart-broken grief. But their sympathy wore thin when Dougless's tears went on day after day after day. They became so annoyed that they began to ask themselves what use the woman was. Lady Margaret had given Dougless everything, but now Dougless was giving nothing in return. Where were the new games, the new songs the woman should be providing?

On the fourth day, Lady Margaret called Dougless to her.

Dougless, weak from fasting and endless tears, stood before Lady Margaret, her head down, her cheeks wet, her face swollen and red.

Lady Margaret was silent for a moment as she looked at Dougless's bent head and heard the soft weeping. "Cease!" Lady Margaret commanded. "I am most tired of your tears."

"I can't," Dougless said, hiccuping. "I can't seem to stop."

Lady Margaret grimaced. "Have you no spine? My son was a fool to believe himself to love you."

"I agree. I'm not worthy of him."

Sitting down, Lady Margaret contemplated Dougless's bent head. She knew her younger son well enough to know that this woman's tears would wrench his too-soft heart. Before he left, Nicholas was saying he could not do his duty and marry the Culpin woman. How would their marriage fare if he returned and found this strange red-haired wench crying for love of him? Lady Margaret had always been able to reason with Kit, but Nicholas, like his father, had a stubborn streak. She did not think Nicholas would do it, but what if he returned, saw the red-eyed face of this Dougless, and attempted to set his marriage aside?

Lady Margaret continued to look at the bent head before her. The woman *must* go from this house. Yet why did she hesitate in sending her away? For that matter, why had she allowed this woman into the Stafford house? At first Nicholas had been enraged that his mother had so trusted the oddly dressed, oddly spoken young woman enough to take an unknown tablet from her. Yet Lady Margaret had taken one look at the woman's face and she *had* trusted her. Trusted her with her life.

Nicholas had been so angry after that. Lady Margaret smiled in memory. Nicholas had locked the girl in a filthy cell at the top of the house, and she'd stayed up there, eaten by fleas, while Lady Margaret had argued with her son over the girl's fate. Nicholas had wanted to toss her into the road, and, in truth, Lady Margaret had known he was right. But something prevented her, something inside her, made her refuse to thrown the girl out.

It was Nicholas who had gone to get the girl. He had been "trying to reason" with his mother ("reason" is what he called his stubborn insistence that he was right) when, abruptly, he got up, left the room, and went to fetch the girl.

Lady Margaret smiled more broadly when she thought of the girl's absurd story of being a princess from far off Lanconia. Lady Margaret hadn't believed her for a moment, but the foolish story had given her a reason for keeping the girl near her, against Nicholas's strenuous protests.

Those first days had been divine. The girl was lively and entertaining beyond all reasoning. Even her speech was amusing. And her actions never failed to delight, puzzle, and fascinate. The girl was stupid about so many things, such as dressing and even eating, yet she was very clever about some things. She knew more about medicine than any physician. She told curious stories about the moon and the stars and the earth being round. She had devised a short, wide chair that was stuffed with down and had fabric nailed over it. She called it an "easy chair" and had given it to Lady Margaret. She didn't know it, but she had half the household rising early to hide in the gardens to watch her bathing in the fountain, using a marvelous foam on her hair and skin. In private Lady Margaret had inspected the wonders in her bag, had even used the little brush and something called toothpaste.

Oh, the girl was entertaining, all right. At one point, Lady Margaret had hoped she would never leave.

But then Nicholas had fallen in love with her. Lady Margaret had not at first cared. Young men often fell in love. At sixteen Kit had been in love with one of her ladies-in-waiting. Lady Margaret saw that the woman took Kit to bed and taught him a thing or two; then she'd sent Kit to the kitchens, where she knew a voluptuous servant girl was working. Within a week Kit had been "in love" with the serving wench.

Lady Margaret had had no such troubles with Nicholas. Nicholas had never needed an introduction to women. Over the years he had given his body freely, but never his heart.

She should have known that when Nicholas did give his heart, he would give it so completely that a hundred voluptuous serving girls would not be able to take it back. At first Lady Margaret had been glad when Nicholas had shown such extraordinary interest in this Dougless Montgomery. Lady Margaret had thought that when Nicholas returned with his bride, since Dougless loved him, the red-haired woman would not be tempted to leave the Stafford household. Lady Margaret would miss the girl's humor and knowledge if she were gone.

But as the days progressed, Lady Margaret refused to see just how attached Nicholas was becoming to her. When at last Lady Margaret had really looked at her household, what she saw did not please her. Her youngest son loved the woman to the point of obsession. Her eldest son spoke of giving the girl great riches, and Kit's future wife talked of little else except what Dougless said or did.

As did the rest of the household. "Dougless says children should not be swaddled." "Dougless says the wound must be washed." "Dougless says my husband had no right to beat me." "Dougless says a woman should have control of her own money." Dougless says, Dougless says, Lady Margaret thought. Who ran the Stafford household? Did the Staffords or this girl who lied about her relatives?

And now she stood before Lady Margaret weeping, weeping as she had done for days. Lady Margaret clenched her teeth when she thought of how the tears of this one woman were affecting everyone.

But worse, she knew that these tears would affect Nicholas. Nicholas who said he loved her, Nicholas who talked of breaking a betrothal because of this woman who had nothing, who was nothing. Yet this woman, to whom Lady Margaret had given so much, now threatened everything in her family. Were Nicholas to disavow his contract with the Culpin family . . . No, she did not like to think what could happen.

The red-haired woman *must* go.

Lady Margaret's mouth set into a firm, hard line. "The runner has come from Lanconia. You are no princess. You are related to no one in the royal house. Who are you?"

"J-just a woman. No one special," Dougless said, sniffing.

"We have given you all that our house has to offer, yet you have lied to us."

"Yes, I have." Dougless kept her head down, agreeing with everything. There was nothing anyone could say to her to make her feel worse. The marriage was to take place this morning. Today Nicholas would marry his beautiful Lettice.

Lady Margaret took a breath. "On the morrow you will leave us. You will take what clothes you came in, no more, and you will be sent forever from the Stafford house."

It took a moment for Douglass to understand. She looked at Lady Margaret, blinking at her through tear-filled eyes. "Leave? But Nicholas wishes me to stay, to be here when he returns."

"Do you think his wife will wish to see you? My foolish son has grown too attached to you. You do him harm."

"I would *never* harm Nicholas. I came here to save him, not to hurt him."

Lady Margaret glared at her. "From whence do you come? Where did you live before you came here?"

Douglass clamped her mouth shut. She could say nothing, absolutely nothing. If she told Lady Margaret the truth, Douglass's life would be worth nothing, and there would never be a chance of her seeing Nicholas again. "I . . . I will provide entertainments," Douglass said, her voice desperate. "I know more songs, more games. And I can tell you many more stories about America. I could tell you about airplanes and automobiles and—"

Lady Margaret put up her hand. "I weary of your amusements. I cannot feed and clothe you. Who are you? A peasant's daughter?"

"My father teaches, and I teach too. Lady Margaret, you can't throw me out. I have nowhere to go, and Nicholas needs me. I have to protect him as I protected Kit. I saved Kit's life, remember? He offered me a house then. I'll take it now."

"You asked for your reward and received it. Due to you, my son works as a tradesman."

"But—" Douglass put out her hands, pleading.

"You will go. We harbor no liars here."

"I'll wash dishes," Douglass said, pleading. "I'll be the family physician. I can't do worse than the leeches. I'll—"

"You will *leave!*" Lady Margaret half shouted, her eyes glistening like precious stones. "I will have you no longer in my house. My son asked to be released from his betrothal for you."

"He did?" Douglass almost smiled. "He never told me."

"You disarray my household. You bewitch my son till he does not know his duty. Be you glad I do not have a whip taken to you."

"This is better? Sending me out there, into those . . . those people? Sending me away from Nicholas?"

Lady Margaret stood up, then turned her back on Dougless. "I will not argue with you. Say your farewells this day, and on the morrow you will be sent from my house. Now go. I do not wish to see you again."

Numbly, Dougless turned and left the room. Not seeing anything, she made her way back to Honoria's room. Honoria took one look at her face and guessed what was wrong.

"Lady Margaret has sent you away?" Honoria whispered.

Dougless nodded.

"Do you have a place to go? One who will take care of you?"

Dougless shook her head. "I will be leaving Nicholas to that evil woman."

"Lady Lettice?" Honoria asked, puzzled. "The woman is cool perhaps, but I do not believe she is evil."

"You don't know her."

"You do?"

"I know a great deal about her. I know what she's going to do."

Honoria had learned to ignore these odd remarks of Dougless's. She thought perhaps that she didn't want to know all there was to know about Dougless. "Where will you go?"

"I have no idea."

"Do you have relatives?"

Dougless gave a weak smile. "Probably. I imagine there are some sixteenth-century Montgomerys about somewhere."

"But you do not know them?"

"I only know Nicholas." Nicholas who was by now, no doubt, married. She had thought she had choices, that she could choose to stay or go, but now it looked as though her fate had been decided for her. "I know Nicholas, and I know what will happen," she said tiredly.

"You shall go to my family," Honoria said firmly. "They will love your games and songs. They will care for you."

Dougless managed a bit of a smile. "That's very kind of you, but if I can't stay with Nicholas, I don't want to stay here at all."

Honoria's face whitened. "Suicide is against God."

"God," Dougless whispered and tears came to her eyes. "God did this to me, and now it's all going wrong." She closed her eyes. "Please," she whispered, eyes closed. "Please, Nicholas, don't marry her. I beg you, please."

Concerned, Honoria went to Dougless and felt her forehead. "You are warm. This day you must remain in bed. You are ill."

"I am past ill," Dougless said as she allowed Honoria to push her down on the bed. She barely felt Honoria's hands unfastening the front of her dress as she closed her eyes.

Hours later she opened her eyes to see a darkened room. She was in Honoria's bed wearing only her linen gown, her hair down. Her pillow was wet, so she knew she had been crying while she slept.

"Nicholas," she whispered. Married now. Married to the woman who would kill him, who would eventually kill all the Staffords. Dougless closed her eyes again. When she awoke next it was night outside and the room was very dark. Honoria was asleep beside her.

Something is wrong, Dougless thought. Very wrong. She remembered Lady Margaret telling her that she must leave the Stafford family, but there was something else.

"Nicholas," she whispered. "Nicholas needs me."

She got out of bed and went into the hall. All was quiet. Barefoot, she went down the stairs, her feet moving about under the dried river rushes on the floor. She went out the back toward the garden, following where instinct and some indefinable pull led her.

She went across the brick terrace, down the stairs, along the raised walk, then turned into the knot garden. There was only a quarter moon, so it was very dark, but she didn't need to see, for she had an inner sight.

As she approached the garden, she heard the fountain splashing, the fountain where she had showered each morning until Nicholas left. She had not been outside since Nicholas rode away.

There, standing in the fountain, his body nude, covered in soap lather, was Nicholas.

Dougless didn't think, and certainly used no reason. One minute she was outside the fountain, and the next she was in Nicholas's wet arms, holding him, kissing him with all the desperation and fear that she felt.

Everything happened too suddenly for her to stop and think. She was in his arms; they were on the ground; she was nude. They came together with a clash of pent-up desire that made Dougless cry out. Nicholas, not gently, no, not gentle at all, bent her body backward over a stone bench and rammed into her with blinding force. Dougless held on to his shoulders, her nails digging into his skin, put her legs about his waist, and held on.

Fast, furious, frantic, they tore at each other. Their bodies, covered with sweat, stuck together as they rose and fell together, again, again, again.

When at last they finished, Nicholas put his strong hands under her and lifted her to meet his final deep, deep thrust. Dougless cried out as the world darkened and her body stiffened as she found release.

It was a while before she recovered herself and could see again, think again. Nicholas was grinning at her, his teeth white. Even in the darkness she could see his happiness.

But Dougless was beginning to think. "What have we done?" she whispered.

Nicholas unwrapped her legs from his body and pulled her to stand before him. "We have just begun."

She was blinking at him, trying to make her mind work, because her body was trembling at the touch of him. The tips of her breasts were touching his chest and they were tingling. "Why are you here? Oh, God, Nicholas, what have we done?" She started to sit on the bench, but he pulled her into his arms.

"Later there will be time for words," he said. "Now I will do what I have much wanted to do."

"No," she said as she pushed away from him. She was fumbling about for the remnants of her gown. "We have to talk now. There will be no time later. Nicholas!" Her voice was rising. "We will have *no more time!*"

He pulled her back into his arms. "You do still insist you will disappear? Here, look you, we have tasted—merely tasted—of one another, yet you do remain."

How could she tell him? She collapsed on the bench, her head down. "I knew you were here. I felt you. And just as I knew you needed me, I know that this is our last night together."

Nicholas didn't speak, but after a moment he sat down on the bench beside her, very close, but their nude bodies were not touching. "I have always felt you," he said softly. "This night you heard my call, but it has always been so with me. After I left I . . ." He paused. "I felt your tears. I could hear nothing but your weeping. I could not see Lettice for seeing you in your tears."

Putting out his hand, he took hers. "I left the woman. I said naught, not even to Kit. I took my horse and rode. When I should have been saying vows, I was riding to you. It took until now to reach you."

This is what she had wanted, but now that it was here, the enormity of what he'd done scared her. She looked at him. "What will happen now?"

"There will be . . . anger," he said, "anger on both sides. Kit . . . My mother will . . ." He looked away.

Dougless could see how torn he was between duty and love. But now she wouldn't be here to help him. She squeezed his hand. "You will not marry her even after I'm gone?"

He turned blazing eyes toward her. "You would leave me now?"

Tears came again to her eyes as she flung herself against him. "I would *never* leave you if I had a choice, but I don't. Not now. Now there is no choice. I will go soon, I know it. I can feel it."

He kissed her, then smoothed her hair back. "How much time?" he whispered.

"Dawn. No more. Nicholas, I—"

He silenced her with a kiss. "I would rather hours with you than a lifetime with another. Now, no more talk. Come, we will love away these hours."

He stood up, then pulled her up beside him and led her into the still-running fountain, where he began to lather her with the last of her soft soap. "You left this behind," he said, smiling at her.

Forget that this is the end, Dougless thought. Forget it. Time *must* stand still for this one night. "How did you kn-know I showered here?" she asked, her voice stumbling.

"I was one of those who watched."

She stopped soaping herself, and Nicholas's hands stilled at her look. "Watched? Who watched me?"

"All," he said, grinning. "Did you not notice the men's yawns? They rose most early to hide themselves."

"Hide!" Her anger was rising. "And you were one of them? You *allowed* this? You let men spy on me?"

"Were I to have stopped you, I would have halted my own pleasure. It was a dilemma."

"Dilemma! Why, you—!" She lunged at him.

Nicholas sidestepped, then caught her, pulling her close to him. He forgot about soaping her as he bent his head and began kissing her breasts, the water pouring down on top of them. "I have dreamed of this," he said, "since my vision."

"The shower," she murmured. "The shower." Her hands were entangled in his hair as his mouth moved lower and lower. He was on his knees before her. "Nicholas, my Nicholas."

They made love again, as they had done before, in the water. For Nicholas it was a discovery of her body, but for Dougless, she had had weeks of remembering and wanting. Her hands were all over him, memorizing, remembering, finding new places she had not touched or tasted before.

By the time they finished, it was hours later. The water had stopped flowing, and Dougless guessed that whoever was turning the wheel was too tired to continue. She and Nicholas lay in each other's arms on the sweet grass.

"We have to talk," she said at last.

"Nay, do not."

She snuggled closer to him. "I must. I wish with all my heart that I didn't have to speak, but I must."

"On the morrow, when the sun touches your hair, you will laugh at this. You are no woman from the future. You are here with me now. You will remain with me for all time."

"I wish . . ." Her voice grew hoarse and she swallowed. Her hand was roaming over his body, touching him. The last time. The last time. "Nicholas, please," she said. "Listen to me."

"Aye, I will listen, then I will love you again."

"When you left before, no one remembered you. It was as though you hadn't existed. It was so horrible for me." She buried her face in his shoulder. "You had come and gone, but no one remembered. It was as though I'd made you up."

"I am most forgettable."

She raised on her elbow to look at him, to touch his beard, his cheek, to caress his eyebrows, to kiss his eyelids. "I will never forget you."

"Nor I, you." He lifted a bit to kiss her lips, but when he wanted more, Dougless pulled away.

"The same may happen when I leave. I want you to be prepared if no one remembers me. Don't . . . I don't know what to say . . . Don't make yourself crazy trying to make them remember."

"No one will forget."

"They probably will. What if the songs I taught you were remembered? It could ruin some very good Broadway shows in the twentieth century." She tried to smile but didn't quite make it. "I want you to swear some things to me."

"I will not marry Lettice. I doubt now I will be asked again," he said sarcastically.

"Good. Oh, very, very good. Now I won't have to read about your execution." She ran her fingertips over his neck. "Promise me you'll take care of James. No more swaddling, and play with him sometimes."

He kissed her fingertips and nodded.

"Take care of Honoria; she's been so good to me."

"I will find her the best of husbands."

"Not the richest, the *best*. Promise?" When he nodded, she went on. "And anyone who's delivering a baby has to wash his or her hands first. And you have to build Thornwyck Castle and leave records behind that show that *you* designed it. I want history to know."

He was smiling at her. "Naught else? You will have to remain by my side to remind me of all this."

"I would," she whispered. "I would, but I cannot. May I have the miniature of you?"

"You may have my heart, my soul, my life."

She clasped his head in her arms. "Nicholas, I can't bear it."

"There is naught bad to bear," he said, kissing her arm, her shoulder, his lips traveling downward. "Perhaps Kit will give me a small estate, and we—"

She pulled away to look at him. "Wrap the miniature of you in oiled cloth, something that will protect it over the next four hundred years, and put it behind the . . . What's the stone thing that holds up the beams?"

"A corbel."

"At Thornwyck Castle you'll make a corbel that's a portrait of Kit. Wrap the miniature and put it behind the corbel. When I . . . when I return, I'll go get it."

He was kissing her breast.

"Did you hear me?"

"I heard all. James. Honoria. Midwives. Thornwyck. Kit's face." With each word, he punctuated it with a little sucking-kiss on her breast. "Now, my love," he whispered, "come to me."

He lifted her body and set her down on top of him, and Dougless forgot everything on earth except the touch of this man she loved so much. He stroked her hips, her breasts as they moved together. Up and down. Slowly at first, then building faster.

Nicholas rolled with her until she was on her back, and his passion rose as he entered her deeply, her body rising to meet his. They arched together, both with their heads back, then they collapsed, Nicholas on top of her, holding her very tightly.

"I love you," he whispered. "I will love you for all time."

Dougless clung to him, holding him as tightly as she could. "You will remember me? You won't forget me?"

"Never," he said. "Never will I forget you. Were I to die tomorrow, my soul would remember you."

"Don't speak of death. Speak only of life. With you I am alive. With you I am whole."

"And I with you." He rolled to one side and pulled her close to him. "Look, you. The sun comes up."

"Nicholas, I'm afraid."

He stroked her damp hair. "Afraid of being seen unclad? It is not something we have not seen before."

"You!" she said, laughing. "I'll never forgive you for not telling me."

"I will have a lifetime in which to make you forgive me."

"Yes," she whispered. "Yes. It will take a lifetime."

He glanced at the lightening sky. "We must go. I must tell my mother what I have done. Kit will no doubt be here soon."

"They will be very angry. And my part in this won't help matters any."

"You must go to Kit with me. I will be shameless. I will tell my brother he must give us a place to live in memory of your saving him."

Dougless looked up at the sky, saw it was growing lighter by the minute. She could almost believe she was going to be able to stay with him. "We'll live in a pretty little house somewhere," she said, her words beginning to gain speed. "We'll have only a few servants, fifty or so," she said, smiling. "And we'll have a dozen kids. I like kids. And we'll educate them properly and teach them how to wash. Maybe we can invent a flush toilet."

Nicholas chuckled. "You wash too much. My sons will not—"

"*Our* sons. I'm going to have to explain to you about women's equality."

He stood up, then pulled her into his arms. "Will this explaining take long?"

"About four hundred years," she whispered.

"Then I will give you the time."

"Yes," she said, smiling. "Time. We will have all the time we need."

He kissed her then, kissed her long and hard and deeply; then his kiss lightened. "Forever," he whispered. "I will love you throughout time."

One moment Dougless was in his arms, his lips on hers, and the next she was in the church at Ashburton, and outside a jet flew overhead.

THIRTY-THREE

ougless didn't cry. What she was feeling was too deep, too profound for her to cry. She was sitting on the floor in the little church in Ashburton, and she knew that behind her was Nicholas's marble tomb. She couldn't bear to look at it, couldn't bear to see the warm flesh of Nicholas translated into cold marble.

She sat where she was for a while and looked at the church. It looked so old and so plain. There was no color on the beams or on the walls, and the stone floors looked bare with no rushes on them. In the first pews were some needlepointed pillows, and now they looked crude. She was used to seeing Lady Margaret's women's exquisite needlework.

When the door of the church opened and the vicar came in, Dougless sat where she was.

"Are you all right?" the vicar asked.

At first Dougless couldn't understand him. His accent and his pronunciation were foreign sounding. "How long have I been here?" she asked.

The vicar frowned. This young woman was so very strange. She walked in front of speeding vehicles, she insisted she was with a man when she was alone, and now she had just walked into the church and was asking how long she had been here. "A few minutes, no more," he answered.

Dougless gave a weak smile. A few minutes. A lifetime in the sixteenth century and she had been away only a few minutes. When she tried to stand, her legs were weak and the vicar helped her rise.

"Perhaps you should see a doctor," the vicar said.

A psychiatrist perhaps, Dougless almost answered. If she told her story to a psychiatrist, would he write a book and make what happened to Dougless into a Movie-of-the-Week? "No, I'm fine, really," she whispered. "I just need to get back to my hotel and—" And what? What was there for her to do now that Nicholas was gone? She took a step forward.

"Don't forget your bag."

Dougless turned to see her old tote bag on the floor by the tomb. The contents of that bag had helped her throughout her time in the Elizabethan age. Looking at it, she felt a closeness to the bag. It had been where she had been. She went to it and on impulse unzipped the top of it. She didn't have to inspect the contents to know that everything was there. The bottle of aspirin was full; none of the pills she had given away were missing. Her toothpaste tube was full, not flat. No cold tablets were missing, no pages gone from her notebook. Everything was as it had been.

She lifted the tote bag, slung the strap onto her shoulder, then turned away. But abruptly, she halted; then she turned and glanced back at the base of the tomb. Something was different. She wasn't at first sure what it was, but something had changed.

Careful not to look at the sculpture of Nicholas, she stared at the base.

"Is something wrong?" the vicar asked.

Dougless read the inscription twice before she realized what was different. "The date," she whispered.

"The date? Ah, yes, the tomb is quite old."

Nicholas's death date was 1599. *Not* 1564. Bending, she touched the numbers, trying to make sure she was seeing correctly. Thirty-five years. He had lived thirty-five years past when he was supposed to have been executed.

It was only after she had touched the date that she looked up at the tomb. The sculpture was of Nicholas, but it was very different now. It was not a portrait of a young man, dead in his prime, but of an older man, a man who had been able to live out his life. She looked down the length of him, saw that his clothes were different. He wore the longer knee breeches of 1599, instead of the short slops of thirty years earlier.

She caressed his cold cheek, traced the lines the sculptor had put at the corners of his eyes. "We did it," she whispered. "Nicholas, my love, we did it."

"I beg your pardon," the vicar said.

When Dougless looked at him, she gave him a dazzling smile. "We changed history," she said; then, still smiling, she walked outside into the sunshine.

She stood in the graveyard for a moment, feeling disoriented. The gravestones were so old, yet an hour before stones with these dates had been new. Dougless gasped in horror at the first sight of a car. And as she gasped, she felt her lungs expand; no steel corset confined her ribcage. For a moment she had a deep sense of everything being wrong. She felt naked and drab in her plain clothes. She looked down at her boring skirt and blouse with distaste. And her back felt as though it had nothing to support it now that her corset was gone, and her leather boots pinched her feet.

Another car went by, and the speed of it made Dougless feel dizzy. She walked to the gate, opened it, then stepped onto the sidewalk. How odd to have concrete under her feet. As she walked, she looked with awe at the buildings about her. There were huge expanses of glass; the shop signs had writing on them. Who can read them? she thought, remembering that where she had been few people could read, so signs were painted with pictures of what was sold in the shops.

How clean everything was, she thought. No mud, no chamber pot emptyings, no kitchen slops, no pigs foraging. The people in the street were odd-looking too. They all wore the same drab clothes as she did.

And they all seemed to be equal, no beggars dressed in filthy rags, no ladies with pearls on their skirts.

Dougless slowly walked down the street, staring wide-eyed, as though she'd never seen the twentieth century before. The smell of food made her turn and enter a pub. For a moment she stood in the doorway and looked about. Obviously, the place was supposed to be a facsimile of an Elizabethan tavern, but it missed by a long way. It was too clean, too quiet, too . . . lonely, she thought. The people sitting at the tables were isolated from one another. Not at all like the gregarious, nosy Elizabethans.

At the back of the pub was a chalkboard with the menu on it. Dougless ordered six courses, taking no notice of the waitress's raised eyebrows; then she went to a table to sit down and sip her beer. The thick glass mug felt odd and the beer tasted as though it were half water.

On the bar was a rack of guidebooks to the historic houses of Great Britain. Dougless handed the barman a ten-pound note, then took the book back to her booth and began to read it. Bellwood was open to the public, just as it had been before. She looked for Nicholas's other houses and found that they were no longer listed as being ruins. All eleven of the houses Nicholas had once owned were still standing. And three of them were owned by the Stafford family.

Dougless blinked hard as she reread the passage. The guidebook said that the Stafford family was one of the oldest and wealthiest in England, that in the seventeenth century they had married into the royal family, and that the present duke was a cousin to the queen.

"Duke," Dougless whispered. "Nicholas, your descendants are dukes."

When the food came, Dougless was a bit startled at the way it was served, without ceremony, all the dishes being put on the table at once.

As she ate, she kept reading the guidebook. Except for Bellwood, all Nicholas's houses were private residences and not open to the public. She turned to Thornwyck Castle. It too was a private residence, but a small section of it was open to the public on Thursdays. "The current duke feels that the beauty of Thornwyck, designed by his ancestor, the brilliant scholar Nicholas Stafford, must be shared with the world," she read.

"'Brilliant scholar,'" she whispered. Not the ladies' man he had once been called. Not a rogue, not a wastrel, but a "brilliant scholar."

She closed the guidebook and looked up. The waitress was hovering over her with an odd expression on her face.

"Something wrong with your fork?" she asked.

"Fork?" Dougless couldn't think what the woman was talking about. The waitress continued to stare at Dougless until she looked down at her empty plate. There beside it lay an unused fork. Dougless had eaten her meal with a spoon and a knife. "It's all right. I just—" She couldn't think of what to say, so she gave the woman a weak smile and looked at the bill. The amount—enough to buy a hundred medieval dinners—made her blanch, but she paid it.

And before she left, she asked the waitress what day of the week it was—something she couldn't remember—and was pleased to find out that it was Wednesday.

Outside again, she didn't allow herself to stand still. If she stayed in one place too long, she knew that she'd start to think; she'd think about Nicholas, about losing him, and about never seeing him again.

She practically ran to the train station to catch the first train to Bellwood. She had to see what had changed. On the train ride she made herself read the guidebook, anything to fill her mind.

By now she knew the way to Bellwood from the train station very well. According to twentieth-century time, she had visited the house only the day before—the day when she'd heard of Nicholas's execution. The guide hadn't been very pleasant. After all, she remembered Dougless as having opened and closed the alarmed door and disturbing her tour.

Dougless bought her ticket and guidebook for the tour, and when she got in line, the same guide was at the head.

In the house, Dougless, who had once thought it was so beautiful, now saw it as bare and drab and lifeless. There were no plates of gold and silver on the hearths, no exquisite needlework on the tables, no cushions on the chairs. But most of all there were no richly dressed people moving about, no people laughing, and no music anywhere.

They were at Nicholas's room before Dougless could recover from her distaste for the barren house. She stood to one side, looked up at

Nicholas's portrait, and listened to the guide. The story was different now—very, very different.

The guide could not use enough superlatives when describing Nicholas.

"He was a true Renaissance man," the guide told them, "the epitome of what his era hoped to achieve. He designed beautiful houses that were a hundred years ahead of his time. He made great advances in the field of medicine, even writing a book on disease prevention that, had it been adhered to, would have saved thousands of lives."

"What did the book say?" Dougless asked.

The guide gave her a hard look, obviously remembering the door-opening incident. "Basically, Lord Nicholas talked of cleanliness and said that doctors and midwives must wash their hands before touching a patient. Now, if you'll follow me, we shall see—"

Dougless left the tour after that, went out the entrance, and walked to the village library.

She spent the afternoon reading the history books. Every scrap of information was different now. She saw the names of people she had known and come to love. They were just names in history books to other readers, but to her they were flesh and blood people.

After three husbands, Lady Margaret never married again, and lived into her seventies.

Kit had married little Lucy, and one book said Lucy had come to be a great benefactress who encouraged musicians and artists. Kit had run the Stafford estates well until he died of a stomach ailment at age forty-two. Since he and Lucy had had no children, the earldom and estates went to Nicholas.

As she read about Nicholas, she touched the printed words, as though they could make him seem closer. When she read that Nicholas had never married, quick tears came to her eyes, but she blinked them away.

Nicholas had lived to the grand old age of sixty-two, and during his life he had done many great things. The books went into detail about the beauty and creativity of the buildings he had designed. "His use of glass was far ahead of its time," one author wrote.

One book told of Nicholas's ideas about medicine, how he had crusaded for cleanliness. "Had his advice been taken," the author said, "modern medicine would have had its start hundreds of years earlier."

"Far ahead of his time," the books said again and again.

She leaned back in her chair. No Arabella-on-the-table. No diary being found that told of what a womanizer Nicholas was. No betrayal. No conspiracy between his wife and his friend. And, most important, no execution.

She left when the library closed, walked to the station, and took a train back to Ashburton. She still had a room at the hotel and her clothes were there.

Once in her hotel room, she had difficulty adjusting to the modernness of it, especially the bathroom. She took a shower, but couldn't bear the hot water or the hard, sharp forcefulness of the showerhead. She turned the knobs until the water was a lukewarm drizzle and felt more at home.

The flushing of the toilet seemed like a waste of water to her, and she kept staring at the big mirror in wonder.

After a room service supper, she put on her flimsy nightgown and felt like a lewd woman. And when she went to bed, she felt lonely without Honoria beside her.

Surprisingly, she went to sleep immediately, and if she dreamed, she did not remember doing so.

In the morning she had difficulty with the hotel when she asked for beef and beer for breakfast, but the English, better than any other people on earth, understood eccentrics.

She reached Thornwyck Castle by ten A.M., just as the gates were opening. She bought a ticket and started on the tour. The guide talked at length about the Stafford family, some of whose members still owned the house, and especially about their brilliant ancestor, Nicholas Stafford.

"He never married," the guide said with twinkling eyes, "but he had a son named James. When Nicholas's older brother died and left no children, Nicholas inherited, and when Nicholas died, the Stafford estates went to James."

Dougless smiled, remembering the sweet little boy she had played with.

The guide continued. "James made a brilliant marriage and tripled the family fortunes. It was through James that the Stafford family really made its money."

And he would have died if Dougless had not intervened.

The guide went on to the next generation of the family and the next room, but Dougless slipped away. When she'd seen Thornwyck before, it had been half in ruins, but Nicholas had shown her the corbel with Kit's face high on the wall of what would have been the second floor. Unfortunately, the second floor was not open to the public.

But Dougless had been through too much to allow anything to stop her. She opened a door that said NO ADMITTANCE, and found herself in a small sitting room furnished in English chintz. Feeling like a spy, but also knowing that she had to do what she did, she went to the doorway and peered out. The hall was clear, so she tiptoed down it, thinking that carpet on the floor made sneaking much easier than noisy rushes.

She found a staircase and went up to the second floor. Twice she had to hide when she heard footsteps, but no one saw her. In Nicholas's time there would have been so many servants running about that it would have been impossible for an intruder to get to the second floor unnoticed, but those days were long gone.

Once on the second floor, she had trouble orienting herself as she tried to remember just where the corbel would be. She searched three rooms before she entered a bedroom and saw it, high up above a beautiful walnut dresser.

She plastered herself between the dresser and the wall as a maid walked out of the adjoining bath. Dougless held her breath as the maid straightened the bedspread, then left the room.

Alone again, Dougless went to work. She pulled a heavy chair beside the dresser, climbed on it, then, after three tries, managed to climb on top of the dresser. She had just put her hand on the old stone corbel when the door opened. Dougless flattened herself against the wall.

The maid came in again, this time with an armload of towels that blocked her from seeing Dougless. She didn't breathe until the woman left.

When the door closed, Dougless turned and touched Kit's stone face. The stonework looked to be solid and she wished she'd had the foresight to bring a screwdriver or small crowbar. She pulled and tugged at the face and was almost ready to give up when the stone moved in her hand.

She broke her nails and skinned her knuckles, but she was at last able to pull the face away. A long piece of stone protruded from the back of the face and fit neatly into the corbel.

Standing on tiptoe, Dougless looked behind the head. Inside a hollowed-out place was a small cloth-wrapped package. Quickly, she took the package, slipped it into her pocket, then shoved the corbel back into place and climbed down. She didn't take the time to put the chair back as she hurried from the room.

She made it, without being seen, back to the tour just as the group was in the last room.

"And here we have the lace display," the guide was saying. "Most of the lace is Victorian, but we do have a very special piece of lace from the sixteenth century."

Dougless gave the guide all of her attention.

"It seems that although Lord Nicholas Stafford of the sixteenth century never married, there was a mysterious woman in his past. On his deathbed he asked to be buried with this piece of lace, but there was some confusion and Lord Nicholas went to his grave without the lace. His son, James, said the lace was always to be kept in a place of honor in the family, since it had meant so much to his beloved father."

Dougless had to wait for the other tourists to move before she could see into the case. There, under glass, yellowed now and worn-looking, was the lace cuff Honoria had been making for her. The name *Dougless* was worked into it.

"'Dougless'?" a tourist said, laughing. "That's a man's name. Maybe ol' Nick didn't marry because he was a little"—he waved his hand—"you know."

Dougless spoke before the guide could. "For your information, 'Dougless' was a woman's name in the sixteenth century, and I can assure you that Lord Nicholas Stafford was *not* a little"—she glared at him— "'you know.'" Storming past him, she left the house.

She walked into the gardens, and while other tourists exclaimed over their beauty, Dougless thought they looked messy and neglected. She went to a quiet corner, sat on a bench, then took the package from her pocket.

Slowly, she unwrapped it. Touching the waxed cloth bindings that had last been touched by Nicholas so long ago, made her fingers tremble.

The miniature portrait of Nicholas came to light, as rich and bright as the day it had been painted. "Nicholas," she whispered as she put her fingertips on the painting. "Oh, Nicholas, have I truly lost you completely? Are you gone from me forever?"

She looked at the miniature, touched it, and when she turned it over, she saw something engraved on the back. Holding it up to the light, she read the inscription.

Time has no meaning
Love will endure

He had signed it with an *N,* a *D* over the top of it.

Leaning back against the old stone wall, she blinked away tears. "Nicholas, come back to me," she whispered. "Please come back to me."

She sat there for a long time before she rose. She'd missed lunch, so she went to the tea shop and sat down with a plate of scones and a pot of strong black tea. She'd bought a guidebook at Bellwood and one at Thornwyck, and as she ate and drank, she read.

With every word she read, she told herself that what had happened had been worth the pain of losing the man she loved. What did the love between two people matter when, by giving up their love, they had changed history? Kit had lived, Lady Margaret had lived, James had lived—and Nicholas had lived. And with their lives, the family honor had been saved, so that today a Stafford was a duke and part of the royal family.

Against all that, what did one piddling little love affair mean?

She left the tea shop and walked to the train station. She could go home now, she thought, home to America, home to her family. No more would she be an outsider, and never again would she have to pretend to be someone she was not.

On the train ride back to Ashburton, she told herself that she should be jubilant. She and Nicholas had accomplished so much. How many other people had had the good fortune to be able to change history? Yet Dougless had been given that opportunity. Through her efforts the Stafford family was doing well. There were beautiful buildings standing because she had encouraged Nicholas to use his talent for designing. There were . . .

Her thoughts trailed off. It was no use telling herself what she *should* feel, because what she did feel was miserable.

In Ashburton she slowly walked back to the hotel. She'd need to call the airlines and make reservations.

In the lobby, Robert and Gloria were waiting for her. At the moment she didn't think she could handle a confrontation. She hardly looked at Robert. "I'll get the bracelet," she said, then turned away before he could speak.

Catching her arm, he halted her. "Dougless, could we talk?"

She stiffened, preparing herself for his abuse. "I told you I'd get the bracelet for you, and I apologize for keeping it."

"Please," he said, and his eyes were soft.

Dougless looked at Gloria. Gone from the girl's face was the smug, I'm-going-to-get-you look. Wary, Dougless went to sit on a chair across from father and daughter. Lucy, and Robert Sydney, Dougless thought. How much Gloria looked like Kit's bride-to-be and how much this Robert resembled a sixteenth-century Robert. Dougless thought of how she and Nicholas had changed the lives of both of those people. Robert Sydney had been given no reason to hate Nicholas because Arabella had not been impregnated on a table. And Dougless had helped Lucy gain some self-confidence.

Robert cleared his throat, then spoke. "Gloria and I have been talking, and we, well, we decided that maybe we weren't quite fair to you."

Dougless stared at him, her eyes wide. At one point in her life she had looked at Robert while wearing a blindfold. She saw only what she'd wanted to see; she had endowed him with characteristics that he didn't have. Now, looking back at their life together, she saw that he'd never loved her. "What do you want from me?" she asked tiredly.

"We just wanted to apologize," Robert said, "and we'd like for you to join us on the rest of the trip."

"You can sit in front," Gloria said.

Dougless looked from one to the other, puzzled, not by their words, for Robert would often apologize to get her to do what he wanted, but by the sincere looks on their faces. It was almost as though they really meant what they were saying. "No," she said softly, "I'm going home tomorrow."

Robert reached out and took her hand. "Home to my house, I hope." His eyes were bright. "To the house that will be ours as soon as we're married."

"Married?" Dougless whispered.

"Please, Dougless, I'm asking you to marry me. I was a fool not to see how good we were together."

Dougless gave a bit of a smile. Here was what she'd wanted so much: marriage to a respectable, stable man.

She took a deep breath and smiled more broadly, for suddenly she didn't feel like selling herself so cheaply. She was no longer the baby of the family who wasn't as good as her big sisters. She was a woman who had been transported to a foreign time, and not only had she survived, she had succeeded in accomplishing a monumental task. No longer did she need to prove herself to her too-perfect family by bringing home an achieving husband. No, Dougless was the achiever now.

She picked up Robert's hand and put it back on his lap. "Thanks, but no thanks," she said pleasantly.

"But I thought you wanted to get married." He looked to be genuinely confused.

"And Daddy said I could be your maid of honor," Gloria said.

"When I do get married, it will be to someone who wants to give to me," Dougless said, then looked at Gloria. "And I will choose my own bridesmaids."

Gloria turned red and looked down at her hands.

"You've changed, Dougless," Robert said softly.

"I have, haven't I?" she answered, wonder in her voice. "I really, truly have changed." She stood up. "I'll get your bracelet now."

When she started toward the stairs, Robert followed her, Gloria remaining in the lobby. He didn't speak to her until she unlocked her room and went inside. Following her inside, he shut the door behind him.

"Dougless, is it someone else?"

She took the diamond bracelet from where she'd hidden it in her suitcase and held it out to him. "There is no one," she said, feeling the loss of Nicholas.

"Not even the man you said you were helping to research?"

"The research is done, and he's . . . gone."

"Permanently?"

"As permanently as time can manage." She looked away a moment, then back at him. "I'm quite tired now, and I have a long flight tomorrow, so I'll say good-bye. When I get back to the States, I'll clear my things out of your house."

"Dougless, please reconsider. We can't end what we've had because of a little argument. We love each other."

When she looked at him, she thought about how at one time in her life she'd thought she loved him. But now she knew their relationship had been one-sided, with Dougless doing all the pleading, all the trying-to-please. "What has changed you?" she asked. "How could you leave me stranded in a foreign country with no money just a few days ago and now be here asking me to marry you?"

Robert's face turned a bit red, and he looked away sheepishly. "I really do apologize about that." When he looked back at her, his face was filled with sincerity—and also a little confusion. "It was the oddest thing. You know, all your family's money used to make me furious. I put myself through medical school while living on canned beans, yet you'd always had everything. You have a family who adores you and a history of wealth that goes back centuries. I hated the way you used to play at living on your teacher's salary, because I knew you could get all the money you ever wanted if you'd just ask. When I left you at that church, I knew Gloria had your bag, and I was glad. I wanted you to see what it was like to have to survive without money, to have to rely on yourself as I've always had to."

He took a breath and his face softened. "But then, yesterday, everything changed. Gloria and I were in a restaurant, and quite suddenly I wished you were with us. I . . . I wasn't angry at you anymore. Does that make sense? All the anger I felt for your having been given everything just evaporated. Gone, as though it'd never been there."

He went to her and put his hands on her shoulders. "I was a fool to let someone like you get away. If you'll let me, I'll spend the rest of my life making it up to you. We don't have to get married if you don't want to. We don't have to live together. I'll . . . I'll court you if you'll allow me. I'll court you with flowers and candy and . . . and balloons. What do you say? Give me another chance?"

Dougless stared at him. He said that yesterday his anger had left him. All her days in the sixteenth century had passed in just a few minutes of twentieth-century time, and during her time with Nicholas, she had defused the anger of Robert's and Gloria's look-alikes. Could this Robert's anger have been based on his bitterness over what had happened in the sixteenth century? When Robert had first seen Nicholas, he had looked at him with rage. Why? Because Nicholas had once impregnated his wife?

And Gloria seemed to be no longer angry with Dougless. Because Dougless had helped an earlier incarnation of Gloria? Because an earlier Gloria no longer believed the man she loved wanted Dougless?

Dougless gave her head a shake to clear it. *Were I to die tomorrow, my soul would remember you,* Nicholas had said. Did Robert and Gloria have the souls of people who had lived before?

"Will you give me another chance?" Robert repeated.

Smiling, Dougless kissed him on the cheek. "No," she said, "although I thank you very much for the offer."

When she pulled away from him, Dougless was glad to see he wasn't angry. "Someone else?" he asked again, as though his ego could stand that rejection better than her choosing to have no one rather than him.

"Sort of."

Robert looked at the bracelet in his hand. "If I'd bought an engagement ring instead of this . . . Well, who knows?" He looked back at her. "He's a lucky S.O.B, whoever he is. I wish you all the luck in the world." He left the room, shutting the door behind him.

Dougless stood in the empty room for a moment, then went to the telephone to call her parents. She wanted to hear the sound of their voices.

Elizabeth answered.

"Are Mother and Dad back yet?" Dougless asked.

"No, they're still at the cabin. Dougless, I demand that you tell me what is going on. If you're in one of your scrapes again, you'd better tell me so I can get you out of it. *You* aren't the one in jail this time, are you?"

Dougless was amazed to find that the words of her perfect older sister didn't anger her, nor did they make her feel guilty. "Elizabeth," she said firmly, "I would appreciate it if you didn't speak to me in that manner. I called to tell my family that I am coming home."

"Oh," Elizabeth said. "I didn't mean anything; it's just that usually you're in one mess or another."

Dougless did not speak.

"Okay, I apologize. Would you like me to meet you and Robert at the airport, or does he have his car?"

"Robert won't be with me."

"Oh," Elizabeth said again, allowing time for Dougless to explain. When Dougless was silent, Elizabeth went on. "Dougless, we'll all be very glad to see you."

"And I'll be glad to see you. Don't meet me, I'll rent a car, and, Elizabeth, I've missed you."

There was a pause, then Elizabeth said, "Come home and I'll cook a celebration dinner."

Dougless groaned. "When did you say Mother was returning?"

"All right, so I'm not the world's best cook. You cook, I'll clean up the kitchen."

"It's a deal. I'll be there day after tomorrow."

"Dougless!" Elizabeth said. "I've missed you too."

Dougless put down the telephone and smiled. It seemed that not only had history changed, but so had the present. She knew, felt inside herself, that never again was she going to be the butt of the family's jokes, because no longer did she feel incompetent, as though she couldn't handle her own life.

She called Heathrow, booked her flight, then began to pack.

THIRTY-FOUR

*D*ougless had to get up very early to catch the train to London; then she took a long, expensive taxi ride to the airport. The sense of accomplishment that had sustained her since she'd left the sixteenth century was leaving her. All she felt now was very tired and very alone. She'd fallen in love with Nicholas twice. Every passing second seemed to bring memories back to her. She remembered when he'd been in the twentieth century and the wonder on his face as he'd touched a book of color photographs. She remembered the way he'd been fascinated with watching the taxi driver shift gears. And the *Playboy* magazine in the drawer at Arabella's!

When she went to the sixteenth century and he hadn't remembered her and he'd even seemed to hate her, she'd thought he'd changed. But he hadn't. He was still the man who put his family before himself, and when he began to include Dougless in his family, he had loved her as completely as he did them.

When the boarding of the plane was called, Dougless waited until the last minute to get on. Maybe she shouldn't leave England. If she remained in England, she would be closer to Nicholas. Maybe she should buy a house in Ashburton and visit his tomb every day. Maybe if she prayed enough, she would be returned to him, or him to her.

She tried to control herself, but the tears started anyway. Nicholas was truly and completely gone from her. Never again would she see him, hear him, or touch him.

Tears were blinding her so much that as she boarded, she walked into the man in front of her and her tote bag slid off her shoulder onto the lap of a first-class passenger.

"I'm so sorry," she said; then she looked into the blue eyes of a very handsome man. For a moment her heart pounded, but she made herself turn away. He wasn't Nicholas; his eyes weren't Nicholas's eyes.

She took her tote bag from the man while he stared up at her with interest. But Dougless wasn't interested. The only man who interested her was sealed inside a marble tomb.

She made her way back to her seat, shoved her tote bag under the seat in front of her, then looked out the window. As the plane began to taxi down the runway and she realized that she was leaving England, she began to cry in earnest. The man in the aisle seat beside her, an Englishman, buried his face deeper into his newspaper.

Dougless tried to make her tears stop. She gave herself little pep talks about how much she'd been able to accomplish, and reminded herself that losing Nicholas was a small price to pay for all the good she'd done. But each thought made her cry harder.

By the time the plane was aloft and the FASTEN SEAT BELT sign was off, she was crying so hard that she didn't see what happened next to her. The man from first class, a champagne bottle and two glasses in his hand, asked the man next to Dougless to exchange seats.

"Here," he said.

She could see through her tears a tall glass of champagne being held out to her.

"Go on, take it. It'll do you good."

"You're an A-American," she said through tears.

"Yes. I'm from Colorado. And you?"

"M-Maine." She took the champagne, drank too fast, and choked. "I-I have cousins in Colorado."

"Oh? Where?"

"Chandler." Her tears weren't flowing as fast.

"Not the Taggerts?"

She looked up at him. Black hair and blue eyes. Just like Nicholas. The tears sped up again. She nodded.

"I used to go to Chandler with my father sometimes, and I met some of the Taggerts. I'm Reed Stanford, by the way." He held out his hand to shake hers, but when she didn't move, he picked up her hand off her lap and clasped it in his. "Nice to meet you." He didn't release her hand, but looked at it, saying nothing, until Dougless snatched her hand away.

"Sorry," he said.

"Mr. . . . ?"

"Stanford."

"Mr. Stanford," she said, sniffing, "I don't know what I did to give you the impression that I'm an easy pickup, but I can assure you that I'm not. I think you'd better take your champagne and return to your own seat." She was trying to be regal, but her effort lost something, since her nose was red, her eyes swollen, and tears were running down her cheeks.

He didn't take the glass and he didn't leave.

He was beginning to make Dougless angry. Was he some pervert who liked crying females? What in the world had happened in his childhood to cause him to be turned on by tears? "If you don't leave, I'll have to call the attendant."

He turned to look at her. "Please don't," he said, and there was something in his eyes that made Dougless halt as she reached for the call button. "You must believe me; I've never done anything like this in my life. I mean, I've never accosted a woman on a plane before. Or even in a bar, for that matter. It's just that you remind me of someone."

Dougless wasn't crying any longer because there was something eerily familiar in the way he moved his head. "Who?" she asked.

He gave a little grin, and Dougless's heart skipped a beat. Nicholas sometimes grinned like that. "You wouldn't believe me if I told you. It's too far-fetched."

"Try me. I have a lot of imagination."

"All right," he said. "You remind me of a lady in a portrait."

Dougless was listening now.

"When I was a boy, about eleven, I think, my parents, my older brother, and I came to England for a year to live. My father had a job here. My mother used to drag my brother and me to antiques stores, and I'm afraid that I wasn't very gracious about going. That is, until one Saturday afternoon when I saw the portrait."

Pausing, he refilled Dougless's empty glass. "The portrait was a miniature oil, done sometime in the sixteenth century, and it was a picture of a lady." He looked at her, and in spite of her swollen face, his eyes were almost caressing.

"I wanted that portrait. I can't explain it. It wasn't that I just wanted it; I *had to have it.*" He smiled. "I'm afraid I wasn't exactly sweet-tempered about voicing my wants. The portrait was quite expensive and my mother refused to listen to my demands, but I've never taken no for an answer. The next Saturday I took the tube, went back to the antique shop, and offered everything I had as a down payment on the portrait. I think it was about five pounds."

He smiled in memory. "Looking back on it, I think the old man who owned the shop thought I wanted to be a collector. But I didn't want to collect; I just wanted *that* portrait."

"Did you get it?" Dougless whispered.

"Oh, yes. My parents thought I was crazy and said an Elizabethan miniature was no possession for a child, but when they saw me, week after week, giving all my allowance toward the purchase of that miniature, they began to help me. Then, just before we left England, when I'd begun to feel that I was never going to get enough money together to buy it, my father drove me to the antique shop and presented the portrait to me."

The man sat back in his seat, as though that were the end of the story.

"Do you have the portrait?" Dougless whispered.

"Always. I'm never without it. Would you like to see it?"

Dougless could only nod.

From his inside coat pocket, he withdrew a little leather case and handed it to her. Slowly, Dougless opened the box. There, on black velvet, was the portrait Nicholas had had painted of her. It was encased in silver and around the edges were seed pearls.

Without asking permission, Dougless lifted the miniature from the case, turned it over, then held it up to the light.

"*My soul will find yours,*" Reed said. "That's what it says on the back, and it's signed with a *C.* I've always wondered what the words meant and what the *C* stood for."

"Colin," Dougless said before she thought.

"How did you know?"

"Know what?"

"Colin is my middle name. Reed Colin Stanford."

She looked at him then, really looked at him. He glanced down at the portrait, then up at her, and when he did so, he looked at her through his lashes, just as Nicholas used to do. "What do you do for a living?" she whispered.

"I'm an architect."

She drew in her breath. "Have you ever been married?"

"You do get to the point, don't you? No, I've never been married, but I'll tell you the truth: I once left a woman practically at the altar. It was the worst thing I've ever done in my life."

"What was her name?" Dougless's voice was lower than a whisper.

"Leticia."

It was at that point that the stewardess stopped by their seats. "We have roast beef or chicken Kiev for dinner tonight. Which would you like?"

Reed turned to Dougless. "Will you have dinner with me?"

My soul will find yours, Nicholas had written. Souls, not bodies, but souls. "Yes, I'll have dinner with you."

He smiled at her and it was Nicholas's smile.

Thank You, God, she thought. Thank You.

The Writing of *A Knight in Shining Armor*

Jude Deveraux

In the fourteen years since I wrote *A Knight in Shining Armor*, I've received many queries about the book, especially about how I came to write it. Many times I've been told that it is "a perfect love story," but I think that the appeal of the book for me—and, yes, it's my favorite of my books—and for readers is the underlying theme.

What people don't know is that *A Knight in Shining Armor* is about alcoholism.

Before I start a book, I think, I want to write about . . . I fill in the blank with something that's of interest to me, then build the plot on that subject. Sometime during the 1980s I was researching another book when I came across some information that startled me. I read that, in many cases, alcoholism is as much a state of mind as it is a physical problem. I had assumed that a person who had stopped drinking, would no longer be an alcoholic.

But what I was reading—and forgive my paraphrasing, as I'm not an expert on this—said that there was such a thing as an "alcoholic personality." In fact, a person didn't even have to drink to have this personality, and in that case, he was called a "dry drunk."

What interested me about this personality was that a person who had it desperately needed to break the spirit of another human being. A "dry drunk" will choose the strongest, most moral, and most generous person he or she can find, then dedicate his life to trying to control, and therefore change, this person. The ultimate goal is to be able to say, "I'm not so bad. Sure, I do bad things, but look at this person. Everyone thinks she (or he) is so good, but I've just proven that she, too, can be bad."

An example of this thinking at work is depicted in the movie *Dangerous Liaisons*. The characters played by Glenn Close and John Malkovich search for the strongest, most highly moral person they can find, portrayed by Michele Pfeiffer, then set out to destroy her.

After I spent some time reading about the alcoholic personality, I knew I wanted to write about it. I also wanted a heroine who was strong but believed herself to be weak, who was generous, the kind who'd help another human even if it caused her hardship, yet thought her generous spirit was a weakness.

I wrote down my goal, then set about creating a story that would show what I wanted. However, I knew my heroine had to be in a non-drinking relationship, because I was sure that if she were involved with an active alcoholic, I'd lose the sympathy of the reader. Unfortunately, there are a lot of people—including many therapists—who say, "All you have to do is leave," and they truly believe leaving a bad relationship is that easy. Also, I didn't want to give away the problem in one sentence. All I'd have to do is have the heroine's boyfriend drink his fourth whiskey and everyone would know they were reading about an alcoholic relationship. No, I wanted more subtlety than that. In fact, at the time, I told my editor that I wanted to write a book about alcoholism but that I was never going to mention the word in the book.

As some of you know, I often write about a family named Montgomery. The Montgomerys are all brilliant, rich, and afraid of nothing. They are true heroes. I thought, What if someone was born into that family but felt she didn't fit in? What if she was intimidated by her glorious relatives and felt that she'd never live up to their standards?

From these questions, I created Dougless Montgomery, a young woman who had three formidably perfect older sisters and had, all her life, felt inferior to them.

It was easy to imagine Dougless being swept away by a man with an alcoholic personality. Robert Whitley was a successful man, and on the surface, he seemed like someone Dougless could show to her family with pride. If Dougless herself couldn't be the tower of accomplishment her siblings were, then she'd do the next best thing and bring such a person into her family.

Once I had my idea of Dougless's background, I needed a story that would change her. First of all, I needed to get her away from the family that made her feel inferior. But how to do that? Part of the Montgomery creed is that they always help each other. How could I put my heroine in a situation dire enough to fundamentally change her personality yet prevent her relatives from bailing her out?

It was this idea of taking my heroine "away" that made me think of writing a time travel novel. I'd always loved to read time travel stories, so I thought it would be interesting to write one. Right away, I saw that I needed two things from my plot. First, my heroine needed to discover that her generosity and kindness were worthy traits. And, second, Dougless needed to accomplish something that made her truly proud of herself, and this accomplishment had to be so big that she could overlook her past failures, her bad boyfriends, and all the embarrassing situations she'd been in.

From these two needs, I constructed a basic time travel plot in which a medieval man comes forward in time and Dougless helps him. She'd be reluctant at first, but her sweet nature wouldn't allow her to abandon him. In order for Dougless to learn that she was actually a very strong woman who could rely on herself, I decided to send her back to the Elizabethan era, where she'd have to use all her wits just to stay alive. And since I didn't want her disappearing under the protective arm of a man, I had her return to a time when the Elizabethan man didn't remember her.

After I had my plot, I spent months researching. When I had read time travel novels in the past, I had always been bored by the long explanations of political history. What I wanted to read about, and certainly to write about, was what the people wore, what they ate. I wanted to know how they *thought*. I wanted to know every detail of Elizabethan *life*—with no boring politics!

I enjoyed the research very much, and as I discovered things that fascinated me, I added to my plot so I could include what I'd learned. For example, I'd never thought about what people did with their children before there were day-care centers. While the serfs were out working all day, who took care of the toddlers that were too young to work but old enough to wander into trouble? I can tell you that I was shocked to read that the children were bound tightly enough to put them into a stupor, then hung from a peg in the wall!

When I had many pages of plot and hundreds of Rolodex cards full of research, I went to my cabin in the Pecos Wilderness in New Mexico and isolated myself for three and a half months while I wrote the book. I got up at daybreak, ate a bowl of cereal, then wrote by hand until noon. After lunch I went for a walk and plotted the next day's scenes in my head. Since my cabin was at a nine-thousand-foot altitude, this meant climbing above the tree line, often to eleven and twelve thousand feet. That summer I climbed so much that when I got into bed at night, my calves were so heavy with muscle that my heels didn't touch the sheet.

When the book was finished, I'd poured so much of my heart into it that, instead of mailing it, I flew to New York to personally deliver the manuscript to Pocket Books.

I was pleased with the book for several reasons. For one thing, I felt I'd done what I'd set out to do: I'd written about alcoholism without ever mentioning the word. And I'd made my heroine realize that she was strong enough to stand up to her controlling boyfriend—and to her overbearing sister. On the day I wrote the scene where Dougless tells her sister not to speak to her in a disrespectful manner, I did a dance of triumph.

In the years since *A Knight in Shining Armor* was first published, I'm happy to say, readers have seemed to like the book as much as I loved writing it. However, in the last few years, I've thought that I'd like to go back through the book and apply some of what I've learned over time about writing. So, in January of 2001, that's what I did. I didn't change the plot, didn't really add any new information, but I somehow managed to add fifty pages to the book. In the end, I think it's now a smoother read, and, maybe, it's a bit more understandable why Dougless wanted to marry a jerk like Robert.

I thank all of you for your kind words about a book that has been so close to my heart for so many years, and I hope you continue to enjoy the book for a long time to come.